APACHE SPRINGS

This Large Print Book carries the
Seal of Approval of N.A.V.H.

A YAKIMA HENRY WESTERN DUO

APACHE SPRINGS

FRANK LESLIE

WHEELER PUBLISHING
A part of Gale, a Cengage Company

Farmington Hills, Mich • San Francisco • New York • Waterville, Maine
Meriden, Conn • Mason, Ohio • Chicago

Copyright © 2019 by Frank Leslie.
Wheeler Publishing, a part of Gale, a Cengage Company.

LIBRARY OF CONGRESS CIP DATA ON FILE.
CATALOGUING IN PUBLICATION FOR THIS BOOK
IS AVAILABLE FROM THE LIBRARY OF CONGRESS

ISBN-13: 978-1-4328-4716-6 (softcover alk. paper)

Published in 2019 by arrangement with Peter Brandvold

Printed in the United States of America
1 2 3 4 5 6 7 23 22 21 20 19

CONTENTS

■ ■ ■ ■

BLOODY ARIZONA

■ ■ ■ ■

CHAPTER 1

Yakima Henry swung around from the man he'd just sent flying through a saloon window to see a fist arcing toward him. The man behind the fist had a big, bearded, bullet-shaped head. His fist was large, brown, and scarred and clenched so tightly the knuckles were white.

The man was grimacing, nostrils flaring, brown eyes pinched to slits.

Yakima started to duck the blow, but the fist connected before he could do more than flinch. It was a hammering punch, and, on the heels of so many more that had weakened the big, raging half-breed, it drove Yakima straight down to the floor.

The next thing he knew — and he wasn't sure how much later he knew it — he was waking up on the saloon floor, feeling as though he'd been run over by a fully loaded ore dray. He stared up at the handsome young, mustached, blue-eyed face of the town marshal of Apache Springs, Arizona Territory. Lon Taggart stared down at Yakima, lips curved downward in unrestrained reproof.

Two sets of lips, two faces beyond a watery blur.

Both the lawman's faces jerked from side to side, hazily, as the young, disapproving marshal shook his head. The man's lips moved beneath his neatly trimmed mustache, and, as though from the top of a deep well, at the bottom of which the big half-breed lay sprawled, came the warbling, barely intelligible words: "Margolis, Sanchez, take this damn fool over to the jail and turn the key on him, will you? I'll buy you each a scuttle of beer for your trouble."

Boots thumped loudly around Yakima. His tender brain rebelled at the din. It also rebelled at the brusque hands grabbing him, lifting his arms and legs up off the floor, digging into his tender muscles and bruised bones. The liquid trickling into his mouth from his upper lip owned the new-penny taste of blood.

The young marshal gazed down at Yakima again, blue eyes filled with acrimony. Taggart withdrew a long, black cheroot from between his fine, white teeth and, letting the smoke trickle out his nostrils, said,

"What the hell kind of stunt was that?"

He appeared to be awaiting an answer as the two men heaved the semi-conscious half-breed up off the floor, but Yakima's only response was a guttural groaning against the many aches in his body, including the hammering of a large, nasty maul against his tender brain and the grinding of what felt like several broken — or at least badly bruised — ribs.

Taggart followed Margolis and Sanchez as they shambled toward the batwings, the big half-breed sagging between them. "You're going to do a good month in the cooler, and then you're going to work off the price of this mess. Right down to the last half penny!"

"Hell of a price it's gonna be, too," yelled Cleve Dundee, the owner of the Busted Flush and the big, egg-headed, rock-fisted gent who'd delivered Yakima's final and decisive blow. He'd been a mule skinner and track-layer in his younger days. "Look at this place!"

Yakima didn't have time to look around, because suddenly he was outside on the street, squeezing his eyes closed against the unforgiving Arizona sun that stabbed his eyes like bayonet blades. But he had a pretty good idea of the devastation he'd left in his

11

wake — broken tables and chairs and likely a shattered lamp or two, not to mention the broken front window, maybe a couple of other windows . . . and the back bar mirror.

He remembered ducking to avoid a thrown chair and glancing over his shoulder to see the chair caroming over the bar and smashing into the mirror, as well as several liquor-laden shelves . . .

A fleeting glance behind him told him the man he'd sent flying through the front window was just now rising up on all fours from the boardwalk, broken glass all around him, and shaking his bloody head as if to clear the cobwebs.

Another man rose from the street, brushing red Arizona dirt from his pants. He swung around to follow Yakima and his chaperones with an indignant gaze. The man's lips were split, one eye was swelling, and blood streamed over his spade-bearded chin. Yakima vaguely remembered tossing the man through the batwings near the start of the dustup. He was a stagecoach driver, name of Shipley, if Yakima remembered. He wore no hat, and his hair hung in his eyes.

Shipley gritted his teeth, raised an arm to point at Yakima, and shouted, "That breed is *loco*! Pure *loco* — you hear me, Taggart! He's due for a hangin'! Time to play cat's cradle with his rock-worshippin', dog-eatin' head!"

"Hangin's too good for that son of a bitch!" bellowed another battered gent just then stumbling out through the batwings to cast his own incriminating gaze toward Yakima. He wore a shabby gray suit with a flowered vest and was swatting at his trousers with a dusty bowler. Yakima merely groaned, gritted his teeth against the sunlight's merciless assault, and lifted his bloody-knuckled left hand to return the suited man's indictment with a raised middle finger.

That riled the battered gent even more.

"See that there? See that there, Taggart? Just shoot the savage son of a bitch and throw him in Reynolds Wash! Feed the strays with him, I say!"

Taggart, following close behind Margolis, who shambled at the half-breed's ankles, Yakima's boots jostling against the man's thighs, shook his head in disparagement. The young lawman said, "You do yourself no favors, Yakima. None at all. The man you just saluted is none other than Apache Springs's mayor, you stupid son of a bitch!"

Yakima finally found reason to smile, albeit fleetingly. The smile quickly transformed into a pained wince as the man holding him by the shoulders let his head smack against the side of a wooden door frame as he carried him into the office of Apache Springs's town marshal. He squeezed his eyes closed against the pain, heard the metallic squawk of steel hinges, and felt a metal-framed cot fly up to smack him hard about his tender head and aching shoulders.

"Oh!" he grunted just before unconsciousness closed its merciful fist around him.

He woke later and lay there for a time, eyes closed, taking quiet inventory of his aches and pains, silently cursing the throbbing in his head. He could hear horse and wagon traffic out on the street, the monotonous, wooden ticking of the Regulator clock over Taggart's desk. He'd been hearing that for a long time, he realized. How long, he wasn't sure. But too damned long . . .

Finally, when he realized sleep was not about to claim him again, to rescue him from the pain and misery of this earthly realm, including the Regulator's relentless hammering or the shrill squawks of a dry wagon axle assaulting the exposed nerve of his brain from out on the street, he sat up on the cot and swung his white-socked feet to the floor.

He held his tender head in his hands, closing them over his eyes. Gradually, he slid his fingers away and opened his eyes very slowly.

Light seeped through his slitted lids. He was surprised that the light's assault didn't hurt all that bad. He was also a little surprised that sitting up seemed to actually make his head hurt less than it had when he was lying down.

Lowering his hands to his knees, he found himself staring at Marshal Lon Taggart, who stood at the potbelly stove in the middle of the office, pouring coffee from a battered, speckled black pot into a stone mug. Taggart returned Yakima's gaze with a critical, slightly amused one of his own.

"The lion awakes," Taggart said. "Probably feeling a little worse for the wear, no doubt."

He strode over toward Yakima's cell against the adobe brick building's rear wall, where it was lined up with three others, all empty. Yakima had the honor of being Taggart's lone guest. "Ain't that so . . ." Taggart asked with an ironic smile. ". . . lion?"

Yakima hacked up phlegm and spat it into the slop bucket to his right, which, he vaguely noted, was not empty. "I'll admit I've felt some better. But right now I'm feelin' about the best I have in . . ."

He let his voice trail off and frowned curiously as he slid his gaze to the two barred, curtained windows in the front wall, to either side of a zinc-topped wooden stand on which a porcelain washbowl perched. By the angle of the light through the canvas curtains, it appeared between eight and nine in the morning. "How long have I been here?"

"Since yesterday morning," Taggart said. "You've been in here a little over twenty-four hours, you crazy bastard. Get comfortable. You're going to be here a whole lot longer."

Yakima hadn't been unconscious the whole time. At least, not completely so. He half remembered half waking up a few times to evacuate his bladder into the slop bucket in the cell's near corner, and to note the misery of his continuing hangover before flopping back down on the cot and letting sleep overtake him once more.

The tall, slender young marshal slid the cup through the bars. "Have a cup of mud. It's fresh. I'd offer you a little hair of the dog, but I don't keep it around. The skull pop is what killed my old man, and it's what got you locked up in here. You're gonna be here for a month . . . if I can stand the stench of your ugly red hide that long."

16

The young lawman gave a mocking snort, and a good-natured smile twitched at the corners of his mouth. Taggart was basically a good sort, as far as lawmen go. In fact, he was probably the only lawman Yakima remembered ever getting along with.

Taggart had introduced himself to Yakima when the half-breed had first ridden into Apache Springs for supplies. Yakima had taken up residence in an abandoned prospector's shack a few miles outside of town and had started doing a little prospecting of his own, having heard in Tucson that several men were finding good color on the north side of the Javelina Bluffs, which most men would call mountains.

Taggart had introduced himself to Yakima, the half-breed knew, because he was a good lawman who liked to keep track of strangers. But unlike most lawmen when encountering the big, broad-shouldered, green-eyed, buckskin-clad half-breed riding a half-wild black stallion, Taggart had made no threats and offered no warnings. He'd merely engaged in pleasant, subtly inquiring conversation, friendly palaver that he and Yakima had picked up again when Taggart had visited Yakima's shack a few times over the past couple of months, on the trail of claim jumpers and, once, a pair of bank-robbing desperadoes.

Yakima had come to regard Lon Taggart as not just the town marshal of Apache Springs, but, improbably, a friendly acquaintance who, in time, he might even find himself calling a friend.

From their conversations, Yakima knew that Taggart's father had once been a deputy US marshal — a good, fair one. Bass Taggart's reputation had preceded him. Lon was following well in his old man's footsteps, minus the tangle-leg, which was a good thing. Yakima had felt no more strongly about that than he did right now, wrung out and feeling twice his age due to his own most recent bout with the coffin varnish.

A bout he'd lost.

Yakima accepted the cup and blew on the black liquid. "Obliged, Lon."

"You ready to oblige a meal, or will your belly rebel?"

Yakima sipped the hot coffee, then hiked a shoulder as he sat down on the edge of the cot. "I don't know. I reckon it's worth a shot. Might be able to hold something down."

The young lawman gave a wry snort. He leaned a shoulder against the door of the cell, regarding Yakima with a pensive expression, his brows shaping a V over the bridge of his nose. "What happened?"

Yakima looked up at him. "What do you mean, what happened? You saw the mess over there. I reckon I got into the firewater. I know I shouldn't drink the stuff, but I did. It was Friday night, and I got to stompin' with my tail up. So there you have it. You locked me up, and when you let me out, I'll work off the debt. It ain't my first rodeo."

"That's not you, Yakima. I don't know you well, but I know you well enough to know that much. You're not a drunken Indian. You don't brawl for no reason. You're a man of honor. A man who can control his emotions . . . most of the time. Until something sends you off the rails."

"It's the Injun in me." Yakima sipped the coffee. It felt good going down, bracing him. "Me an' firewater don't mix."

"Who's Faith?"

Yakima was about to take another sip of the coffee but lowered the cup quickly and looked sharply up at Taggart. "What?"

"The whore you were with, before you went downstairs, said you were muttering 'Faith' in your sleep. Then you woke up covered in sweat. That's when you went downstairs, joined that poker game, and started pounding the whiskey. You got drunk, started cheating, and when you were

19

called on it, you exploded like a hundred-pound keg of dynamite.

"Who is she?" Taggard paused, canted his head to one side, studying Yakima closely. "Who's Faith, Yakima?"

CHAPTER 2

Hearing her name was like having a fist buried in his solar plexus.

Yakima sat there for nearly a minute, coffee steaming in his hand, staring at the floor.

"Faith."

Just her name slipping off his tongue threatened to annihilate him, conjuring as it did the flaxen-haired beauty with cornflower-blue eyes and a smile like Christmas morning. It also reminded him of her unmarked grave near the ruins of Thornton's old roadhouse in Colorado, and the marker the half-breed had erected as a memorial on the small wild horse ranch they'd shared for way too short a time. The little shotgun spread lay on the slopes of Mount Bailey just north of here in this wild Arizona Territory.

Faith.

Yakima cleared his throat, said haltingly, "She was my wife."

"Was?"

"Dead."

Taggart stretched his lips back from his teeth as though he'd somehow been expecting the answer. "I'm sorry." He paused. "You want to tell me about her?"

Yakima stared at the floor, slowly shook his head. "Not much to tell. We weren't together long. A rabid polecat by the name of Thornton had her killed. Now they're both dead, and . . . I'm alive." *To remember. To reflect every waking hour on what might have been.*

Yakima drew a deep breath and sipped his coffee, blinking away the scurry of emotions within him.

"I'm sorry for your loss, Yakima. But it don't give you the right to —"

"No, it doesn't," Yakima finished for the young lawman, quickly. "It gives me no right to do what I did. You done right, lockin' me up, Lon. And when I'm out of here, I'll work off the damages. And then I'll pull my picket pin." He nodded, sullen-faced. "I know when I've burned my bridges. I know when it's time to leave."

"You can't run forever."

Yakima looked up at him again, curiously.

Taggart shook his head. "Especially when it's yourself you're runnin' from."

Yakima was a little taken aback by the young man's philosophical insight. Taggart was right. Yakima had been running a long time, and this was the first time he'd been confronted with the notion that it might be himself he was running from. Not just from life's circumstances, most of which were out of his control. He and Taggart held each other's understanding gazes for a time, and then footsteps tapped on the wooden gallery fronting the lawman's office.

The latch clicked, and the door shuddered open.

A young woman poked her head in the door and cast her shy but piercing gray-eyed gaze quickly around the office before finding Taggart standing outside Yakima's cell. Her face was heartbreakingly beautiful with its wide, high cheekbones, smooth skin, fine slender nose, and lush lips.

Her wide, red mouth broke into a delighted smile, making the stunning gray eyes dance. Her lips stretched farther back from even, white teeth as she skipped playfully into the office, clutching a beaded black reticule in both hands in front of her.

"Well, good morning, there, Marshal Taggart!" Her voice was fetchingly raspy, slightly husky, but all feminine.

She left the door standing open behind

her as she flounced up to the young law-man, whose own face broke into an enchanted smile of its own as he said, "Julia, what are you doing here? I thought you'd be off to church by now."

"I am off to church by now," she said, lifting one of her white-gloved hands to adjust the string tie knotted at the lawman's throat. Dropping her chin slightly and looking up into the handsome young man's face enticingly from beneath her thin, brown eyebrows, she added, "I was hoping I might be able to coerce you into joining me. It's a beautiful morning, all fresh and clean after the rain, and I'm told by the preacher's housekeeper, Mrs. Pritchett, that Reverend Logan worked extra hard on his sermon this week."

That this young beauty was Taggart's wife there could be little doubt. She sported a ring under the glove on her right hand, and she lifted that hand still further to brush a fleck of dust from his cheek with wifely intimacy.

"Shucks," Taggart said, taking the young woman's wrists in his hands and planting a kiss on her own right knuckle. "I wish I could, honey. But I'm afraid I have chores this morning."

He cast a fleeting glance at Yakima. The

young woman glanced Yakima's way, as well, sizing up her husband's prisoner quickly as well as critically, taking the big half-breed's measure where he sat on the edge of the cot, steaming coffee in his hands. Flushing a little with embarrassment, Taggart drew his pretty young wife away from the half-breed's cell, leading her over to his desk standing out from the wall at the far end of the room, under a framed map of Arizona Territory hovering over three wooden filing cabinets and flanked by a thirty-eight-star flag of the United States as well as by the territorial flag of Arizona.

The young woman glanced once more at Yakima, her brows arched with reproof, and said, "Surely your prisoner can get along here alone for an hour, Lon."

"It's not just him, Julia," Taggart said. Then, lowering his voice to speak privately with his wife, whose hands he held in his own, he continued the conversation at a pitch Yakima couldn't make out.

Not that he wanted to eavesdrop. He stared at the stone floor between his white-socked feet, trying to put the obviously in-love young couple out of his mind. As soon as Yakima had seen the young woman enter the office, a knife had poked through his chest and pierced his heart.

There'd been something about Julia Taggart's eyes, the set of her mouth . . . the intimacy of her smile as her eyes had roamed adoringly across her husband . . . that had hit just too damned close to home.

What had once been for Yakima. What might have continued for him and Faith if not for one vengeance-hungry madman in Colorado . . .

Yakima tried to block the intimate whispers from his mind, the playful chuckles, Julia's mild cajoling. He slurped his coffee, staring into the steaming black liquid, and, as he did, hooves thumped loudly outside the jailhouse. Yakima looked through a front window to see several men pull up in front of the building, tan dust sweeping around them. He could hear the horses snorting and the men talking in gruff tones as they swung down from their saddles.

Yakima glanced at Taggart. The lawman was still leaning back against the front of his desk, Julia's hands in his own, smiling down at his young wife as she smiled up at him. Neither Mr. nor Mrs. Taggart was aware of the newcomers, only each other, the love they shared.

Cold fingers of apprehension danced along the half-breed's spine. He wasn't sure why. There was something vaguely threatening in the fast, purposeful drumbeat of the horses' hooves, the obvious heat in the voices of the newcomers.

The half-breed was still considering whether he should say something to Taggart when boots thumped on the gallery and spurs chinked loudly. A big, bearded man in a dust-covered tan duster entered the office quickly, flanked by a slightly shorter second man, a Mexican with mare's tail mustaches and a red sash around his waist. Two other men remained on the gallery, turning to face the street. Yakima heard one of them spit chaw to one side, heard the wet plop in the dirt beside the boardwalk.

Julia gasped at the thunder of boots and the ring of spurs behind her. She turned quickly to cast a startled glance over her shoulder.

"Taggart?" said the big man in a thundering, gravelly voice near the door, sliding a long-barreled Colt from a brown leather holster strapped low on his right thigh.

"Yes, I'm Taggart," the young marshal said, frowning against the sunlight spilling in through the open door and gently nudging his wife to one side. He straightened, stepped away from the desk. "What can I help you men with?"

"We got us a little message from Rebel

Wilkes," the big man said, chuckling and raising the long-barreled, silver-chased Colt in his gloved right hand. "You remember him, don't ya?"

Yakima jumped as the Colt roared. It sounded like a cannon blast echoing off the building's adobe walls. Smoke and bright orange flames lapped from the barrel.

The young lawman jerked backward sharply, grimacing, his coffee-brown Stetson falling onto the desk behind him. Julia screamed and slapped her gloved hands to her face, staring in horror at her husband falling backward against his desk while lowering his hand to the Remington holstered in the cross-draw position on his left hip.

"This is Wilkes's thank-you note for that stunt you pulled against the spur line!" the bearded man shouted, laughing again as he triggered his Colt a second time . . . a third time . . . and then a fourth, each bullet slamming into the marshal's body, each time evoking an agonized grunt.

"We're gonna spread Wilkes's message to the whole rest of your town, Marshal!" the big man bellowed, firing one last shot into Taggart.

With the second shot, Taggart had fallen farther backward against his desk, knocking over an unlit Tiffany lamp. The last shot, punching into his belly, doubled him over forward, and, his screaming wife reaching for him with her gloved, outstretched hands, he dropped to his knees on the floor in front of his desk.

Yakima could only stare with hang-jawed, disbelieving exasperation into the smoky room outside his cell, his muscles suddenly turned to stone. His ears rang from the gunfire.

"Lon!" Julia screamed, crouching over Taggart as the young marshal slumped sideways to the floor, his eyes dull with shock.

The big, bearded man strode forward, yelling, "Forget him, honey — he's a goner!" He holstered his smoking Colt, jerked Julia Taggart up off the floor, grabbed her around the waist, and threw her over his shoulder. "I'm gonna take you over to the Busted Flush, and you an' me is gonna have us a good, old-fashioned mattress dance!"

The short, mustached Mexican threw his head back, laughing, as the big man strode past him with the kicking, screaming woman on his shoulder. The Mexican wheeled and followed him out the door.

Neither one had so much as glanced toward Yakima.

The half-breed heard beneath Julia's screams and sobs the big man say, "Bonner, Griggs, head on over to the church. Don't forget the torches. Me an' Tio's gonna go over to the Busted Flush and introduce ourselves to the marshal of Apache Springs's purty li'l widow . . . after killing everyone on the premises, that is!"

"Save some for us," one of the other two yelled as they mounted their horses.

"We'll see about that," the big man returned, laughing, Julia Taggart's cries dwindling into the distance.

Yakima had dropped his coffee cup to the floor. The steaming liquid pooled around his socks. He'd worked free of his stony muscles to rise from his cot and stand at the cell door, staring out the jailhouse window toward where the big man, Julia Taggart, and the Mexican called Tio angled off toward the saloon on the other side of the street.

"Julia!"

Yakima turned toward Taggart. He'd thought the man was dead, but he'd been wrong. Taggart was crabbing belly down along the floor, clawing his way forward, leaving a thick smear of blood on the adobe bricks behind him. His face was deep red, purple veins bulging in his forehead, blue

30

eyes sharp with pain, horror, and fury.

"Julia!" he rasped out again.

Yakima dropped to a knee, so that he was nearly eye level with the dying marshal. "Taggart! The key!"

The young marshal stopped in front of Yakima's cell. He looked around as though for the key to the cell door, then glanced over his left shoulder. Yakima followed the lawman's gaze to the key ring hanging from a spike protruding from the wall by his desk. Inwardly, Yakima cursed. Taggart didn't have the strength to retrieve the ring.

The young lawman had a better idea. He lowered his right hand to his Remington, stretched his lips back from his teeth as he worked the revolver free of the keeper thong and the holster. With a fierce groan, he swung his arm around in an arc toward Yakima, slammed the Remy against the bars.

Yakima reached between the bars and grabbed the gun.

Taggart's hand dropped to the floor, and the rest of him remained there, as well — belly down, cheek against the cold bricks. He was breathing hard, a pool of blood growing beneath him.

Yakima straightened, cocked the Remy's hammer, aimed at the lock, and fired. He fired three times before the lock finally blew open. Yakima shoved the door out against Taggart's slumped figure, then walked to the back of his cell and stomped into his boots. He donned his low-crowned, wide-brimmed, black hat, the chin thong dangling against his chest, and stepped out of the cell and over Taggart. He dropped to a knee beside the lawman, and rolled him onto his back.

"Don't worry, Lon — I'll — !"

He stopped. The two blue eyes staring up at him were as opaque as isinglass. Lon Taggart was dead.

CHAPTER 3

"I'll get her back," Yakima assured the dead man staring up at him unseeing. The half-breed raked his fingers down Taggart's face, closing his eyes.

Swallowing down a hard knot in his throat, he quivered with an anger that was building now on the lee side of his shock at what had just so quickly and decisively occurred. With everything that had happened, he'd forgotten his hangover, though the hangover hadn't forgotten him. His head still ached, and his body was sluggish, limbs heavy from all the hours he'd been slumped on the cot. Adrenaline was taking over now that his whiskey-besotted brain was beginning to comprehend what had happened and had decided what he was going to do about it.

Yakima looked at the unfamiliar Remington in his hand. He needed his own gun for the work he had ahead. He turned to the wooden gun cabinet standing against the wall near Taggart's desk. A padlocked chain snaked through the steel door handles. Yakima blasted the lock, removed the chain, and opened the doors.

A minute later, he was striding quickly out of the marshal's office, buckling his own cartridge belt around his lean waist. As he angled over toward the Busted Flush, where he could hear men's angry voices rising, as well as Julia Taggart screaming, he palmed his horn-gripped Colt .44. He flicked open the loading gate, filled the chamber he usually kept empty beneath the hammer with a fresh cartridge from his shell belt, and spun the cylinder.

He'd considered arming himself with his prized Winchester Yellowboy repeater, which he'd also found in Taggart's gun cabinet, but had nixed the idea. He knew from plenty of past experience that the Colt was better suited for indoor work.

As he strode quickly, jaws hard, jade eyes intense beneath the low-canted brim of his black hat, he vaguely noted the quiet of the nearly deserted street. It was Sunday. Everyone in Apache Springs was either in church or at the Busted Flush, the most popular saloon in the little desert town. Not so vaguely, Yakima remembered that the bearded man had sent two of his men over to the church with torches. The half-breed quickened his pace as the shouting got louder in the Busted Flush, and Julia's screams became more muffled, seeming to originate from the second story.

"What the hell you doin', you crazy Mex?" a man bellowed amidst the din of stomping boots and ringing spurs.

A man laughed shrilly. A rifle thundered.

"Holy shit, he's crazy!" another man cried as the din of stomping feet grew louder.

"Going to kill all you sonso' *beeches*!" came the Mexican's heavily accented shout.

Holding his Colt straight down by his right side, Yakima clicked the hammer back. He mounted the boardwalk fronting the Busted Flush and pushed through the batwings just as the short Mexican with the red sash fired a Winchester repeater toward the far side of the room, where six or seven townsmen were cowering behind chairs and tables, two of which were overturned.

The bullet punched a ragged hole through one of the overturned tables, and a man in a bowler hat lifted his head sharply, falling backward, swiping a hand against a bloody gash in his left cheek and shouting, "Holy shit — the crazy fucker means it!"

The Mexican laughed as he ejected the spent cartridge, sending it smoking over his

35

right shoulder to clatter onto the floor at Yakima's boots as the half-breed walked up behind him.

As the Mexican rammed another cartridge into the rifle's action, Yakima stopped.

"Tio." Yakima's voice was flat and dull with menace.

The Mexican jerked with a start, froze, then, holding the rifle at half mast before him, turned an apprehensive look over his shoulder. His black eyes widened as he saw the big half-breed standing behind him, holding his cocked Colt down against his leg.

The Mexican's startled look changed to cunning as he shaped a smile over cracked teeth and turned more quickly, bringing the rifle with him, saying, "You want to die, too, eh, Indio?"

He snapped full around, pulling the Winchester's rear stock back against his shoulder. Or, was just about to pull it against his shoulder.

The puckered, .44-caliber hole Yakima snapped through his forehead, just beneath the brim of his low-crowned straw *sombrero*, halted the action and sent the Mex stumbling straight back toward the bar. The Winchester left his hands to clatter onto a table trimmed with two whiskey bottles, glasses, an ash tray in which a cigar smoldered, and several poker hands. Tio's spurs made a raucous jangling sound, tearing slivers out of the floor before he fell straight back, smacking the back of his head hard against the edge of the bar with a dull thud, then piling up at the base of the bar, jerking as he died, eyelids fluttering like the wings of some hard-dying, panicking moth.

Silence descended over the room. Here and there, a face peered out from behind or over the tops of tables and chairs. Slowly, an egg-shaped bald head rose up from behind the bar. Cleve Dundee stared at Yakima in wide-eyed shock, then leaned forward to look at the Mexican slouched at the base of it, the pool of blood growing beneath his head.

"Dead?" he asked Yakima, tugging on his beard.

Just then a woman's cry from above sliced through the drinking hall's heavy silence. A man bellowed something in anger, and there was the sharp sound of a hand striking flesh. The sounds issued through several barriers — the barrier of the ceiling as well as a closed door, most likely.

One of the men who'd lifted his head above a table on the other side of the room looked at another man who'd done the same and said, "The marshal's wife . . ."

Yakima was already on the stairs to left of the bar, taking the steps two at a time. He swung around on the first landing and, his left hand on the banister, right hand gripping the Colt, continued bounding up the stairs. He gained the second story within seconds of leaving the first, all eyes in the saloon staring after him.

From somewhere on the second-floor hall, a woman screamed again.

Only this time, it was a deep, guttural scream of rage. A man bellowed. The din was coming from the door just ahead on Yakima's left. Loud thuds issued from behind the door. The door opened, and the big, bearded man stumbled out. He was naked from the waist down, pale dick jutting out from between his shirttails that brushed the tops of his fish-belly-white thighs. He wasn't wearing a hat. Thin, red-brown hair sparsely covered his pink scalp.

He stumbled toward Yakima, who'd raised the Colt and tightened his index finger against the trigger. The half-breed held his fire. The bearded man stepped into the hall, throwing his head back and bellowing like a pole-axed bull as he clamped a hand to the left side of his neck, trying to stem the blood geysering from a deep cut behind his jaw and splashing the blue-and-gray papered wall of the hall, above the pine wainscoting.

"You bitch!" he wailed, stumbling into the wall his blood had just painted. "You *bitch-hhhh*!"

He dropped to his knees with a heavy thump.

Instinctively, Yakima swung his Colt toward the half-open door when he glimpsed someone stepping through it. He let the gun sag in his fist as Julia Taggart walked into the hall. Her dress was torn in several places, and her dark-brown hair, which had been pinned into a bun beneath a yellow felt hat when Yakima had first seen her, hung in mussed tresses about her shoulders. The front of her dress was torn down to her waist, barely covering her breasts.

She let both arms drop to her sides, mindless of her near nudity. In her bloody right hand she held a broken lamp chimney from which the bearded man's blood dripped.

She stopped just outside the door and glared down at the bearded man, who was wilting like a big, lumpy flower and groaning as his blood drained out of him. Julia hardened her jaws, gray eyes flashing with rage, and threw the jagged chimney at the miserable bearded man, who was merely whimpering now as his face and chest hit the floor, his body spasming.

The young woman turned to Yakima, her eyes glassy with shock. She studied him as though she weren't quite certain she could believe what her eyes were telling her. Suddenly conscious of her torn dress, she reached for the tattered laps of the shirtwaist and drew them across her pale, blood-splattered breasts.

Again, she turned to Yakima. "The church," she said, raspily, wearily. "The other two were going to burn the church."

Yakima holstered his Colt and walked up to her, placing his hands on her shoulders. "You're . . . all right?"

She frowned up at him, as though taken aback by the question, and shook her head slightly as she said, "No."

Of course she wasn't all right. Feeling chagrined for asking the fool question, the half-breed wheeled and jogged back along the hall and down the stairs. As he ran across the main drinking hall toward the batwings, Cleve Dundee turned from where he and several other men were standing over the body of the dead Mexican.

"Where's Taggart?" he called.

"Dead," Yakima said without turning toward the barman but pushing through the batwings.

Several horses stood tied to the hitch racks fronting the saloon. Yakima's own black stallion was in a livery corral, so Yakima quickly picked out a fine blood bay and ripped the bridle reins from the rack, swinging lithely into the saddle. As he batted his heels against the bay's flanks and the big horse lunged into an instant gallop, heading west, Yakima tossed a quick glance from one side of the street to the other.

The town was eerily silent. The fact that virtually no one was out on such a fine, bright morning meant that nearly the entire population of Apache Springs was in church — toward which the other two tough nuts were heading with torches.

Yakima leaned far forward and whipped the rein ends against the bay's right hip, urging more speed. The big horse obliged, and the relatively new wood-frame or adobe-brick buildings whirled by in a blur on both sides of the street.

Peering along the horse's sleek neck, Yakima saw a dog running toward him from the direction of the church. The yellow-brown mutt ran hard, ears laid back, fear in its eyes. It whipped past Yakima and the bay without so much as a glance at horse and rider, heading straight east at a full-out sprint.

Just as the church slid into view off the street's right side, sitting back near where the old cavalry outpost had been only a few years ago, under the lip of a wave-shaped, sandstone rimrock, women's screams and men's shouts and howling laughter reached the half-breed's ears. Yakima swung the bay off the main street and onto the trail bordered by white rocks that led to the church and the cemetery behind it, both sitting on a knoll a hundred yards away.

The horrified screams and shouts were coming from inside the white-painted, wood-frame church capped with a bell tower. The howling laughter came from outside, around where two horses stood ground-tied near the two hitch racks where several other saddled horses were tied and before which sat a good dozen buggies and wagons.

The two laughing hard cases were just then ramming their rifle barrels through the two long, slender windows, one on each side of the church's covered entrance, and opening fire on the panicked worshippers.

CHAPTER 4

Yakima rammed his boot heels harder into the bay's flanks, following the trail up the knoll at a breakneck pace, sliding the Colt from its holster.

He could see, as he neared the wagons fronting the church, that the killers had shoved a board through the handles of the two front doors, locking the worshippers in from the outside. Meanwhile, smoke was slithering out around the door frame as the panicked churchgoers hammered on the doors. Smoke also ebbed outward from the broken windows the hard cases were pouring lead through, having broken the glass when they'd thrown their lit torches into the church.

Screams and wails rose from within.

The killers' rifles thundered loudly. The killers howled victoriously.

Inside, women screamed, men shouted and bellowed curses, and young children and babies wailed.

The shooter flinging lead through the church's right window must have heard the bay's drumming hooves as Yakima approached. He swung around, cocking a fresh round into his Winchester's breech, and sent a slug curling the air six inches to the right of the half-breed's head. That alerted the second shooter, who also turned from the window.

Yakima didn't slow the bay but turned it slightly right, sending it off at an angle away from the church as he dropped out of the saddle, hitting the ground and rolling up behind a small box wagon to which was harnessed a jittery steel-dust mare. The wagon jerked back and forth as the mare, who didn't like the shooting a bit, pulled against her ground anchor.

Yakima clicked the Colt's hammer back as he swiped his hat from his head and edged a look over the top of the wagon. The two shooters were moving toward him, crouching, running wide of the horses tied at the hitch rack and weaving around the buggies and wagons. The one on the right stopped suddenly near the end of a surrey fifteen yards from Yakima, snapped his rifle to his shoulder, and fired.

Yakima dropped quickly behind the box

wagon. The round barked into the wagon near where Yakima's head had just been.

The shooter howled merrily. The mare whinnied horrifically, said to hell with the ground anchor, and bolted forward, dragging the wagon and the anchor along behind it. The wagon slid to Yakima's left, and suddenly he was without cover and facing the shooter standing just ten yards away and just now pumping a fresh cartridge into his rifle's action.

Yakima extended the Colt straight out from his right shoulder.

The shooter, finding himself also exposed, and squinting against dust from the wagon billowing against him, blinked his surprise. Seeing that Yakima had the drop on him — as he himself was only then ejecting his last spent cartridge casing — he opened his mouth to scream. He only got out a grunt as the half-breed's Colt lapped smoke and flames, hurling a bullet through the killer's heart, driving him backward to the ground, where one of the startled horses at the hitch rack reared and kicked the fast-dying man in the head.

Hearing running footsteps ahead and left, Yakima turned to see the second shooter — a short, potbellied man with a double chin and a short, fat cigar clamped down in one corner of his mouth — run toward him around a leather-seated chaise. Yakima had swung his Colt along with his gaze, and now he squeezed the trigger.

The second shooter fired his rifle into the ground halfway between himself and Yakima, as he stumbled backward, gazing down in shock at the hole spurting blood in his upper left chest. He regained his balance, sort of. His torso wobbled on his hips, and then he dropped to his knees in the dirt.

He looked up at Yakima, fury glazing his brown eyes beneath shaggy, cinnamon brows. The cigar dropped from his mouth to spark in the dirt. He gritted his teeth at Yakima. "You . . . you are sooo dead, you cocksucker!"

Yakima gave a wry snort and sent another round through the man's broad, pale forehead, where his hat had shaded it from the sun, finishing him.

Holstering the Colt, the half-breed ran up the church's front steps, jerking the board free of the doors. He opened both doors and stepped back as the crowd burst through the entrance, screaming and coughing on a roiling cloud of heavy smoke.

When everyone who could get out by themselves was out, Yakima and two other men ran into the church and helped several older folks and one wounded man get out, as well. There were two dead men and one dead older woman inside, killed by the shooters. Yakima managed to get the dead woman out but couldn't get back inside for the two dead men before the entire building, its boards dried out from the desert air, was fully consumed. It looked like a giant orange torch, heating up the air around it so that the horses bolted from the hitch racks. Those hitched to the wagons pulled away, as well.

Nearly overcome from the smoke, Yakima dropped to a knee just outside the perimeter of unbearable heat, and for a time he felt as though he were about to cough up both lungs. His eyes stung. Soot covered him. The sleeves of his buckskin shirt were smoking where flames had nipped him.

When he could catch a breath, he sat back on his heels and looked around.

The scene before him resembled the aftermath of a small battle. The church minister was wrapping the arm of one of the wounded with cloth from his own torn shirtsleeve. Several people were down, overcome with smoke or wounded from the lead the shooters had flung into the burning church.

A hysterical young woman sat rocking a

wailing baby in her arms, a bearded young man wrapping an arm around her. An older, gray-bearded man waved his hat in the face of an older woman, likely his wife, who lay prostrate on the ground, coughing. A little girl in a pink, Sunday dress sat beside him, cheeks smudged, eyes wide with shock.

Just then a buggy swung up to the edge of the crowd. Julia Taggart jumped down from the seat and, hitching her torn skirts above her ankles, ran over to the old woman being administered to by her husband.

She glanced at Yakima, looked away, then turned her gray eyes to him again, holding his gaze with a vaguely puzzled one of her own before averting her eyes once more and helping the old man lift the old woman to a sitting position. Yakima took a moment to marvel at the young woman's spleen. Her husband had just been murdered in front of her, and she'd been mauled by the bearded desperado.

Still, she had sand enough to know she was one of the more fortunate today, and heart enough to offer a hand to those who needed it.

Yakima heaved himself to his feet and stood staring at the church, which was now clad in a thick, furry gown of orange flames that caused the air all around it to ripple and weave. One wall had already fallen inward, on top of the burning roof and bell tower. Another wall appeared to be getting ready to collapse, as well. The two dead shooters lay in front of the church, where the saddled horses, wagons, and buggies had been, inside the perimeter of unbearable heat. They were likely crispy as burnt toast by then.

Yakima wondered who they and the bearded gent and the Mexican were. What was their beef with Apache Springs? They'd been intent on wiping out every living soul on the face of this rocky pass east of Tucson.

Yakima didn't think on it over long. It wasn't any of his business. He had no stake in this town, aside from using it as a supply, drinking, gambling, and fornicating hub. He'd gone after the shooters for the same reason he'd have intervened against a pack of blood-sniffing wolves stalking a herd of helpless cattle. No reason at all, really. Just the instinct to help those who couldn't, for whatever reason, at any time help themselves.

He'd done all he felt obligated to do here. There being no more wolves on the prowl, he'd ride on.

He started looking around for the bay, spied it standing down the knoll a ways with several other saddled mounts, pulling at tufts of needle grass. As he started toward the horse, he caught Julia Taggart's eye again. He stopped and returned her gaze. She regarded him pensively, with the same curious scrutiny as before, then returned her attention to the leg of a wounded young woman. A man whom Yakima recognized as the local sawbones was suturing the wound with catgut.

Yakima strode on down the slope. The bay was spooky, but Yakima was eventually able to grab the reins. Swinging into the saddle, he rode back into town and pulled up in front of the Busted Flush. Several men, including the owner/bartender, Cleve Dundee, stood over the bodies of the bearded man and the Mexican they'd laid out on the gallery, conversing in dark tones.

They turned as Yakima swung down from the saddle. A slender, freckled, red-haired gent in a cheap suit raised an arm to point an accusing finger.

"There he is!" he cried, holding a beer in his other hand. "That's the green-eyed Injun who stole my hoss!"

Dundee gave him an incredulous look. "Shut up, you damn fool!"

Yakima looped the reins over the hitch rack.

Ignoring the red-haired gent, he said to Dundee, "I'll be back in a few days to work off the damages."

He turned and began tramping west along the deserted main street.

"Where you goin'?" Dundee called behind him.

"Home," Yakima said without looking back.

Yakima sure as hell wasn't going to return to jail. His jailer was dead, and Taggart had had no deputies. He'd work off what he owed Dundee in the days ahead.

At the moment, he wanted to get shed of this town. Obviously, things had gotten a little complicated here. He preferred simplicity and clarity. He was curious as to why the four tough nuts had wanted to massacre everyone in Apache Springs, starting with a man he'd come to call a friend despite Yakima's jail time, but he'd get over it.

Besides, he was still hungover and sore from the dustup in the Flush, and he yearned for a long sleep in his own cot. At least, the cot that he'd called his for the past four or five months, since he'd ridden into this country around the Sierra Estrada of south-central Arizona Territory, northwest of Apache Pass, having won a gold map off a one-eyed, bib-bearded prospector in Phoenix during the previous Christmas Eve.

He didn't know if the map was good or not. It might have been a fake. It didn't matter. Yakima hadn't had anywhere else to go, anything else to do. His woman was dead. He'd never find another like her. He was of the firm belief now, after Faith, that there was only one woman for every man. Or maybe there was only one woman for him.

Now, with Faith gone, there was only time to fill. A long stretch of lonely years ahead. He'd be licking his wounds for a long time, and he didn't feel foolish about that. He had a right to feel sorry for himself.

To fill some time recently, as well as to make some money, he'd led a party of miners into Mexico to retrieve silver bullion owned by an American mining company under siege by a corrupt Mexican general. He'd had to shoot his way in as well as out. Not a bad way to pass the days, with the possibility of death like the chili peppers in an otherwise bland plate of beef.

After that, he'd made his slow, cautious way south again and had spent a few months along the Sea of Cortez with the lovely Mexican *revolutionaria* Leonora Domingo, eating carne asada and drinking tequila and *bacanora* and smoking Mexican marijuana.

He'd fished a little. Mostly, he and Leonora had enjoyed each other's mattress sacks on the sand of the Mar de Cortes. Her brown body was long and supple and full-breasted, and if Leonora knew one thing, it was how to please a man.

She wasn't Faith, of course, but she'd eased his pain for a time, and that's all he'd asked.

When they'd damned near worn each other out, and she'd found another revolution to fight and possibly die in, Yakima had headed back north. He didn't believe in revolutions. It was as good a way to die as any, but he just didn't give enough of a damn to fight in one. You owed it to the people you fought with to at least give a shit. He felt the pull to head north, if only to die a little closer to his dead love's grave.

Now, as he entered the livery corral, his fine black stallion, Wolf, stood facing him, pawing the ground playfully, kicking up thick, tan dust and snorting and shaking his head. The other horses ran in jittery circles around the corral, brushing the rails and snorting. The stallion had spent nearly a week in the corral behind Scudder Early's Feed & Livery Barn, and while Wolf liked to tussle with the fillies as much as his rider did, he was always ready to hit the trail again.

He had that, too, in common with his rider.

The horse's excitement made him hard to saddle and bridle, and the shuffling around kicked up the hammering in Yakima's brain again. The half-breed didn't hold it against the horse, however. The stallion had some stable green to run off, but then, what was the old saying? A horse without pitch was like a woman who couldn't dance.

When he'd finally gotten the latigo pulled taut and tied through its ring, he led the stallion out through the gate. He closed the gate and then had to hop along beside the horse, as Wolf sidled playfully away while craning his neck to nip the rider's left ear, before Yakima could finally swing his right leg up and over his bedroll. Yakima sighed as he shoved his boot into its stirrup and seated himself in his old, familiar saddle.

He chuckled despite the ache between his ears and brushed his hand across the fine walnut stock of the Yellowboy repeater jutting up from the scabbard he'd strapped over the right saddle fender. The rifle had been a gift, years ago, from a Shaolin monk he'd once laid track with and who, during their sparse spare minutes, had taught him

Eastern fighting techniques. The man had called himself Ralph with a big grin on his round, perpetually smiling, slant-eyed face, knowing that no one on this side of the sea could have pronounced his actual handle.

Ralph had been a good poker player, but he'd only played for fun. He'd won the Yellowboy in a game of stud in a smoky tent at end-of-track and given the prized rifle to Yakima.

Ralph had had no use for such a weapon. He'd had an old Sharps and a rusty Green River knife he'd used for hunting. That was all he'd needed. Although he could fight like a mountain panther with cubs to defend, moving like the wind itself, he wasn't a fighter. He wouldn't have fought to save his life, and apparently he hadn't. Yakima had found Ralph hanging from a tree near end-of-track one early morning, where apparently sore poker losers had lynched him the night before and left him to the crows.

Smiling now at the overall memory of Ralph, because there was as much to smile as to weep about, Yakima adjusted the rifle in its scabbard, then took up his reins and touched spurs to the stallion's loins, heading west along Apache Springs's still-deserted main street. He glanced in passing at the jailhouse in which Taggart had been murdered only a little over an hour before, then urged the horse into a lope. Soon, Apache Springs and its troubles were behind Yakima Henry and his fine stallion, Wolf, and the rider noted a definite attenuation in the severity of his hangover, knowing it was no coincidence.

He didn't know why he ever went to town.

For the whores and trail supplies, of course, but he should always just stick to those two things and leave the fucking firewater alone.

Mental note.

The warm dry breeze, tanged with sage and creosote, was fresh against his face. His long, coarse black hair blew behind his ears. He drew the air deep into his lungs and sat easily in his saddle, letting Wolf pick his own route across the bristling, rocky desert, heading southwest from Apache Springs and into the magnificently stark, wild, and broken country of the Sierra Estrada, a spur range of the majestic Chiricahuas — his current, if only temporary, home.

But a perpetually homeless man couldn't ask for much better. A vast lonely country. A great country to get lost in.

But when he heard a horse whinny as he neared his cabin, he reined Wolf to a sharp halt and slid the Yellowboy from its sheath, wondering with a cold feeling of dread if someone had found him.

CHAPTER 5

Yakima slid the Yellowboy from its scabbard, then swung his right foot over Wolf's mane and dropped smoothly to the ground. He threw the reins back over the horn, patted the horse's left wither with his gloved hand, and said, "Stay till I whistle."

He pumped a cartridge into the Winchester's breech, then stepped off the ancient trading trail he'd been following — a faint trace cutting right through the heart of the sierra and no doubt leading to California or Baja, maybe even straight through Mexico to South America.

He moved carefully around some *cholla* and catclaw, then began climbing up through a jumble of solid and broken humps of limestone and granite forming a ridge of sorts east of his cabin, flanking it. He quickly scrambled over the top of the dyke, not wanting to be silhouetted against the sky for longer than he had to be, then dropped into the clearing in the rocks and desert scrub in which the stone, brush-roofed hovel sat, facing a boulder- and cactus-choked gulch.

Beyond the cabin lay a small corral and stable built of woven ocotillo branches. When he'd been on the dyke, he'd glimpsed a horse milling inside the corral and a saddle draped over the corral fence by the gate.

Anger welled in him. If someone else thought they were going to crowd him out, they had another think coming. His "guest" might even be some desperado on the run from Mexican *rurales,* as the remote Sierra Estrada was often home to *banditos* with bounties on their heads.

Yakima ran, crouching, to the rear of the cabin, passing the privy and a pile of mesquite branches he'd gleaned from near arroyos for firewood, and continued to the cabin's rear wall. Holding the Yellowboy straight up and down before him, he made his way around to the cabin's wooden front stoop, crouching beneath the end rail to mount the gallery. He pressed his shoulder against the front wall near the hovel's lone window and crouched to peer inside.

He couldn't see much through the warped, dirty glass. Only shadows and the sunlight reflecting off the sashed panes. The door on the other side of the stoop was open, however, and he could smell the aroma of cooking beef.

Again, anger burned.

He passed the window quickly, striding on the balls of his boots, then turned in the open doorway, raising the Yellowboy and clicking back the hammer and yelling, "Make yourself at home, *amigo!*"

There was a shrill scream. The figure facing the small stove in the middle of the earthen-floored cabin swung around sharply, knocking a sizzling skillet onto the floor with a clattering thud. Hazel eyes burned in the shadows by the stove, glaring at the big half-breed filling the doorway.

"Yakima, you son of a bitch! Lower that goddamn rifle!"

"Emma?" Yakima depressed the Yellowboy's hammer and let the rifle sag in his hands. "What in the hell are you doing here? You almost got yourself shot — do you realize that, young lady? Sneakin' around in a man's home . . ."

"Sneakin' around in a man's home," Emma Kosgrove mocked, crouching to poke the steak she'd dropped to the floor with a fork. She straightened, setting the skillet back on the stove. The pretty, coarse-tongued blonde walked brusquely past Yakima, anger still sharpening her pretty hazel eyes.

She gave him another acrimonious glance as she dipped water from his clay *olla* hanging from beneath the gallery's brush roof and poured it over the steak she held out over the rail, washing off the floor dirt. "I came to cook your dinner, you ungrateful heathen. When I didn't find you here, I decided to cook a steak for myself."

"You did, did you?"

"Yes."

Yakima reached over and plucked the steak off the fork. He inspected the nicely marbled beef, then bit off one end and chewed. "You still can't cook for shit."

"Why, you — !"

"But this'll do. I'm so hungry I could eat a sun-seasoned javelina layin' four days in Chiricahua wash." He leaned his rifle against the cabin's front wall and took another bite of the steak. "Which probably wouldn't taste a whole lot different than this," he added, chewing the stringy, charred beef.

He gave a wry chuckle as he hung his hat on a peg in the front wall, then sagged into the hide-bottom chair near the window and facing the stable and corral. He saw now that it was Emma's buckskin out there, hanging its head over the fence and facing the cabin, working its snout, testing the air.

That reminded Yakima of his own horse. When he'd finished chewing the meat he had in his mouth, he swallowed, stuck two fingers between his lips, and whistled.

Emma was leaning against the door frame, scowling at him bitterly. "How long you been gone?"

"Jeepers," Yakima said, taking another bite of the steak. "Three or four days? I can't remember."

"Must be longer than that. I stopped here last week, and you weren't here."

"Checkin' on me again?"

"I was bored."

Yakima grunted wryly at that and continued eating the steak.

"What were you doing in town?" She answered the question herself, bitterly, with several more questions that were more like accusations. "Drinking and gambling and *whoring*?"

Yakima frowned in mock befuddlement. "Emma, did we go and get married and I plum forgot? I'd swear, you talk like one of those old, married harpies I do my best to steer wide of."

"You'd be lucky to have me," the girl said,

flaring her nostrils angrily. "You'd be lucky to *win* me. I'm too good for you." She paused, canted her head to one side and studied him while he chewed the steak, no doubt scrutinizing the cuts and bruises on his face.

Yakima heard hoof thumps and turned to see Wolf galloping into the yard from the northwest.

"You were fighting again," Emma said, her voice softer now, more sympathetic than accusing, though the accusing was still there.

Again, Yakima hiked a shoulder.

"Was it over a woman?"

"Can't rightly remember what it was over," he lied, knowing that he'd been cheating at cards because he didn't have enough money to cover his bets, and because, in his besotted state, he'd thought it might be a nice distraction from the dream he'd had in the whore's room. He rarely cheated just to up his odds but for the thrill of cheating, and he couldn't remember cheating while sober.

Emma came over and knelt beside his chair. He'd just finished the steak and was wiping the grease from his hands on his denims while chewing the last bite. Emma took his left hand in both her own and ran her thumbs across the bruised, cracked knuckles. "You damn fool. Look what you've gone and done."

"I've done it before. I'll do it again."

"Don't you know you don't need to go to town to seek your pleasure, Yakima Henry?"

He narrowed an eye at her. "Does your father know you're here?"

Emma's father was Hugh Kosgrove, owner of the Conquistador mine only five miles as the crow flies from Yakima's cabin. Kosgrove, a wealthy easterner, was a man not to be trifled with, as he had a whole passel of tough nuts riding for him, making sure no one tried usurping his mining rights or stealing the bullion he shipped weekly through Apache Springs to the Southern Pacific railhead at Tucson.

Yakima wished the man kept as good track of his daughter as he did his gold.

"Pa and a couple of mining engineers headed into the Dinosaur Hills day before yesterday, looking for more color. Likely won't be back for days." Emma smiled as she lifted Yakima's hand to her cheek and stared up at him enticingly. "We have all the time in the world to get to know each other better, Mr. Henry. You are welcome to take that however you'd like to take it."

She pulled his hand down against her breasts and beamed up at him. She wore a red calico blouse and gray denims that hugged her exquisite figure. He could tell by what he could feel of her breasts caressing the backside of his hand that she wasn't wearing much beneath the blouse. Certainly no corset. Probably only a thin chemise. The firm globes pressed against his knuckles as she breathed. Yakima had an unwelcome image of the girl's bosoms snuggling behind the shirt and knew a moment's male discomfort before he pulled his hand away.

"Since I'm welcome to take that how I'd like to, you're welcome to saddle your buckskin and go on home."

She leaned back in shock. "Why?"

"Because you're too damn young." Yakima rose and stared down at her as she scowled up at him. He slid a lock of her flaxen hair away from her tan, marble-smooth cheek bearing a single mole that gave an exotic definition to her face. "And too damn pretty."

That caused her eyes to brighten.

Yakima turned away and walked down the gallery steps. He went over to Wolf, grabbed the reins, and led the horse into the corral, where the buckskin gave a greeting whinny. Wolf thrashed his tail, whickered, and flicked his ears. The stallion was a whole lot happier about the current company than its rider was.

Yakima just wanted to be left alone. He wanted to get a good night's sleep and clean up the mess he'd left in his mine before heading back into town to settle up with Dundee. Of course he was attracted to Emma Kosgrove. What man wouldn't be? A beautiful young blonde whose body had been sexily sculpted by years of riding her horses through these desert mountains. Although she'd refused to tell him her age, he knew she was too damned young and inexperienced for a man in his thirties to get entangled with, and her father had too much power. Yakima had all the trouble he needed without messing with the alluring daughter of Hugh Kosgrove.

He'd informed her of that on several occasions already.

Besides, there was an innocence about the girl, however reckless she may have been, that he didn't want to blemish.

He'd met her out in the desert nearly two months ago. They'd both been hunting, and he'd shot the black-tailed deer she'd been aiming at. She rode her buckskin over, fighting mad and sassy as hell, the way rich, privileged girls could be. She'd piped down when Yakima had silently field-dressed the deer and thrown it over the back of her horse.

"What're you doing?" she had said, startled, as he shoved his Arkansas toothpick back into the sheath behind his neck.

"I figure one bullet and one deer is a small price to pay for a little peace and quiet."

With that, he'd swung up onto Wolf's back and ridden off to find another deer for his cellar.

He didn't know if she'd followed him home that day or just figured he must be occupying the stone cabin in the Javelina bluffs, but she showed up there two days later. She'd been showing up unexpectedly ever since. Eventually he'd learned that she'd joined her father at the Conquistador five years ago when her mother had died in Boston, and she'd been expelled from her girls' school for failing grades and general delinquency.

Learning that, he'd softened toward her. They shared a bond of sorts. The bond of the black sheep, though he, being a halfbreed in a white man's world, was decidedly blacker and not half as pretty . . .

Now he watered and grained Wolf and forked hay from the crib fronting the corral. He took his time rubbing the horse down with a scrap of burlap and then took an even longer time with currying. The half-breed enjoyed such chores. At such times, he and the horse were one, and a strange but welcome calm overtook him as he could tell it did Wolf, who stood with his tail arched, head down, ears up, eyes closed.

The calm overtook Yakima so thoroughly that he didn't realize a storm was rolling in over the near peaks to the north. A refreshing wind was building, spitting large, cool drops of rain that plopped in the cabin yard with soft thuds, rolling the dirt into little mud beads.

He closed the corral, latched it with the wire loop, and jogged toward the cabin. He saw Emma sitting in his chair as he climbed the gallery steps. She was leaning back against the cabin's front wall, her long, strong legs stretched straight out before her. Her feet were bare, and she gripped the edge of the mesquite rail with her toes. She'd fried a steak for herself, and she was eating it the way Yakima had eaten his, with her fingers, occasionally wiping her hands on her trousers.

"You still here?" Yakima said.

"We're about to get a gully-washer." Not looking at him, talking with her mouth full and plucking the fat from the T-bone with her fingers, she said, "My pa would get powerful mad if you sent me off in this storm and I drowned in a flooded arroyo." She swallowed, glanced up at him insouciantly, and said, "I got a pot of coffee on the range."

Yakima grunted. He went inside and came out lugging his cot, nudging the girl's legs out of his way. He stumbled with his load along the gallery, banging the cot off the rail.

"What're you doing?" she asked.

"Gonna take a long nap. I sleep better out here." Yakima set the cot down, arranging the pillow and the blankets, and turned to her. "As soon as the storm quits, go home. Don't let me wake up and find you here."

"What the hell are you so afraid of?" She looked genuinely puzzled.

"Your old man."

"No, you're not." Emma laughed caustically. "You're not afraid of any man, Yakima Henry, least of all a fifty-six-year-old man with the gout."

"Haven't you noticed all the men he has ridin' with him?"

"I bet you whipped that many in town with those bruised fists of yours."

"Those were townsmen. You could beat them up. Probably with one hand tied."

She'd lifted her bare foot to the edge of

her chair and was hugging her knee, looking around it at Yakima. She shook her head slowly as she watched him unbutton his shirt. He turned away from her with a grunt, tossing his shirt onto the floor.

Thunder rumbled in a sky sooty with lowering storm clouds. Lightning forked.

He kicked out of his boots, removed his cartridge belt and Colt, and hung them on a hook in the wall. He hung the toothpick there, as well, snugged in the small sheath he often wore behind his neck. He'd retrieved the toothpick from Taggart's office when he'd retrieved his rifle. Keeping his back to the girl, he skinned out of his denims, tossed them aside, then sat on the cot to remove his socks.

He lay back on the cot, enjoying the cool, fresh air blowing over him, drying the sweat on his body. The rain was coming hard now, in buffeting white sheets. The wind blew a cool mist under the gallery roof, and Yakima smiled as it cleansed his face. There was nothing as soothing to the soul as a desert rain in high summer.

He rested his head back against his bent arms and closed his eyes. Slowly, sleep began cat-footing around him.

It stepped away when he heard a young woman's delighted laughter mingling with the drumming of the rain on the roof. He opened his eyes and turned his head to stare out through the gallery's slender, crooked rails.

Emma stood out in the yard, naked in the rain.

CHAPTER 6

Emma was dancing around and laughing, her face tipped toward the sky, letting the rain wash over her.

Her tender, pale breasts jostled. Her soaked hair was a couple of shades darker than it was when dry, and it hung pasted to her head, neck, shoulders, and back, several wet tendrils clinging to the sides of her breasts. She danced around like an Indian, face up, holding out her arms, then bringing them to her chest and rubbing the rain into her breasts.

"Come on out here, Yakima," she called, teasing. "It's wonderful! Come out here and wash your sins away!" She winked and smiled and added thickly, lustily, "We know you have your share of those!"

Yakima watched her through the gallery rails. She moved like a dancer or a white Indian, her long-limbed, large-busted body pale as marble. She was like a desert sprite, thrilling to the storm gods. Watching her young, supple body caressed by the rain, Yakima became aware of all the layers of sweat and filth encasing his own brawny frame, fairly gluing his long handles to him. He stared at the rain falling like a billowing curtain, pouring off the gallery roof to drum onto the mesquite rail.

"Ah, hell."

He rose from the cot and walked to the top of the steps. She was out in the middle of the yard now, between the cabin and the stone well coping, arms out, twirling, laughing, smiling up at the sky, where thunder continued to crackle and drum, witches' fingers of lightning sparking over the rocky western ridges cloaked in the fluttering sequins of the hard-falling monsoon rain.

Yakima started skinning out of his long handles. He peeled them down his chest and arms and crouched to roll them down his legs. Naked, he walked down the gallery steps and held the filthy, sweaty garment out to the water pouring off the gallery roof. He let the rain soak the wash-worn red cloth, then wrung them out and soaked them again. Finally, when they were relatively clean, he tossed them over the mesquite rail.

He turned to Emma. She stood still now

73

in the yard, facing him, gazing at him, a faint smile tugging at her mouth corners. Yakima looked down his broad, flat-bellied body painted copper by his mother's Cheyenne blood. His manhood stood at full mast. It throbbed with raw desire.

He stepped under the water cascading off the roof, tipped back his head, and let the fresh, pure water from the sky wash over his face. He smoothed his wet hair back with his hands, let it trail, sleek as a soaked badger tail, down his heavy shoulders and back, and then brushed the rain from his eyes.

He looked at Emma. She returned his gaze. She stood absolutely still now, arms down at her sides. Her pale breasts were swollen, cherry nipples jutting from pink areolas. Her face was hard as stone, her eyes serious, flinty with unbridled desire.

Slowly, she lifted an arm, stretched out her hand to him. She gave an alluringly crooked smile and beckoned him with her fingers.

Yakima walked to her, the rain drumming off his heavy shoulders, his mast jutting out before him, throbbing with his need.

He stopped before her, their bodies so close they were nearly touching. She let her gaze trail across his chest, brushing her fingers across the various scars — knife scars, bullet scars, whip scars, rock scars, glass scars, even the scar from an arrow loosed by a renegade Apache when he'd been scouting for the cavalry at Fort Hell, not all that far from here, but years ago now.

Emma pressed her thumb to the largest scar, just beneath his slab-like left breast, then leaned forward and pressed her lips to it. She looked up at him, her eyes soft now and doughy with gentle, dreamy passion.

Yakima placed his hands on her face, cupping her jaws with his thumbs, and tipped her head back. He lowered his head to hers and kissed her. She returned the kiss, parting her lips for him, gradually sticking her tongue out to flick it teasingly against his own.

Yakima's blood grew hot. He could feel her heart beating more and more quickly against his hands splayed across her slender back, just beneath her shoulder blades. He could feel the furnace of desire burning in her own body, despite the chicken flesh rising across her breasts pressed nearly flat against his chest.

As he kissed her, he felt her fingers trail down his chest, past his belly. Her hands traced the long, thick line of his staff, flicked across the heavy, bulging sack of his scrotum. Yakima's heart thumped heavily. He groaned. He pulled his mouth from hers, leaving her gasping, and crouched to suckle her swollen nipples.

"Oh!" she cried, the scream nearly being drowned by a thunderclap that caused both their bodies to jerk as though lightning struck.

Yakima moved his mouth back to hers and placed his hands on her wet buttocks. He slid them lower, splaying his fingers against the insides of her upper thighs. This evoked another cat-like groan from Emma, who, shuddering with craving, obeyed his urging by lifting her legs and wrapping them around his back. She folded her arms around his neck and clung to him tightly while he carried her over to the well and set her on the edge of the stone coping.

"Hurry," she said, pressing her trembling hands against his jaws and looking down between their bodies, down past their quickly expanding and contracting bellies. "Hurry!"

She grabbed his manhood in one hand, then looked up at him, eyes flinging javelins of desire at him as she drew him into her. She shuddered more violently as he slid inside her, her warmth engulfing him.

He placed his hands beneath her rump, cushioning her from the unforgiving stone of the well, and began bucking against her.

"Yes," she said. "Oh, Yakima . . . *yes!*"

They frolicked like horny desert nymphs, like unsupervised adolescents for the rest of the stormy day and night.

They retreated into the cabin where, clad in only socks and a blanket, Emma cooked them another meal — a proper meal of beans and bacon and baking powder biscuits and hot, black coffee. They sat out on the gallery, warmed by a fire from the kitchen range behind them, watching the clouds thin and scud off to the south, letting the stars wink through the trailing vapors.

Finally, they collapsed onto the cot together, on the gallery, where the rain-silky air lulled them to sleep after they made love one more time — slowly, luxuriously, Emma straddling him, the starlight flashing off her uptilted breasts and dancing in her round, dark eyes.

The heavy wings of sleep were so tightly wrapped around Yakima that he was only vaguely aware of Wolf's warning whinny. Gradually, other sounds tugged him up out of the clinging fingers of slumber.

Lying belly up on the cot, he slitted his eyes, then groaned and closed them again quickly against the buttery wash of sunlight filtering beneath the gallery roof. But, having seen something off the side of the gallery, he opened them again quickly and pushed up onto his elbows with a startled grunt.

Emma, curled against him, one arm flung across his belly, her cheek resting on his chest, gave a soft grunt of complaint against his movement.

Yakima was still blinking against the light, shading his eyes with one hand, as a woman's arch voice said, *"Emma?"*

Emma gasped as she jerked her head up off Yakima's chest and turned to the three horseback riders sitting about ten yards off the gallery, facing the lovers lying all but naked on the cot, the blankets twisted and hanging askew.

Yakima blinked again, heart thudding, at once realizing how exposed he was and recognizing the three riders as none other than Lon Taggart's wife, Julia, sitting a cream horse between the short, stocky mayor of Apache Springs and the owner/bartender of the Busted Flush, Cleve Dundee. The mayor — whose name was Cliff Sykes, if Yakima remembered right — wore a white bandage over his nose, which was twice its normal size, and the man's eyes were both ringed in a sickly yellow and black, the whites red.

The mayor had been one of the men who'd accused Yakima of cheating at cards and had received the broken nose for his trouble. He was also the one who'd stumbled out of the saloon as Yakima was being carried off to jail, demanding a necktie party in the half-breed's honor.

Now, apparently, he was here to stretch some hemp.

But . . . what were Julia Taggart and Cleve Dundee doing here, as well?

The young widow's exasperated gaze was on the girl Yakima had spent most of yesterday afternoon and evening frolicking with, and who returned Julia's gaze with an equally incredulous one of her own, pulling a blanket up to cover her breasts and inadvertently uncovering Yakima's privates.

Julia's eyes flicked to the organ of topic, then returned her fiery gaze to Emma and said, "Does Father know you're here, dear sister?"

Yakima wondered if he'd heard her right. *Sister?*

"Oh, Christ," Emma said. "What in the hell are *you* doing here?"

"We're here to see the breed," said Sykes, the light of amusement dancing in his bruised eyes, above the broken nose and the bandage that glowed way too brightly in the mid-morning sun.

Mid-morning?

Yakima must have been more tired than he'd realized, distracted as he'd been by Emma, who wasn't nearly as innocent as he'd thought, it hadn't taken him long to realize . . .

Julia gave Sykes a sharp glance of reproof, then turned back to Yakima. "We're here to see Mr. Henry. Emma, why don't you go inside and get some clothes on. You're liable to catch your death of cold out here."

"I managed to stay pretty warm, dear sister," Emma shot back snidely, rising from the cot and wrapping the blankets around her shoulders, "until you came."

As she padded off to the cabin door, leaving Yakima naked on the cot, he reached back to pluck his hat off a hook behind him and set it on his privates. Holding the hat in place and feeling like seven kinds of a fool, lounging around out here naked in front of visitors, he swung his bare feet to the floor. He sat on the edge of the cot, facing the newcomers, blinking sleep from his eyes and reminding himself that if he, a man with no few enemies, continued to be so careless, letting folks ride up on him like that in broad daylight, he should probably scout

80

around for a burial plot.

Amidst all the other confusion in his brain, he was still having trouble wrapping his mind around Julia Taggart being Emma Kosgrove's sister . . .

He cleared his throat and returned Julia's incriminating gaze with his own sheepish one. "What, uh . . . what can I help you with, Mrs. Taggart?" He glanced at Sykes, gave a guilty smile, and added, "Mr. Mayor . . . ?"

Both men seemed to be deferring to the woman. They glanced at her sidelong, as though hoping she would take the lead. Julia's horse lowered its head and shook. She jerked the mount's head back up with the bridle reins and said, "Mr. Henry, after yesterday we now have a situation in Apache Springs. A situation in which we find ourselves without a town . . . without a town marshal." Her voice trembled slightly, as did her upper lip. She was trying to control her emotions in much the same way she was controlling her horse, reining them in commandingly.

Yakima waited, not sure what was coming next but wishing she would get on with it. He was feeling damned awkward, sitting here on the cot in his birthday suit, with his hat over his privates.

"Lon knew you. I mean, before you ended up in his jail." She'd added that last with a fleeting cast of irony in her gaze. "He talked about you . . . to me . . . a couple of times. You made an impression on him. I guess you could say that yesterday you made an impression on me and the rest of the town when . . . when you broke out of jail when Lon was killed and, instead of running away, as some would . . . as *most* would . . . you saved a good many lives."

Sykes spat to one side, ran his sleeve across his mouth, and turned to Yakima. "I hate to say it after you broke my nose an' all, Henry, but you might have got to the church just in time to save most of the town."

"I seen how you could fight," Cleve Dundee added his two cents. "Sure didn't care for it much, but I reckon now in hindsight I was right impressed by your accounting of yourself in my saloon. I mean . . . I don't cotton to card sharpies, but" — he turned his head to one side and narrowed a shrewd eye at Yakima — "somethin' tells me maybe you don't make a habit of that."

When Yakima didn't say anything but only studied the three through incredulously slitted lids, Dundee added, "I never seen a man take on a dozen men, hold 'em off for as long as you did, until I got the drop on ya. And the way you took down that Mex, why . . ." He paused, drew a deep breath. "I'm just sayin', uh, we'll forget the damages to my waterin' hole if you'll take the job."

Yakima scowled. "What job?"

"The town marshal's job," Sykes said.

"The town marshal's job," Yakima said, mostly to himself, trying to understand.

"Your husband's job." Maybe they weren't here to play cat's cradle with his head, after all.

"My husband's job, Mr. Henry. Lon's job." Julia reached into the pocket of the man's canvas coat she wore and held her husband's badge out toward Yakima. It glinted in the sunshine. Yakima started to get up but then, remembering his state of undress, gave another sheepish smile and hiked a shoulder.

Julia flipped the badge over the gallery rail. Yakima snapped it out of the air, opened his hand. The five-pointed town marshal's star was marked with dark-red spots turning brown against the polished tin.

"It still has my husband's blood on it," she said, meaningfully, her jaws hard, her gray eyes flinty beneath the broad brim of her man's felt Stetson.

CHAPTER 7

Yakima brushed his thumb across the badge in his hand, staring down at it.

He glanced up at the three people sitting their horses before him in the mid-morning sunshine. "This isn't just about pinning a badge on my shirt, is it? About walking around town after business hours, making sure the shop doors are locked, and hauling drunks out of saloons."

"No, it's not," Julia said without hesitation. "If that's all we needed, we could probably find the right man sitting in the Busted Flush in Apache Springs at this very moment."

"It's about somebody havin' one hell of a chip on his shoulder. One hell of a beef with you folks — with the whole town."

"Rebel Wilkes." Julia had spoken the name as though it were a curse. "He sent those men to kill Lon and the rest of us. To burn the town to the ground." She paused, staring directly at Yakima, her eyes dark with foreboding beneath the brim of her hat. "He'll send more. Until the deed is done. That's the way he is."

"Or until he himself is dead," Cleve Dundee said, sharing a dark glance past Julia with Sykes.

"What's got this fella Wilkes's neck in such a hump?" Yakima asked.

"He wanted to run a spur railroad line through Apache Springs," Sykes said. "From the Southern Pacific Line in Tucson. The town voted against it. He'd discovered a gold-bearing quartz vein just east of Apache Springs. Due to the topography of the area, the only way to get the bullion out was through town. We said no to the spur line. Didn't want the trouble the railroad brings."

"Unfortunately, Wilkes had put his cart in front of his horse," Dundee said, nibbling a wad of chaw off the blade of a folding Barlow knife. "He got a pool of investors together, and they started buying up right-of-ways northeast of Tucson, certain-sure that when they got to Apache Springs, we'd be more than willing to let him hammer his rails right through the heart of town and off to his mine in the east. See, there was no other way for the rails to go, the country bein' what it is to either side of the pass the town sits on."

"When he got to Apache Springs with his offer and we turned him down, his investors backed out," Sykes said.

"And he was left holding the empty money sack," Dundee said.

Julia said, "In his desperation, he made certain threats. He tried to bully the town. He tried to bully Lon into convincing the town to change its mind. But we didn't want a railroad through Apache Springs. Most of the people in Apache Springs came here to get away from the noise and crime of most frontier towns, to earn their modest livings and to raise their families in peace."

The young widow shook her head, lips pursed stubbornly. "The town wouldn't cave to Wilkes's bullying. So now, apparently, he is trying to make good on his threats. It didn't work yesterday because of you, Mr. Henry. That's why we're offering you the job. Rest assured, we don't expect you to stand alone against the men Wilkes will no doubt send next. But we'd like to have a formidable leader, a leader like Lon himself was, in the office of town marshal. If, considering what you know now about Apache Springs and its history with Rebel Wilkes, you choose not to accept our offer — our offer of fifty dollars a month plus free room and board for as long you want the job — simply return the badge to me in Apache Springs. But I do hope you'll at least consider our offer" — she blinked once with a vague beseeching — "and our plea."

Yakima looked down at the badge again, then squinted up at Julia Taggart once more. "Why not bring your father in? Hire one of his men. Surely . . ."

"My father isn't trustworthy, Mr. Henry. Nor are any of his men. My father lives for one thing and one thing only — gold. He pays the border toughs he has riding for him very well to do just that. And only that." Julia gave a bitter smile. "The county has a sheriff, of course, but his office is in Tucson, sixty miles away. Stafford's too undermanned and has too much ground to cover to be of much help to Apache Springs. He has his hands full with the trouble the railroad has brought to Tucson.

"So . . . there you have it, Mr. Henry. We need your help. Take a couple of days to consider our offer. And, please . . ." Glancing at the cabin's front window, she edged her tone with a persnickety crispness. "I'm sure you're quite lonely out here. But don't let yourself be exploited by my sister's weaknesses, of which she has many."

She neck-reined the cream around, chin

in the air, and galloped away.

The two men glanced at the cabin, wry casts to their gazes, then pinched their hat brims to Yakima and galloped off into Julia Taggart's dust.

Yakima sat staring after them, fingering the star.

The cabin door latch clicked. The door shuddered on its dry leather hinges as it opened inward and Emma stepped out, still wrapped in her blankets. She almost appeared in a trance. Her face was pale and drawn. She stopped at the top of the steps and stared out across the yard, her gaze edged in deep thought.

Her voice was soft, stricken. "Lonnie . . . dead . . . ?"

Yakima frowned. "Lonnie?"

She turned to Yakima. "He was killed . . . yesterday? In town?"

Yakima nodded. He rose, set his hat on his head, and, otherwise naked, walked over to where he'd draped his long handles over the mesquite rail. "You know him pretty well, I take it — Lon Taggart?"

"I knew him first. Before my sister met him."

Yakima stepped into his long handles. They weren't quite dry, but they were dry enough for him. It looked like another hot, dry day shaping up. They'd dry soon enough. As he sat down on the cot to pull on his socks, he considered what Emma had just told him about herself and Taggart and decided that things were right complicated in these parts. More complicated than things had seemed at first.

But, then, wasn't everything?

"You and your sister don't get on too well, I take it?" Yakima reached for his shirt, drew it onto his knees, and plucked his makings sack and small, tin matchbox from the breast pocket. "Did the bad blood start with Taggart?"

Emma continued to stare out across the yard, seeing nothing there, but only some vision in her head. Probably Taggart, Yakima guessed. The handsome young marshal had also apparently been considerably more complicated than he'd at first seemed.

But, then, wasn't everybody?

As Yakima took his time building a smoke, Emma turned to him suddenly. Her brows furled with deep consternation, she padded over to him barefoot and knelt before him. She placed a hand on his knee. "Yakima, don't do it. Don't take the job."

"Why not?" he said, looking at her as he slowly rolled the wheat paper closed.

She studied him closely, suspiciously.

"You're considering it, aren't you?"

Yakima hiked a shoulder, poking the quirley in and out of his mouth, sealing it. "I been playin' at rock-breakin' long enough, maybe. I'm not really a prospector at heart. Too damn much like work."

He gave a dry chuckle.

"It's her, isn't it?"

"Huh?"

"You got Julia stuck in your craw."

"What do you mean?"

Fuming, Emma stood and, planting her fists on the mesquite rail, stared off into space again. Beneath her Arizona tan, her cheeks turned dark with anger. "Oh, Miss Prissy-Pants and her queenly ways! The way butter wouldn't melt in her mouth — or so everyone thinks! My sister, treated like royalty wherever she goes!" Emma glanced at Yakima snidely, with bitter accusation, and snapped her fingers. "Men fall in love with her just like that!"

"Is that what happened with Taggart?"

"Damned right it is." Emma stared down at the rail now, her jaws hard. "I met him first. He saw her, and she took him away from me. I didn't think it would work out. I didn't think it would work out any better with Lonnie than it had with Wilkes."

Yakima had just struck a match to life and

91

was about to touch the flame to his cigarette but stopped and looked at the girl in shock. *"Wilkes?"*

Emma glanced at him, nodding. "Rebel Wilkes was Poppa's chief mining engineer. Until he betrayed Poppa and went out on his own, found that quartz vein, and registered his own claim in secret. Julia had been engaged to Wilkes. They'd been set to marry the next spring. When Poppa found out what Rebel had done, that he would now be operating a competing mine, Poppa forced her to cancel the marriage."

Emma shook her head. "Not forced. *Allowed* her to cancel it. Julia never loved Wilkes. She'd agreed to marry him as a favor to Poppa, who was rewarding Wilkes with his daughter's hand for what he saw as the man's previous loyalty. And, back then, Julia did whatever Poppa asked of her."

Yakima opened his mouth to speak, but then the lucifer burned his fingers. "Ouch!" He tossed the match into the yard, rose from the cot to stand beside Emma, and continued with, "How did Taggart work into it?"

"I met Lonnie in Tucson. He wasn't a marshal yet. Just a handsome young shotgun rider for the local stage. I was smitten. It was love at first sight. So . . . I invited Lonnie out to the mine, where Julia and I both lived together with Poppa, in a house he'd built out there, after Mother died back east.

"By the end of the meal, I could sense that Lonnie had fallen head over heels for my sister, as so many had before him. Don't ask me how I knew. I kept close watch, but I never once saw them so much as glance at each other across the table."

She paused, brushed a tear from her cheek with the back of her hand. "Looking back, I guess that's how I knew. They didn't look at each other all night long. They didn't dare. What they felt was so real that it scared them both. Two weeks later, Lonnie broke off our courtship. Two weeks after that, Julia announced that she was seeing him. Two months after *that,* they announced their marriage. Our father wouldn't have it, of course. Lonnie was a former ranch hand who now rode shotgun for a stage line. He'd been raised in Missouri, the product of a hillbilly family who'd taken part in the border wars. His father went on to become a decorated deputy United States marshal here in the west later in his life, but that wasn't good enough for Poppa. Two of Lonnie's brothers were dead, and another one was in the federal pen!"

Emma was staring off across the yard now,

past the corrals and the two horses — her buckskin and Wolf — both staring back toward the cabin. She was smiling, but tears streamed down her cheeks.

"Lonnie," she said softly. "Dead. However he may have treated me, he was a good man. And that scoundrel Rebel Wilkes killed him." She sobbed. "I knew there was something off about Wilkes the first time I met him. A craziness in his eyes. The craziness of blind ambition."

Yakima wrapped his arm around her shoulders and drew her to him.

"I'm sorry," he said.

Emma looked up at him. "It happened in front of you?"

"Yeah. I was, uh . . . behind bars at the time." Yakima sighed and added guiltily, "Taggart had locked me up for drunk and disorderly. Your sister was there when it happened. The man who killed your brother-in-law dragged her off, kicking and screaming, but he paid the price when she raked a broken lamp chimney across his neck."

Emma gave a snort. "That's Julia. You pay a high price when you cross her."

"Good to know."

Fatefully, smiling crookedly up at Yakima, Emma said, "So, you're in love with her . . . ?"

"Hell, no!" Yakima chuckled without mirth. "I don't even know the woman, for chrissakes, Emma!"

He walked to the top of the gallery steps. The quirley still dangled from between his lips. He snapped another luficer to life on the ceiling support post and lit the cigarette. Puffing smoke, he said, "I do know what I saw, though. Her husband killed in front of her."

His rage at the memory kindled within him, and a gnawing ache assaulted his heart as he remembered his own love dying in his arms as he screamed her name at the top of his lungs, trying in vain to bring her back. Instead, he'd buried her in Colorado and erected a marker at the home they once shared on the slopes of Mount Bailey in Arizona.

Faith's killer, Bill Thornton, was dead. Sometimes Yakima wished he wasn't. The man's being dead meant he couldn't kill him again.

Emma walked up to him, placed her hand on his arm. "Tell me about her."

Yakima glanced at her sharply. "What?"

"What was her name?" Emma's voice was gentle. "What happened to her?"

Yakima drew deep on the quirley, blew

out the smoke. "I don't want to talk about it."

"All right." Emma rubbed her forehead against his upper arm, snuggling against him. "Let's not say another word for the rest of the morning."

He heard a faint rustling sound and a soft plop. He looked down at the girl pressing her cheek against his right arm, smiling alluringly up at him. She'd dropped the blankets to the floor.

CHAPTER 8

Yakima lay with his head resting on his bent arms, staring up at the gallery roof, but seeing only the startled, agonized look on Lon Taggart's face as the bullets had hammered into him, one after another.

He heard Julia's screams. They mixed with his own cry of unendurable perplexity, depthless incomprehension: *"Faith!"*

Emma stirred beside him, her head moving on his chest. He felt the soft caress of her lashes as she opened her eyes. She lifted her head with a tired groan, glanced into the yard bathed in the softening light of the late afternoon, and looked up at him, eyes red from sleep.

"You're awake."

"Slept out, I reckon."

"I'd best skedaddle on home before Poppa returns. I'm not sure Three Moons will buy my story of getting lost in the desert during the storm."

"Three Moons?"

Julia kissed Yakima's chest, then rolled over and dropped her feet to the gallery floor. "Our Apache housekeeper." She snorted an ironic laugh. "Full-blood Chiricahua. Or, one of *the People,* as he calls them."

Yakima laughed. "A housekeeper? Way out there in the desert?"

Emma chuckled as she began to stumble around sleepily, gathering her clothes. "Poppa has never believed in roughing it, even far out in the desert. Three Moons guided him into the desert nearly fifteen years ago now, when Poppa first come out here to find his El Dorado. Three Moons was an orphan raised by wealthy missionaries and educated back east. A friend of a friend introduced him to Poppa. Now Three Moons rules the Kosgrove roost, you might say. He keeps Kosgrove House, as Poppa calls it, in tip-top eastern shape." She raked her pink pantalets across Yakima's face and smiled down at him. "Maybe I'll wrangle you an invitation to dinner sometime, and you can see how we Kosgroves live way out there in the godforsaken desert . . . with indoor showers and everything else. It's quite decadent, actually."

Yakima chuckled, sat up, and swung his

legs over the side of the cot. He ran his hands through his long hair, yawning. "I ain't heeled well enough for dinner in no Kosgrove House. I'll stay right here and throw my scraps to the javelinas and mountain lions."

"You do that," Emma said, dressing. "You stay right here, Yakima. Don't go to town. Leastways, don't pin that badge on your chest."

Yakima frowned up at her as she dropped her chemise over her head, covering her pale breasts. "Why do you have so much interest in me an' that badge? If it's about your sister —"

"It's not just about Julia." Emma dropped to a knee beside him, ran her fingers through his hair. "It's about you. I like you too much to see you killed. And that's what will happen to you if you take the job as town marshal of Apache Springs. If Rebel Wilkes sent four men last time, he'll send double that many next time. I know. I saw the rage in his eyes when he rode out to our house and asked to buy a right-of-way through Conquistador property and Poppa turned him down."

"I don't understand. Why did Wilkes need a right-of-way through your father's property?"

"The only way he could get ore wagons from his mine to the smelter in Lordsburg was either through Poppa's chunk of desert, or straight over the pass Apache Springs sits on. It was after Poppa turned him down that he came up with the spur railroad idea, believing the town would go for it because the town would benefit from a railroad connecting it with the Southern Pacific and Tucson and the whole rest of the world. Poppa made Rebel mad. Literally spitting mad! But he was even madder when the town turned down his idea for those rails, because that was the last nail in the coffin of his gold discovery. With no way to get that ore out to the smelter and to the US Mint, the gold was no better than the quartz it's buried in. He spent all of his own and his investors' money on railroad right-of-ways, so now he's broke. Broke and no doubt working for his father in Prescott."

"What's his father do in Prescott?"

"Owns the High and Mighty."

"A dance hall and saloon?" Yakima knew of the place. A glorified brothel that catered to freighters and railroad workers, mostly. The half-breed whistled. "That's quite a takedown from a gold fortune."

Emma was sitting on the cot beside Yakima, pulling on her gray denims. She chuckled. "Probably even more of a takedown since his father put Rebel through engineering school back east. His father didn't see any reason for higher learning. Rebel's father wanted Rebel to go into business with him there at the High and Mighty. What was good enough for Rebel's father was good enough for Rebel. But now that Rebel lost all his and his investors' money — and I have no doubt Zeke Wilkes was one of Rebel's biggest investors — Rebel's probably cowering like a whipped dog behind his old man's bar at the High and Mighty. Likely getting kicked regularly, too."

"How do you know so much about Rebel Wilkes, Emma?"

Emma, standing now and throwing her blonde hair out from behind the collar of the shirt she'd slipped into, blushed. She hiked a sheepish shoulder. "Well, you see . . . Rebel an' me, for a while there . . ."

Yakima frowned, incredulous. "You mean, while he and your sister . . . ?"

"Were fixing to get married. Yes, yes, I know. I'm a bad girl. So what else is new?" Emma donned her hat and dropped to a knee before Yakima once more. She placed her hands on his thighs, ran them up toward his belly. "Would you want me any different?"

Yakima wasn't sure what to say to that. He was no saint himself. Still, he was a little taken aback by the wildcat he'd just tangled with. Here he'd thought she was so young and innocent. Young, maybe. But sure as hell not innocent.

"All I have to say," he said, wagging his head slowly, "is that you and your sister sure have one hell of a complicated relationship."

"Doesn't everybody?" She sandwiched his face in her hands and kissed his nose. "Don't go to town, Yakima. Dangerous there. Believe me. I know Rebel Wilkes. You're better off out here" — she gave a lusty wink — "where I know where to find you."

She kissed his lips. She held the kiss a long time, hungrily flicking her tongue against his. She pulled away, nipping his chin, and rose. "I'll see you again soon."

She blew him one last kiss, flounced off to the corral, saddled the buckskin, and rode away.

Yakima stared after her. He turned to Wolf, who'd been staring into the dust of horse and rider, as well. Wolf twitched his ears dubiously at Yakima, who chuckled.

Then he dressed fully for the first time that day, went into the cabin, and brewed a pot of coffee. Sipping the coffee and smoking a cigarette, he fried up a couple of venison steaks and the last two potatoes from his root cellar. He'd worked up one hell of an appetite tussling with the Wildcat of the Sierra Estrada, or so he'd come to know Emma Kosgrove.

Thinking of the sassy blonde set him to thinking about her sister again. He wanted to help Julia Taggart, because he knew the rawness of watching someone he loved die, as Julia had watched Lon die. At the same time, he didn't owe her or the rest of the town a damned thing. He owed Cleve Dundee money for damages, but he could work that off in a week or two and have his life little more complicated for his trouble.

And that's why he was in this godforsaken desert, after all — holed up in this crude, ancient prospector's shack in the heart of the remote Sierra Estrada. Because he'd wanted to be alone and know the simplicity of a quiet life for a change. Except for the rare trip to Apache Springs to drink, gamble, fuck, and tear apart a saloon or two, that is . . .

He didn't owe Taggart anything, either. He'd liked the man. But Taggart had chosen to wear the badge. He'd been no fool. He'd known what the job entailed and that badges were often targets. So, he'd been targeted. It wasn't up to Yakima to take up arms whenever he was privy to a grave injustice. If it was, he'd be shooting his way in and out of this life the way he'd had to shoot his way in and out of Mexico not all that long ago.

No, he had to think about himself once in a while. There was nothing in that fight for him. He was only one man, after all. Apache Springs had plenty of able-bodied men among its citizenry who could take up arms against Rebel Wilkes and those the obviously deranged mining engineer sent to exact his revenge.

Yakima would stay out here and break rocks until he found enough color to fund another trip to Mexico for the winter and maybe track down the beautiful *revolutionaria* Leonora Domingo, with whom he'd like to hole up for the winter again on the shores of the Sea of Cortez.

Until then . . . well, he'd made a special friend in Emma Kosgrove. She'd surely keep him well sated in the pleasures of the flesh until October, say.

Tomorrow, Yakima would crawl back into his mine.

His mind was made up, he decided, pushing his empty plate away and refilling his empty coffee cup from the steaming pot on the stove. He stood, stretched, stepped out through the door propped open to the early evening breeze, and set his coffee on the gallery rail to drag the hide-bottom chair up from the cabin's front wall.

There was a sharp *ping!*

The coffee cup disappeared from the mesquite rail to clank onto the floor by the open door, coffee spraying in all directions.

The clank of the cup was nearly drowned by the cough of a distant rifle.

Yakima threw himself to the gallery floor and lay belly down, wincing as another bullet screeched through the air over the rail and slammed into the front of the cabin, trailed closely by another hiccupping rifle roar.

Another bullet hammered the rail, and he squeezed his eyes closed against the spray of mesquite slivers.

When another bullet did not come hurtling toward the cabin within seconds of the last one, Yakima rose to his knees, palming the Colt strapped to his waist. He flung the Colt up over the top of the rail and, aiming in the general direction from which the rifle had thundered, clicked the hammer back and fired. He flung six quick rounds toward the brushy arroyo and the rocks beyond, south of the corral in which Wolf was running around in distress, buck-kicking and whinnying angrily.

When the echo of his sixth shot was still chasing itself around the canyon, Yakima rose, ran crouching into the cabin, and grabbed the Yellowboy leaning against the wall by the door. He racked a round into the chamber, stepped outside, putting his back to the cabin wall so he wouldn't be outlined against the door, and raised the butt to his shoulder.

He held fire as he saw a man-shaped shadow just then crawl up and over the top of a rock outcropping on the arroyo's far side. Yakima cursed, lowered the Winchester, and leaped off the gallery. He ran across the yard, past the corral in which Wolf stood, shaking his head in protest of the din, and leaped into the arroyo. He hotfooted from boulder to boulder until he was across the arroyo, and then he climbed the outcropping, noting several brass cartridge casings strewn along the gravelly side of the slope.

As he neared the crest over which the shooter had slipped, he paused, shoved his hat back of his head, letting it dangle by its thong between his shoulders, then edged a slow, careful peek up over the top of the ridge crest.

He pulled his head back down, quickly, to

avoid another possible bullet.

When one didn't come, he drew a quick breath and jack-rabbited up and over the crest, landing on the opposite slope several feet down from the top.

A bullet smacked the slope two feet below his position and slightly left.

Seeing the last, dying rays of the sun glancing off a rifle barrel aimed at him from beside a wagon-sized, flat-topped boulder on a rise of chaparral forty or fifty yards straight beyond, he threw himself right and rolled up behind a low, cactus-spiked knoll.

Two bullets hammered the front of the knoll, rifle reports bellowing.

Yakima snaked the Yellowboy around the knoll's right side. The shooter was running up the rocky spine capping the slope, above the boulder he'd been covering behind. Yakima cut loose, the Winchester leaping and roaring in his hands, the kicks feeling firmly satisfying against his right shoulder.

Cartridge casings arced back over his shoulder to clink to the rocky ground behind him.

He was aiming for the man's legs, but the man was moving, making a hard target. One of Yakima's bullets thumped into a small shelf of sandstone just as the fleeing shooter put his boot on it. The shelf broke. The man's right foot jerked down. He gave a yell and fell backward, dropping his rifle and rolling heels-over-head down the slope toward the boulder.

He was still rolling as Yakima leaped from behind his own cover and ran down the slope, then up the opposite rise. He saw his assailant land atop the flat-topped boulder with a snarling groan, flopping around like a landed fish and clutching his left shoulder.

Yakima leaped onto the boulder and stood over the man, aiming his cocked Yellowboy straight down at the man's head. His opponent was short and thick-bodied, broad-shouldered, and boasting a considerable paunch, which was fish-belly white as it stuck out between two torn buttons of his hickory shirt. He had a thick head with very little neck and a double chin. His eyes were blue beneath sandy brows and a nearly bald head with thin hair of the same color crowning his ears. His battered, funnel-brimmed Stetson lay up the slope a ways.

He wore a red neckerchief and suspenders, and the sleeves of his hickory shirt were rolled up to the thick slabs of his biceps.

Two Remingtons hung from double cartridge belts strapped around his thick waist; he'd started to reach for the one on his right hip but stopped the motion when he looked up to see Yakima staring down at him from over the smoking barrel of the cocked Yellowboy.

"Give me one good reason why I shouldn't drill a bullet through your fat head," the half-breed grated out.

Chapter 9

The man stared up at Yakima uncertainly, stretching his thin lips back from his teeth in misery.

"Well?" Yakima said when a response wasn't forthcoming. "Tell me why I shouldn't kick you out with a cold shovel."

"I can't think of one!" the man bellowed.

That rocked Yakima back on his proverbial heels. "Huh?"

"I can't think of one, so . . . go ahead and finish the job." The man turned his head to one side and squeezed his eyes closed. "I sure come a long way, fought a bunch of nasty, dirty Injuns on both sides of the con-sarned border to get killed by a lone Apache out here in the middle of nowhere. Go ahead! What're you waitin' for?"

"I'm not Apache."

The man slitted one eye open as he gazed curiously up at Yakima. "Comanche?"

"Half-Cheyenne." Yakima lowered the Yel-

lowboy, then stooped to rip both Remingtons from the man's holsters and toss them
down the slope behind him. "Who're you,
and why were you tryin' to trim my wick,
you son of a bitch?"

"I was tryin' to kill you so I could steal
your horse and your minin' claim. I aimed
to bury you in the nearest ravine, plunder
your possibles, and follow your color . . .
hopefully to the mother lode! If you got a
woman in the cabin, she'd be mine, too!"

Yakima scowled dubiously down at the
man. He wasn't accustomed to such bald-
assed, unqualified honesty. "Huh?"

The man returned Yakima's scowl, as
incredulous as Yakima was. "I'm Johnny
Day," the man said.

Yakima continued scowling.

"Johnny Day! Don't you hear, breed? I'm
the outlaw *Johnny Day*. Some folks know
me by the handle 'the Rio Grande Kid.' "
He waited, brows hooding his eyes. "Ring
any bells?" he asked, impatiently. "Rio
Grande's a real bad apple in these parts and
over Texas-way. Has been fer years."

Yakima depressed his Yellowboy's hammer, then used the barrel to poke his hat
brim back off his forehead, pondering.
"Johnny Day, Johnny Day. That does . . ."
He widened his eyes. "Oh, the Rio Grande

Kid! I remember that name from when I was scouting at Camp Hildebrandt."

"Hildebrandt?"

"Better known as Camp Hell," Yakima said.

"Yeah, I remember ole Camp Hell. Near Apache Pass. Real wild country in them days!"

"And I remember the Rio Grande Kid. Small-time outlaw who stole cattle on this side of the border, ran 'em down to Mexico, changed their brands, then ran 'em back to this side of the border to sell to the Indian agencies. Heard a lot about him, but we had bigger fish to fry, so we were never sent after him. Small potatoes."

"Small potatoes! Bigger fish to — ! Well, you sure as hell were not privy to the full extent of my depredations, then! No, sir. I was as wild as the javelinas!"

"I heard the US marshals ran you down in a hog pen along the border and sent you to the federal hoosegow."

"I wish you'd go ahead and shoot me if you're otherwise just gonna remind me of things I'd as soon forget."

"I think you're too soft in the thinker-box to shoot."

"More insults!"

"Get up."

Johnny Day, aka the Rio Grande Kid, rolled onto his left shoulder and flopped around some more, like the proverbial landed fish. "You're gonna have to give me a hand here, Red. I sprung my shoulder and about every other bone in my body, rollin' down that hill."

Yakima took his rifle in one hand and extended his other hand to the Rio Grande Kid, who grabbed it. Yakima set his boots and assisted the man to his feet. The outlaw was only about five feet eight, but he was nearly as wide as Yakima, and he was as solid as a rain barrel. His belly flopped over the buckles of his double cartridge belts. Each thigh was nearly as wide as both of Yakima's own. Just the work of gaining his feet had winded him and turned his face as red as an Arizona dawn.

The Kid — Yakima inwardly chuckled at the moniker — leaned forward, hands on his knees, and shook his head, making a blurbling sound with his flapping lips.

Yakima said, "How old are you, anyways?"

"Nineteen."

Chuckling dryly, Yakima said, "Nineteen plus fifty, give or take."

"You got a mouth, for a half-breed addressing a white man."

"This half-breed has a rifle and about

thirty less years than you do, you old reprobate. I still haven't decided if I shouldn't go ahead and shoot the over-the-hill outlaw who bushwhacked me, damn near blew my head off with the intention of stealing my horse, my woman, my possibles, and my gold claim . . . though if there's any actual gold to claim, I haven't found it yet."

"Well, shit." The Rio Grande Kid straightened. His beefy face sagged on the raw bones of his skull, crestfallen. "How 'bout a woman? You got a woman here?"

"One left a few minutes ago, but you'd be better off tangling with a hydrophobic bobcat in a one-hole privy."

The Kid grinned. One of his large, rectangular, yellow front teeth was chipped. "Sounds like fun."

Yakima looked the raggedy-heeled former outlaw up and down. "How long you been out of jail?"

"Well, I was in a couple of times, but my last stint ended two months ago."

"How long were you in for? *Last* time."

"A year. I got a year off for good behavior. I robbed the bank in Snowflake; would have made off with twelve thousand dollars if . . ." Again, a miserable, crestfallen expression caused the muscles in his big, meaty face to slacken, a practice they seemed accustomed to. ". . . if my damn hoss hadn't spooked at a tumbleweed and run off, leaving me alone in the street. The locals took no pity on ole Rio Grande, I can tell you that for sure. They went at me with sticks and stones and axe handles and even a rake. Busted me up somethin' awful. I was thankful when the law finally came! They broke this here arm in three places, and I think I might have reinjured it good right here an' now. Ah, lord o' mercy!"

He flexed the limb of topic in the air above his head and to the side, wincing.

"My heart bleeds for you," Yakima snorted. "By rights, I should shoot you for nearly blowing my head off, not to mention wasting a good cup of coffee."

"Wouldn't blame you a bit."

"You best find your horse and be on your way, Rio Grande. I find you around my cabin again, I'm not gonna be as obliging as I've been here tonight."

"Don't blame ya a bit, Red," the oldster said.

Yakima stepped off the boulder and started walking back toward his cabin. He heard the Kid sigh heavily. He glanced back over his shoulder to see the old man sitting down again atop the boulder, draping his arms over his upraised knees. Yakima turned his head forward and continued walking. Something was making his feet grow heavy. He took a few more steps, then stopped and turned back around.

The Kid sat atop the boulder, head lowered. He was a bulky, man-shaped silhouette there against the tawny slope reflecting the salmon and yellow light of the setting sun.

"Goddamnit." Yakima walked back up the slope and stepped onto the boulder.

"You forget somethin', Red?" the Kid asked.

"The name's not 'Red' or 'Breed' or 'Injun' or anything else. It's Henry. Yakima Henry."

"That what you came to tell me?"

"You got a camp?"

The Kid patted the rock beside him. "I reckon this'll do right here. I was just about to fetch my hoss and some firewood."

"It's damn near dark."

"Yeah, well, ole Rio Grande can see best at night. He's like a cat that way." He pointed a dirty, sausage-like finger at his eyes and grinned.

"Fetch your goddamn horse and your goddamn guns and get over to my cabin. It rubs my fur in the wrong direction to feed and house some old mossy horn who just tried to shoot me off my own gallery — and take my horse, my gold, and my woman if I had one — but I reckon even broken down old coyotes need to be fed and watered."

"No, shit, Red? Er . . . I mean Yakima . . ."

The half-breed had already turned and was striding off toward his cabin again.

Behind him, the Rio Grande Kid said, "I'll be damned if you ain't half bad for an Injun."

Yakima gave a caustic chuff and kept walking.

An hour later, it was nearly as black as the bottom of a grave outside. The only relief was the stars like chips of glistening silver dancing over the black velvet of jutting ridges.

The hurricane lamp hanging on a hook over Yakima's small, square wooden eating table issued black smoke from its sooty chimney as the old outlaw known as the Rio Grande Kid dropped his wooden-handled, three-tined fork on his empty plate, which he'd swabbed free of venison grease with several of Emma's baking powder biscuits, then sat back in his chair, making it creak beneath his considerable girth.

He gave a loud belch, then leaned forward, stretching a thick arm toward Yakima's making sack. "You mind? I'm fresh out."

"Help yourself."

"What's this?" Reaching for the sack, the Kid found the town marshal's star lying between the sack and Yakima's coffee cup. He fingered the blood-speckled badge curiously.

"Nothing," Yakima said and sipped his coffee.

The Kid dropped the badge and grabbed the Durham. Yakima watched as the old outlaw, his eyes bright with the anticipation of the rich tobacco smoke invading his lungs, slid the hide sack toward him and poked two fingers inside. He appeared not to have indulged in a coffin nail for a long time, which prompted Yakima to voice his curiosity, which he normally kept on a short leash, knowing impropriety was often met with a bullet out here in the tall and uncut, but also knowing that the Rio Grande Kid was too sore and tired to do any more lead slinging this evening.

"What're you doing for jingle these days, Kid?"

"Jingle?" the Kid said, looking across the table at Yakima as he troughed a wheat paper between the first two fingers of his right, ham-sized hand. He quirked a customarily devilish grin. "Hell, the Rio Grande Kid steals his jingle! In no small amounts, neither. What? You don't think I'd lower myself to working for a living, do you? No, sir, I ain't one o' them guys. Never been tied to a woman or a job!"

He chuckled in delight at himself.

"When was your last shakedown, Kid?"

The oldster gave a subtle wince, really just a slight rising of his right cheek, as he sprinkled chopped tobacco into the crease on the paper. "Uh, let's see . . . maybe three, four months ago now. I reckon I'll ride into some little border town soon and relieve the local banker of his coinage, pop a few caps in the air just to hear the ladies scream. That gets right addictive. Never get tired of hearing town wimmen scream, the Kid don't."

"Don't forget to tie your horse," Yakima said, taking a deep drag from his own quirley, then adding on the exhale, "or avoid a day when the wind's blowing the tumbleweeds around."

Slowly rolling the quirley closed, making flakes of tobacco dribble out both ends, the Kid flared a nostril at him. "I reckon since I'm eatin' your food and smokin' your tobacco, I can let that slide."

"Thanks."

"Don't mention it." The Kid scratched a lucifer to life on the table, touched the flame to the quirley, then leaned back in his chair, blowing smoke at the hurricane lamp, the smoke cloud glowing as bright as a miniature sun. "Tell you what I will do, though."

"What's that?"

"Since you been so good to the Kid, as few are, I'll let you in on a deal I got goin'."

"A deal you got goin'?"

"Yeah." The Kid took another deep, luxurious drag off the quirley, half-shutting his eyes in an almost erotic delight. "A big one." Another cloud of exhaled smoke melded with the first, billowing over the table and around the light.

"I'm really not up to big deals these days," Yakima said. "I'm going to stick to following gold veins in the mountains out there until I get sick to death of it." He was well on his way to that death, but picking and shoveling was the best thing going at the moment. Besides, he'd found just enough color to fill his larder from time to time, and to keep him interested. He mashed his cigarette out in the ashtray he'd cut from an airtight tin and started to rise. "I'm off to bed. I like to get an early star —"

"Hold on, hold on, Yakima." The Kid looked up at the half-breed from beneath the low-hanging lamp. "Hear me out. Could be something big in it for both of us."

Yakima thought he'd done enough for the

man, since he really didn't owe him anything except a bullet for the ambush, but he eased back down in his chair. The Rio Grande Kid deserved his respect, if only because he was a good bit older and probably lonely, since he apparently had no gang to speak of. Outlaws were like buffalo that way. When one grew old, they turned him out and let the wolves take care of him.

Besides, there was something more than a little endearing about the old scoundrel, in the way he clung to his old reputation despite the obvious ravages of the years, as though Johnny Day's old handle were a life raft in a storm-tossed sea.

"Make it fast," Yakima said. "My pillow's calling."

The Rio Grande Kid smiled like a kid with a secret as he reached into the breast pocket of his sweaty, dirty hickory shirt and pulled out a leaf of parchment paper. He unfolded the yellowed, coffee-stained, cigarette-burned sheet that Yakima could see by the writing and drawing on the front was an old Wanted circular. The name printed in large block letters across the top was Edgar K. "Nasty Eddie" Logan.

"This here's a wanted dodger for a friend of mine, now deceased, God rest his wicked soul." The Kid chuckled and smoothed the parchment down on the table before him, dribbling ashes from his cigarette onto the paper, then brushing the ashes onto the floor. "Eddie drew this map a long time back, on the back of this wanted dodger he carried to show off to the whores up here an' the *putas* down in Mexico. Eddie was right proud of bein' wanted for a full six-hundred-and-fifty dollars by the marshals up in Oklahoma. Ah, Eddie . . ."

The Kid wagged his head fondly at the memory of his dead outlaw partner, took another deep drag from the quirley, and blew the smoke over the lamp. "Anyways, Eddie and I was on the run from the *rurales* down in Baja one time, oh, fifteen, twenty years ago now. Or maybe it was longer than that . . . Shit, how the time flies! Anyways, it don't matter how long ago it was. We split up at the border, see, because we knew a couple of stock detectives were waiting for us on this side of the line. We heard about those detectives from a soiled dove Eddie knew in — Oh, well, that don't matter, neither.

"Anyways, we forked trails, and I rode up through the Mojave Ridges, and Eddie came up through the Sierra Estrada, not too damn far from here, in fact. We met up in a little *cantina* outside of Phoenix. Oh, the *putas* in that place! There was one li'l brown-eyed *senorita* there who could — Ah, shit, there I go again. Hah!"

The Kid slapped the table and bellowed his self-deprecating laugh.

"Anyways, when Eddie was comin' up through the Estrada, he stumbled on an old abandoned mine and a Mexican church in a deep canyon. There was gold every-where . . . and what looked to Eddie like a treasure box from some Spanish galleon. Spilling over with jewels of every shape, size, and color. And you know what else Eddie found in that canyon?"

"A cathouse filled to its seams with purty *putas*?"

"What?" The Kid scowled, puzzled. "Ah, you're funnin' ole Rio Grande! No, no — Eddie found a cannon made of pure gold!"

CHAPTER 10

The Kid stared across the table at Yakima.

Yakima stared back at him, expressionless.

"And you know what else?" the Kid asked.

"No."

The Kid held up the Wanted circular and turned it so that its backside faced the half-breed. A map had been penciled on the back — squiggly lines demarking canyons and arroyos, no doubt, and rectangles of various shapes and sizes delineating mountains, with several snake-like arrows pointing the way through the rugged terrain to a large, black X.

Yakima looked up from the map to the round, beefy face of the man holding it. The Kid was smiling like the snake that followed the rabbit down the hole.

"The Kid wrote this map as he made his way out of the canyon to Phoenix. We was gonna follow it back when our trails cooled, but by an' by the law tracked us to Emory-

ville, Nevada, and bushwhacked us walkin'
out of a —"

"Whorehouse?"

"How'd you know? Pshaw, you're funnin'
the Kid!" He laughed. "Eddie took a bullet,
and we got away, but Eddie died along the
trail. Before he died, he turned over the map
to me, said even if we couldn't go together
to seek our El Dorado, at least I could, and
he gave me his blessing. He said he'd save
me a cloud in the land beyond the pearly
gates, Eddie did!" By now, the Kid was sobbing, tears dribbling down his cheeks.

"So, why didn't you head off to find
Eddie's El Dorado?"

The Kid rubbed a hand across his cheeks,
brushing away the tears. "Because, gall-
blastit, the next day the law caught up to
me. I hid the map under a rock. Wouldn't
you know that when I got out of prison, I
couldn't remember which rock I hid the
map under? Well, shit, I was damn near six
years behind bars that first time. The second
time it was four, the third time two. But on
one of my last days in the Colorado pen, I
had a dream. I seen that rock as plain as
day, and the land around it. And you know
what?"

Yakima stared at him.

"I rode right up to that rock in the Nevada

desert, six miles west of Las Vegas. There it was, just like in the dream. And I reckon that dry desert air preserved it." The Kid held up the map again and brushed loving fingers down its surface. "You're the only one who knows about this map — aside from me an' Eddie, of course. An' Eddie's dead. I need a young man's eyes to help me find it."

"Sorry," Yakima said, sliding his chair back and gaining his feet. "Ain't interested."

"Why not? Didn't you hear what I told you?" The Kid leaned far over the table, wielding his big face like a club. He raised an arm and pointed toward the southeast. "There's a canyon out there. Filled with gold! What you got to do that's so damn more important than looking for El Dorado an' become the richest man on earth? Least-ways, one of two."

The oldster grinned.

Yakima reached down and plucked the town marshal's star off the table. "Wearing this badge, that's what." He looked down at the five-pointed star, raked a thumbnail across a fleck of dried blood. "I think it looks right good on me, matter of fact."

"You're crazy," the Kid said, sitting back in his chair in astonishment. "You can't be no lawman. You're an Injun!"

"I may be an Injun," Yakima said, outside on the stoop now, dipping water up from his *olla*. "But at least I'm not some crazy old man living in the past and still looking for El Dorado. If I stay out here, though, that's likely what will happen."

He took a long drink from the gourd dipper, then looked at the Kid again, sitting at the table glaring at him. "Thanks, Kid." He winked and dropped the dipper back in the clay jar. "The tables have turned. I owe you a big debt."

Yakima strode over to his cot and began shucking out of his clothes; time for bed. He could hear the Rio Grande Kid grumbling inside at the table.

Yakima lay back against his pillow, feeling a wave of relief wash over him. He was content to have his mind made up. A grief-stricken young widow had asked him for help, and he'd been about to turn her down for a thin vein of quartz and a few pinches of gold dust.

The Kid's bitter voice from inside: "Can I roll another quirley?"

Yakima gave a droll chuckle. "Sure. I'll pick up some more Durham tomorrow. In town."

He rolled onto his side, punched his pillow, and went to sleep.

■ ■ ■ ■

The next day around mid-morning, Yakima halted Wolf on a low knoll overlooking Apache Springs from the southwest. The little town, still relatively new and spread somewhat haphazardly across the ragged pass between bald crags, baked in the late-summer sun.

On a hill to Yakima's right lay a cemetery surrounded by a low hip-and-rail fence freshly painted white. A few sycamores and an almond tree offered sparse shade. Outside the fence's front gate, several buggies were parked where five or six saddle horses stood, heads hanging, reins tied to a wooden hitch rack shaded by a bushy mesquite.

Inside the cemetery, two sets of mourners clad in the somber colors of grief stood around two coffins and fresh dirt piles. One group was singing "Bringing in the Sheaves." They finished as Yakima rode down the slope, and the group began dispersing and moving in smaller groups over the hill toward the buggies and the saddled horses.

As Yakima skirted the cemetery, he saw Julia Taggart standing by one of the buggies, holding a black parasol over her head, her face partly concealed by a black mourner's veil dangling from the brim of a small, black felt hat pinned to her immaculately coifed and pinned-up brown hair.

She was shaking the hand of a gray-haired man standing beside a gray-haired, thickly built woman. The man was smiling gently and speaking in dulcet tones while the old woman shook her head sadly beside him, also muttering her condolences. Several others stood around her, apparently waiting their turn to console the young widow of Apache Springs's dead town marshal.

Yakima was going to ride on past the mourners, having no place among them, but the young widow looked up at him as he approached, having heard the clomps of Wolf's hooves. Her eyes caught his, and she frowned at him from behind the veil, vaguely curious. The others followed her gaze to the big half-breed on the rangy black horse and stopped talking, also frowning curiously.

Yakima reined in Wolf a few yards from the small gathering, pulled his hat down from his head and held it against his thigh.

"Mrs. Taggart, my condolences for your loss. I didn't know your husband well, but well enough to know he was a good man."

"Thank you, Mr. Henry." Julia's eyes flicked toward the five-pointed star he'd pinned to his shirt. "I see you've come to a decision."

"I've decided to accept your offer. I don't know if I can solve your problem, but I'm here to give it a try."

"What's this about?" asked a dapper gent in his mid-thirties and tricked out in a tailored gray suit, stepping up beside Julia and staring incredulously at Yakima. He wore round spectacles and a Van Dyke beard. "Why is he wearing that badge?"

"This, ladies and gentlemen," Julia said, extending a black-gloved hand toward Yakima, "is the new town marshal of Apache Springs — Mr. Yakima Henry."

"Julia . . . er, I mean Mrs. Taggart," the dapper gent said, correcting himself quickly and gesturing toward the half-breed, "this man is a . . . an . . . an *Indian*!"

The others around him and Julia muttered their own reproof, scowling up at the half-breed still holding his hat on his thigh. Julia turned sharply to the dapper gent and said crisply, "What does his being an *Indian* have to do with *anything,* Mr. Garland?"

When the dapper gent just stared at her aghast, she continued with: "It certainly didn't seem to come between him and saving you and most of the rest of the town when you were locked in the burning church last Sunday."

"That was *him*?" one of the women asked no one in particular.

The dapper gent said, "Yes, but . . . but . . . but . . ."

Yakima smiled reassuringly at Julia, donned his hat, winked, and booted Wolf on down the trail. Behind him he could hear the townsfolk conversing in low but contentious tones, the voices dwindling as he put more distance behind him and them. He entered town at a trot.

The wide sun-baked street was virtually deserted. One ranch wagon was parked in front of the large mercantile building with a broad front-loading dock propped on fieldstone stilts. Two men in range garb were tossing fifty-pound flour bags into the box. Two dogs, one large and one half its size, were fighting playfully over a forked mesquite stick, kicking up dust, the small one rolling and then rising to squeal and pull at the stick the larger dog carried proudly and with no little taunting.

"Simple little savages," Yakima muttered, chuckling. Life was so much simpler for the beasts.

As he passed the wagon, one of the men in range garb glanced at him, glanced away, then snapped his gaze back to him sharply, likely picking out the badge winking on the half-breed's chest. The first man elbowed the other man and stared in surprise as Yakima pinched his hat brim to them and continued on by.

He pulled off to the street's right side, approaching a raw-boned, thick-set man in pinstriped overalls sawing wood propped on two sawhorses between the open doors of a wide, deep adobe-brick building identified by a sign over the door announcing *Haugen's Fine Furniture & Undertaking.* The man had a stone coffee mug steaming on a covered rain barrel near to hand.

He likely had a lot of work to do and needed to stay fortified. Yakima saw several dead men reclining atop planks stretched between barrels deep inside the building. It was an odd sight — one that Yakima had seen before. But it was still strange to see fully clothed men reclining on boards like that, as though merely sleeping when, of course, they were sleeping the longest sleep known to man or beast.

Yakima stopped Wolf near the big, raw-boned gent sawing a board likely to add to the pile of sawed boards piled on the ground nearby and that were likely waiting to form coffins. The undertaker/furniture maker wore no hat; his head was capped in a thick but close-cropped, bristling thatch of dark-red hair. His face was wide and square and sandwiched between thick muttonchop whiskers.

Yakima's and Wolf's combined shadow slid across the man, who stopped sawing and looked up, a little breathless. He studied Yakima closely, with the same skepticism as most white folks upon seeing the big, copper-skinned man with long, coal-black hair and jade eyes shaded by the broad brim of his black hat.

This man's skepticism deepened when his brown eyes drifted to the badge on Yakima's chest.

"You . . . you're the . . . new . . . ?"

"Town marshal, that's right." Yakima had seen the man before, who no doubt knew Yakima from one of the half-breed's previous trips to town or from the Sunday morning dustup. Hell, he might have even been in the Busted Flush the night Yakima had busted up the place, but he appeared no worse for the wear. At least, he bore no visible scarring. "Those the scoundrels back there?"

The undertaker glanced over his shoulder. "Four of 'em are."

"Do me a favor, will you?"

"What's that?"

"Box 'em up and set 'em out in the street."

The undertaker scowled, planted his fists on his hips, and stuck his chest out. "Now, why in hell would I do that, breed?"

Yakima blinked. His smile belied the anger kindling inside him. He gave a fateful grunt as he swung down from his saddle and stood in front of the undertaker, who was nearly as tall and broad as he was.

"What's your name?" Yakima asked the man.

The undertaker lifted an index finger to indicate the sign above his open double doors. "If you can read, it's just like the sign says. Haugen."

"Well, Mr. Haugen, it looks like you and I have gotten off on the wrong foot. Or, I should say that you got off on the wrong foot with me. Would you like to feel how that foot tastes in your mouth, or can we straighten this thing we seem to have between us out in a friendlier fashion?"

Haugen glowered, deep lines forming around his eyes and mouth. "If you think pinning that badge on your chest means you can push me around, *breed,* then you got another think comin'!"

Yakima leaped two feet straight up and spun full around.

His left leg whipped out first, and the back

of his left boot slammed into the left side of the undertaker's neck.

The man fell as though his legs had been torn out from under him. He lay in the dirt of the street, on his side, right cheek pressed to the ground, unmoving. He blinked, staring at the dirt as though not quite sure where he was. Dust wafted over him.

"Ho-holy . . . Ch-Christ!" he wheezed out after several stretched seconds, peeling his lips back from his teeth and raising his left hand to his neck, where a bright red welt was growing.

"An old Chinaman taught me that," Yakima said. "I could have broken your neck if I'd wanted to."

"Christ!" the undertaker wheezed out again, massaging his neck with his hand and lying where he'd fallen, stunned.

Yakima dropped to a knee beside him. "Get this straight — the name is not 'breed.' Calling me that again is going to get you planted like just now. Maybe a little worse. I probably won't kill you unless I've gotten into the firewater. If I've gotten into the firewater, all bets are off. If not, the very least that will happen is that you're going to turn a lot of money over to your local dentist, possibly even the sawbones. The name is Yakima Henry. I'm going to make an exception for you, however. *You* can call me *Mister.* Understand?"

"Ch-Christ!" the undertaker wheezed out again.

"I'll take that as a yes. Now, what I was about to *ask* you to do but what, under these fast-changing circumstances, I am now going to *order* you to do, is box up the four tough nuts and lean 'em against the front wall of your fine establishment here. For all to see. Hang a painted board over them. Leave 'em there till I say to plant 'em."

Yakima gestured with one hand, as though indicating the painted words in the air before him. " *'Rebel Wilkes's Town Killers.'* Have the local schoolmarm help you with the spelling if you need it. I don't know about you, but I always have trouble when it comes to apostrophes showing possession."

Yakima swung up onto Wolf's back and rode over to the town marshal's office to officially begin his first day on the job.

CHAPTER 11

Yakima's kick to the undertaker's neck must have been the kick felt around the entire town of Apache Springs.

The next four days were relatively quiet. Most folks steered clear of the town marshal's office and the badge-wearing halfbreed who, when not making the rounds around the little town, could usually be seen sitting on the front gallery, holding his prized Yellowboy repeater across his thighs, boots crossed on the gallery rail before him.

Yakima's only real challenge over those four days was a cat.

Not even a wild cat. A domestic cat.

Two elderly ladies, both widows who shared a little frame shack on the town's south end, rode up to the marshal's office in their little, red-wheeled phaeton, sobbing over the fact that their three-month-old kitten, Boris, had tumbled into an unused, open well in their yard. The cat had managed to scramble up out of the water at the bottom of the well and perch, meowing desperately, on a root protruding a few inches out from the well's wall.

Yakima rode over to the ladies' house in their prissy carriage and, on his knees beside the well, the two old widows sobbing behind him, briefly evaluated the situation. Little Boris gazed up at him, meowing beseechingly from his root, yellow eyes flashing in the light filtering into the well.

Yakima gave a sigh, kicked out of his boots, and peeled out of his socks.

He'd brought a rope, but he didn't think he'd need it, as he saw plenty of foot and hand holds in the sides of the old well, which was only about five and a half feet in diameter. Yakima and Ralph had climbed steep ridges in mountain country back when they were laying rails for the Transcontinental Railroad. Ralph had been a good free-climber, and the Chinaman had taught Yakima a few tricks as well as the art of fluid, mindful movements, feeling as well as seeing the terrain around him and how to handle fear.

Yakima had an innate fear of heights, so challenging those fears had unexpectedly offered a heady exhilaration. The climbing hadn't banished his fears altogether, but it had taught him that parrying with them could be an amusing Sunday afternoon distraction.

This wasn't Sunday but Thursday, but what the hell. Yakima wasn't exactly running himself ragged around Apache Springs just now. Rebel Wilkes was probably still trying to figure out his next move.

Besides, the widows were genuinely worried about their cat, who was in genuine trouble, so Yakima, who could use the exercise anyway, made the best of the situation. He scrambled down into the well, using his bare feet to negotiate one side and his shoulders to scrape along the other side, and climbed back up using fingers and toes, with Boris riding his shoulders and digging his claws painfully into Yakima's back.

The widows rewarded Yakima with a cup of tea in their parlor, which was really the most strenuous part of the situation. A half-breed drifter and sometime-gunslinger had very little in common, conversation-wise, with two elderly widows of English extraction. They'd both come to the fledgling town of Apache Springs with their shopkeeper husbands, who'd died on them soon after.

Now they had their days to fill, house to keep, sheets to boil, and their cats to care for. Nice ladies, both. But there was very little to talk about once they'd gotten beyond the usual chatter about the weather. Having lived most of their lives in Apache country, they were both obviously and understandably a little cowed by the dark hue of Yakima's skin, not to mention his size.

Yakima wasn't offended. He was just as cowed by them and their overly nipped and tucked home made especially somber by the infernally dolorous ticking of a Waterbury cabinet clock.

He slurped his tea and ate his lemon muffin as fast as was seemly, in his unheeled judgment, then gave his thanks and took his leave. The widows offered to drive him back to his office in their phaeton, but he said he'd prefer to walk. So, walking back in the direction of the heart of Apache Springs, down a gravelly little avenue fronted by widely spaced adobe and wood-frame houses, he saw the dapper, bespectacled gent Julia had addressed as Mr. Garland walking toward him on the opposite side of the street.

Yakima knew by now that Garland was one of two attorneys in town who'd read for the law under the tutelage of his own father and occasionally did work for Julia's father, Hugh Kosgrove. Garland was a bachelor in his mid-thirties and had an eye for the ladies. Apparently, he had an eye for one young beautiful widow, Yakima saw, as the man turned through the gate in the white picket fence surrounding the house Yakima knew belonged to Julia Taggart.

As Yakima approached the gate on the street's opposite side, he heard Garland knocking on Julia's front door.

"Julia?" he called, stubbornly continuing to knock. "It's Wayne. I'm just checking on you. I wanted to make sure you were all right . . . er, as well as possible . . . uh, given the circumstances."

Pause.

Yakima stopped and looked at the young widow's small, neat, frame house sitting back from the gate and abutted on two sides by palo verde trees that cast sparse shade over the front gallery. Garland stood on the gallery, holding the screen door open and canting his head to listen through the inside door.

He knocked again, three times. "Julia, are you there? It's Wayne."

Again, Garland canted his head toward the door.

Finally, audibly grumbling, he let the screen slap shut and made his way back along the cinder path bisecting the front yard and pushed out through the gate. He stopped when he looked up and saw Yakima standing on the other side of the street from him.

He flushed, grimaced, then walked over to stand before Yakima, hardening his jaws in anger.

"Can I help you, bre— . . . uh, *Mr. Henry*?"

Yakima almost smiled at that. So, his kick to the undertaker's neck had made its way around town, as he'd suspected.

Yakima brushed a thumb across his badge. "Marshal Henry."

"Can I help you, *Marshal Henry*?"

"Nah, I was just on my way back from fetching a cat out of a well and heard you knocking on Mrs. Taggart's door."

"What's that to you, if I may ask?"

"Oh, I don't know — it appears to me the woman wants to be alone, that's all."

Garland's flush grew crimson. "Are you suggesting I'm bothering Jul— . . . I mean, Mrs. Taggart?"

"That's what I'm suggesting, all right," Yakima said, meeting the angry attorney's gaze directly and quirking his lips in a faint, challenging smile.

Garland blinked slowly and drew a deep, slow breath, trying to keep his rage on a leash. "Listen, *Marshal Henry,* I am a member of Apache Springs's six-man town council. Just so you know, I and the other councilmen allowed Mrs. Taggart to hire you out of deference to her and her murdered husband, a man we all admired. She has no actual standing with the council. It is not her job to hire the town marshal. We allowed her to do so as a *favor.*"

"Are you firing me, Mr. Garland?" Yakima asked with the same bland smile.

Garland glanced at the house, to each side of which the palo verdes were swaying in a sudden breeze, leaves flashing silver, then turned back to the half-breed. "Not yet. In a few weeks, however, we will be relieving you of your obligation. You see, Julia hired you at a time when she was under extreme duress, having just witnessed the passing of her husband and all. And when you just happened to be in the right place at the right time . . . and sober enough to shoot straight enough to gun down those four obviously *drunk* gun wolves."

"They seemed sober enough to me," Yakima said. "But get on with what you have to say, Garland."

"Oh, thank you for granting me permission to speak." Garland sneered.

Anger flared inside Yakima, but he managed not to show it, his bland smile in place.

Garland continued. "The town council is scouting around for a more permanent lawman. One more suited to the job. When we've found our man or men — we'll probably need more than one, considering the current threat — you will be free to go. I will explain the situation to Julia when the time comes. I'm sure in a few more days she'll be more clear-headed than she was when she insisted that she and Sykes and Dundee ride out to offer you the job — a man who'd been in jail at the time her husband was killed!"

The attorney chuckled dryly but at some length at the irony of that.

"And by the way, I am ordering Haugen to get those four dead men off the street no later than noon tomorrow. Everyone downtown is tired of the stench, and it's cutting into the business traffic!"

The attorney chuckled again as though at the absurdity of having a half-breed wearing the town marshal's badge and said, "Good day, *Marshal.*" Patting Yakima's shoulder condescendingly, he turned and walked away, shaking his head.

Yakima watched the attorney's diminishing back, gritting his teeth. He drew a deep, calming breath. He heard the whine of a door hinge and turned toward the Taggart house. Julia stepped outside and eased the screen door closed behind her.

She stared at Yakima, crossing her arms over her breasts. She wore a cream dress with a matching shirtwaist and a white apron. Her brown hair was pinned into a thick bun, but renegade strands blew around her heart-shaped face in the breeze.

She gazed inquiringly at Yakima, who crossed the street, stepped through the gate in the picket fence, and walked up to the house, stopping at the bottom of the gallery steps. Julia looked washed-out and tired, her features gaunt.

She was still a beautiful woman, but her gray eyes owned little of their previous luster, which was to be expected. There was a smudge of flour low on her right cheek. She'd been baking. That was good a sign that she was starting to come out of the depths of her despair. Or trying, anyway. Yakima knew how it went.

"What were you two talking about?" she asked.

"Mr. Garland was giving me a job evaluation."

"And . . . ?"

The half-breed shrugged. "I reckon he thinks I should be doing more than hauling kittens out of wells."

Julia's eyes crinkled at their corners, and her lips spread a rare smile. "Ah, you've met Apache Springs's two notorious widows and at least one of their cats, I would imagine." She chuckled. "Lon was called over there at least once a week to get their cats out of one situation or another."

"Don't doubt it a bit."

"Would you like to come in? I made a pie, and I could use someone to help me eat it." Julia's eyes said that she'd made the pie for her husband, despite knowing he wouldn't be there to enjoy it. It was the sort of thing grieving people did.

A little puzzled, Yakima glanced off toward where Garland had disappeared.

"He's impertinent," Julia said, following Yakima's gaze. "He tried to spark me long ago and apparently thinks he can again now, so soon after . . ."

Yakima glanced around again and smiled. He knew that a small town had many sets of eyes, and they were everywhere. "It might not look so good."

"I don't care."

Julia pulled the screen open and stepped inside. Yakima doffed his hat and held it as he followed her through a small, neat parlor, the curtains drawn over the windows, and into a small kitchen at the house's rear. The

146

range had heated the room up something fierce. A pie sat on the ledge of an open window, baked apple juice oozing up from slits in the sugar-sprinkled crust. The back door was propped open with a chair.

The house was still very much haunted by Lon Taggart's presence. What were obviously his coats and rain slicker hung from hooks on the wall by the door. A man's pocket watch was open on the table. Julia had apparently used it to time the pie's baking. A manly smell still lingered — pomade, leather, and sweat — beneath the aroma of baked apples, cinnamon and sugar, and a buttery brown crust.

"Too hot in here," Julia said, reaching to pull two small plates off a shelf. "Let's sit outside. Lon built a brush arbor out back." Her voice cracked midway through that sentence but did not break. "You go ahead. I'll be along in a minute."

Yakima stepped outside. He didn't care for any pie after having tea and muffins with the widows, but Julia needed company, and he sensed his company might be more welcome than that of anyone else from town. Not knowing her very well, he carried less historical weight.

Yakima sensed Julia had few close friends, if any. He wasn't sure what it was about her that told him so. A certain chill reserve, perhaps, which didn't work well in the intimacy of a small town. Besides, she was beautiful, if a little icily so. She also came from a wealthy eastern family. All of that would put her at some distance from the rest of Apache Springs.

Yakima sensed, in a way a man can sense such things, that she was attracted to him. Maybe intrigued was a better word. She might not realize it herself, but he did. He also sensed that she shared her sister's sexuality, though in a much more restrained way, and not only because her husband had just passed. Emma was the wild one. Julia was the more intelligent, cerebral one who, under certain conditions, could be wild in her own right. Her passions lay a little farther beneath the surface than Emma's did, and it took a little more digging to stir them.

But they were very much there, all right.

Yakima saw a two-person swing hanging beneath the brush arbor. It was fronted by a wooden table hammered together from three vegetable crates. He followed a gravel path out to the arbor, looked around once more for another chair but, not finding one, sat down on one end of the swing. As far to one side as he could.

The unrelenting sun seeped through the arbor in places, but the shade was still a welcome relief. Yakima hiked a boot on a knee, set his hat beside him on the swing, and waited.

Shortly, Julia stepped out of the back door bearing a wooden tray with two pieces of pie and two china coffee cups on saucers. She looked at Yakima sitting on the swing and then glanced around as though for another, less intimate place for herself to sit. Not finding one, she smiled a little incredulously and kept walking toward him.

"I'll sit over here on the ground," he said quickly, rising from the swing and grabbing his hat.

"Don't be ridiculous!"

"It's no trouble." He glanced around. There was a house to each side of the Taggart place. Both were constructed of adobe brick and a good distance away. No one was outside, but he was aware of the impropriety of him and Julia possibly sitting on the swing together so soon after she'd buried her husband. "I can grab a chair out of —"

Julia stopped and, flushing a little as though with anger, said, "Mr. Henry, if you're that afraid of me, you can sit on the ground. I'm a grieving widow, not a sex-hungry harlot. Besides, my neighbor to the north, who lives alone, is visiting his son in Lordsburg. Both neighbors to the south, a man and wife, are off at their own shop on Main Street. Their children are grown up and gone. There is no one around to see us sitting together on this swing . . . not that I would care if there were."

"All right, then." Yakima sat back down on his end of the swing.

CHAPTER 12

"Your pie and coffee," Julia said, holding the tray out to Yakima.

He removed the coffee and the pie, capped with fresh whipped cream, from the tray and set them on the low wooden table. "Much obliged."

Julia set her own pie and coffee on the table, set the tray on the swing beside Yakima's hat, and sat down on the swing herself, smoothing the skirt of her plain house dress against her thighs. "I'm sure you were well fed by the widows, but I do appreciate your indulgence, Mr. Henry."

"Call me Yakima, if you've a mind."

"All right, then. I am of a mind." She smiled at him briefly but warmly. "You may call me Julia. I started making the pie automatically, out of habit. I continued even after realizing what I was doing, because I guess I'm just not ready to stop yet. I've always made a pie on Thursdays, for some reason. Lon always came home in the afternoons for dessert and coffee, and we'd sit right out here on this swing and catch up on the day's events."

She sipped her coffee, then set it on the table, atop the saucer, and picked up her pie, running her fork through the cream.

Yakima sipped his own coffee and turned to her, setting his cup down on its own saucer. "I know what you're going through, Julia."

She looked at him as she forked a chunk of cream-smothered pie into her mouth. She chewed for a time, studying him closely, then swallowed and said, "I sensed that you did." She took another bite of pie, chewed and swallowed, and then set the plate down on the table, picking up her cup once more. Staring into the steaming black liquid, she asked, "Does it get better?"

Yakima sighed after he'd swallowed a bite of pie. "In time," he said finally, "you forget. But like a friend of mine once said, that's part of the sadness."

Julia drew the corners of her mouth in and nodded.

Yakima decided to change the subject, asking, "Your father and sister weren't at the funeral? At least, I didn't see Emma there."

Swallowing a sip of coffee, Julia turned to

him. "How do you know Emma?"

"We met out in the desert. We were after the same black-tail. I thought for sure she was going to ventilate me."

Julia looked at him, raking a coy glance across his shoulders, then twitched the corners of her mouth with a knowing smile. "How well do you know her? I mean, I know you know her intimately, but . . . ?"

Yakima shrugged, feeling his ears warm a little, discomfited by the topic. "She came around the cabin from time to time. The day you saw us together was the first time we were together in that . . . fashion."

"In that fashion." Julia took another sip of her coffee. "No, she didn't come to the funeral. Neither did my father who, for all practical purposes, disowned me when I married Lon. You probably know why Emma didn't come." She slid another coy glance at Yakima.

"She told me about the, uh . . . family trouble."

"So I'm sure she also told you that I'm the man-stealing devil of the family."

"Not in exactly those words."

Again Julia laughed, but there was only a little humor in it. "She's always felt in competition with me, even before we came out here together to live with our father after our mother died. She is a very competitive young lady, Miss Emma. And very much the apple of our father's eye. I've always wondered if Father would have disowned Emma the way he disowned me, if she'd been the one to marry Lon."

She flared her nostrils as she used her fork to cut off another piece of her pie and said, "How ironic that the one he wanted me to marry was the one who really betrayed him. His mistake should be plain. Lon was a good man. He must realize that by now. Still, he stayed away from the funeral. That's the way he is. He would never admit a mistake . . . or give up a grudge. Even against his older daughter."

"Emma told me he was off on a gold-searching expedition."

"Yes, but even if he wasn't . . ." She chewed and swallowed again. "I'm sorry to go on about all that. It just galls me, of course. Now . . ." She set her plate down, picked up her half-empty coffee cup, and set it on her thigh. "Now . . . I find myself quite alone. With Lon dead. Written out of my father's will." She smiled ironically. "And living in a town that has been targeted by the very man my father wanted me to marry . . . because we wouldn't let him run his railroad through Apache Springs and spoil the peace and quiet of this still fairly peaceful and quiet place."

"Wouldn't your father have helped in this matter if you'd asked? Deep down, he still must love you and . . . worry about you."

"Father thinks about one thing and one thing only. He always has. Two things really. Himself and his gold. Well, three things if you count Emma. Still, himself and gold come first. Even before Emma. That's why she rides all around the Sierra Estrada, looking for companionship." She glanced at Yakima quickly, sheepishly. "I didn't mean to diminish what you might mean to her."

"I understand. I'm one of many."

Julia slid another demure glance toward him, giving a crooked smile. "Just as Emma probably is for you . . . ?"

Yakima smiled thinly and looked off.

"But one stands out," Julia said, probing him subtly.

"Just one," Yakima allowed, nodding.

"Purely hell, isn't it? Life and all." Julia finished her coffee and set the empty cup on the tray, beside her half-eaten piece of pie.

"Purely hell," Yakima said, still nodding.

She turned to favor him with a direct look. A little of the previous luster had returned to her eyes. "Why did you accept my request, Yakima?"

He thought about it. "I don't know. Maybe for you, after seeing what happened. Maybe for the one who stands out for me."

Julia pulled her mouth corners in again and stared toward the open back door of her house, nodding. "That's as good a reason as any."

Yakima left Julia Taggart sitting alone in her two-person swing a few minutes later.

He felt bad about leaving her there. He didn't think she'd been ready to be left alone just yet. But she'd wanted him to pin the marshal's badge to his chest for a reason, so he had a job to do.

Besides, at such a time you were alone even when you weren't actually by yourself. He knew that from experience. Julia would know it soon.

He stepped outside the Taggart house and drew his shell belt up higher on his hips, then strode out through the gate in the fence and headed south. As he gained the main street and turned right, walking toward the town marshal's office, he slowed his stride before stopping in the middle of the street.

Six riders sat their horses outside of Haugen's Undertaking & Fine Furniture. They were staring down at the coffins leaning up against Haugen's front wall, to the right of the open double doors.

Two of the riders held colorful hankies over their mouths against the stench. The lead rider lowered his hanky to speak to Haugen, who stood near the coffins. Being an undertaker accustomed to the stench of death, or maybe having just gotten used to the stench of those dead four, because they'd been out there for days, Haugen held nothing over his mouth.

His mouth and head moved as he spoke to the lead rider.

Suddenly, he turned toward Yakima, then lifted a big arm and pointed in Yakima's direction.

All six riders turned their heads to follow his stare.

Yakima's heart quickened.

Six, huh? he thought, knowing he'd left the Yellowboy in the office. *Oh, well — I've gone up against six before. Just have to make each shot count, that's all . . .*

Yakima stared back at the six horseback riders. The lead rider wore a suit with a string tie and a broad-brimmed, white planter's hat. His face was deeply tanned behind a thick, black beard. He held a cigar in his right, black-gloved hand. One of the other riders moved up from behind to sit beside him and turned his head slightly toward the lead man, whose name came to Yakima at just that moment — Bryce Dixon.

A regulator from the Deep South somewhere.

Alabama?

Via the frontier grapevine, Yakima had heard that Dixon, a former officer in the Rebel army whose family lost their slave plantation to Sherman's Bummers, specialized in range wars. In other words, he hired his guns — as well as the five men who rode for him, all former Rebels in their own right — out to the highest bidder.

It appeared now that they'd broken with tradition.

It appeared now that they'd signed up to take down a whole town, no doubt starting with its half-breed marshal.

When Dixon and the other man stopped conversing, they sat their mounts, staring at Yakima for a time, gazes unwavering. They were roughly a block away. The other four sat behind Dixon and the other man, staring past them toward Yakima. Haugen stood staring in the same direction, a vaguely sheepish slouch to his shoulders.

Dixon touched spurs to his horse's flanks and moved ahead. The others followed suit, spreading out around their leader. Yakima's heart increased its pace. He drew a deep breath and swung his hand across his Colt's hammer, releasing the keeper thong and nudging the pistol loose in its holster.

But the group of six killers did not continue toward him. Instead, they swung off to their left and Yakima's right, pulling up in front of the Busted Flush sitting across the street from the town's marshal's office.

They swung down from their saddles, tossed their reins over the hitch racks, loosened their horses' latigo straps, and slipped the bits from the beasts' mouths so the horses could drink from the stock troughs. The southern killers mounted the boardwalk fronting the Busted Flush. They batted their hats against their thighs, making dust billow.

Then they disappeared into Cleve Dundee's watering hole. All but Dixon, that is. He lingered on the boardwalk a moment, turning his head to stare up the street at Yakima. The old Rebel held his planter's hat down by his side. His dark-brown hair was thick and long, but the top of his head was nearly bald.

He held Yakima's gaze with his own, faintly challenging one, then twitched a smile before lifting his cigar to his mouth and pushing through the batwings, disappearing inside the saloon.

Yakima walked to the town marshal's office — *his* office, however temporarily, he had to keep reminding himself — and filled the chamber he usually kept empty beneath his Colt's hammer. He retrieved the Yellowboy from where it leaned against the wall by the door and rested the barrel on his shoulder.

He went outside and paused on the jailhouse's gallery, staring at the Busted Flush. Two men were running out of the place — businessmen in three-piece suits and bowler hats. Another in a green-checked jacket — a drummer who'd ridden into town last night — also bolted into the street, heading toward the Apache Springs Hotel.

Two more men ran out through the batwings, one on the heels of the other. The second man, whom Yakima recognized as a cowpuncher from a small shotgun operation just down the pass from Apache Springs, dropped his hat and stopped to retrieve it with an anxious curse. He glanced once more over the batwings, then swung up onto a horse at the hitch rack and galloped out of town to the west.

Laughter drifted out through the Busted Flush's batwings.

Yakima set his jaws hard, racked a cartridge into the Winchester's action, lowered the hammer to half cock, and stepped down the gallery steps. He strode slantwise across the street, holding the rifle low in his right hand.

He knew no other way than to confront such obvious trouble straight on. He saw no reason to waste time trying to figure out how to even the odds against him. There were six of them and only one of him. He'd discovered that the best way to confront such men as the ones he was about to confront, and whom he'd been invited to confront, was boldly.

Often boldness and lack of hesitation displayed in extreme situations rocked his opponents back on their heels, causing them to make the grave error of hesitation.

That wasn't to say Yakima knew no fear. As he approached the Busted Flush, cold sweat broke out across his back and down his chest, and his hands were clammy inside his thin buckskin gloves.

That was all right. Fear kept an edge on the blade of his mind.

Yakima mounted the boardwalk fronting the Busted Flush, just off the building's right front corner, wide of the widows. Holding the Yellowboy in both hands across his chest, he moved quickly past the windows toward the batwings. Something moved in the left periphery of his vision. He stopped and swung around to see a man aiming a rifle at him from the roof of the building directly across the street from the Flush.

Yakima started to bring his rifle up.

He was too late. The bushwhacker's own rifle thundered.

No. Not the bushwhacker's rifle.

The would-be shooter jerked suddenly forward, his hat tumbling from his head. He stumbled off the edge of the roof and released his rifle. Leaning forward, he turned a slow somersault, limbs windmilling, and thumped into the street on his back, head facing the building from which he'd fallen, boots facing the Flush.

His rifle clattered into the street a half-dozen feet to his right.

Dust lifted around the man and his rifle. The man lay still.

Yakima frowned up at the silhouette of another man with a rifle just then moving up to take the place of the first rifleman. The second man was just then slamming another cartridge home. The barrel swung toward the Busted Flush. Smoke and flames lapped from the barrel. Yakima jerked with a start, at first believing the second man was shooting at him, then realizing he'd aimed too high.

Above Yakima, a man grunted. The ceiling over Yakima's head creaked.

Another grunt. And then a man tumbled into Yakima's field of vision, dropping straight down from the roof above the half-breed's head to land in the street, between the two sets of horses tied to the hitch racks, on his belly. He was still clutching his Colt rifle.

The horses pushed up hard against the hitch rack and looked at the fallen man behind them.

He pushed up onto his hands and knees, grunting and cursing. He'd lost his hat, and thick, red-brown curls spilled to his shoulders. He turned his head to glare at Yakima. His head jerked as another bullet plowed into it, and he dropped belly-flat in the dirt as the report of the shooter's rifle across the street echoed off the false fronts of the Main Street business buildings.

The horses gave another start. One whinnied indignantly.

The two would-be ambushers had been shot from their respective perches in less than five seconds. They both lay still in death, the harsh golden sunlight bathing them.

Yakima glanced up at the roof of the building across from the Busted Flush. His guardian angel set his rifle on a thick shoulder, doffed his hat from his balding head, and gave a little bow, spreading his lips away from grimy yellow teeth in a grin.

"The Rio Grande Kid," Yakima muttered, giving a wry snort.

He turned around and stepped resolutely through the batwings to confront his other six enemies.

CHAPTER 13

Yakima let the batwings slap shut behind him as he stepped quickly to the right, away from the door, aiming his Yellowboy straight out from his right shoulder and clicking the hammer back to full cock.

A man seated with two others to his left jerked back in his chair, raising his gun-filled right hand. Yakima drilled a slug into the table. The man yelped and jerked back in his chair again, making a face. His eyes were wide and pain-wracked beneath the brim of his cream Stetson.

Yakima curled half of his upper lip in a wry smile. The bullet must have clipped something important beneath the table.

"Stand down, gentlemen!" Bryson bellowed, holding both of his black-gloved hands up, palms out. He sat to the right of the table at which the wounded man was sitting, now squirming around in his chair and grinding his back teeth.

"Stand down! Stand *down*!" Bryson ordered.

All six hired killers had tensed as they sat in their chairs at the two separate tables, the tables about ten feet apart, ahead of Yakima and to his right and left. But now the six men eased back in their chairs, removing their hands from the hoglegs strapped to their sides.

Five of the six eased back, rather. The one who'd gotten something important goosed beneath the table sat with his back taut, glaring up at Yakima, chomping down hard on his lower lip.

He was the tallest of the bunch — long-faced with yellow horse teeth and wearing a tattoo of a naked dancing girl on his long, tan neck.

To him, Bryson said sternly, "That was your own damn fault, Ryder! What makes you think you can jerk iron on our lawman here? Damn fool!" The former Confederate turned to Yakima. "I'd like to apologize for my friend here. In fact, you can have his beer. I don't think he's in any condition for beer at the moment."

He glanced toward where Cleve Dundee stood holding a wooden tray bearing six filled beer schooners. Dundee stood near the bar at the back of the room, straight beyond Yakima, sliding his wary gaze tensely between the newcomers and the half-breed lawman. He was visibly sweating, and Yakima didn't think it was just because he was afraid he was going to have his saloon busted up again, either.

Yakima looked at Dundee. "Hot day. Sure, I could go for an ale."

Dundee strode forward, lowering his tray to the men to Yakima's left, two of whom lifted a schooner of the frothy ale. Ryder was leaning forward over the table, glowering toward Yakima, his face looking washed out and haggard. Dundee lowered the tray to the men on Yakima's right, and when those three each had a beer, he brought the tray with the last beer on it to Yakima.

Dundee gazed anxiously at the half-breed. Yakima gave the saloon owner a mild smile as he lifted the beer from the tray and raised it in salute. Dundee retreated behind the bar, where he stood, hands on the bar top, looking anxious. His mouth moved inside his thick beard.

Yakima held his beer in his left hand. He held his rifle in the other hand.

The six men at the two tables gazed at him, flint-eyed. They were at a stalemate. They might have outnumbered Yakima, but they hadn't been aware that the lawman's play was being backed. Yakima hadn't known that, either. They'd expected him to be dead by now, and that they'd be drinking their beers in peace.

That hadn't happened. They'd been caught sitting, their guns in their holsters. Yakima had the drop on them. So now they were just going to have to bide their time and see what the future brought.

Yakima raised his beer again in salute. "Shall we drink to those two poor devils in the street?" He glanced over his shoulder. "They're turning that Arizona dirt a darker shed of red."

Dixon glowered at Yakima. Then he forced a smile and looked at the other men sitting around him. "Why not? Of course! Why the hell not?" He chuckled and took several deep swallows of his beer.

The others followed suit, as did Yakima.

Dixon lowered his beer schooner and raked a sleeve across his bearded lips. He held his gaze on the tall half-breed standing near the door, and his eyes darkened. "Who are you?"

"The name's Yakima Henry."

"The new law in town," said a man at the table to Yakima's left, casting a dimple-cheeked, jeering grin at Dixon. "Fuckin' Indian!"

The others laughed. All except Dixon, who just smiled mockingly at the lawman.

Yakima narrowed his eyes at the dimple-cheeked fellow, and said through gritted teeth, "What did you call me?"

He moved forward, still holding his beer in his left hand, rifle in his right hand.

The dimple-cheeked fellow's dimples slowly disappeared as Yakima approached.

Yakima stopped before the man's table and, keeping the others in the periphery of his vision, on the alert for sudden moves, he glared at the suddenly dimpleless, stone-faced man before him.

"Apologize," Yakima said, tightly, "and I'll think about letting it go."

The man drew his lips together in a white line. His brown eyes blazed, and his hairy nostrils flared.

A man rose suddenly to Yakima's right, filling his hand with a big Remington.

"No!" bellowed Dixon, beside whom the now-standing man had been sitting.

Yakima swung the Winchester around and pulled the trigger, the rifle roaring, flames stabbing.

The man beside Dixon screamed and dropped the Remy as he flew straight backward and landed on a table, kicking.

Another man jerked to his feet — this one

to Yakima's left. Yakima dropped his beer on the table of the hairy-nosed fella and shot the second would-be shooter before he could get his six-shooter unsheathed.

The hairy-nosed fella jerked his arm down beneath the table, reaching for a pistol, and Yakima shot him before quickly dispatching two more, the Yellowboy thundering like an angry god, red-flashing bursts lighting up the room, cartridge casings arcing back the lawman's shoulder and pinging onto the floor around his boots.

Yakima racked another round into the Winchester's action and, holding the stock up close to his cheek, looked around through the wafting powder smoke. Four men were down. Two were still sitting — the man whom Yakima had pinked in the nether regions beneath the man's table, and Dixon.

Two men lay dead around Dixon, one lying on the table behind the ex-Rebel gang leader. Two others lay dead near the other man, who sat at a table ten feet from Dixon. He sat with his hands extended halfway across his table, palms down. He hung his head, wagging it slowly, long hair hanging down around both sides of his face. He looked fearfully up at Yakima from beneath shaggy brows, bunching his lips dreadfully.

Dixon sat straight-backed in his own chair, hands raised to his shoulders, smiling. He looked cool and calm, except for the single sweat bead rolling down the left side of his face to disappear into the tangle of his dusty beard.

"Well, well, well," said the ex-Confederate. "Aren't you special?"

"All I know is you got six men dead and" — Yakima glanced at the other man still shaking his head and grimacing at the half-breed with the Yellowboy repeater — "two more soon to follow."

"I'll admit I misjudged the situation."

"Rebel Wilkes sure holds a grudge."

"He does at that. It's a southern thing." Dixon smiled.

"He also must have deep pockets, meaning the stillborn railroad must not have cleaned him out entirely."

"Oh, it did. He's working for his father now, trying to dig himself out of the hole this town put him in. Tom Wilkes is one wealthy old Rebel, most of it stolen, of course, but I heard he invested well." Again, the self-satisfied smile.

"Rebel's father pay you?"

"No one paid us. True, I owed Rebel's old man an old debt from years back — a little matter concerning a deputy US marshal on my trail and sporting a federal warrant in his saddlebags — but it's not every day an old killer like me is turned loose on a whole town . . . with the whole town and all its riches . . . including its women . . . including the pretty wife of the dead town marshal . . . as my reward. Makes it some bit easier, knowing that Tom Wilkes, the old Rebel outlaw himself, has the county sheriff in his back pocket. Old Tom bought the sheriff as a Christmas present, shall we say, for his boy."

Yakima had wondered why he hadn't heard by now from even an over-worked, spread-too-thin county sheriff, under the prevailing circumstances. Word of the Apache Springs situation must surely have spread to the county seat in Tucson.

Well, now he knew.

"Get up," Yakima said, wagging the Yellowboy. "I got a room ready for you. One with a barred door."

"I don't think so."

Yakima arched a brow in question.

The old Confederate quirked a challenging smile.

Yakima set the rifle down on a table to his left. Then he brushed his hand across his holstered .44, unsnapping the keeper thong.

"Get up," he ordered the other man.

Dixon slid his chair back and rose slowly, keeping his hands raised to his shoulders until he was standing. Then he lowered them slowly to his sides.

He stared at Yakima.

Yakima stared back at him, unblinking.

Dixon's right hand dropped to the holster thonged to his right thigh. He had the converted Griswold & Gunnison .44 half-raised and cocked when Yakima's Colt danced in the half-breed's hand.

Dixon stumbled backward, kicking his chair. Grimacing, he fired the Confederate pistol into his table, shattering his beer schooner and sending frothy ale cascading across the table's scarred wood. He wobbled on his hips but maintained his feet, looking suddenly as though he'd swallowed something foul down the wrong throat.

He glanced at the growing stain on his light-brown wool vest and white shirt, then rolled his fast-fading eyes up at Yakima. "Fast . . . fast fuckin' half-breed," he grunted through a grimace, stumbling sideways. He smiled coldly at his killer, eyes bright with mockery. "Fast fuckin' Injun!"

Yakima pumped two more bullets into him. The ex-Confederate jerked two more times, violently.

"Go to hell." Dixon got his boots tangled

up in his chair and fell hard with another grunt and a long, final sigh.

Yakima turned to the man he'd pinked through the table.

"Can you ride?" he asked him.

The man's pain-sharp eyes widened in surprise. Then he nodded.

"Tell Wilkes if he sends anyone else, I will personally lead those men back to him, tied belly down across their saddles. And he'll be so full of lead he'll rattle when he walks."

The man rose stiffly. He had his right hand clamped over the inside of his upper right thigh. Blood streaked the inside of his pant leg all the way to the man's high-topped, black boot. He strode toward the batwings as though he had a full load in his drawers. He pushed through the batwings, hobbled across the gallery, climbed onto a rangy chestnut, and, leaning forward and gritting his teeth, rode away.

"Christalmighty," Dundee groused behind his bar, looking around at the dead men, the growing blood pools on his floor. "Why does my place have to take the brunt of this little disagreement?"

"You serve good beer," Yakima told him, grabbing the Yellowboy and starting for the batwings. "I'll be back to finish mine later."

He pushed through the batwings. The Rio

Grande Kid sat in the hide-bottom chair to the left of the door, legs stretched out, boots crossed at his ankles. His chin was dipped toward his chest, as though he were napping, and his thick hands were laced over his broad belly still poking out through the missing buttons of his hickory shirt.

"What're you doing here?" Yakima asked him. "I thought you were headin' out for El Dorado."

The Kid lifted his head and inhaled deeply. "I was, but . . . turns out I was a tad short on supplies. Came to town to fill the larder. When I got to town I realized I had a hole in my damn pocket!"

"You had a hole in your pocket?"

"All my jingle musta dropped straight down my leg!"

"That's too bad."

"I'll just have to work for a week or two, build up a grubstake. Maybe I can find a rancher who needs some broncs broke."

The Kid turned to look toward the adobe-brick bank sitting across the broad street and outside of which several townsfolk — three men and two women, one holding a parasol against the desert sun — were standing and staring toward the Busted Flush. "Or maybe I'll hold up the bank." The Kid rubbed a big paw across his jaw as

175

though thinking it over. "Sure, maybe I'll hold up the bank. Why don't you take tomorrow off? Go fishin' up in the mountains. I don't want to have to shoot you since I ate your grub, drank your mud, and smoked your tobacco, an' all."

"Hold on, now, Kid," Yakima said. "Don't go off half-cocked."

"Easier said than done!"

"If you need a job, you can work for me for a while. How 'bout pinning a deputy town marshal's badge on your shirt for a few days? I need a fresh set of eyes, and the cool, cunning eyes of the Rio Grande Kid would more than fill the bill to help me keep an eye on things around here."

The Kid squinted up at him and quirked a devilish grin. "Pretty good shootin', eh?"

"Not bad."

"Not bad? Hallkatoot — look at 'em!" The Kid gestured at the two dead men lying in the street. Haugen was kneeling beside the corpse on the street's far side, going through the dead man's pockets and just now holding a pocket watch up to his ear. "Two shots. One for each. Killin' shots, both!"

"Preening doesn't become an outlaw of your stature. What do you say?"

The Kid raked a nail along his jaw, squinting into the sun. "I don't know — a badge?

On the Kid's chest? Shit, I'm an outlaw. The worst of the worst. Might be a tall order for the Kid to keep his town manners . . . follow the law instead of breakin' it, like usual. But, oh, all right, since you seem to be in such a tight spot, an' I ate your grub, drank your mud, and smoked your tobacco." He looked up at Yakima. "What do you pay?"

"Fifty cents a day? Plus one beer?"

"Make it sixty cents and two beers, and you got a deal."

"I'll pay you out of my own salary," Yakima said. He flipped the Kid a silver dollar. "There's a dollar to start, with a bonus. Help Haugen haul the dead men over to his undertaking parlor. You and the gravedigger can fight over what you find on their persons. They looked pretty well heeled. Just on them alone, you'll probably find enough for mining supplies."

Yakima stepped off the Busted Flush's boardwalk. "And take these horses over to the livery."

"It's going to take me some time to get used to takin' orders from an Injun," the Kid yelled behind him.

"You'll get the hang of it," Yakima said.

He glanced at the undertaker, who was pulling a boot off one of the dead men and inspecting the man's socks. "Hey, Haugen," Yakima called. He slid his gaze toward where the four dead men were propped against the front of the undertaker's shop in their wooden overcoats. "Why don't you plant those smelly bastards before you bait in the wildcats?"

Haugen scowled and gritted his teeth as Yakima continued to the marshal's office. He stopped when he saw a familiar buckskin tied to the hitch rail fronting the building, and the flaxen-haired girl standing on the gallery.

CHAPTER 14

Emma Kosgrove gazed back at Yakima, her eyes strangely cold.

Finally she blinked, turned around, chin in the air. She thrust out an arm to throw the marshal's office door open with a haughty flourish and disappeared inside, leaving the door open behind her. A princess disgruntled with one of her minions.

Yakima sighed, climbed the gallery steps, and walked through the door.

Emma sat in his chair, behind his desk, spurred boots on the desktop, ankles crossed. She had her hands laced behind her head. She slitted her eyes as she said, "I have a bone to pick with you, Mr. Marshal of Apache Springs."

"Get in line." Yakima pegged his hat on the wall and shoved her feet to the floor. "Boots off my desk."

She bounced up out of the chair and swung toward him as he took her place in the chair, crossing his ankles atop the desk and resting the Yellowboy across his thighs.

"I saw you sitting with my sister," Emma accused. When he didn't respond, she said, "I was riding up the draw behind her place, to extend my condolences about Lonnie. Imagine my shock to see you two sitting on the swing together — the swing that Lonnie built for the two of them right after they were married — happy as two birds in a nest."

"You shouldn't be spying on the law of Apache Springs. Now I'm gonna have to mark you down as trouble." Yakima snorted ironically at that.

Emma crossed her arms on her breasts. "Her husband has been dead only a little over a week. Don't you have any sense of propriety?"

"No."

"She told me you told her about us."

Yakima was pinching cartridges from his shell belt and thumbing them through the Winchester's loading gate. "Wasn't much more I could tell her that she hadn't already seen."

"I didn't want her to know I'd been riding out to see you. I mean, often."

"I didn't realize you were so shy about

letting folks know about your stable of studs."

"How dare you, you bastard!" Emma took a step forward, cheeks flushed with anger. "You take that back!" Suddenly, her lips trembled, and her eyes filled with tears. She jerked around abruptly, closing a hand over her mouth, sobbing.

"Holy Christ," Yakima said, stopping his work to gaze up at her in surprise. "Are you crying?"

Emma swung back around, sniffing back her tears, brushing her sleeve across her nose. "Didn't I mean anything to you?"

Yakima didn't know what to say to that. His lower jaw hung, and he felt his lips working, but no words came out.

"Nothing?" Emma said, shrilly, bent forward at the waist.

"What the hell did you want it to mean?"

"I thought it meant as much to you as it meant to me!"

"Well, I reckon I thought it did!" Yakima paused, staring up at her, trying to figure out what the hell was going on. He was truly puzzled. He hadn't realized she had taken what they'd done so seriously.

"Look," he said, "I'm sorry if it meant more to you than what it was, but . . ."

She pinched her face in an angry grin.

"You got her stuck in your craw, now, don't you?"

"What?"

"She's taken you away from me, just like Lonnie!"

Yakima set the rifle on the desk and rose from the chair, staring down at the girl in exasperation. He placed his hands on her shoulders. "You never had me. All you ever had was what was happening when we were together. That was all. I thought you understood that it was all just a . . . a . . . *dalliance.* If I'd known that you —"

"You like me. I know you do, Yakima."

"I do like you, Emma. Like is far different from love."

"Do you love her?"

Yakima's exasperation kept growing until he thought his head would explode. He almost laughed as he said, "No! I hardly know her. Like you said, her husband only died a week ago, fer chrissakes, Emma!"

"Then what were you doing, sitting in the swing with her?"

"Eating pie!"

"She's pretty, isn't she?"

"No more than you."

That seemed to float right past without Emma so much as noticing. "She's working on you. I could tell by the way she talked about you."

"That's ridiculous. She's grieving over her husband."

"Strange way of grieving — inviting a strange man into the house for pie and coffee. A man she knew I'd taken a fondness for."

Yakima lifted his arms, drawing a deep breath and raking his hands back through his long, sweat-damp hair in frustration. "Look, Emma — you two have a complicated relationship. I understand that. But I do not have your sister stuck in my craw. I assure you. Now, if you'll forgive me, I have more important concerns than —"

"I think we should get married."

Yakima's jaw dropped nearly to his chest. He stared down at Emma in wide-eyed shock. *"Huh?"*

She pushed him back down into his chair. She leaped into his lap, folding her long legs over the chair's right arm, and wrapping her own arms around his neck. "You don't have to answer right away. I realize it's a big decision. But I think you should think about it. I love you, Yakima, and I can tell by the way you responded to me — you know, out at your cabin in the desert," she purred, nibbling his right earlobe, "that you have some pretty strong feelings for me, too."

She squirmed around in his lap and the sensation of her heart-shaped rump caressing his crotch had exactly the effect she desired. He grabbed her arms to heave her off his lap, but then she turned full around to him and pressed her mouth against his, kissing him hungrily. Oh, she was a devil! He wanted with every ounce of his being to throw her off of him, but his arms and legs had suddenly turned to melting putty.

Her tongue just felt so damned good, sliding against his own.

Her breasts felt wonderful, swelling against his chest, making him remember how she'd looked that stormy night, dancing naked in the rain.

"Okay, okay, okay," he groaned, managing to call up enough willpower to push her away from him. "That's enough."

"You know it's not," she groaned back at him, lunging toward him once more, mashing her lips against his own.

"No, it's not, but it's gotta be!" he finally said, breathless, holding her away from him, his hands on her arms. "You've already gotten the wrong idea, and I need you to realize that this right here is as far as it's ever gonna go again, Emma!"

"I knew it," she cried, leaping away from him, running the back of her hand across her mouth as though to rid herself of his taste. "You got her stuck in your craw!" Her eyes glazed in rage as she leaned forward at the waist to berate him with: "I need you to know that you've had the pleasure of me in your mattress for the last time, you no good half-breed son of a bitch!"

Lunging forward, she smashed her hand across his face, then turned and ran out of the marshal's office, sobbing. She ran into the Kid just then coming up the gallery steps and nearly sent the old outlaw sprawling.

"Lord o' mercy!" the Kid cried, clinging to the rail as Emma grabbed her reins off the hitch rack and swung up onto the buckskin's back.

She galloped off to the east, hunched low in her saddle.

Yakima stood in the office's open doorway, staring after her.

The Kid turned to him and shook his head. "Well, you got you a way with women, anyway."

Another lull settled over the town.

Over the next week and a half, Yakima worked from early in the morning to mid-evening, leaving the Rio Grande Kid to fill in the gaps when Apache Springs was

185

relatively quiet. Especially quiet, rather. The town was always quiet save for when a small pack of local ranch hands came to town to stomp with their tails up on Friday and/or Saturday night, or a local prospector struck a vein, fell off the wagon, saw snakes, and decided to trigger an old-model pistol through the shop windows on Main Street.

In other words, it was raucous just often enough to keep Yakima from growing so bored that he wanted to leave town at a dead run, howling like a gut-shot coyote.

He'd been sleeping in the jailhouse up until he'd deputized the Rio Grande Kid. When the Kid came on board, he rented a small, mouse-infested room at the local inn. He still spent most of his time in the jailhouse or eating in one of the cafes or saloons, but he slept at the inn — when he wasn't hearing mice scuttling around under his bed or in the walls, that is.

Or when that desert-addled prospector wasn't in town, turning his inner animal loose.

One day a couple of cow punchers, recently fired from one of the ranches, came to town, held up the Johnson Brothers Mercantile, and lit off for the tall and uncut to cool their heels and head to Mexico. One of the Johnson brothers alerted Yakima after the fact, and the half-breed mounted Wolf and headed out after the robbers, who, despite having taken down only one hundred and twenty-five dollars in their ill-conceived robbery the morning after the Johnson brothers had deposited the previous day's earnings in the bank, decided to make an all-or-nothing stand from a low ridge.

They weren't up to the task.

Yakima led them back to town wrapped in their blanket rolls and tied belly-down over their horses' backs. Just as he made it into the outskirts of Apache Springs, the monsoon storm that had been threatening for the past half hour hunkered low and began spitting rain.

As he skirted the cemetery rising on the rocky knoll to his right, he saw a figure standing on the top of the knoll. He stopped Wolf and stared up at the slender figure wearing a long skirt, ruffled blouse, and small, black hat pinned to her pulled-up hair.

Julia Taggart had her back to Yakima. She was staring down at the freshly mounded grave of her dead husband. As Yakima watched, she slowly crouched and set a spray of what were probably flowers atop the mounded rocks. Seemingly oblivious to the building storm and the rumbling thunder, she dropped to her knees beside the grave and threw herself forward atop the mound. Her shoulders jerked as she cried.

A knife of deep sorrow pricked Yakima's heart.

He turned his head, giving the young widow her privacy, and nudged Wolf on ahead, jerking the reins of the two pack-horses behind him. He delivered the dead men to Haugen, whose business was doing so well of late that the man was adding another room to his building, and headed over to the livery barn with Wolf and the dead men's horses.

He'd just turned all three mounts over to the hostler and was heading back to his office when the storm cut loose, rain coming down in lacy white sheets, thunder clapping like giant, rolling boulders breaking against one another in heaven. Yakima put his head down and started running slantwise across the street, boots splashing in the instant puddles.

He glanced toward the cemetery and stopped despite the rain hammering against him, soaking him.

"Shit!"

He ran across the street, opened the jailhouse door, and leaned his Yellowboy against the inside wall. He headed back outside, closing the door behind him, and ran east along the muddy, rain-battered street. He hadn't run far before he was as wet as he would have been if he'd jumped into a river fully clothed. He ran with his head down, hat pulled low over his eyes, boots splashing in the puddles, the noise covered by the hammering drive of the rain and the thunder.

He ran up the knoll. Julia sat with her back against Taggart's freshly chiseled stone. She sat with her knees raised beneath her skirt, arms encircling them, one cheek resting against her right kneecap as she cried, her entire body convulsing. The rain had driven the small, black hat from the bun atop her head, and it clung to a few strands of her wet, disheveled hair, over her right ear.

"You're gonna catch your death up here!" Yakima yelled above the storm.

She looked up at him with a start. Because of the storm, she hadn't heard him approach. She blinked once, shook her head in defiance, and placed her cheek back atop her knee. Her shoulders continued shuddering. Beneath the booming thunder, he could hear her crying.

He grabbed her arm, yanked her to her feet.

"No!" she cried, trying to pull away from him.

He regained his grip on her arms, gave her a violent jerk, and, before he knew what he was doing, he'd closed his mouth over hers. She tried to pull away, but he held her fast and closed his mouth over hers once more. She squirmed in his arms, tried to shove him away, but he held her close, kissing her.

Thunder rumbled and lightning flashed. The rain hammered down around them.

Yakima drew his head away from hers. She stared up at him in open-mouthed shock, gasping, chest rising and falling heavily. Rainwater streamed down her face, washing away her tears.

He felt the burn of guilt at what he'd done, but the impulse had overtaken him as suddenly and unexpectedly as the storm had overtaken Apache Springs. He didn't think he could have stopped it any more than he could have stopped the storm.

He was at a loss for what to say for a time, but then he blurted out, "You're alive. He's dead. He's buried under those rocks." He gestured at the grave, then hardened his jaws as he regarded her again, sternly. "He's not comin' back, Julia! They never come back!"

She stared back at him, and a little of the defiant anger left her gaze.

Her eyes continued to soften. Then she threw himself into his arms once more and kissed him. He drew his arms tighter around her and tipped her head back, returning her kiss, relishing the sensation of her warm, wet lips against his own. The rain beat down, dribbled off his hat brim.

Finally, he pulled away.

"Come on," he said, taking her hand and starting down the hill. "Going to get you home!"

CHAPTER 15

Julia's knees buckled as Yakima led her down the cemetery hill. She dropped to the muddy trail, sobbing and yelling, "Leave me alone! I want to stay here . . . with him!"

"He's not here!" Yakima scooped her up in his arms and carried her the rest of the way down the hill.

When he got to the bottom of the hill, he turned right and continued walking north, tipping his head against the pouring rain the wind blew at him from straight ahead. It was one hell of a gully washer. The gullies and arroyos would literally be gushing for a long time after this one. As it was, the trail he strode along under his burden of Julia Taggart had nearly become a stream. High ground lay ahead, so the water was running toward Yakima, rising nearly to his ankles in places.

Julia had stopped fighting him and now lay slack in his arms, her own arms around his neck, sobbing against his ear. He tried to ignore the way her supple, trembling body felt against his own, the occasional brush of her nose against his neck. He pushed through the gate in her fence, mounted the gallery, fumbled with the doorknob, and stepped inside.

"Upstairs," she said, clinging to him tightly now. She was staring into his eyes, her gaze penetrating. Yakima looked away. He felt a raw ache in the pit of his belly.

Yakima strode through the small parlor and climbed the carpeted stairs. At the top, she thrust a wet arm out toward an open door. "In there."

Yakima stepped into the bedroom and laid her on the canopied bed abutted by two small, round tables adorned with hurricane lamps on doilies. Lightning flashed beyond the curtained windows. The rain hammered the roof.

Yakima released the young woman. As he straightened, she raised a hand toward his chest as though to pull him back down to her. The tips of her fingers brushed his wet shirt. She stared up at him with the same, odd, penetrating gaze as before. She was no longer crying. Her expression seemed one of great concentration.

He turned away. "I'll build a fire. Then

you'd better get out of those wet clothes."

He walked to the small black stove in the room's far corner. An apple crate filled with piñon and mesquite branches and kindling sat beside the stove. He opened the stove door and tossed in some kindling from the apple crate — feathersticks, dried pinecones, and strips of old newspaper.

A tin matchbox sat on a shelf above the stove, beside a tintype photograph of Lon and Julia Taggart. Yakima's glance caught on the photograph, obviously taken just after their wedding, probably at a photographer's studio in Tucson. Julia wore a gauzy white wedding gown, and she held a spray of flowers in one hand on her lap. She was sitting in an upholstered chair, Taggart on one knee beside her, his hand resting on the wrist of her hand holding the flowers.

As was the fashion of the time, the couple was not smiling, but their eyes were lit with a barely contained joy.

Yakima wished that he and Faith had sat for a photograph like that. He wished he had a photograph of any kind to remember her by. As it was, he had only his memories. It horrified him at times, noting that some of the details of her face and body were beginning to fade. The harder he tried to remember them, the more they faded, giving him a desperate, breathless sensation, as though he himself were teetering on the edge of a steep cliff.

He scraped a match to life on the stove door, then touched it to the neat pile of kindling he'd arranged on the grate. The paper and pinecones caught, the flame growing, spreading, gray smoke lifting and swirling around inside the stove. Yakima dropped the match and then grabbed a featherstick from the crate, broke it up in his hands, and added it to the flame. While the bits of broken wood were being consumed, he added a couple of sizeable branches, which threatened to snuff the fire until he leaned forward and blew on it, making the flames instantly lick up around the freshly added wood and dance, whispering more and more loudly.

He added two more branches, and then, deciding the fire would take, he closed the door, latched it, and stood. "There — that should . . ."

Turning toward the bed, he stopped suddenly. She stood before him, holding a baby-blue cotton towel in front of her breasts. She was naked, only the towel concealing her, and it wasn't concealing much.

She lifted the towel to him. "Here."

Yakima's heart fluttered. "Thanks, but I'll
—"

She reached up, pulled his hat off his
head, dropped it to the floor beside the
stove, and used the towel to dry his face
and neck, working gingerly, staring up into
his eyes. Her lips were slightly parted, showing the tips of her two front teeth. The towel
danced between them, the ends caressing
her pale breasts, at times covering her pale
pink nipples, at times revealing them.

He drew a deep breath, his heart quickening, his loins aching with his nearly instant,
full arousal.

"I'll do it," he said, trying to take the towel
from her.

She wouldn't release it.

"Get undressed," she said, softly.

He opened his mouth to speak, but she
placed a finger across his lips, hard. He
could feel her pulse in the tip of that finger.
"I do not want to be alone." She shook her
head, and tears glazed her eyes, her upper
lip quivering. "I do not . . . want . . . to
be . . . alone!"

She released the towel and began unbut-
toning his wet shirt.

He tried to stop her again, but he couldn't.
There was so much that wasn't right about
what he was about to do. She was grieving

deeply over her dead husband. On the other hand, Taggart was dead, and she was grieving. What could ever do more harm than that?

Besides, he was no longer in control of the situation. She was. And his lust was.

She pulled off his shirt and then unbuckled his cartridge belt. She let it fall to the floor. He kicked out of his boots and unbuttoned his pants. She helped him remove them and then shoved him down on the edge of the bed to peel his long handle top from his thick arms. Kneeling before him, she was about to peel them down his legs but stopped when she saw that his erection had burst free of the long handles' fly.

She stared at it, breathing hard, her nipples pebbling.

She lowered her head, cupped the mast in her hands and then slowly lowered her mouth over it. She sucked him slowly, softly, teasing with her tongue. After a time, he felt the wetness of her tears on him. He reached down and, with two fingers beneath her chin, lifted her head toward him, frowning.

Tears dribbled down her cheeks. But she was laughing, lips trembling. Then she was crying . . . laughing again . . .

Yakima gentled her up in his arms and laid her on the bed.

She lay naked before him, lifting her arms, extending her hands, reaching for him, tears running down the sides of her face to the pillow.

Yakima crawled atop her, between her spread legs. He smoothed her damp hair back from her cheeks. Her whole body trembled beneath him. He could feel her heart hammering against his chest. He placed his lips over hers, slid inside her.

She tipped her head back, digging her fingers into his shoulders, and gave a guttural, nearly deafening groan that teetered on the edge of a scream.

A couple of hours later, the storm rumbled off to the southeast.

Yakima found himself walking along Main Street, stepping around mud puddles, wet boots squawking. Julia had wanted him to don dry clothes from her husband's closet rather than wrestle back into his own duds, which hadn't had time to dry even though, after his and Julia's first fevered coupling, he'd taken time to hang them out near the stove.

He'd turned down the offer, feeling an impractical revulsion against donning the clothes of a man so recently expired. The clothes of the man he'd just cuckolded, if a dead man can be cuckolded, which he probably couldn't, but there had been very little that was rational about the stormy night that had passed in a blur of grief-driven lust.

Making his way back to his hotel for a couple hours of shuteye and dry clothes — he had a second pair of duds in his war bag — he paused across the street from the jailhouse. There was a light in the office's front window, the wick turned halfway down. In the light beyond the half-closed sackcloth curtains, the Rio Grande Kid slumped back in the office chair, boots crossed on the desktop, arms folded across his chest. His chin was dipped down and to one side, his shoulders dangerously slanted to that side, as well. The Kid looked as though he would soon fall out of his chair.

The night was so quiet that amidst the pleasant sounds of the rain dripping from the eaves around him, Yakima could hear the snores beyond the dully lit window and closed office door.

The Kid.

Yakima snorted at the appellation. "The Kid" hadn't been a kid in a good forty, maybe fifty years. (He refused to reveal his actual age.) He looked even older without the hat that usually covered his balding pate. Seeing the oldster sitting there, asleep on the job, the weak lamplight revealing the wrinkles in his craggy face, beneath the thumb-sized pockets sagging beneath his eyes, Yakima felt a razor-edged sympathy pang.

Johnny Day could cling to the Rio Grande Kid as furiously as he wanted, but the Kid had galloped into the sunset long ago, and it was only aging Johnny Day sitting there now, half-asleep in a dead man's chair, about to suffer the insult of a hard stone floor.

Yakima weighed his options. He could walk over and wake the Kid, but would that be any less of a rebuke than him falling to the floor?

He'd known the Kid slept on the job. That was all right with Yakima. If there was any trouble, someone would knock on the jailhouse door. If the Kid needed help, he'd been instructed to trigger three quick shots into the air over Apache Springs, and Yakima would come running. Having the Kid on the job allowed him to get a few hours' sleep at night; without the Kid, he'd get none and would be no good against trouble when it came.

And he was sure more trouble was on the way. A man who'd already sent the kind of trouble Rebel Wilkes had sent to Apache

Springs would surely send more. Probably a lot more.

Yakima continued moving east toward the hotel only to get sidetracked again when the rich aroma of a good cigar touched his nostrils. He stopped and turned to his left once more. A small dull crimson circle of light shone in the darkness fronting the building whose second story housed the office and living quarters of the attorney, Mark Garland. The light, growing slightly as the smoker drew on the cigar, hovered at the base of the stairs rising to Garland's office.

Suddenly, the light went out. Yakima saw a man-shaped silhouette standing there in the darkness at the bottom of the stairs. The silhouette was obscured by a thick, web-like wreath of cigar smoke. The crimson light appeared again as the attorney took another drag off the stogie, and when it faded, more gray smoke issued as the man's voice said, "You've had a late night, Marshal Henry."

The man's voice had been no louder than if Yakima had been standing two feet away from him, but it had been edged in no vague accusation.

Before Yakima could respond, Garland spat to one side, turned, and started up the stairs to his office, the soft soles of his slippers tapping on the risers. By the light of a sickle moon rising on the other side of the building, Yakima saw that Garland wore a garment that hung down to just above his ankles and that was probably a night robe.

The attorney hadn't been able to sleep. Maybe thinking about Mrs. Taggart?

Knowing how the man felt, Yakima continued to his room.

CHAPTER 16

Two days later, Yakima and the Rio Grande Kid were sitting on the gallery of the jailhouse, watching the mid-afternoon traffic idle by, when three strangers rode into town from the west.

Yakima couldn't see them well, as they were coming into town with the west-slanting sun behind them, but what he could see was the sun's reflection off the well-tended pistols bristling on their persons, and the handsome, silver-chased Henry repeater jutting up from the sheath on one of the rider's horses.

They were a fine-looking trio — straight-backed, square-jawed, serious-eyed, and well-groomed. At least, what Yakima could see of them. The man with the Henry appeared to sport a waxed handlebar mustache. He was the tallest of the three, and he held Yakima's gaze with a direct one of his own until he and the other two riders swerved abruptly to the side of the street on which the attorney's office sat, above a barber shop.

"Well, well, well," the Kid said. "What do you suppose we have here?"

"Yeah," Yakima said, keeping his eyes on the three newcomers. "What do you suppose . . . ?"

The Kid, who was here when he didn't need to be because he didn't have anything else to do and he could drink the coffee for free, took a long drag off his loosely rolled quirley and said, "That's a Texas crease in the hat of the steely-eyed gent who finds you a specimen of uncommon interest." He glanced at Yakima, narrowing one cautious eye. "Regulators?"

"Possibly."

"If so, they must wanna look their best before they start to work." The Kid amended his estimation of the three when, instead of heading into the barbershop after tying their three handsome but hard-ridden horses to the hitch rack fronting the two-story building, they headed up the stairs hugging the place's east wall. "Or . . ."

"Yeah," Yakima said. "Or . . ."

"Or maybe they're gonna sue us!" The Kid slapped his thigh, laughing.

Yakima started to think that very thing

might be true when all three headed toward the jailhouse like four geese crossing a road, following the mother goose in the person of the attorney himself, Mark Garland. Garland wore his crisp brown bowler tight on his head, and a smile of unabashed delight made his eyes sparkle behind his spectacles as he strode forthrightly along the boardwalks, jauntily swinging his left arm while taking frequent drags off the fat stogie he held in his right hand.

The lawyer looked so happy that Yakima thought he might break out in song.

"Mr. Henry!" Garland called as he approached the jailhouse gallery. "Oh, Mr. Henry!"

"Well, Mr. Garland," Yakima said, "to what . . . or whom . . . do we owe the pleasure?"

"I'm glad to see you're both here — you and your, uh, deputy." The attorney snorted.

The Kid scowled at him. "What's that supposed to mean — you're, *uh,* deputy? Or did you break wind?"

The attorney glared at the Kid.

"The Rio Grande Kid, my ass," he sneered. "The *real old man,* more like!" He chuckled. The three men flanking him laughed, as well.

"Why, you little gutter snipe!" The Kid

dropped his coffee cup and started to rise from his chair.

Yakima grabbed his arm and pulled him back down. "Easy, Kid."

"You're both fired," Garland said, smiling like the bull snake that ate the rat, tugging on the lapels of his black, claw-hammer coat, his string tie blowing over his shoulder in the hot breeze kicking up dust and swirling it along the main street.

"Fired?" the Kid said, incredulous.

"I wrote a letter to the US marshal's office in Phoenix, explaining the situation. The US marshal agreed with my assessment that, since the entire town's safety is at stake, and that the US Post Office resides within the city limits of Apache Springs, making it also at risk, the threat posed by Rebel Wilkes is a federal matter. I requested that a good friend of mine, Deputy US Marshal Tennyson Kinkaid, be sent to the town's rescue and relieve the current sitting town marshal and his, uh, *deputy,* of their duties."

Garland glanced at the tall gent with the handlebar mustache, who smiled grimly beneath the brim of his Texas-creased Stetson and slid the lapel of his tan corduroy jacket back from his gray wool shirt to reveal the moon-and-star badge of a deputy

US marshal.

"This is Ten Kinkaid." Garland glanced at the other two men, in turn announcing, "And this is Deputy United States Marshals Stanley Wellman and R. C. 'Raging Ronnie' Holbrook, colleagues of Kinkaid's under orders from Chief US Marshal Brian Donleavy of the Southwestern District."

Wellman was nearly Kinkaid's height, roughly six-two and wearing his red-brown hair pulled back in a mare's tail dangling down his back. He had brown eyes and sun-bleached brows, and a scar on his upper, mustached lip that made him appear to be perpetually sneering. Or maybe he was just always sneering; Yakima vaguely revised his estimation of the man's character.

R. C. "Raging Ronnie" Holbrook could have passed for a thirty-a-month-and-found cow puncher if not for the stylish cut of his three-piece suit, complete with gold watch chain and the pearl-gripped Colt residing in a holster over his belly beside the glistening gold buckle of his shell belt. He was under six feet and stocky, with little mean eyes set back in doughy sockets. He was a hard-jawed blond with tiny freckles and practically no lips at all. Those he did have had no smile lines around them.

He stared at Yakima with his chin down,

thumbs hooked behind his cartridge belt. If he'd been a bull, he'd have been ready to charge.

"This, gentlemen," Garland said, addressing the three hard-eyed lawmen and gesturing toward Yakima and the Rio Grande Kid, "are the current town marshal and his, uh, *deputy*, both of whom you'll be relieving until this matter with Rebel Wilkes has been resolved."

"I don't see why you have to keep calling me 'his, *uh*, deputy,' Garland," the Kid said, snarling through gritted teeth, his big nose as red as the tongs in a smithy's forge. "Why, you're makin' my ass so hot, I'm like to vault right over this railing and kick the shit out of both ends of your mean little person!"

"You are fired, sir!" Garland retorted, crisply, giving his coat lapels another tug.

"Rebel Wilkes should no longer be a problem," said Deputy US Marshal Tennyson Kinkaid, addressing his friend Garland. "We've sent a man to investigate Wilkes in Prescott. If it can be proven that Wilkes sent the gunslicks to Apache Springs, he'll be behind federal bars soon. We might have to have a few citizen witnesses from town here go up to testify. This will all be over soon, and you'll likely be able to seat a *permanent, bona fide lawman* within a couple of weeks. In the meantime, we'll take over, on the off-chance Wilkes has more gunmen en route."

He spoke the words "permanent, bona fide lawman" while gazing darkly, meaningfully at Yakima.

"Mr. Garland!" a woman's voice called from across the street. "Mr. Garland, what is going on over there?"

All eyes, including Yakima's, turned to where Julia Taggart was waiting for a ranch wagon to rattle on past her. She was staring with concern toward the men grouped before the town marshal's office, squinting her eyes against the ranch wagon's dust. When the wagon had passed, she hurried across the street, carrying a reticule in one hand and using her other hand to lift the hem of her orange-and-brown-patterned day dress above the ankles of her black, side-button half boots.

"Julia, this is none of your concern," Garland said as she stood before him, scrutinizing the well-dressed newcomers, then shuttling her curious gaze to Yakima. "I am simply dismissing the half-breed, or *Mr. Henry,* rather, and his deputy, the Rio Grande Kid, as he calls himself," the attorney added with an ironic snort, causing the Kid's eyes to flare once more. "The US marshal in Phoenix, having decided to intervene in the matter, has sent my friend Ten Kinkaid and his colleagues, Wellman and Holbrook, to take over the law-enforcing duties in Apache Springs."

"Why wasn't I notified?"

"Look, Julia, I and the rest of the town council allowed you to hire Mr. Henry as a special courtesy, given that your husband —"

"I don't understand, Mark. Why are you firing Mr. Henry . . . after all he's done for us? After the several times he's risked his life for this town? He's done nothing but an exemplary job — he and the Rio Grande Kid, I might add."

"I do appreciate that, Missus Taggart," the Kid said, doffing his hat and holding it over his heart before casting another snide glance at Garland and the federal lawmen.

Yakima cleared his throat and rose from his chair, holding his coffee cup in his right hand. "Mr. Garland has a point, Mrs. Taggart. It's time to bring the federals in. The situation calls for bona fide lawmen. Besides, I seem to have worn out my welcome here in Apache Springs."

He'd glanced at Garland as he'd uttered those last few words, and the attorney acknowledged the hidden meaning with a bitter twitch of his mustached mouth.

"I think this is all very unfair," Julia said, crossing her arms on her breasts. "Especially the way this has been handled. I don't mean your neglecting to consult with me. I realize I have no official standing in this town, as no women are allowed seats on the town council. But I think you would have saved yourself the appearance of extreme impropriety, Mr. Garland, if you'd at least have given Mr. Henry and his deputy some notice instead of confronting them like this with their replacements standing behind you like common thugs."

The federal lawmen frowned and shifted their feet, looking insulted.

Yakima held up his hands in supplication. "Really, Mrs. Taggart, I take no offense." He unpinned the town marshal's star from his shirt and held it out to Garland. "Here you are, Garland. My deputy and I will take our time and get out of your hair."

But Garland wasn't looking at him. He was looking at Julia, his cheeks flushed with anger, a sour smile on his mouth. "Impropriety, Julia? Really? I've noticed that your cheeks have been rather quick to regain their color after your husband's death. Judging by the lightness of your step lately, and the flash in your eyes, I'd say your grieving period is over. I — and much of the rest of the town, I might add — have been wondering if that healthy color and jauntiness of step is from having the half-breed take your husband's place — in the town marshal's office or perhaps your *bedroom*?"

Garland started to smile with a devilish satisfaction in his comments, but Yakima's right fist promptly rendered the smile stillborn. Garland screamed as he stumbled backward against the three federals. He screamed again as Yakima's bunched right fist smashed him again in the dead center of his mouth, splitting both lips.

Garland fell like a hundred-pound sack of feed corn.

As the three federals stumbled backward, Yakima reached for Garland once more, intending to drag him back to his feet and resume hammering away at the attorney's smug mouth.

"Yakima, no!" Julia cried, positioning herself between the half-breed and the fallen attorney. "Please, don't!"

Gun hammers clicked as two of the three lawmen drew their pistols, aiming at Yakima, while Kinkaid dropped to a knee beside Garland, one hand on the lawyer's shoulder. Kinkaid glared up at Yakima, ordering,

"Throw him behind bars. Assault and battery!"

"No!" Julia cried, swinging around to face Tennyson and the others, pressing her back against Yakima's chest. "Garland, don't you dare let them arrest this man. You had that coming!"

"Let him go," Garland said, dabbing at his smashed, bloody lips with a handkerchief, his mussed hair in his eyes. His glasses had fallen to the street. He stared up at Yakima, fire flashing in his gaze. "Get the hell out of town, and don't you ever come back — you hear me, breed?"

Yakima jerked forward, fists clenching once more, rage burning through him. He wanted to kick the attorney senseless, and if he'd had a few shots of firewater in him, he likely would have done just that and more. As it was, he was as sober as a judge, and Julia pressed back against him while the Rio Grande Kid grabbed his arm and pulled him away from the jail office.

"Come on, Yakima," the older man said. "We don't need this sack-of-shit town and its sack-of-shit attorney." The Kid spat. "Nor its sack-o'-shit *federales*!"

"My rifle," Yakima said, glaring down at Garland.

"I'll fetch it." The Kid climbed back up

the gallery steps and disappeared into the jailhouse.

Julia turned to Yakima and placed her hands on his chest, pushing him away from Garland and the lawmen. "Please, Yakima — just go. It's all right. Garland's nothing." She turned to glare at the man. "He's less than nobody!"

When the Rio Grande Kid had fetched the Yellowboy and slapped Yakima's shoulder, urging him in the direction of the livery barn, Yakima turned to Julia. She'd already started walking away, back in the direction of her house. Several townspeople had gathered in a ragged half circle around the town marshal's office. Word of what had been said here today would likely spread fast. In her humiliation, Julia wanted only to retreat to the sanctuary of her home.

Alone.

Yakima wanted to follow her, to comfort her. But that would be a mistake. Because of him, she would likely be a marked woman here in Apache Springs. Whispered about and shunned.

No. Not because of Yakima. Because of the envious Mark Garland.

As he shambled behind the Rio Grande Kid in the direction of the livery barn, Yakima cast one more glare toward Garland,

whom the three federal lawmen were helping to his feet. They dusted him off and
conversed in hushed, hard tones, glancing
back at Yakima.

The half-breed clenched his left fist at his
side, squeezed the neck of the Yellowboy
residing on his right shoulder, and forced
himself to keep walking.

His business here in Apache Springs was
over. He didn't care if Rebel Wilkes burned
the place to the ground.

CHAPTER 17

"Well, it wasn't the first job I ever been fired off of," the Kid said as he and Yakima took their time heading back toward the old prospector's shack huddled in a canyon of the remote and rugged Sierra Estrada. "Prob'ly won't be the last, neither. Not that I work honest jobs all that much. I tend to steer away from such tedium. Let the weak and simple work for livings, I say. The Kid mainly steals what he needs. Pillages an' plunders it!"

He pondered that, glancing speculatively off toward the southern horizon that was a blur of misty blue mountains beyond the salmons, greens, and duns of rolling chaparral. "Still, it was sorta nice havin' a real job an' . . . an', well . . . feelin' like a feller who belonged in a place."

He glanced at Yakima riding in brooding silence beside him. "Know what I mean?"

Yakima had brooded since leaving the

jailhouse, unable to tamp down the burn of anger deep in his belly. He'd only vaguely half heard what the Kid had said.

"I say there, Yakima," the older man said, raising his voice, "it was sort of nice livin' like the civilized folk there for a while, don't you think?"

Yakima looked over at him, scowling. "Like the civilized folk?" He snorted. "I'll tell you what I'd like to do. I'd like to ride back into Apache Springs, get good and soused on firewater at the Busted Flush, and turn those civilized folk who gave us the bum's rush inside out!"

He stopped his horse, heart thudding, and turned to stare back in the direction of town.

"Now, now, settle down there, Yak!" the Kid said. "Jeepers, you been around me too long, I reckon. You got the fightin' furies, same as me. Er . . . at least me a few years back. Leastways, you better put them civilized folk out of your mind. You ride back into town and try to get even with them, you'll only do jail time. *Federal* jail time. The federal prison ain't nothin' to fool with, neither; I can tell you from my own experience."

Since that didn't seem to be working, the Kid tried another tactic. "Besides, it wouldn't do her no good, neither, you ridin' back into Apache Springs and paintin' the town red. The locals would think you're doin' it for her, and they'd hold it against her. You don't want to do that to her. She's a rare one, that Mrs. Taggart. I could tell that from what little I seen of her. The Kid knows women. Er . . . I once did. Still, I know what I'm talkin' about. No, sir, you don't want to cause her no more trouble."

"I reckon I've already caused her enough," Yakima allowed after nearly another minute's pondering, feeling his burning heart slowing its beat and lowering his gaze to the rocky ground around him.

He wasn't seeing the ground, however. He was seeing Julia Taggart turn away from him and the attorney and the three federals — seeing her turn away from the entire town in shame and hurry back to the sanctuary of her house, in which she would continue to live with only the company of her dead husband's ghost.

"You know what your problem is?" the Kid said, chuckling, trying a little too hard to lighten Yakima's mood. "You like women too much. And, hell, they like you too much!" He laughed. "That's another thing you an' me got in common. Leastways . . . we had it in common a few years back. Two or three."

Yakima swung Wolf back around and continued riding south in the same sullen silence as before. The Kid rode beside him, casting frequent anxious glances toward him.

Finally, with one more attempt to break the half-breed out of the testy silence he'd cloaked himself in, the older man said, "Besides, if you rode back into Apache Springs and got likkered up, I'd have to ride back with you. To back your play, I mean, since we're pards an' all. And I for one am not ready to see the inside of a jail cell again just yet. Hell, just bein' in the same office as them cells made me feel itchy all over my body."

He chuckled, then narrowed an eye at Yakima and said, tentatively, " 'Cause . . . 'cause that's what we are now, ain't we?"

"What?" Yakima muttered as he reined Wolf wide of a nasty-looking *cholla* patch.

"Pards."

Yakima turned to the older man and slitted one lid. "Say again."

"Pards, goddamnit!" the Rio Grande Kid fairly bellowed, getting red-faced himself now with peevishness. "You know — trail partners. I mean, shit, we worked in the same office for a few days, wore the same badge . . . drank the same coffee. I smoked your Durham!"

Yakima stopped his horse suddenly and turned his jade eyes toward the man sitting his beefy sorrel that owned a spray of white spots across its withers and chest. The Kid stared back at him, eyes looking suddenly apprehensive, as though he thought he were about to become the target of the big half-breed's condemnation; as though, from his experience with others, he expected nothing less.

"You saved my life, Kid."

The Kid's brows furled beneath the brim of his ragged hat. "Huh?"

"If you hadn't pinked those two sonso'bitches from the rooftops a few days ago, I'd be snuggling with the diamondbacks about now. I'd be deader'n a beaver hat. So, yeah, we're pards. And I'm right happy and proud to call you partner. Make no mistake."

The Kid looked suddenly stricken, befuddled. "You . . . you . . . *are?*"

"Hell, yes." Yakima shaped a slow smile. It was true. By now he would have known by instinct, even if the Kid hadn't saved his hide, that the Kid was a friend. It was a harsh world. A man needed friends whether he wanted to believe it or not. Yakima would have been a fool not to see that the Rio Grande Kid, or whatever he wanted to call himself, could be counted among his own sparse stable of friends.

The one thing he knew about friends was that you took them at face value. You didn't judge them. At least, you didn't judge them any more harshly than you would want yourself to be judged.

The Kid said, "You, uh . . . you don't see me as just some washed-up old scalawag . . . an old, lyin' blowhard clingin' to wilder days . . . ?"

"Hell, you were and always will be the Rio Grande Kid. Who in their right mind wouldn't be happy and proud to be trail partners with the Rio Grande Kid? Not to mention have the privilege of being able to tell his grandkids — if he ever has grandkids, that is — that his life was at one time saved by none other than the famous Kid himself."

"Infamous."

"What's that?"

"The *in*famous Kid himself. The *in*famous Rio Grande Kid. That's what folks call me — those who've witnessed my deprivations, that is, even though most of those deprivations occurred some years back."

"Oh, right," Yakima said. "I'll tell my

grandkids how my hide was once saved by none other than the *in*famous Rio Grande Kid."

"And they'll look at you in a whole new light, sure enough!" the Kid said, slapping his thigh in delight. "They'll see you as somethin' more than their toothless old granddad fartin' and leanin' on a cane. Yessir!"

"Don't push it, Kid," Yakima warned.

"Right, right," the Kid said, snorting another laugh.

Yakima's smile faded as he stared back toward town.

"Don't worry about her," the Kid said.

Yakima looked at him, arching one brow.

"She'll be all right," the Kid said. "She's Kosgrove's daughter. No one'll pester her."

Yakima pursed his lips, nodding.

Finally, he touched spurs to Wolf's flanks, and the two men continued south.

They gained the old shack just as another monsoon storm cut loose.

Before the ground had become muddied by the falling rain, Yakima noted relatively fresh horse tracks in the yard between the cabin and the corral. It didn't appear that anyone had moved in and taken over the cabin, but someone had visited. The tracks were from the same horse, and they were of various ages, indicating that the same person had visited the cabin at least a couple of times since Yakima had become town marshal of Apache Springs.

Emma Kosgrove.

Yakima knew he had no reason to feel sheepish. He'd promised Emma nothing, and what had happened between him and her older sister was between them and them only. Still, the matter of having made love to two women in the same family aroused his guilt and his own sense of impropriety. Worse, it complicated his mind.

How could things get complicated way out here? Was anywhere safe from the hassles of the populated world?

He felt oddly distracted and restless for the next three days, through which he and the Rio Grande Kid occupied themselves by making minor repairs to the cabin, stable, and corral, and cutting and splitting firewood. Just keeping the place up for whomever moved in next. Between chores, they gambled for matchsticks. During the frequent, late-day storms, they sat out on the gallery, drinking black coffee, smoking, and watching the rainwater tumble over the edge of the gallery roof and splatter into the mud by the hitch rack and stock trough.

The morning of their fifth day back at the cabin, Yakima rose early, gathered his gear, saddled Wolf, and led the horse back to the cabin. It was a little after dawn, and the sun was a brightening pat of butter between the eastern ridges, casting copper-tinged light across the boulder-strewn, brush-choked arroyo beyond the corral. The cool, damp ground sent up writhing snakes of steam as it warmed.

Yakima was filling one of his two canteens at the *olla* hanging from the gallery roof, dribbling water into the spout with the gourd dipper, when he heard the Kid stumbling around inside the cabin, hacking and coughing like he did every morning. The cabin door opened and the Kid looked out, blinking groggily, his beefy face bleached and crinkled from sleep.

"What you doin'? Goin' huntin' or somethin'? Shoulda woke me. I'd go —"

"I'm pullin' my picket pin," Yakima said, dribbling water into his second canteen. "I figure I'll head down to Mexico for the winter."

"What's the matter? I snore too loud or somethin'?"

"No." Yakima chuckled. "It's just time. When I get to feelin' grass growin' under my boots, I get restless."

Or when things, like women, make his life more complicated than he was comfortable with. Faith had been a different thing altogether. He'd loved the complication of that woman, had intended to spend the rest of his life trying to figure her out, in fact. There was only one Faith for most men and for Yakima most of all. He might have fallen in love with Julia Taggart if the circumstances had been less disjointed — her being freshly widowed and the sister of an even younger woman he'd sought a lighthearted distraction with.

And if he'd been the type of man who could fall in love twice in one lifetime, which he thought he probably wasn't.

"Sorry — I would have told you, Kid, but I only decided late last night, layin' out here unable to sleep."

"Mexico, eh?"

"Somethin' about crossin' that border always makes me feel new again. Or at least like I'm getting a fresh start. You stay here as long as you want. The place is yours now, as far as I'm concerned. Use it as a base to scout your El Dorado."

"Well, hell, I figured we'd both scout it as soon as we had enough grub laid in."

Yakima shook his head as he used the heel of his hand to shove the cork into his canteen's mouth. "I'm gonna head south," he said with a sigh, staring off in that very direction, toward the dun mountain rising above the still-dark horizon. "Maybe I'll head back this way again come spring. If you haven't found El Dorado by then and still need a partner, maybe I'll throw in for a few months."

"Well, shit," the Kid said, running a hand down his face and yawning. "All right." He extended his hand to Yakima. "Good luck in Mayhee-ko. Don't catch nothin' from the *senoritas* down there that the sawbones can't . . ."

The Kid let his voice trail off as the drum of hoofbeats grew in the south, gaining volume fast.

"What in tarnation?" the Kid said, staring in that direction. "Who could that be so early in the — ?"

He cut himself off again when horse and rider galloped into the yard, turning around a large boulder and two scrawny mesquites, then jogging up to the cabin. Tawny blonde hair bounced around Emma's slender shoulders clad in a checked shirt and an Indian-beaded buckskin vest.

"Yakima!"

Aw, shit. He'd thought he was going to make a clean break.

But then he saw that something was wrong. It wasn't just that Emma had been missing him, either. Her cheeks were flushed, and her eyes were frightened. He also saw that she was trailing a second, unsaddled horse behind her.

As she put her buckskin up to the hitch rack, she flung an arm out to indicate north. "Flames!" She swallowed, sucked a shallow breath. "Earlier this morning I saw red flames in the sky in the direction of Apache Springs!"

CHAPTER 18

"Flames?" the Kid said.

Yakima stepped off the gallery and strode into the yard a ways, peering north. "I don't see . . ." But then he smelled the smoke. He'd smelled it before, but he'd thought it merely smoke from a forest fire higher in the mountains. Now he realized that didn't make sense. After last night's downpour, nothing in the mountains would be dry enough to burn.

"It's Apache Springs, I tell you!" Emma said. "There's a fire! A big one! A big chunk of the northern sky was lit up orange!"

"I believe you." Yakima hooked his canteens over his saddle horn, then swung up into the leather.

"Holy shit — you think Rebel Wilkes would . . . ?" Then the Kid answered his own question, running another big paw down his face. "Well, I reckon he would at that, wouldn't he? Hold on, Yakima! Let me get dressed and throw a kak on my hoss. I'll ride with you!"

But the half-breed had already wheeled Wolf away from the hitch rack. Telling Emma to stay there, he touched spurs to the black's loins, and Wolf lunged off his rear hooves, dashing across the yard toward the northern trail.

"Forget it!" the girl called behind him. "I brought a second horse because I knew Rowdy'd be blown out by the time I got here. I'm just gonna switch my saddle. Hey, wait up, dammit, Yakima!"

He only vaguely heard her above the drumming of Wolf's hooves against the still-soggy ground and the drumming of his heart in his ears. Apache Springs was home to over a hundred people, but the fate of one was foremost in his mind. Given her history with Rebel Wilkes, Julia would likely not be spared from another onslaught.

Yakima pushed Wolf hard for nearly three miles. He knew the horse had the endurance for it. Only when he began to feel fatigue shortening the stallion's stride did he slow him to a trot. After another quarter mile, he stopped the mount altogether and, though his heart hammered impatiently, took a moment to swab the black's mouth and nose and give him a two-minute breather. No water yet. They still had three miles to cover quickly, and Yakima didn't want him bogged down.

While Wolf blew, his powerful chest expanding and contracting, Yakima glanced along his back trail. In the far distance, maybe half a mile behind, he thought he detected a slim curl of tan dust catching the morning sunshine. Then he saw the thumb-sized silhouette of a horse and rider mounting a low, rocky ridge. That would be Emma.

Horse and rider dropped down the top of the ridge and continued heading toward Yakima.

The half-breed cursed. He didn't want her with him when he reached Apache Springs. He didn't want to have to worry about her. He wanted free rein when he went after the fresh batch of killers Rebel Wilkes had sent. If it was Wilkes's hired killers who'd started the fire, that is. Buildings burned all the time, especially out here in the desert that turned green wood to tinder in a matter of months. A shattered coal-oil lamp was all it took to take out a quarter of a good-sized town, depending on the quickness of the town's response and its access to water. A town the small size of Apache Springs could be entirely engulfed in a matter of minutes. Yakima had seen it happen several times in the past — a quick, roiling fire leaving the town's inhabitants either dead or in shock.

Julia.

Yakima cursed again as he swung up into the leather and nudged Wolf with his spurs. After another ten minutes of hard riding, he saw gray smoke tinged with black rising ahead, atop the rocky pass on which the town sat. For several minutes, he couldn't see much more than the smoke, but as he crested several hogback ridges and drew within a mile of Apache Springs, he saw the fire-blackened buildings strewn out across the top of the pass, between the two flame-shaped stone ridges.

Some buildings appeared to still be standing, but a good many had been turned to black rubble. Several ragged columns of smoke rose from various rubble piles, combining into one thinning column as they climbed toward the peaks looming in the north and south.

Yakima shot up the side of the pass, skirted the hill the cemetery was on, curved into the town, and reined Wolf to a skidding halt. He sat staring in shock at the broad main drag before him, lined on either side by burned-out buildings, several of which were still afire.

Flames licked up from collapsed walls and

the sides of collapsed brick chimneys. Most of the adobe-brick structures were still standing, but they'd been hollowed out by flames, some of which still licked out through broken windows, the wooden frames of which were gone. The mercantile, easily the largest building in town, had been a combination of wood and brick, with a wooden front loading dock. It was a charred ruin still being chewed at by large, orange flames.

Maybe a dozen people — both men and women — lay dead in the street. Even a boy lay dead. Yakima recognized him as the kid who earned nickels by shoveling the dung and tumbleweeds off boardwalks for the shopkeepers, and who also mucked out the livery barn stables. Pistols and rifles lay near some of the bodies. At least they'd put up a fight — or tried to.

What caught the bulk of the half-breed's attention was a cottonwood tree on the street's right side, between the smoldering ruins of the livery barn and a harness shop. Three men hung from a stout limb that angled out over the street. As Yakima kneed Wolf ahead, he saw that all three dead men, decked out in stylish frontier attire, were wearing sun-and-moon deputy US marshal badges.

Tennyson Kinkaid hung between Stan Wellman and R. C. "Raging Ronnie" Holbrook. Bloodstains on the three indicated they'd been shot before they'd been hanged, but they'd likely died from the hanging, as none of the bullet wounds had been killing shots. Kinkaid's eyes were wide open, and his lips were snarling as though in both rage and agony at his horrific fate.

Holbrook's eyes were only half open and staring at the ground. If he'd gone out raging, it didn't show in his current expression. Wellman's face was badly bruised, both open eyes swollen. He'd been beaten severely before he'd been shot and hanged with the others. He'd kicked out of one of his boots, which lay on the ground beneath his gently swinging body.

Whoever had done this had taken their time.

And then, true to Wilkes's word, they'd burned the town.

Yakima swung Wolf around the hanging men and rode on down the street, avoiding piles of still-burning wood. He rode past the Busted Flush, or what was left of it. Three of its adobe-brick walls had collapsed from the heat of the fire. A half-burned man lay on the charred boardwalk fronting the place. Yakima paused a moment to recognize the attorney, Mark Garland. The man's glasses lay on the boardwalk's charred boards, just beyond an outstretched hand.

Yakima had negotiated the urge to kill Garland himself, but he felt little satisfaction at the irony of the man's demise, given all of the innocent folks lying dead around him.

As he continued riding, Yakima spied several women dead in the street. Two had obviously been raped, for their clothes had been torn, lewdly exposing them. They'd been raped and shot. The neck of the woman who owned a woman's clothing store, a pretty brunette in her early thirties and a widow, had a gaping red wound across her neck, reaching nearly from one ear to the other. She'd been stripped almost nude, her frilly pink dress lying in bloody tatters around her.

As Yakima passed her, she seemed to be staring up at him through lilac eyes in silent pleading.

Near the west end of the devastated town, Yakima reined Wolf to a sudden halt. He hadn't expected to see anyone alive, but he saw now that at least one man had survived the pillaging and plundering of Apache Springs. The man sat on the edge of a raised boardwalk fronting Isaacson's Grocery, which for some reason didn't appear burned. The man's feet were on the ground, knees spread, elbows on his thighs. He appeared to be staring off into the western desert.

As Yakima approached, he turned his head sharply, startled, nearly losing his seat on the boardwalk.

"Dundee?" Yakima said.

The bald man only stared back at him through one good eye. The other eye was bloody. A knife slash cut over the socket. Dundee's clothes were scuffed and torn, and his dusty cheeks and lips were cut, bruised, and swollen, his fire-singed beard covered in dust and ashes.

"H-Henry?" the man said.

Yakima halted his horse.

Dundee stared up at him, his one eye wide and sharp with shock and horror.

"What happened?" Yakima asked. He wanted to ride over to the Taggart house, but something kept him from doing so. He'd get to it soon, but he was afraid of what he'd find there. Likely, more of the same.

"Small army of 'em," Dundee said, shaking his head, a tear rolling down from both eyes, one tear red with blood. "Thundered in from the west, firing every which way.

Started with the saloon. Shot everyone inside the place except for me. They dragged me out and beat me while they shot up the rest of the town, gallopin' their hosses, runnin' in and out of stores, spilling coal oil, dropping matches. Them three federals didn't have a chance. One was in the saloon with Garland, and they dropped him first and took away his guns, made him watch while they pillaged and plundered . . . burned the stores and houses . . . raped the women an' young girls. *Ah, shit!*"

Dundee pressed the heels of his hands to his cheeks, shook his head, lowered his hands again to his thighs. "I'll never get those screams out of my head. Men . . . women . . . children — all screaming while those bastards laid waste!"

"How many?"

Dundee shook his head as though it had all been a blur. "Maybe a dozen." He blinked, looked up at Yakima. "Wilkes was one of 'em. He told me he wanted me left alive to tell Kosgrove."

"Kosgrove?" Yakima said. "Tell Kosgrove what?"

"That he had his daughter. That he was gonna take her down to Mexico, way deep down in Mexico where he'd never find her, and sell her to the nastiest Mexican pimp who ran the filthiest Mexican whorehouse south of the border."

Yakima stared at the man in silent fury.

Dundee stared back at him, eyes glazed in shock.

"How long ago did they ride out?"

Dundee shook his head. "I don't know. I just came to my senses a few minutes ago. I was layin' out in the street. They must've figured I was dead."

Yakima reined Wolf around and galloped back down the street to the east. He turned left at the first cross-street and galloped north. The Taggarts' small, white-frame house was still standing, as were several others around it. Apparently, the gang hadn't bothered to burn the entire town. They'd probably been too busy with other distractions — namely, raping and looting. One old woman scurried into her own house as Yakima galloped past, casting the buckskin-clad half-breed on the black stallion a dark, fearful look over her shoulder.

Yakima dismounted outside the Taggart picket fence, pushed through the gate, and went inside the house.

"Julia?" he called, knowing she wasn't there but unable to stop hoping that Dundee had had it wrong. Some townsfolk had survived the raid. Not many, it appeared.

But a few. Maybe Julia was one of those.

He knew it wasn't true.

Still, he called her name again, running through the house, knowing she was gone, and knowing he needed to get after her and Wilkes.

Hooves drummed outside. Wolf whinnied. Drawing his Colt, Yakima walked onto the front gallery. Emma was just then pulling her second horse, an applewood bay, up to where Wolf stood near the open fence gate. She leaped out of the saddle and ran up to where Yakima stood atop the gallery.

"Is she here?" the girl asked, her voice trembling, fear in her eyes.

Yakima shook his head. "Wilkes has her." He stepped around Emma and strode toward the horses. He had to pick up their tracks.

A woman's voice called, "Emma?"

Yakima turned to his left. The old woman who'd run into her house now stood out on her front gallery, holding her front door open and staring toward Emma.

"Mrs. Cena!" Emma said. "Where's my sister?"

"They took her, screaming. Last night! Those men with their guns!" She let the door close behind her and brought her hands to her head, sobbing. "It was awful,

Emma!"

"Which way?" Yakima said.

The woman lifted a heavy arm and pointed east.

CHAPTER 19

Hours later, just after dark and several miles east of Apache Springs, Yakima scooped the last of his beans and bacon from his tin plate and shoveled them into his mouth. He stopped chewing when he looked up to see Emma staring at him dubiously from the other side of the low, dancing fire on which a coffee pot steamed.

She turned away, pinching her mouth corners.

Yakima chewed the beans and meat, swallowed, then set his pan aside. He grabbed a leather swatch and reached for the coffee pot. While he poured himself a fresh cup of coffee, the Kid looked from Emma to Yakima, then back again. He shook his head and said, "You two sure aren't much for conversation this evenin'."

Emma gave a caustic chuff as she stared off into the night, arms resting atop her upraised knees.

"I know when three's a crowd." The Kid took the last sip of his coffee, tossed the dregs onto the fire, picked up his empty plate and his fork, and rose with a grunt. "Think I'll go scrape my plate clean and keep the first watch." He glanced at Yakima. "I'll wake ya at midnight."

He picked up his old Spencer repeater, swung it over his shoulder, letting it hang by its leather lanyard, and walked off through the rocks lining the spring-fed arroyo, the sheltered bank of which they'd chosen for a camping spot when it had become too dark to continue tracking the marauders. A good dozen overlaid hoof prints had led a gradual southeasterly course from the plundered and half-burned Apache Springs.

Yakima and Emma hadn't exchanged a single word since they'd picked up the killers' trail. Yakima wasn't sure what to say to the girl. He'd slept with her sister, two-timing Emma. At least, that's how he knew she saw it. He didn't see it that way. Still, he felt chagrined. He didn't want to talk about it. They had bigger fish to fry — namely, catching up to the human raptors and extracting Julia from their bloody talons.

Then he'd head to Mexico as he'd planned

before Wilkes had burned the town and kidnapped Julia. His life had become too complicated in these parts, as it had a tendency to do everywhere he went.

In the meantime, his worry about Julia's fate was a raw ache in his gut. He hadn't been hungry, but he'd shoveled the food down anyway. He needed sustenance for the hard ride and likely even harder fight ahead.

"I knew she'd get to you," Emma said, staring off toward the darkening arroyo in which a gilded flicker peeped. "She gets to every man I set my hat for."

"You didn't set your hat for me, Emma."

Yakima lifted his coffee and blew on it.

She turned to him sharply, the fire's orange flames flickering in her eyes. "I did so. I'll admit at first I just wanted . . . you know." She hiked her shoulder a little and crooked a sheepish half smile. "I don't see anything wrong with it. I'm a grown woman. Women have their needs, same as men. I saw a handsome man, and I wanted him, that's all. But . . . later . . . I felt something more for you, Yakima."

She stared at him directly now, her head turned toward him, her arms still draped over her raised knees. He could see she was speaking the truth, and the knife in his belly, the one there for Julia, twisted for his sister, too.

"I'm sorry, Emma. I didn't . . . realize."

"Do you love her?"

Yakima opened his mouth to say no, he didn't, but then he didn't hear any words come out. Christ, had he fallen in love with Julia? Had their shared grief nudged him that close to her?

He knew only that he felt miserable, thinking about what could be happening to her right now while he was sitting here by this fire with her sister. The need to get her away from Rebel Wilkes and his hired killers was a living, breathing monster inside him. An insatiable one.

It made him want to keep tracking them even now, at night. The only thing that kept him from trying was knowing how impossible it would be to follow a trail through this rocky, broken country with only starlight illuminating the way. The moon wouldn't be up for another couple of hours. Trying to follow them now would be a waste of time. He had to get some sleep, start fresh in the morning.

"Do you?"

He'd been so distracted by his worry about Julia that he hadn't realized that Emma had gotten up and walked over to him. She settled down beside him now, placing a hand on his shoulder and sliding her face up close to his.

He frowned at her, only vaguely hearing the question.

"Do you love her?"

He didn't know how to answer, so he deflected the question with one of his own. "Why did you come along if you hate her so much? Why didn't you just ride back to the mine like I wanted you to do?"

"Do you have any siblings, Yakima?"

He shook his head.

"If you did, you'd know how you can hate . . . and *love* . . . your sister at the same time." Emma shook her head and studied the fire, her eyes anxious. "I'm as worried about her as you are." She glanced up at him. "You didn't answer my question. Do you love her?"

"Of course not," he said, not knowing if was a lie, no longer caring, only wanting to get Julia back.

Emma slid her face closer to his. Her lips brushed Yakima's mouth. He pulled away from her.

Emma frowned, eyes darkening with injury and anger. She stared at him for nearly an entire minute before rising, walking over to the other side of the fire, and rolling up in her blankets. She rested her head back against her saddle and turned away from him.

The next morning, in the first light of dawn, the morning birds piping in the brushy arroyo, they broke camp and continued riding east and south, following the killers' trail. Not long after sunrise, Yakima reined Wolf to a halt and leaned far out from his saddle.

He looked over the stallion's ears and then off to his right, lifting his gaze steadily before he was peering off toward the southern horizon.

"They split up," said the Kid as he also studied the ground.

Yakima swung down from his saddle and looked around at a twisting path through the rocks and cactus, picking apart the individual sets of horse tracks and counting them. "Seven angled this way."

The Kid was standing thirty or forty yards to Yakima's left, also scouring the ground with his gaze. "Six this way." He lifted a thick arm, pointing. "This bunch headed southeast."

"This one southwest."

"You suppose they know we're following 'em?"

"They probably figure someone will follow. They cut the telegraph lines in town, so word wouldn't get out any time soon, but they're a cautious bunch."

"I got a feelin' this wasn't their first rodeo," the Kid said darkly.

"Which bunch do you think Julia's riding with?" Emma asked, sitting her applewood bay and staring fearfully down at where the two sets of forking tracks disappeared into the desert.

"No way of knowin'." Yakima ran a buckskin sleeve across his forehead, wiping away the sweat. "I guess the odds say she's one of the seven."

"We could split up," the Kid said.

"You want to stand alone against six or seven yourself, Kid?"

"I've gone up against more than that," the Kid said, glancing at Emma and puffing out his chest.

Emma rolled her eyes and said, "Let's stick together. I think my sister is one of the seven."

"Those're the odds." Yakima stepped back into the saddle.

He reined up again just after noon, when they were dropping into a shallow valley choked with boulders, saguaro and barrel cactus, and mesquites, with a high, sawtooth mountain ridge looming straight south, maybe ten miles beyond. Yakima squinted straight ahead along what he figured was an old Spanish trading trail that had been cut deep into the middle of a narrow, ancient riverbed long ago. The deep ruts of the traders' wagons still shone.

Yakima's heart quickened slightly as he stared, for Wolf's ears were twitching, and he could hear the almost inaudible, discontented rasping of the horse's breath.

The horse had scented something ahead.

Then Yakima saw the riders — two men riding abreast — top a distant ridge and drop down the near side, heading toward Yakima, the Kid, and Emma.

The Kid wouldn't give his age, but his eyes were still young, for he'd seen the riders at the same time Yakima had. "Now, who you suppose that is?"

"Only one way to find out." Yakima neck-reined Wolf abruptly off the trail. The Kid and Emma followed suit.

They put their horses a good distance off the east side of the old riverbed and tied them in a nest of brush and black volcanic boulders likely spewed up from the earth's bowels beneath that distant ridge several eons ago. They disturbed a Mojave green rattler that had been sunning itself atop one of those boulders, and the angry viper slithered into a crack running vertically through the boulder, its quivering button tail causing a chill of instinctive revulsion to run down Yakima's sweaty back.

Five minutes later, he, the Kid, and Emma lay against a low hummock of black gravel and Mormon tea, staring through greasewood toward the riverbed only a few feet beyond. They waited, hearing only cicadas and the scratching of the dry brush around them as a hot breeze rose and fell.

Hoof thuds invaded the breezy silence.

Looking left through the lime-green brush, Yakima glimpsed the two riders approaching. He glanced at the Kid lying just beyond Emma, to his right, and the old man returned the glance with a brief, acknowledging nod.

Yakima would make the first move. The Kid would back his play.

When the horses were a dozen or so yards up the trail, Yakima gained his feet and stepped onto the trail, turning to face the two riders, who instantly jerked back on their horses' reins. He'd left his Yellowboy in its saddle sheath, and he'd left his Colt in its holster. He could get to it fast enough if he needed it. There was no point in coming off as an immediate threat.

If the two men in the wash were part of

the bunch he was after, he'd likely know soon enough. Besides, he just now heard the Kid clicking his Spencer's hammer in the brush behind him, backing him.

The two horseback riders each held carbines across their saddle bows, and they were not one bit reluctant to use them. Both men snapped their rifles up at the same time, apparently deciding to shoot first and ask questions later. That told Yakima all he needed to know at the moment.

The Colt was instantly in his hand, exploding.

The Kid's Spencer roared.

Both saddles emptied at nearly the same time, and the two suddenly riderless horses curveted, crow hopping, stirrups flapping like wings.

"Goddamnit!" wailed one of the fallen riders who'd just been kicked by his own horse. He rolled off toward Yakima's right, screened by billowing dust as both horses wheeled and galloped back in the direction from which they'd come. The kicked rider had lost his hat, and his blond hair danced about his head as he rolled up onto his haunches.

The other rider lay on his back, gasping, coughing.

The blond reached for a sidearm.

Yakima extended his Colt at him, clicking the hammer back once more. "Hold it."

The blond froze. His cold blue eyes were pinched to slits. He was fair-skinned, and he had thin sideburns and a mustache and spade beard. He had a long, thin cut on his left cheek, just beneath his eye. The cut was jellied, beginning to scab. He gritted his teeth as he crouched there on his haunches, one gloved hand on the gutta-percha grips of his holstered Smith & Wesson. He wore a greasy, sweaty long-handle shirt patched at the elbows, and a dirty red neckerchief.

Frothy blood oozed from a hole in his upper right chest.

"Toss the hogleg," Yakima told him, glancing at a second gun residing on the man's left hip. "Both of 'em."

"Who're you?"

"Toss the hoglegs, and then we'll powwow."

Grimacing against the pain of his bullet wound, the blond lifted each gun from its holster in turn and tossed it into the brush. He eased onto his butt and brushed a hand against the bloody hole in his chest.

"Lung shot," he said, glaring up at Yakima, slitting his little eyes. "You killed me for no goddamn good reason!" He looked at his partner, who now lay still, staring skyward through death-glazed eyes. "Tucker, too! For no good reason!"

"Who are you?"

"Levi Antrim from the Bridlebit Ranch." He tossed his head toward the west. "Over that way."

Yakima glanced at Emma, who'd stepped out of the bushes and was moving up from behind him. "There such a ranch over that way?"

Emma nodded.

"Why were you in such a hurry to ventilate me with your carbine?" Yakima asked Antrim. "My gun was holstered."

"You see a big Injun step out in front of you in these parts, you shoot!"

"Hold on." This from Emma, who was just then bending over to pick something up off the ground. Turning toward Yakima, she held up what appeared a fancily cut, purple dress made of fine silk and taffeta. It danced and fluttered in the breeze, flashing in the harsh sunlight. "This must've fallen out of his saddlebags."

She turned her angry, dark eyes on the man who called himself Levi Antrim. "I saw this on one of the dummies in Mrs. McReynolds's ladies' wear shop in Apache Springs." She brought it to her nose and sniffed. "Smells like smoke." She tossed the dress at Antrim. "A gift for some *senorita* down in Mexico?"

"I bought it for a gal last week," Antrim said. "Haven't had a chance to give it to her yet."

The Rio Grande Kid said, "How'd you get that scratch on your cheek there?"

Antrim turned to the Kid and spat. "Tree branch, you old fool!"

The Kid stepped forward, raising the butt of his Spencer. "Why, you . . . !"

"A woman's fingernail more like," Emma said, hardening her jaws at the man, then sliding her dark gaze at Yakima. "From last night in Apache Springs!"

"Shut up, you little bitch!"

Emma stepped forward and buried her right boot in Antrim's belly. He lurched back from the impact of the blow and then bent forward, crossing his arms on his midsection, groaning and cursing.

Yakima planted the ball of his boot against Antrim's forehead and shoved him onto his back, where he lay groaning and bleeding. "Why were you riding back this way?"

"Go to hell, you red-skinned bastard!"

Yakima dropped to a knee beside him and poked the barrel of his Colt into the bullet wound in the man's upper right chest. Antrim screamed and recoiled but Yakima held the pistol firm.

"Why were you heading back this way?"

"Wilkes sensed trouble behind us! He sent us back to clean our backtrail!"

"Wilkes is part of your group, then? The one headed southwest?"

"Yes! Oh, Jesus Christ — pull that pistol out of my lung, you merciless son of a bitch!"

"One more question."

"What? *What?!*"

"Is Mrs. Taggart part of your group?"

"Yessssss!"

Yakima removed the Colt's barrel from the man's wound.

"There," he said. "That wasn't so hard — now, was it?"

Antrim glared up at him, jaws hard, writhing.

"Now, you got a decision."

"What's that?"

"We can either leave you out here to die slow and alone, or I can do you a favor. One that, after seein' your handiwork back in Apache Springs, you sorely don't deserve."

Yakima clicked the Colt's hammer back and held up the pistol to show the wounded man.

"No!" Antrim yelled, indignant. "Get away from me, you fuckin' rock worshiper!"

Yakima depressed the Colt's hammer and holstered the weapon, snapping the keeper thong home. "Let's get after 'em," he said to the Kid, glancing at Emma, who was still glaring down at the grunting, slow-dying killer.

When Yakima, the Kid, and Emma had retrieved their horses and rode back onto the trail, Antrim was on his back, not writhing as much as he had been. He appeared to be weakening. Blood matted his chest and dribbled down over his ribs to soak the caliche beneath him.

"I . . . I changed my mind," he said, fear replacing the anger in his voice. "I'd . . . I'd like that . . . I'd like that bullet, I think."

"Too late," Yakima said and spurred Wolf south along the arroyo.

As Emma passed Antrim, she leaned out over her saddle and spat in the killer's face.

The Kid chuckled. "Girl, I like your style."

CHAPTER 20

They rode for another hour more cautiously than before. There was a good chance Wilkes and the other killers had heard the gunfire. Yakima wished he'd kept Antrim alive long enough to answer one more question: how far up the trail were the others?

But he hadn't. So now he kept their own pace slow, and he scrutinized the terrain ahead and around them carefully for signs of an ambush.

The Kid rode off Yakima's right stirrup. Emma brought up the rear, also looking around carefully, occasionally twisting around in her saddle to make sure no one was coming up from behind.

Ahead, the ridge grew larger and turned from a dark, misty gray to light tan as the sun caressed its mostly bald north side. The terrain around the three riders was breaking up, low mesas and volcanic dykes shelving around them, and the trail was rising toward the massive mountain. Soon they were within a mile of it, then half a mile, and then the arroyo developed a fork, the two tines angling around to the left and right of a rocky escarpment jutting maybe a hundred feet in the air and bristling with cactus of all shapes and sizes. In bunch grass and Mormon tea at the base of the formation lay what was left of what appeared a javelina after some predator, probably a wildcat, had killed and mostly devoured it, leaving a sickly stench in the air around it.

Yakima scoured the ground. He hadn't seen any tracks for over half a mile; the arroyo had turned too rocky to show any. As it was, his and his trail partners' horses stood on a slanting slab of solid black stone that paved the dry riverbed in places. Dinosaur bones and seashells were embedded in it — natural decorations in an ancient floor tile.

He glanced from the arroyo's left tine disappearing around the left side of the dyke, to the right tine disappearing around the formation's right side.

"*Now* we split up?" the Kid asked.

"Reckon." Yakima swung down from the saddle. "We'd best leg it, too. I got a feelin' they're close. Maybe waiting."

Emma swung down from her bay's back,

and Yakima, sliding his Yellowboy from its scabbard, turned to her. "Wait here with the horses. Find some shade. Stay out of sight."

"Oh, no." Emma shook her head obstinately. "I'm going with you. It's my sister they —"

Yakima cut her off with: "You're staying here, and that's that. We need someone to watch the horses and keep an eye on our back trail. If anyone comes up behind us" — he glanced at the Bisley .44 she wore holstered on her right hip — "trigger two quick shots into the air."

Emma drew in the corners of her mouth and sighed.

Yakima glanced at the Kid, who stood ready, his Spencer in his hands.

"You go left," he said. "I'll go right. Keep your eyes peeled."

"The Rio Grande Kid's eyes was born peeled!"

The older man spat to one side, adjusted the set of his battered Stetson, and began tramping up the arroyo's left fork. Yakima glanced once more at Emma, who stood holding the reins of the three mounts and staring back at him, edgily, worriedly.

"We'll get her back," he vowed.

Emma didn't say anything, and her expression didn't change. Wolf pawed the ground anxiously behind her, the stallion's eyes on its rider.

Yakima swung around and headed up the arroyo's right tine. He stayed close to the base of the escarpment so that he would have to worry about an attack from only three sides — ahead, behind, and to his right. He moved slowly, chill fingers of dread drumming along his spine. Ahead, he could see a break in the wall of the ridge looming over him. It appeared a large crack running nearly vertically from the ridge crest to the ground, a hundred to two hundred yards wide. Probably carved out by the ancient river that had formed the arroyo a couple of million years ago.

Had Wilkes holed up in there?

Or did the chasm extend all the way through the ridge, and had the killers ridden on through to the other side?

Yakima paused, shifted the Yellowboy to his left, gloved hand, and used his right shirtsleeve to nudge his hat brim up and scrub sweat from forehead. It was over a hundred degrees out here. The cicadas whined. There was no breeze now, and the scrub around him bristled dryly, the sun's merciless rays limning every branch and clump of cacti.

Ahead, the cool darkness of the declivity beckoned.

Yakima drew his hat brim down, shading his eyes from the sun, and continued walking. Just ahead, the arroyo was blocked with boulders likely fallen from the top of the ridge looming above him, so the half-breed followed a game path up the right bank through scattered mesquites, around the obstruction, then continued walking forward, toward the ridge.

Now he could see a few shod hoof prints marking the ground, and a pile of horse apples lay scattered amongst beans fallen from the branches of a near mesquite. Yakima crouched to pick up a crumbling apple and sniffed. Fresh. Likely dropped within the last half hour.

Cigarette smoke touched Yakima's nostrils. He caught only a fleeting whiff, but then, sniffing again, he caught it again. Tobacco, all right. Coming from not far ahead.

Yakima straightened, his heart quickening. He clutched the Yellowboy in both hands, squeezing, as he started forward. He'd taken only a half-dozen more steps when a man's voice said, "Any sign of 'em?"

No response. Whoever the man ahead had spoken to might have merely shaken his head.

"I'm pretty damn sure I heard gunshots behind us," said the man who'd spoken before.

A deeper voice said on a long inhalation, "I didn't hear a thing."

"That's because you an' Wilkes was talkin'. I was ridin' drag and keepin' my mouth shut. And" — there was a sudden smacking sound — "I sure as hell wasn't smokin' a quirley!"

"Hey, goddamnit — I just rolled that!"

"You damn — !"

The first man cut himself off abruptly as he swung his head to peer behind him, at the half-breed just then stepping out from behind a small boulder. Yakima held the Winchester straight out from his right hip and bunched his lips and hardened his eyes in challenge.

The first man, big and muscular — probably from breaking rocks in a prison quarry — and not wearing a shirt, held his own Winchester down low in his right hand. Sweat glistened on his fair-skinned, deeply-tanned torso over the thick shoulders of which were looped suspenders. The other man, short, stocky, and black-haired, was frozen in the crouch he'd assumed to retrieve his quirley, which smoldered on the ground near his right, spurred, black boot decorated with red Mexican-style stitching.

The first man had a thick, pewter-colored mustache dripping down over the corners of his broad mouth. As he swung slowly toward Yakima, his mustache lifted in a faint, shrewd smile. The other man straightened slowly, his mud-brown eyes turning shrewd and glassy as he regarded the newcomer from beneath the brim of his low-crowned *sombrero* banded with a lady's gaudy, pink garter belt.

No other men were around. No horses, either. Wilkes must have sent these two back to keep an eye on the entrance to the canyon standing dark beyond them.

"Who're you?" asked the bare-chested man slowly, his voice deep and even, eyes hard and touched with a vague apprehension.

"The man who just killed you."

Yakima snapped the Yellowboy to his shoulder. The rifle thundered twice. He winced at each explosion and winced again at the loud echoes vaulting toward the crest of the ridge, alerting everyone with twenty square miles of the canyon. The reports couldn't have been helped, however. The two men before Yakima had needed to die like the dogs they were, and there'd been no way to do it quietly.

As the dust rose over where the two men had been punched back into the rocks and brush behind them, Yakima ejected the second spent cartridge, hearing it clatter onto the gravel over his right shoulder, and levered a fresh round into the action. Staring at the two men who lay still in death, their blood trickling onto the gravel around them, the half-breed thumbed two fresh cartridges from his shell belt and shoved them through the Winchester's loading gate.

Holding the Yellowboy at port arms across his chest, he stepped between the two dead men, through his own wafting powder smoke, and continued moving forward. He walked even slower now, more cautiously, taking one step at a time, and looking around warily, sometimes turning completely around as he walked.

Ahead, the canyon's entrance grew, cold and dark as doom.

CHAPTER 21

Near the canyon's opening, the escarpment slid back over Yakima's left shoulder.

As it did, the Rio Grande Kid walked out from around the opposite side of it — a hundred yards away at least. The Kid was moving slowly, holding his Spencer's butt on his right hip. Turning his head toward Yakima, he stopped suddenly, began to bring his rifle to bear, but stopped the motion when Yakima tossed out an arm, waving. The Kid returned the gesture, then stood looking into the canyon ahead of him, as was Yakima.

The deep cleft in the ridge was an awesome sight. It would have been called a tunnel if not for the open ceiling a good three or four hundred feet above, slanting brassy light into the chasm. Two hundred yards wide, the canyon's steep walls were partly hidden by an ancient Indian cliff village — crumbling towers, turrets, walls, fireplaces, circular fire and milling pits, and stacked caverns constructed of mud adobe bricks terraced into the back-sloping wall like giant swallows' nests.

The two parts of the village were separated by the arroyo running through the heart of the canyon. The arroyo was choked with rocks, boulders, brush, and driftwood probably strewn there by previous floods. The banks on each side of the arroyo were capped with ancient adobe-brick walls, and above and beyond these walls lay the cliff dwellings — a mud empire that connoted hotbeds of swirling human industry and activity beyond the mists of an incomprehensible length of time.

Ahead of Yakima, the canyon floor rose steeply to the right of the arroyo. The half-breed climbed, noting fresh horse prints in the dust beneath his boots. To his far left, on the chasm's other side, the Kid climbed the canyon floor to the ruins on his side of the arroyo. As Yakima neared the level the dwellings were perched on, he glanced to his left again.

A man moved atop one of the hovels on the canyon's far side.

A sunbeam flashed off the barrel of the rifle in the man's hands.

"Kid!" Yakima shouted, pointing, his voice

echoing.

The Kid stopped and dropped to a knee as his would-be assassin's rifle barked, the discharge sounding at once flat and loud in the close confines, flames lapping from the barrel. The bullet plumed dust two feet in front of the Kid. The old outlaw snapped his Spencer to his shoulder and aimed upward at a slant.

The Spencer roared. The bullet caromed through the would-be assassin's chest just as he finished cocking his own long gun again and was about to bear down once more on the Kid.

The man jerked backward, dropping his rifle, his hat tumbling off his head.

Movement flicked in the right periphery of Yakima's vision, and he instinctively threw himself forward and down, piling up behind a circular fire pit as another rifle crashed — this one from among the ruins on his side of the canyon. He pushed up taut against the wall of the pit as the rifle belched again, again, and again, the reports echoing shrilly, the bullet tearing gobs of ancient adobe out of the fire pit's wall, the slivers of mud peppering Yakima's hat.

The shooting stopped, though the echoes continued to vault skyward.

Yakima edged a look over the top of the

pit, saw the shooter — or the man whom he assumed was the shooter — running along a ledge fronting the ruins, about thirty yards up from the canyon floor. He wore a fancy black suit with a white shirt and string tie, and he was running at a crouch from Yakima's right to his left, holding his rifle in his right hand.

Yakima cursed as he whipped up the rifle and cut loose, hammering lead at the running rifleman, the bullets tearing bits of adobe from the wall of the hovels around him. The man stopped suddenly and threw himself into a cave-like opening to his right.

Yakima cursed again, rose, ran around the side of the fire pit, and sprinted toward the back-sloping wall ahead, heading for a stone ramp that would take him into the upper tiers.

He saw the rifleman's orange flash a quarter second before he felt the pinch in his left side. It was a quarter second after the pinch that he heard the belching thunder of the shot that had just punched a bullet into his flesh. He slowed, stumbled, staggered sideways, then, suppressing the pain and the wet feeling in his side just beneath his ribs, ran forward, climbing the incline and triggering his Winchester at the spot in the ruins where he'd seen the shooter's rifle flash.

As he ran, he wended his way around ruined walls and piles of adobe fallen from the mud hovels higher on the cliff.

The shooter returned fire, the bullets whistling through the air around Yakima's head and spanging off rocks around and behind him. He ran up two spans of steeply angling adobe steps. At the top of the second span, which had brought him to the level of the ruins from which the shooter had been firing, Yakima suddenly found himself on his knees.

His legs had given out, seemingly turning to warm sponges. The canyon pitched and rolled around him.

He leaned forward on hands and knees, trying to catch his breath while gritting his teeth around the dog fangs of pain chewing into his left side. Looking at the ground beneath him, he saw blood oozing from the ragged tear in his shirt to spatter onto the dirt and crumbling mud.

"Shit," he wheezed.

Footsteps sounded to his left, along the eight-foot width of open ledge giving access to the mud caverns on this level of the ruins. Yakima reached for the Yellowboy. It was gone. He must have dropped it while running up the last flight of steps.

"Shit," he wheezed again, hearing the anguished befuddlement in his own voice.

He turned to his left. A tall, lean man walked toward him, his tailored duds caked with dust from the desert trail. This was Rebel Wilkes. Of course, Yakima couldn't be certain — he'd never met the man — but he knew it just the same. Wilkes wore a crisp, tan Stetson on his large, square-hewn head with a rawboned but boyishly handsome, clean-shaven face. The hair showing beneath the hat was close-cropped and dark-brown. The man's small, round, steel-framed spectacles added an educated, studious air.

The eyes behind the glasses, however, were flat and hard with a cruel, cunning fury.

As the former mining engineer approached Yakima, he leaned his smoking Winchester against the front of the nearest cavern. He wore two stylish pistols on his hips, both pearl-gripped. He flicked the keeper thongs free of the right one and slid it from its holster. He stopped beside Yakima and smiled coldly down at him.

"Who the hell are you," he asked, adding tightly, "breed . . . ?"

Still on his hands and knees, Yakima

268

glared up at him. "Where's . . . where's Julia?"

Wilkes's nostrils flared. "What's she to you, a lowly Injun?"

Yakima pushed himself up off his hands, slapping his right hand toward his Colt, but he hadn't gotten either hand a foot off the ground before Wilkes buried the toe of his right boot into Yakima's left side. An agony like none other he'd ever felt ripped through the bullet wound. The force of the man's kick knocked him up and over onto his back, screaming.

That rabid dog was biting him hard now, rending and tearing as though to chew through to his heart.

He pressed both hands to his sides and gritted his teeth, every muscle and bone in his body drawn taut, waiting for the pounding pain to abate. It did not. In fact, when Wilkes pressed the heel of his boot directly down onto the wound, the misery grew even more unbearable.

Yakima arched his back and howled.

Wilkes's face turned crimson as he smiled savagely down at his helpless victim, hardening his jaws. Forked veins bulged in his forehead.

Yakima wasn't sure where the energy or dexterity came from — maybe from his dead Chinese mentor, Ralph, maybe from his own unbridled fury and drive to kill the killer looming over him — but he watched himself with an almost objective remove as he bounced off the ground beneath him and flung his right boot straight up and back, slamming the heel into Wilkes's belly.

The man's lower jaw sagged in sudden shock.

As he grunted and stumbled backward, he triggered his pistol into the air before dropping the weapon, then giving a shrill scream as Yakima bucked up off the ground again, whipped both legs upward this time, and sliced them sideways, cutting Wilkes's own legs out from beneath him. Wilkes hit the ground with an agonized, enraged cry.

Yakima rose, parceling his agony off to a back room in his brain, the way Ralph had taught him, and lunged toward the writhing, wailing killer who was reaching for the pistol he'd dropped. Yakima slashed the side of his left hand down on the man's right wrist, breaking it with an audible crunch.

Wilkes howled.

Yakima heaved up onto his knees and, leaning forward over Wilkes, slammed his right fist into the man's face — two hard blows followed by a third, smashing the man's glasses, breaking both lenses.

Somehow in his desperation to survive and free himself of his own agony, Wilkes lifted his own legs and kicked Yakima off of him, throwing the half-breed straight back into the dirt he'd bloodied before. Yakima had been reaching for his Colt, but the force of the blow had ripped the pistol from his hand, and it went sailing back behind him.

Wilkes heaved himself to his feet, his face a mask of rage and agony, his broken, twisted glasses hanging from one ear. He staggered over to Yakima, palmed his second pistol in his left hand, and clicked the hammer back. He took another step forward and stepped down once more on the wound in Yakima's side.

Yakima gritted his teeth against the unrelenting agony shooting all through him, setting a savage fire in his bowels.

Wilkes aimed his cocked Colt at Yakima's head and curled his upper lip in silent victory.

Yakima flinched, blinked, turned away.

A gun's roar caused the ground to jump.

He looked back up to see Wilkes no longer looking at him but over him, beyond him. Wilkes's eyes were large and round and growing larger and rounder. The gun sagged in his hand. Then it hung by one finger. It slid from the finger to drop onto the ledge beside Yakima.

Wilkes glanced down at the blood spurting from the hole in the dead center of his chest. He looked up once more, again casting his gaze beyond Yakima.

"Bitch," he grunted.

Then his eyes rolled back in his head, and he fell straight backward like a felled pine.

Yakima rolled his eyes up and back. Julia stood behind him, holding Yakima's Colt in both her hands, aiming at where Wilkes had been standing. Gray smoke curled from the barrel. Rope was tied around her right wrist, a frayed length dangling. Her left wrist was purple and raw from having been tied.

Slowly, she lowered the Colt and looked down at Yakima. She dropped to a knee beside him. Her hair hung in dusty tangles around her head, and trail dirt streaked her face. But she appeared all right. Dirty and battered, but all right.

Yakima's heart lightened.

"Yakima," she said, softly, giving a sob, tears rolling down her cheeks. "Oh, Yakima . . . how . . . bad . . . ?" She brushed her fingers lightly over his bloody shirt.

Yakima heaved himself to a sitting position, scuttled back against the wall of a mud cavern, and drew a deep breath, wincing as the pain continued to batter him. "Not sure," he wheezed, cold sweat bathing his face. "I think the . . . think the bullet went all the way through."

"Yakima!" another woman's voice sounded amidst the thuds of running feet.

Julia jerked with a start, as did Yakima, both turning their heads to see Emma gaining the top of the steps. The young woman paused, breathless, eyes bright with worry and looked down at Julia and Yakima.

"Oh, God, you're alive!" the girl cried, though Yakima wasn't quite sure whom she was addressing.

Both him and her sister, he decided, as Emma dropped to her knees beside him and Julia. She looked at Julia and then at Yakima, and then she turned to her sister again. She flung herself at her, wrapping her arms around Julia's shoulders, bawling her relief.

Julia sobbed and squeezed her eyes closed, returning Emma's hug.

Finally, the sisters broke their embrace and turned to Yakima, sniffing and brushing tears from their cheeks.

"We have to tend that wound," Emma said. "We have to get you out of here and gather wood and build a fire." She grabbed the half-breed's right arm and looked at her sister. "Julia, help me, please. We have to get that wound tended. If Yakima dies, I'll kill him!"

Julia at once sobbed and laughed. "I'll kill him, too!"

Each taking an arm, they hoisted the half-breed to his feet.

"What's this female chatter I heard about killin'?" the Kid said, wheezing breathlessly as he, too, reached the top of the steps and turned his red, puffed-up face and exertion-bleary eyes to Yakima and his harem.

Seeing Yakima's bloody side, he said, "Holy jeepers — you been hit, Yak!"

"Ain't as bad as it looks," Yakima grunted as the women led him past the Kid and over to the adobe steps, each holding one of his thick arms around her neck.

The Kid looked at Rebel Wilkes. He picked up Yakima's Colt and shoved it behind his cartridge belt. He turned to where the women were helping Yakima down the steps.

"You need any help, Yak?"

The half-breed glanced over his shoulder at the Rio Grande Kid and hooked a smile. "Nah. I'm well cared for, Kid. Thanks."

He winked and turned his head back around.

"I'll be damned," the Kid groused, scratching the back of his head with a thick finger. "I climbed all the way up here, riskin' a heart stroke, fer nothin'." Watching the three descend the steps together, he shook his head. "Oh, to be a few years younger." He amended that with: "Well, maybe twenty, thirty years younger . . ."

He chuckled dryly, scooped up Yakima's hat, and started the long descent to the canyon floor.

WILDCAT OF THE
SIERRA ESTRADA

CHAPTER 1

Bullets blew up dirt and gravel inches behind Yakima Henry's desperately running feet.

The half-breed ran hard, scissoring his arms and legs, his breath raking in and out of his lungs.

Rifles cracked and belched. Bullets ricocheted with wicked whines. One kissed the heel of Yakima's right boot. The two shooters fifty yards ahead of him whooped and hollered.

A boulder lay ten feet from Yakima. He bounded off the toes of his boots and was caroming through the hot, dry desert air, hot lead screeching around him, when he saw the rattler idling in the shade behind the rock he was heading for with no way to change his course.

"Ahh, shitttttt!"

The snake was slithering for a small hole opening along the base of the rock, but

Yakima landed on the viper before it could poke its head into the hole. Yakima fought against his impulse to recoil, knowing that if he did, the serpent — a Mojave green rattler, one of the deadliest snakes in the Southwestern desert — would likely pump him so full of poison, he'd bloat up like a javelina lying five days dead in a wash.

Instead, he pressed his chest and belly down hard against the snake, which he could feel writhing furiously beneath him, filling every nerve in the half-breed's tall, brawny body with instinctive revulsion.

At the same time, he could hear the two shooters running toward him, their boots grinding rocks and snapping cacti as they continued to whoop and holler and trigger lead in Yakima's direction. Several bullets screamed off the rock behind which Yakima lay flat, grinding his chest down hard against the panicking snake likely trying to twist its head around so it could sink its teeth through the man's buckskin tunic.

Yakima had once known a man who'd been bit in the chest by a rattler. His name had been Samuel Otter, and he'd been laying train rails with Yakima in western Kansas when he'd stepped away from the rail bed to take a piss, slipped on a rock, and fallen in some bushes. A sand rattler had sunk its fangs into his chest, just beneath his breast-bone, filling his heart with black poison.

Otter had died screaming an hour later, clawing at his chest as though to dig out the burning organ.

The shooters were closing on Yakima, shooting and yelling like coyotes on the blood scent. Soon, they'd have in their sights the half-breed, who was now the town marshal of Apache Springs, Arizona Territory. The bullets were getting closer. As the men's shadows began to slide toward Yakima's rock, the lawman shoved his hands under his chest and closed them around the piss-burned serpent's writhing body, one hand clenched just beneath the diamond-shaped head, the savage jaws open to expose the long, curved fangs.

The body curled up around itself and Yakima's gloved hands, the button tail arched and rattling shrilly.

Keeping his head down, Yakima took the snake in one hand and tossed it up and over the rock. The rattling increased as the snake plopped into the dirt. Suddenly, the shooting stopped.

One of the shooters yelled, "Snake, Goose!"

The warning hadn't entirely left the mouth of the first man, whose name Yakima knew was Curley Buck, a small-time criminal who'd robbed a whorehouse and cut a percentage girl the previous night in Apache Springs, before the other man, Buck's partner named Chuck "Goose" McGowan, gave a shrill, agonized cry.

"Oh, Jesus!" Curly Buck bellowed.

Goose gave another even shriller cry. A rifle belched.

Curley Buck loosed a strident scream.

Yakima grabbed his prized Winchester Yellowboy repeater, pumped a cartridge into the action, and pushed up onto his knees, swinging the Yellowboy's barrel over the top of his covering boulder. He held fire as Curley Buck, standing ten feet away and to Yakima's left, bellowed, "You done shot me, Goose!"

Curly Buck triggered his own Winchester at Goose McGowan, who stood another ten feet to the right of Buck, the viper hanging onto Goose's left leg, its fangs embedded in his thigh, near Goose's holstered six-gun. Goose was facing Curley Buck, whom he'd apparently inadvertently shot when the viper had struck.

Now Goose stumbled backward, dust rising around his spurred boots and billowing deerskin leggings, blood staining the right side of his collarless, pinstriped shirt.

"Fuck you, Curley!" Goose railed, lifting his carbine one-handed and sending another bullet — this one intentional — into the upper torso of his shorter, mustached partner, who already had one wound in his belly, just above his cartridge belt.

Curley Buck gave another enraged, agonized wail. He stumbled backward, nearly tripping over his own gravel-raking spurs, before pumping another cartridge into his Spencer repeater, snapping the butt plate to his shoulder, and hurling yet one more bullet into Goose, who gave his own bellowing cry in response.

He returned Curley Buck's fire.

All Yakima had to do was kneel there behind his boulder and watch in mute astonishment as the two raggedy-heeled, cork-headed criminals continued to exchange lead until they were both down and writhing, and the Mojave green rattler was tracing a quick, serpentine route for the sanctuary of the high chaparral to the south.

"Well, I'll be damned," Yakima said, depressing his Yellowboy's hammer and lowering the Winchester to his side. "I didn't even have to burn any powder." He chuckled dryly to himself. "Can't beat that. Who said law-doggin' was hard?"

He'd taken the job of Apache Springs

town marshal not long after the town had been burned by an especially nefarious criminal element, one with a very particular and deadly grudge against the entire town. The surviving members of the Apache Springs town council had beseeched Yakima to pin the badge to his shirt. Rather, the town council and the widow of the previous marshal — Julia Taggart.

In fact, that was the second time Julia Taggart had asked him to take the job, her dead husband's position. Both times Yakima had found himself accepting the offer, though he was as surprised as anyone who knew him would have been at his actually veering toward such permanent, reputable employment. Yakima Henry — a tall, slab-shouldered, jade-eyed German from his father's side, and a raw-boned, copper-toned, hawk-nosed Cheyenne from his mother's side — was not nor ever had been the law-dog sort.

In fact, anyone who knew him would have said he had more potential as an outlaw than a lawman. But Julia Taggart had had a hold on him.

She still did, sixteen months later.

Such a hold he hadn't felt the likes of since his beloved Faith had been killed by Bill Thornton up in Colorado, in fact.

A very strong hold, indeed. One that had him not remembering Faith quite so often these days. Or not as painfully. At least, he no longer woke from nightmares as regularly as before, screaming her name, his body bathed in sweat. It was nice to think about a living, breathing woman for a change. Also, sort of sad to finally be letting Faith go.

He did not think about this now, however, as he walked over to where Goose McGowan lay belly up, unmoving, in a patch of prickly pear. The recent events with the two criminals he'd tracked out of Apache Springs, and the deadly snake doing his job for him, still had him marveling at his uncustomary good luck.

Maybe the tide was changing for Yakima Henry. A new job, a new woman, finally letting some grass grow beneath his feet . . .

The lawman stared down at Goose McGowan. The man's chest wasn't moving, and his eyes were half closed and glassy. He was a bloody mess, as were the cacti around and beneath him. The snake had chewed two gnarly-looking holes in his breeches, baring his bloody flesh that had already swollen up to half the size of Yakima's clenched fist.

Goose had cut his last whore.

Yakima crouched to dig around in the man's pockets, finding nothing more valuable than the twenty-five dollars in scrip and specie the son of a bitch had taken from Señora Galvez. "The Señora," as most knew her, owned and operated a locally famous parlor house in Apache Springs. The whorehouse, known simply as Señora Galvez's Place, was one of the first new establishments built after half of Apache Springs's business district had been turned to charred rubble by Rebel Wilkes, the ex-mining engineer who'd condemned the town and all its inhabitants.

Wilkes was dead now, and, with several pockets of high-quality, gold-bearing quartz having recently been found in the mountains around Apache Springs, the town had been rebuilt with almost dizzying speed.

In the year and a half since it had met its unceremonious near-demise, Apache Springs had almost doubled its previous size and was quickly growing larger. In fact, the spur line that Wilkes had gone into such a tizzy over not being able to construct himself was now being built by a Texas speculator named James Osgood, who'd convinced Apache Springs's new town council to turn over construction rights for a twenty-percent share of the new railroad's profits, of which he assured the six-man team of boosters there would be many more, what with all the bullion that would be shipped out of the Sierra Estrada — not to mention people pouring in to search for their own El Dorados — in the coming years.

Yakima pocketed the money he'd found on Goose. Señora Galvez would be happy to get it back, though what Goose and Curley had taken from the gold lockbox she kept in her boudoir wouldn't put much of a dent in the Mexican madam's considerable coffers. Yakima rarely saw the large, Victorian-like structure without a fairly steady stream of men issuing in or out, day or night. Señora Galvez kept the red lamp burning in her window twenty-four hours a day — unless one of her girls was giving birth, that is.

On that rare, problematic but understandable occasion, given the nature of the business, the light went out, and the drapes were drawn across the windows. Yakima suspected the shrewd, business-minded Señora didn't want to appall her clientele with the sounds of a wailing newborn, even though the child had likely been fathered by one of them.

Quickly, the child would be shunted off to

an adoption agency in Phoenix or Denver, and the red light would burn with brash seediness once again . . .

Yakima found the rest of the stolen money in Curley Buck's shirt pocket. The twelve dollars he found there was blood speckled and slightly bullet torn, but Señora Galvez would be glad to see it just the same. She'd been in Apache Springs only a few months, but already her parsimony was legendary.

With the stolen money stowed safely in his right boot well, the lawman strode off in search of the robbers' two horses, which had run away during the gunfire. He found them grazing mesquite beans in a gully not far from where the bodies lay, already attracting flies. He whistled for his own horse, and the blaze-faced black stallion galloped in from where Yakima had left him well down the rise when he'd spied Curley and Goose stopping to rest and water their own horses, likely on their way to New Mexico.

They'd been savvier than Yakima had figured, and, spying the lawman on their back trail, they'd opened fire.

Yakima's mountain-bred stallion, Wolf, stopped a good ways off from where its rider was tying Goose belly down across the dead man's saddle. The high-blooded stallion rippled his withers and shook his head so hard, he nearly threw off his bridle. Wolf didn't like the smell of blood any more than he liked the sound of gunfire, and he wasn't sure what to think about the dead men's two horses, both geldings who eyed him warily.

"Stand down, hoss," Yakima told the stallion. "Let's all be friends, all right? That way we'll get to town all the faster with no one's feelings getting hurt. I know you could do with a feed sack, and I sure as hell know I could do with one of Dundee's ales over to the Busted Flush."

Cleve Dundee had rebuilt his saloon in grand style after losing his original place in the fire. Losing his place and his left eye, that is, when Rebel Wilkes's human coyotes had run roughshod over the town. Dundee's establishment sat next to Señora Galvez's place and shared much of the same clientele.

Yakima thought the one-eyed saloon owner and madam might be sharing more than just clientele. Rumor had it that Dundee had been seen leaving the aging but well-preserved Spanish madam's private boudoir. Once, when making his rounds late at night, the half-breed lawman himself had spied Dundee slipping covertly down the whorehouse's back stairs from the third story, adjusting his eye patch and whistling a happy tune.

With his passing, the night air had been so liberally scented with perfume and lilac water, Yakima had stifled a choking cough.

Now he finished tying Curly Buck over his claybank's back, lashing the dead man's tied ankles to his tied wrists beneath the mount's belly, then walked over and untied his own bridle reins from his saddle horn. He swung up onto Wolf's back, scrubbed sweat from his forehead with a sleeve of his buckskin shirt, and took a quick look around, getting his bearings.

Or trying to.

All around was rocky chaparral spiked with cactus. Red mesas and long, spine-like dykes rose in all directions, brightly reflecting the harsh sunlight of the high desert mid-afternoon. Coves of boulder-strewn earth and dinosaur teeth of jutting slabs of granite, limestone, and fire-blackened lava made this eastern leg of the Sierra Estrada a geologic maze. Yakima had been so intent on his quarry's sign that he wasn't sure what route he'd taken to get where he was.

Did his route back to town lie between those two tabletop mesas off to the northeast, or between the slant-topped mesa and jog of low sandy hills off to the northwest?

He could backtrack himself, but that would take a while, given that the ground he'd followed the two robbers across was for long stretches solid volcanic rock blown up eons ago from cones jutting in the far west.

The half-breed almost randomly chose a route in the general direction of Apache Springs and booted Wolf into motion, trailing the two packhorses by their bridle reins.

An hour later, he felt a nettling unease. Chill fingers tapped across the back of his sweaty neck, and his innards squirmed like snakes.

He was lost.

He was also being followed.

CHAPTER 2

Wolf had alerted him to the possible danger, as the horse, even more attuned to trouble than his rider, often did. The stallion had suddenly lifted his head and whickered deep in his chest, casting one brief glance over his shoulder.

Yakima had turned then, as well, and caught a glimpse of a horse and rider descending a steep grade maybe a hundred yards behind him. Horse and rider were a small, light-brown blur against the gray rock behind them, and then, as fast as Yakima had spied them, his shadower was gone, riding on down the grade and out of sight behind the boulders that fairly choked this canyon he'd found himself riding through, following the faint trace of an ancient Indian trail.

Yakima glanced behind him again now. Nothing. Just rocks of all shapes and sizes.

He turned his head forward, nudged the

.44 residing in its holster thonged to his right thigh, and loosened the Yellowboy in its scabbard jutting over his right stirrup fender. He looked around at the canyon whose northern wall, on his right, had grown taller the farther he'd ridden along its base. It must have been two hundred feet high in places — flues and chutes and crenellated, castle-like walls of eroded sandstone. There was virtually no growth except a few patches of wiry brown brush and cat claw, maybe a greasewood tuft or two.

To the south, on Yakima's left, was a massive jumble of boulders that had likely tumbled down from the northern ridge. That ridge, if comprised of all the rock that now nearly squeezed off Yakima's passage in places, must have been as tall as the northern ridge at one time. But something, maybe an earthquake, had caused that wall to collapse into the canyon.

Yakima knew he hadn't come this way. But maybe he'd find a western exit to the canyon. Apache Springs was north and west, and it really didn't matter which way he took to get there.

He cast a cautious glance behind him again. Not seeing his shadower, he kept riding.

The canyon turned this way and that, ever so gradually.

The hot sun's rays were relieved by long shadows angling out from the northwestern wall.

Yakima followed another curve in the wall to his right, turning back toward the north, and abruptly jerked back on Wolf's reins. The horse whickered uneasily, blew. Staring at something on the ground a ways ahead and near the base of the northern wall, Yakima put the horse a little farther ahead, then stopped him again.

He stared down at what remained of a man who'd been staked out spread-eagle on the canyon floor. Little more than a mere skeleton. There were three men, in fact. Two more skeletons lay just beyond the first one.

The half-breed stared at the nearest man — sun-bleached bones to which a few bits of sun-mummified skin and scraps of clothing clung. A few sparse patches of skin also clung to the skull, and hair clung in similar patches to the scalp. The bony wrists were lashed with dried scraps of rawhide to stakes that had been driven into the ground.

Yakima put Wolf a little farther ahead, scrutinizing the other two skeletons, which were in similar shape as the first. He shifted his attention to the sandstone wall beyond them, into which someone had scratched *TURN BACK OR DIE* in both English and Spanish: *RETROCEDEN O MORIR.*

Yakima glanced about, feeling those cool fingers of apprehension once more. He hipped around to peer along his back trail. No sign of his shadower, if the rider back there had been shadowing him. Maybe two people out here in this dinosaur mouth of geologic chaos had merely been a coincidence, and the rider had gone his own way.

Lord knew this devil's playground was home to more than a few prospecting desert rats from both north and south of the border.

Or maybe the rider was the person who'd scribbled the bilingual warning into the canyon wall. Maybe the jake had a mining claim nearby, and the three poor devils lying stretched out on the red caliche of the canyon floor, like sacrifices to Father Sun, had been claim jumpers.

"Don't get nervy, pard," Yakima said to no one in particular as he booted Wolf on down the canyon, running his wary gaze across the rubble strewn to his left and from which a bushwhacker would find plenty of hiding places. "I ain't out to crowd anyone off their diggin'. Just tryin' to find a route back to Apache Springs, that's all. Back to the Springs and a tall, cool, malty ale in the Busted Flush . . ."

He fairly groaned at the imagined malty wetness of Dundee's personally brewed ale, from malted barley he shipped in from Kansas via the Southern Pacific and a regular train of freight wagons. The two packhorses clomped along behind Yakima, shod hooves occasionally ringing off cracked stones. The three dead men of bones fell back over his right shoulder.

Yakima rounded the bend in the trail and stopped once more. He stared into a broad, flat area opening to his right. Ahead, near the base of the canyon wall looming far above, sat a small, box-like adobe structure that looked almost toy sized in contrast to the cliff towering over it. A belfry had been mounted over the apparently doorless front entrance set atop crumbling stone steps.

A church? Way out here?

Yakima nudged Wolf forward, particularly interested in what appeared to be a well sitting in front of the church, within a circular wall of stone coping and shaded by a small brush *ramada*. He was low on water, and the longer he spent out here, he would naturally get lower. He had three horses to water in addition to himself, and Curley and

296

Goose's own canteens were only about one-third full of the warm, brackish substance.

He drew up in the yard of the church, stopped Wolf and the packhorses over which his dead quarry slouched, and looked around once more. Turning to the church, he called, "Hello!"

A slight pause while he watched, listened. "Anyone here?"

His voice sounded inordinately loud, echoing in the canyon's crypt-like silence.

He stared at the church and the flat, hard-packed canyon floor around it. There appeared to be no one here. Judging by the lack of prints in the thin, red soil stippled here and there by chips of red gravel, no one had been here in a while. A gust of a hot breeze rose from behind him, kicked up a curtain of tan dust, blew it over Yakima and the horses, and set it ticking against the side of the church slumped before him like a derelict boat, if boats could be made of cracked, water-stained, sun-bleached adobe.

Yakima's long, sweat-damp black hair rose, dancing across his face. He lifted his low-crowned, flat-brimmed, black hat with one hand and pulled his hair back behind his head with the other. He ran a buckskin sleeve across his face again, swabbing the sweat, then set his hat back down.

The breeze was hot and dusty. Still, a cold thread ran through it. Cold as air blowing across a frozen lake in the North Country.

No. Couldn't be.

The chill he felt came from inside. There was something dark and cold about this canyon. Something that continued to make writhing snakes of his innards and squeeze his heart in a dark fist of doom. It was a foreboding of . . . what?

Evil.

Still, he felt oddly compelled to investigate. Why not? The horses needed water and a rest.

He turned Wolf around and rode over to the well. He swung down from the saddle and peered over the well coping, spying the oily glint of water about ten feet down.

An old bucket sat on the edge of the coping, attached to a wooden winch with a frayed rope. He dropped the bucket into the well, winched it back up, the winch working hesitatingly, spindly with age, and then poured water from the bucket into his hat. He set the hat on the ground before Wolf, then set the bucket on the ground before the two dead men's horses.

The claybank began drinking first while the second horse, a dapple gray, drooped its head and flicked its ears, waiting patiently for its own turn.

Yakima had enough of the old frontiersman in him to allow his horse to drink before he himself did. After all, without a horse — especially out here in this godforsaken desert — a man wouldn't last long.

Patting the black's rump, he told the horse to stay there and then, looking cautiously around once more, feeling a cold thumb of apprehension pressing taut against the base of his spine, he began striding toward the church. As he walked, the breeze continued to gust. He flicked the keeper thong free from over the hammer of his .44 and then mounted the stone steps, treading lightly and carefully, for the mortar between the stones was loose.

The steps had to be a couple of hundred years old.

He stopped at the top of the steps and peered through the broad open door. The door itself, or what was left of it, lay on the floor to Yakima's right — little more than moldering bits of rotten wood. Cobwebs had taken its place, the webs stitched with dead flies, dead leaves, and dust.

Yakima parted the sticky web with his arm and stepped through the doorway to stop just inside. Nothing here but dirt and other debris littering the floor, blown in through several glassless windows in the stout walls to the left and right. The smell of bat guano and mouse shit. Glancing to his right, Yakima saw a partly devoured rabbit carcass, probably left there by some coyote that had entered the ancient church to dine and maybe spend a recent evening. More, similar bones lay strewn amongst the rubble.

Another breeze gust sent more dust through the windows to Yakima's right. Squinting against it, he stared at what appeared to be an altar at the far front of the church. Atop the altar sat a large crate or box of some sort, which shone in a thick ray of golden sunlight spilling into the church from a window to its left. Slowly but steadily he moved down the center of the church, between two rows of crumbling wooden benches where worshipers had apparently sat — how long ago?

He stopped before the altar. The box was a trunk — roughly the size of a large steamer trunk. There was no lock, no padlock or chain. The box sat coated in dust and cobwebs atop the cracked adobe altar.

Yakima's heart quickened inexplicably as he placed both his gloved hands on the sides of the lid and opened it. Dry steel hinges squawked. The lid shifted precariously in the half-breed's hands. Sunlight angling down from the left began to smolder and glisten as the lid rose and fell back away to rest atop the altar on the other side of the trunk.

There appeared a veritable fire inside the trunk. The flames were so bright that Yakima had to look away briefly, then squint.

No, not fire. Sunlight glistened off what appeared to be pure gold trinkets heaped inside the trunk.

Yakima's heart danced, and his legs weakened. His breath became short and strained, like an old man's.

"Holy . . ."

The trinkets were mounded to the top of the box. He plucked up one and scrutinized it — a gold griffin with tiny, demonic eyes and bared fangs. Yakima set the griffin aside and picked up what appeared to be a winged angel with the face of a small child. Like the griffin, it was roughly the same size as his clenched fist.

Setting the angel aside, he picked up another angel and then a cherub and then a crucifix and then a gold, jewel-encrusted ring. Then a jewel-encrusted bracelet. There were many coins of all sizes and bearing Latin crosses. There were necklaces and miniature daggers and molded depictions of what Yakima, not a religious man, figured were saints.

He continued to rummage through the box of solid gold doodads until his face was bathed in sweat and his heart was hammering his breastbone. He'd never had such a feeling before. He'd never figured himself susceptible to such gold fever.

But, then, what man would not have such a reaction when confronted with so much wealth? He had no idea what the contents of the trunk were worth, but he figured likely in the millions of dollars.

"Holy . . . shit," he muttered.

He drew a deep breath and stepped back away from the trunk.

Words of his friend the Rio Grande Kid, also known as the outlaw Johnny Day, who now worked as Yakima's deputy town marshal in Apache Springs, spoke to him with remembered quiet eagerness, with a weird, almost lewd intimacy that untold wealth often inspires in men who rarely had more than a few cents to their names at any one time:

". . . when Eddie was comin' up through the Estrada, he stumbled on an old abandoned mine and a Mexican church in a deep canyon. There was gold everywhere . . . and what looked to Eddie like a treasure box from some Spanish galleon. Spilling over with jewels of every shape, size, and color. And you know what else Eddie found in that canyon? . . . Eddie found a cannon made of pure gold!"

The words seemed have been spoken out loud in the church and were now echoing off the walls.

The walls.

Yakima had vaguely noticed something odd about them.

There was gold everywhere!

Frowning, Yakima stepped around behind the altar. He moved up to the back wall, shoved his face up to within a few inches to study it closely.

It appeared to have been tiled. The tiles were dark, mostly in rectangular shapes roughly twelve inches long by three inches wide. At first, Yakima thought the tiles were some kind of stone, but he'd never seen stones that off-gray, almost copper color.

His heart once again beginning to race. He dipped a hand into a pocket of his denim trousers and pulled out a coin. He shoved his hand forward and scraped the quarter against one of the tiles, plowing up nearly a quarter-inch crust of dust and grime of many years, laying bare a small strip of pure, glistening gold.

Gold so bright that, with the sun from a

near window reflecting off of it, it was like a miniature dagger poking his eyes!

Yakima stepped back, his heart thudding slower now but with more vigor against his sternum. He turned to the right wall. It was tiled in the same stuff. He swung around, breathless, to face the left wall.

Same stuff.

He tipped his head far back on his shoulders to study the ceiling eight feet above his head.

Sure enough. Same stuff.

The walls and ceiling of this church lost in a deep, rubble-strewn chasm were tiled in pure gold ingots!

Not only that, but . . .

Something crouched low against the wall to his right, partly concealed in the wall's heavy shadows. Yakima knelt beside it, laid a hand against the side of a long, tapering barrel. The barrel of a cannon whose wooden wheels were nearly disintegrated. It slumped nearly sideways against the gold wall.

Again, he used the coin to scrape away the grit, revealing another line of pure gold.

The gold cannon from Eddie's treasure tale!

Yakima straightened, stumbled backward, throbbing heart swelling in his chest. He stared up at the ceiling. He didn't realize it, but his mouth was hanging nearly wide open as he continued to study the ceiling as though in a trance.

He closed it when he heard the soft ring of what sounded like a spur outside the front door.

He lowered his head in time to see a man in a long, black duster and brown Stetson standing silhouetted against the outside light, aiming a pistol straight out from his right shoulder.

Flames and smoke lapped from the barrel.

CHAPTER 3

Yakima threw himself to his left as the shooter's bullet screeched over his right shoulder to bark against the gold-paneled wall behind him.

He hit the floor — which he just then realized was also tiled in gold! — and rolled off his left shoulder as the shooter flung more lead, the next bullet spanging off the floor two feet in front of him, the ricochet burning a fine line across his cheek. He rolled again . . . and again, dodging another bullet . . . and on the next roll he came up on his heels and propelled himself nearly straight up and out the low, rectangular window in the church's east wall.

The shooter's pistol thundered hollowly inside the church, on the heels of another bullet slicing through the air over Yakima's head as he hit the ground outside with a grunt and rolled onto his back. His ears rang, and his cheek burned.

"Goddamnit!" yelled a voice near the front of the church.

Spurs chinked angrily.

Yakima slipped his stag-horned .44 from its holster as he rolled up onto his haunches. He clicked the hammer back and extended the pistol straight out from his right shoulder as the shooter strode quickly around the church's front corner.

The Colt bucked and roared in Yakima's hand.

The shooter had just cleared the corner and turned to face him, bringing her gun around — *yeah, a girl* — and now she screamed as the half-breed's bullet chewed into her right arm. She dropped her own smoking Colt and flew backward in the dust, her hat tumbling off her head, and her flaxen hair spilling in thick curls about her shoulders.

Quickly, Yakima gained his feet. "Emma?"

She turned to him, throwing her hair back behind her head, clamping her left hand over her upper right arm. Her hazel eyes were cast with pain and surprise. "*Yakima?* What . . . what are *you* doing out here?"

The half-breed holstered his Colt and dropped to a knee beside her. "I was about to ask you the same thing." He pulled her hand away from her arm. "How bad you hit?"

"I don't know, but it hurts like a devil! Thanks a bunch, *Marshal*!"

"You're lucky I didn't blow your head off. That's what I was aiming for!" Yakima pulled the ragged edges of her bullet-torn duster and checked shirt back away from the wound.

"Ouch!" she cried.

"Hell," he said, giving a wry snort. "I've stubbed my toe worse than that gettin' up at night to evacuate my bladder."

"I bet you don't use such farm talk as that around my uppity sister." Emma Kosgrove's voice was pitched with accusation. She was the younger sister of Julia Taggart, the former town marshal's widow Yakima had taken more than a little fondness to in Apache Springs.

Yakima had met Emma before he'd met Julia, who, at twenty-four, was older than Emma by five years. He'd met Emma out in the desert nearly two years ago, when he'd first come to this country with a mining claim he'd won in a poker game. He and Emma had both been hunting, and he'd shot the black-tailed deer she'd been aiming at. She rode her buckskin over, fighting mad and sassy as hell, the way rich, privileged girls could be. Her father, originally from the east, owned the Conquistador gold mine. Emma had piped down when Yakima had silently field-dressed the deer and thrown it over the back of her horse.

"What're you doing?" she'd said, startled, as he shoved his Arkansas toothpick back into the sheath behind his neck.

"I figure one bullet and one deer is a small price to pay for a little peace and quiet."

With that, he'd swung up onto Wolf's back and ridden off to find another deer for his cellar.

He didn't know if she'd followed him home that day or just figured he must be occupying the old stone cabin in the Javelina Bluffs, but she showed up there two days later. She'd showed up unexpectedly several times after that — a hot-blooded, flaxen-haired, hazel-eyed beauty, her tan, marble-smooth right cheek bearing a single mole that gave an exotic definition to her face.

She and Yakima had become lovers for a time, though that was over now. At least, as far as he was concerned. Eventually he'd learned that she'd joined her father at the Conquistador several years ago, when her mother had died in Boston and she'd been expelled from her girl's school for failing grades and general delinquency.

Learning that, he'd softened toward her. They shared a bond of sorts. The bond of the black sheep, though he, being a half-breed in a white man's world, was decidedly blacker and not half as pretty. He'd come to call her the Wildcat of the Sierra Estrada, because in many ways she was every bit as wild as the pumas and bobcats that stalked these mountains, always hunting . . .

Maybe she was as lonely, too, her father being more interested in finding more gold than spending time with Emma. That's why she could nearly always be found on her fine-boned buckskin, riding these mountains, looking for something, though Yakima doubted even Emma knew what . . .

But then, remembering what he'd found in the church, maybe he did know what she'd been looking for . . . and found.

As he plucked his red handkerchief from his back pocket and wrapped it around the girl's arm, he frowned at her suspiciously. "Let's leave your sister out of this," he said and narrowed one eye. "What're you doing out here, shooting first and asking questions later? Though the way you flung lead at me just now, I doubt you were hoping there'd be anyone alive later to ask any questions."

She winced as he drew the hanky's knot

tight, then glanced at him incredulously. "You saw, I take it? What's inside?"

"I sure as hell did. How did you know about it? We must be a good twenty miles from the Conquistador." She lived in a sprawling house near the remote gold mine with her father and a full-blood Chiricahua butler, Three Moons.

"You're all turned around," Emma snorted, tossing her hair again as she jerked her chin west. "The Conquistador is only five miles as the crow flies . . . and as I ride," she added snootily, "that way. Apache Springs is straight north, a dozen miles or so."

"Well, shit," Yakima said, raking a sheepish thumb down his unshaven jaw and rising to his feet. "I did get turned around."

"Who're they?" Emma asked as Yakima pulled her to her feet. She glanced at the two dead men lying belly down across their horses standing by the well with Wolf.

The stallion hadn't alerted Yakima of the girl's approach because he'd known her and the buckskin that now stood nearby, reins dangling. Wolf had assumed, albeit wrongly, that Emma Kosgrove hadn't been out to trim his rider's wick, the half-breed silently opined, brushing his hand across the bullet burn on the nub of his left cheek.

"Those two fellas cut a whore and robbed Señora Galvez in Apache Springs," he said.

"You brought 'em down, I take it."

Yakima chuckled darkly. "They took themselves down with a little help from a Mojave green sidewinder."

Emma scowled at him. "A *what*?"

"Never mind." Yakima walked over to the front of the church, mounted the steps, and stood peering inside once more, still not sure that he'd really seen what he thought he'd seen before he'd been so rudely interrupted. "How long have you known about this place, Emma?"

He moved inside, and she walked up behind him.

Immediately, he had that feeling again. The jitters.

Gold fever.

It was as though the walls were filled with shimmering lightning, and the fires were oozing through his bones, causing his hands and feet to tingle, his nerves to dance. He still couldn't wrap his mind around how much wealth was here, lining the walls of this small, derelict hovel out here in this likely uncharted, unmapped canyon.

No. It wasn't unmapped. Eddie had mapped it and, dying when a posse had ridden him down and shot him, had turned the map over to his friend, the Rio Grande Kid. The Kid still had the map. In fact, on his days off, the Kid often wandered out here with his map, looking for this very canyon.

The gold fever burned through the half-breed's veins. At the same time, a chill lingered at the back of his neck. That presentiment of evil he'd felt before discovering the gold . . .

"I've known for about three years," Emma said. "That's when I rode in here by accident, heading west. I reckon that's how you did it, too."

"I was heading back to Apache Springs, lost my trail."

Their boots crunched the dead leaves and gravel and other debris littering the church's gold floor — beneath the debris and several layers of desert grime. The half-breed lawman was thinking about the Rio Grande Kid and his treasure map. *My, won't the Kid be surprised to learn just how much treasure was really here?*

"Yakima?"

He turned to the girl again, raking his gaze from the gold-tiled wall to his left. Emma gazed at him gravely, her eyes filled with a deep desperation. "What is it?" He walked over to her, took her hand, and lifted her arm so he could inspect his handkerchief. "You bleeding?"

She pulled her hand away and continued to stare up at him with a strange anguish. Slowly, she shook her head. "Yakima, no one must know about this canyon. The church. Any of it."

He stared back at her, waiting for her to continue.

"I promised old Jesus that I would make sure no one knew about it. At least . . . I promised to do my best."

"I don't get it. Who's Jesus?" Yakima paused, absorbing the information. "Don't tell me you killed those three men staked out —"

Shaking her head, Emma cut him off. "Jesus did. They were outlaws on the run from Mexico. They stumbled into this canyon like I did . . . like you did . . . and started to fill their saddlebags from the gold in the box. They probably would have come back for the rest . . . maybe brought others . . . and . . ."

"Jesus killed them?"

"He had to."

"Why? Who was this Jesus fella — some prospector who stumbled upon this canyon and wanted it all for himself?"

Emma shook her head, frowning. "No. It

314

wasn't like that. It's *not* like that!"

"What do you mean it's *not* like that? Where's Jesus?"

"Dead."

"Who killed him?"

"Rattlesnake crawled into his bed one night for warmth, and Jesus rolled over on it. I found him two days later, near death."

Yakima winced, involuntarily feeling the Mojave Green rattler squirming against his own chest . . .

Emma opened her mouth to continue, but then distant thunder rumbled, and she turned to the west windows. Clouds were scudding across the ground outside the church. She placed a hand on Yakima's arm. "I'll explain later. Let's stable our horses."

"Where?"

Emma strode to the open door. "I'll show you." She stopped and, seeing the big, green-eyed lawman just standing there, gazing at her skeptically from beneath his flat-brimmed, black hat, said, "No more questions for now. I'll explain everything later, once we're in out of the rain."

"In out of the rain where?"

She smiled and gave a coquettish wink. "My secret place."

She flounced out into the yard, buttocks pushing against the worn seat of her gray denim trousers as the black duster blew out behind her. Yakima looked away quickly, not liking the tug the image of her heart-shaped rump gave his loins.

Yakima fired a lucifer to life on the buckle of his cartridge belt.

He touched the flame to the end of the quirley he'd just rolled and drew the smoke deep into his lungs, staring at the rain hammering nearly straight down and forming a billowing white curtain over the desert around him.

He stood on the narrow front gallery of Emma's "secret place" — an ancient, two-room adobe shack with a beehive fireplace, a small eating table, a few chairs — one made of wicker and padded with straw-stuffed deerskin — and a large cot whose legs were formed of crisscrossed ironwood trunks. Its straw-stuffed ticking mattress was covered with threadbare sheets, an equally threadbare quilt, and two sewn-together mountain lion hides. The desert nights got cold, even colder now in the late fall.

Javelina skins acted as throw rugs on the shack's hard-packed earthen floor, which was the color of iron heated to glowing in a blacksmith's forge.

There were rudimentary shelves and a

wooden dry sink and rickety washstand with a rusty tin washbowl perched on top, with a cracked mirror secured to the ceiling beam above, beside a deer antler comb hanging from another nail. Yakima could hear Emma in there now, filling a pan for coffee from a wooden water bucket.

As Yakima smoked, he slid his gaze to the right of the old shack to where Wolf and the two dead men's horses and Emma's buckskin stood beneath a brush *ramada* in a small, stone corral, the corral's fence and gate constructed from woven mesquite and cedar branches. The horses stood still as statues, lined up side by side, watching the rain tumble off the *ramada* into the dirt of the ancient corral.

The cabin and corral were tucked into a notch in the canyon wall, screened from the church by boulders that had tumbled into the canyon when the southern ridge had collapsed. Yakima wouldn't have known the hovel was here unless the Wildcat of the Sierra Estrada had shown him — just in time to avoid the late-summer monsoon downpour, in fact. They'd just finished tending the horses, and Yakima had just finished laying out Goose and Curley Buck behind the lean-to stable attached to the corral, when the skies had opened up.

Yakima hadn't realized how appropriate the name he'd dubbed the girl had been. She'd been living out here only a handful of years, but she must have known every nook and cranny of this remote range, a spur range of the Chiricahuas. She probably knew every gold-seeking desert rat within a hundred square miles and had shared a pan of coffee and pot of beans with him more than once.

The lonely, adventurous sort. Beautiful, too.

Get your mind off her damned ass, you cur.

"What's the matter?" she said now, giving him a mild start as she stepped through the doorway behind him. Her voice had been soft and melodic beneath the steady din of the rain.

"Huh?"

Emma stopped beside him, holding two smoking tin coffee cups. "You were snorting and shaking your head."

"Oh, nothin'."

"Nothin', huh?" Emma curled one side of her mouth as she held up one of the cups.

Yakima's ear tips warmed.

She sipped her coffee and stared out at the storm. "Were you remembering?" she asked him, smiling up at him again, her hazel eyes bright with teasing.

Yakima frowned as he blew on the coal-black, steaming surface of his coffee. "I wasn't remembering a damn thing. I was thinking about this canyon . . . that church . . . the wealth here. All of it."

"I can see by the flush in your cheeks you were thinking about more than the wealth here. Er . . . at least, not just the gold wealth here."

"Be quiet, Emma."

"So you were!"

"What?" he said angrily, his ears fairly burning now.

"You were remembering our first time. You know — the first time we made *love*?" She flounced close beside him. "At your old shack in the Javelina Bluffs. In the rain . . ."

How could he help remembering the vision of her stripping off her clothes and dancing naked in the desert downpour? A vixeny desert sprite. A blonde-headed, ripe-breasted, round-hipped succubus of the Sierra Estrada. He'd joined her naked in the yard, and they'd danced together — if you could call it dancing. He'd lifted her onto the edge of the well and taken her like a love-hungry stallion.

He could still hear her love cries echoing in his head.

He tried hard to listen to the rain, wanting the storm to drive the echoes out.

It wasn't her he'd set his hat for. Not that he'd set his hat for anyone. But, if he had, that person would be her sister, Julia. Not as sexual, maybe. Not as wild. But every bit as beautiful. Besides, he felt a kinship with the older daughter of Hugh Kosgrove, for Julia had lost someone as important to her as he had.

She knew how he felt; he knew how she felt.

Emma set her cup on the gallery rail, walked up to Yakima, placed her hands on his chest. She smiled lustily up at him, began to slide her face toward his. He stared at her mouth, the fullness of her lips, and couldn't help seeing them together in the Javelina Bluffs.

He drew his head back. "Forget it."

"You know you don't mean that," she said, wrapping her arms around his neck, trying to pull his head down to hers.

"Forget it. I want to talk about this canyon."

Suddenly, Emma's eyes hardened. She removed her arms from around his neck and turned her mouth corners down. "Are you going to deny yourself *me* because of Julia?"

"I know how you feel about her, Emma . . . about your own sister. There's no point in talking about it. So take your coffee, sit down, and tell me about this treasure-laden canyon and your friend Jesus."

CHAPTER 4

"No," Emma said, taking her coffee cup in her hands and leaning back against the gallery rail, the pouring rain flanking her. "I won't tell you a thing about this canyon. I won't tell anyone. I promised Jesus I wouldn't, just as he promised the others who came before him."

She turned her head sharply, defiantly, to one side to stare off toward the unseen, gold-laden church.

"Others?" Yakima said. "You mean there were others before Jesus? Other" — he looked around as though for the right word — "*protectors* of the canyon?"

Emma stared at him, holding her cup in both hands just under her chin. "Tell me about Julia, Yakima. What rare trait does my sister have that makes it so easy for her to steal men away from me?"

Anger burned in him. "Men? There was only one you could say she 'stole' from you,

Emma. That was Lon. And it wasn't something she'd wanted to do. She didn't set out to hurt you. It just worked out that way. She and Lon felt something . . . something *lasting* . . . between each other. And it would have lasted, too . . ."

He walked up to the rail several feet away from Emma and stared moodily out at the rain. "It would have lasted if she hadn't been taken from me." He caught himself suddenly and turned to Emma quickly. "I meant — it would have lasted if Taggart hadn't been taken from her. Killed by Rebel Wilkes."

He sipped his coffee to cover his chagrin.

Wilkes, who'd worked as chief mining engineer for Emma's father, had been the first man Julia had been slated to marry. But then he'd gone off on his own and staked his own gold claim, and that had set him at odds with Julia's and Emma's father, Hugh Kosgrove, who'd founded the Conquistador. So Kosgrove had banished Wilkes and made Julia break off the engagement.

"So that's it."

Yakima was staring out at the rain again. He turned sharply, a little surprised to see that Emma had sidled soundlessly up to him. She stared up at him from just below his left shoulder. "That's what you see in her. Her grief." Kosgrove's younger daughter shook her head darkly. "Grief isn't much of a bedrock to lay the foundation of a marriage on."

Yakima snorted. "Who said anything about marriage?"

"You have that look in your eyes. I never would have figured you for a marryin' man. Not when I first saw you out in the desert that day — taking down the deer I was tracking. At first I thought you were Apache. Then I realized you were something even wilder. A half-breed. At home in no world. I couldn't have imagined you falling in love with any woman, much less my uppity sister." She smiled. "Maybe that's what made me so attracted."

"Well, I have." Yakima turned around, giving his back to the storm. He took a deep drag off his quirley and blew the smoke against the hovel's adobe front wall, which had a long, curved crack in it. "I'm in love with her. So you and I, Emma, well . . ."

"He'll never allow it to happen, Yakima."

He narrowed a curious eye at her.

"Hugh Kosgrove will never allow it to happen." Emma had said these words slowly, enunciating each one carefully, a little snidely. "Poppa will never allow Julia to marry you."

Yakima just stared at her. Of course, he knew it was true.

Such was the nature of love — or what seemed to be a sprouting seed of love — that you never really thought it through. If he'd thought through his and Faith's love — a half-breed drifter and a beautiful former whore in the employ of the embittered Bill Thornton — they wouldn't have been together for as long as they had. It wouldn't have made any sense.

No, maybe Kosgrove wouldn't allow such a union. But there were places Yakima and Julia could go to get around such obstacles. Julia's and Kosgrove's relationship being as troubled as it now was, since she'd married Taggart — another man Kosgrove had deemed unworthy of his daughter's hand — Yakima doubted Julia would give two cents for what Kosgrove had to say on the matter.

He could make her and Yakima's life difficult in Apache Springs, but it was a big world. Kosgrove owned but a small chunk of it — the Conquistador.

"On the other hand," Emma said, reaching up to nudge his hat off his head so that it dropped down his back, where it hung by its braided horsehair thong, "he probably *would* let you marry me. Old Hugh Kosgrove's strict eastern rules don't apply to his younger, wilder daughter. He'd love for any man to tame me. Even a wild, green-eyed half-breed!"

"I don't know," Yakima said, tossing the stub of his cigarette out into the muddy yard. "He didn't want Taggart, a town marshal, to marry Julia. I doubt he'd want a wild, green-eyed savage to marry you." He looked at Emma. "I think you might think your old man has a lower opinion of you than he really does."

"How would you know?" she said defensively. "You've never even met the man."

Yakima gave her a wink. "Just got a sneaking suspicion, that's all."

Emma's cheeks colored a little, and she brushed her left breast against his arm. "Don't wink at me like that or I'll start pestering you again, you handsome devil." She turned her head a little to one side and narrowed one eye. "But if you try to plunder this canyon, I'll have to honor my promise to Jesus."

"Shoot me?"

She pressed her index finger against his chest. "Right through your brisket — solid as it is."

Yakima chuckled, then sagged into an old hemp-bottom chair, one leg of which was propped on a flat rock. "Don't worry. The wealth over yonder is way too much trouble for any man. Especially this man. Besides, when I get rich, I like to think it'll be more on account of hard work than plundering a church."

He sipped his coffee, then looked at Emma standing with her back against the gallery rail, arms crossed on her breasts, holding her coffee in one hand.

"I sort of thought you'd see it that way. I'm sorry I shot at you, Yakima. When I think I could have —"

"Tell me about this place, Emma. Tell me about Jesus. Just out of curiosity, you understand," he hastened to add with an ironic half smile, glancing at the New Line .41-caliber Colt revolver she wore strapped to her shapely hip.

She hiked her other hip onto the gallery rail, took another sip of her coffee, then stared out at the rain, which appeared to be lightening somewhat, the thunder dwindling, lightning forks growing less dramatic over the surrounding peaks. "I rode into this canyon the same way as you, looking for a way home. Jesus heard my horse, went for his rifle, fired a shot. Fortunately for me, his eyesight was going by then. He didn't know how old he was — his parents lost track of the years out here — but I figured that when I met him, five years ago, he was in his late sixties. Maybe even seventy."

Yakima had just finished building and firing another quirley. Emma stepped over to pluck the cigarette from between his fingers. She took a drag, half closing her pretty eyes, then blowing the smoke out into the slowly dying storm. She returned the cigarette to Yakima, then went inside for the coffee pot. When she'd refilled both of their cups and had set the pot on the rail beside her, she continued.

"Jesus's shot frightened my horse. He threw me. I wasn't as good on a horse then as I am now." She smirked at this, smiled, ran her index finger around on the rim of her refreshed cup. "Jesus was surprised to find a girl out here. I guess that's why he didn't kill me. He doctored my bruised hip and twisted ankle and helped me run down my horse. While he did, he swore me to secrecy and told me that he'd lived in the canyon all his life. His parents had, as well. He'd had a woman — several, in fact, but they were long dead. Jesus's family, as well as his wives, had been Apache slaves of the Jesuits who'd operated the mines that spotted that ridge up there. Back before the earthquake that collapsed the ridge and killed nearly all of the slaves but a few . . .

including Jesus's grandfather and grandmother.

"The mines had been in operation for many years. Jesus wasn't sure how many. Much gold had been milled and smelted here and shipped back to Mexico City, and from there to Spain. Every ounce dug and milled by slave labor. After the earthquake that killed so many Apaches, one of the survivors, an Apache witch, led an insurgence of the surviving slaves against the Jesuits. When the priests had been killed and their bones scattered, she cursed this canyon. The gold that had been dug out of those mines by the dead slaves shall always remain here, in honor of their memory. No one will ever spend it for private gain. Any taken out of the canyon will cause death and destruction everywhere it goes.

"Most of the surviving slaves left the canyon after the quake, to freely live out their lives. The Apache witch and her husband and son stayed to protect the canyon from interlopers — from anyone who might find this hallowed ground and desecrate it by removing the gold. That son was Jesus's father, who married another former slave and remained here, true to his mother's wishes, after his parents had died."

Yakima stared in wide-eyed interest at

Emma, as the words of the riveting, improbable tale dwindled from her lips.

"No kiddin'?" was all he could find to say after nearly a minute, the quirley drooping from a corner of his mouth.

The sky was only spitting now, the thunder rumbling into the distance.

Emma turned to him. "No kidding. Jesus married descendants of the slaves, their families still living in the area, trading with one another and with other Apaches both north and south of the border. All were sworn to secrecy about the existence of this canyon and the treasure here. Jesus married two more times. He had four children, but all died from one ailment or another. One I think died in a rockslide on the slope yonder, while trapping rattlesnakes, one of their primary foods. Then, after the years had passed . . . there was only Jesus . . . a broken-down, hump-backed old Mestizo — one-quarter Spanish-Mexican and three-quarters Mexican-Apache — when I met him. While he was dying from the snake poison, he asked me to take over for him here, in his people's plight."

"As protector of the canyon?"

Emma nodded.

Yakima sighed, chuckled softly, dubiously, and looked off, blowing smoke out toward the gallery's far end.

Emma frowned. "You don't believe me?"

"Oh, I don't doubt you were told that very tale," Yakima said. "I'm sure ole Jesus told you every word of what you just told me. It's Jesus I don't believe."

Emma looked indignant. "Why on earth not?"

"It's the oldest game in the gold-hunting book. Tell someone the canyon around your diggin's is haunted, they'll stay away. If they're the superstitious sort, that is. I'm not."

Still, he couldn't deny that feeling of evil he'd felt earlier.

"What? You think Jesus was just some old prospector who stumbled onto this place and concocted that story to keep others out?"

"It's happened before."

"Why wouldn't he have just taken as much treasure as he could carry and gotten out?"

"Maybe he was tryin' to figure a way to get it *all* out, without no one else gettin' suspicious."

"For three years?"

Yakima hiked a shoulder. He had to admit it sounded a little far-fetched. On the other hand, so did Jesus's story about the Apache witch's curse on the canyon, and the three generations of his family living out their lives here, watching over this place. He'd sat around many a campfire, listening to long windies blown by old prospectors, but Jesus's tale took the prize.

"Explain the church, then. All the treasure in there."

"Oh, I don't doubt there were mines around here. Probably up on the fallen-down ridge, even. A good chunk of that gold ended up in the church. For one reason or another, the Jesuits or Franciscans, or whoever built it, deserted it. Likely due to Apache or Yaqui raids. They probably planned to return for the gold one day, but it's a long way to Mexico City."

Emma was shaking her head and pursing her lips. "No. Jesus and I were friends. He would have told me the truth. Maybe not right away, but later he would have. I rode out here to visit that kind old man at least once every two weeks since I first stumbled on the canyon. I loved him. And he loved me, in his grandfatherly way. Besides, even if it was a lie, when he was dying he would have told me the truth."

Emma shook her head again, stubbornly. "You're wrong, Yakima. There's a curse on this canyon. Deep down, you know it's true." She paused. When she spoke again, her voice was pitched with low, quiet menace. "And you know what else?"

Yakima flicked his cigarette stub into the yard and leaned back in his chair, entwining his hands behind his head. "What?"

"I think someone knows about it and is trying to find it. One of them is who I thought you were. That's why I was so eager to trim your wick." Emma dropped to a knee before him and placed a hand on his thigh. "You have to help me keep them away, Yakima, or something really awful is going to happen!"

CHAPTER 5

The next morning Yakima waited for the floodwaters of the previous night's storm to recede before saddling Wolf, loading up the two dead men, and following Emma west along the canyon floor. To his left, where previous floods had cut a second, slightly deeper floor in the canyon's center, the last of the floodwaters swirled and gurgled, sending up steam snakes to glisten like melting butter in the high desert sunshine.

After a half hour of slow riding along the base of the northern ridge, the ridge dropped away behind them, and the canyon narrowed and doglegged to the right.

For a moment, Yakima thought the canyon ended just ahead, in a giant rumble of black boulders sprouting tufts of greasewood, cat-claw, and Mormon tea. But then Emma swung her buckskin to the far right, apparently finding an ancient trail of some sort, and Yakima followed, skirting the edge of the rubble, dropping into another shallow arroyo, then swinging sharply right — up a steep, gravelly bank.

The game trail twisted and turned until finally Yakima and Emma were out of the canyon.

They stopped on the canyon's lip, in a fringe of mesquites and palo verdes, to rest the horses. Yakima looked back down into the canyon. Only, from this vantage you really couldn't tell there was any canyon down there. It appeared like a narrow arroyo mounded over with boulders of all shapes and sizes.

"Perfectly hidden from this end," he said, half to himself. "No one could find a way into the canyon from here. And from the other end, about the only way you'd end up in the chasm is by accident."

"That's how I figure it." Emma shook her hair back, then turned to stare off to her left, behind and beyond Yakima. "Someone's been looking mighty hard, though."

"How do you know?"

Emma looked at him, then swung her right boot over her saddlehorn and dropped straight down to the ground. "Right this way."

Yakima dismounted, ground-reined Wolf, and followed the young woman around boulders and mesquites as well as saguaros and barrel cactus. He yawned as he walked, brushed a tired hand down his face.

His sleep had been troubled. He'd bedded down outside, on the shack's gallery, but knowing that Emma was inside, so close, had nettled the maleness in him no end. He was assaulted by discomfiting, remembered images of the times they'd spent together, before he'd begun tumbling for her sister. It didn't help hearing Emma moaning in her sleep only feet away from him, her own dreams likely assaulted by the same memories.

He brushed knuckles over the point of his chin, stifling a wry chuckle.

Ahead of him, Emma stopped suddenly and dropped to her haunches by a small pile of gray ashes from a recent campfire. Yakima looked around. There were a couple of discarded airtight tins and the charred bones of a small animal, probably a rabbit.

"So someone camped out here," Yakima said. "Doesn't mean they were looking for the canyon."

"I wouldn't think so, either," Emma said, "if I hadn't seen two more campsites just like this one about a mile west, and two more on the other side of the canyon, near Hawk's Pass."

Yakima squatted beside Emma. He picked up a charred airtight tin and turned it between his gloved fingers, staring at it. He wondered if the Rio Grande Kid was the one who'd left this fire as well as the others. The Kid had ridden out this way several times with his dead pard Eddie's treasure map in his pocket.

Yakima didn't think the Kid had been out here within the past couple of weeks, however. With all the folks pouring into Apache Springs of late, Yakima had needed all hands on deck. His only two hands at the moment were the Kid and Galveston Penny, a gun-savvy but good-natured and seemingly trustworthy young man, twenty-two years old, who'd taken the job Yakima had advertised in hand-written circulars he'd posted around town. Not long ago, it had become obvious that two town lawmen were no longer adequate to keep the growing population of Apache Springs buttoned down, so Yakima, with the permission of the city council, had added Penny as his second deputy.

All three lawmen — Yakima, the Rio Grande Kid, and the real kid, Penny — had had their hands full for the past several weeks. The Kid hadn't had time to head into the desert looking for his El Dorado.

Yakima had scoffed at the idea of Eddie's treasure. He'd thought for sure Eddie had imagined the whole thing.

He didn't know what to think now. He wasn't sure what to make of that much treasure. Just the idea of so much wealth made his head feel light and his toes tingle. If the Kid ever saw that canyon, he'd likely get so excited he'd die of a heartstroke before he could get any of the gold out of it.

"What're you thinking about?"

Yakima dropped the can. "Nothin'." He didn't want Emma to know about the Kid's treasure map. She had her neck in such a kink about anyone stumbling into that canyon that she might ride into town and back shoot Yakima's older deputy. Of course, he thought he knew her well enough to doubt she'd really do that, but, given her seeming zealousness for keeping Jesus's secret, part of him wondered.

She was a wild one, Emma.

"What is it?" she coaxed, staring at him curiously. "Tell me."

Yakima straightened with a sigh. "I was just thinking it might be wise for you to let this whole thing go. The canyon, I mean. You don't live out here. Your home is the Conquistador. You don't owe Jesus or that canyon a damn thing. If someone finds it, let 'em find it."

Emma straightened, her eyes nearly crossing as she regarded Yakima with her customary defiance. She slid a lock of flaxen hair back away from the mole on her cheek that gave her face bewitching definition. "I can't do that. I know you don't understand, but I can't, and that's that. As long as I live anywhere near this canyon, and as long as I'm still alive, I am going to do everything I can to make sure that treasure stays where it is."

She brushed past Yakima and stomped back to where the horses grazed mesquite beans near the canyon's lip.

"It's a mighty big responsibility," Yakima called after her in frustration. "I don't think Jesus knew what he was askin' you to do, is all I'm sayin'." Never mind that he didn't believe in the curse anyway.

Emma just kept walking, not so much as glancing over her shoulder at him.

Yakima followed her back to the horses. She was already mounted.

"Head back that way," she said, jerking her chin toward a crease between two small, shelving mesas straight north of the canyon. "You'll pick up the trail to Apache Springs in a half hour." She flared a nostril. "Don't get lost again."

She swung her buckskin around and nudged it west through the rocks and gravelly mounds of red grit spiked with cacti, presumably heading back to the Conquistador. Yakima grabbed the reins of the dead men's horses and mounted Wolf. He turned to see that Emma had stopped the buckskin and turned around to face him.

A saucy smirk tugged at her mouth corners.

"How did you sleep last night?" she asked, jeering.

"Terrible."

"Good!" She spat the word out, half laughing, half cajoling, then neck-reined the buckskin around once more and spurred it into a gallop.

Soon she was gone. Then there was just Yakima, Wolf, the dead men and their horses, a loud cicada, and the hot sun beating down. Beyond, to the south, lay the hidden canyon in which wealth too vast for him to imagine was shrouded by the ancient church. As he stared in that direction, a raw fear gnawed at him.

When he'd first spied the treasure, he'd known the ache of gold fever. The fever was tempered by his knowing that he had no use for so much gold. He hadn't realized it, but aside from Faith having been taken from him, he was pretty much satisfied with his life as it was.

His gold fever had been replaced by a churning apprehension. What would happen to whoever found that wealth and hauled it out of the canyon? Of course, someday it would be found. When it was, it would forever change whoever found it, and it would forever change everyone around that person or those people. The entire town of Apache Springs, most likely. As far as Yakima was concerned, the town was changing, growing fast enough, as it was.

He had the undeniable feeling that the treasure down there was like a massive keg of black powder just waiting for its fuse to be lit. And when it exploded, it would take out half of the county. Yakima didn't believe in the curse.

On the other hand, maybe he did.

The feeling of something evil down there had been real. Maybe it was the lingering, tortured souls of the slaves who'd been forced to mine the canyon until they'd died meaninglessly in the quake. Whatever caused the feeling, Yakima didn't care ever to visit that canyon again.

He switched his gaze toward where Emma had shown him the remains of the campfire.

She was probably right. Someone was looking for the treasure. Whoever it was, they were getting close. If they kept looking, they'd find it.

How did they know it was down there? Did they have a map?

The questions lingered in the half-breed's mind as he urged Wolf forward and, leading the two dead men's horses by their bridle reins, began riding to Apache Springs.

Soon, he picked up the main horse trail and followed it through the chaparral, climbing up and over hills and steep, rocky hogbacks. The air was warm and humid from last night's storm. The arroyos were still muddy. Steam rose from them. All around, the intermingling peaks of the Chiricahuas and Sierra Estrada jutted, dark-green and light-yellow with distance, shadows sliding across them.

A hunting Mexican buzzard, a *zopilate,* gave its ratcheting cry.

Ahead, the half-breed could see the high rocky pass on which sprawled the burgeoning town of Apache Springs. The pass was the southern entrance to the Sierra Estrada. To the southwest of the pass, bristling desert rolled away to the Southern Pacific rails forty miles distant. Those rails connected Tucson to Lordsburg in the east, and vice versa. In fact, they connected both coasts, an idea that, for Yakima, born when the Iron Horse was still a foggy notion even in the minds of its creators, was nearly as hard to fathom as the wealth in the canyon he'd put behind him.

Slowly, the trail rose until he found himself on the Apache Springs pass, with the town now dead ahead, sprawling up and down the several rises rolling up and away to the last rise of the pass a mile or so beyond. He reined up on a high hill, on the southeast corner of the town. Wolf curveted, and Yakima rested his right hand on his right thigh, near where his .44's holster was tied to his muscular leg swelling out his denim pant leg, and stared out over the town.

His town.

Yes, it had come to feel like that now. No one could have been more surprised than himself. He'd never felt at home anywhere before. At least, not in any town and not around more than a handful of people. But, for some reason, he felt at home here. Which wasn't to say that the decidedly reddish hue of his skin and the raptor-like cast of his nose didn't cause him to be looked down on by more than a few from time to time right here in Apache Springs.

Still, he and the town, in its earlier, preburn guise, as well as in this current rebuilt, booming manifestation, had been through a lot together. Yakima had known many of the people who'd died here in the fire, just as he knew many of the fire's survivors. (There were far too few of those.) He'd come to know many more people who'd poured in over the past months, after gold had been discovered north and west of the pass.

Those newcomers had seen him more as a native of Apache Springs than a lowly aborigine. He supposed he really was a native of the town in a way, having helped rebuild the place. For that reason folks tended to be more accepting than if he'd been a stranger riding into town for the first time.

Of course, it also helped that he wore a badge and carried its authority on his shoulders. On the other hand, there were a few here and there who resented a redskin bearing any authority at all, much less the authority of a badge-toting town marshal. Because of that attitude, he'd had to bust a few heads. He'd likely have to bust a few more in the weeks and months, maybe years, ahead.

Just the same, he'd sunk a taproot here in Apache Springs, if only a little ways down beneath the thin volcanic soil. It felt good.

He didn't doubt that he'd tire of the place, or that it would tire of him, and he'd eventually ride on. At the moment he felt the warm, familiar feeling of having a home, of belonging in and to a place, and of having a definite connection with others.

That thought got him thinking of Julia Taggart and, as he booted Wolf on down the hill and into the outskirts of the town, the pounding of hammers rising all around him as more houses and businesses were going up, he glanced over his left shoulder. The cemetery in which Julia's dead husband lay buried rose in the north, stippled with rocks, mesquites, and palo verdes. A path climbed the cemetery hill, the base of which was delineated by a freshly painted white picket fence.

Yakima remembered finding her there, just after Lon had been shot in front of both her and Yakima, in the town jailhouse, and how her grief had been so deep and poignant that it had made her want to stay there in the cemetery, despite the monsoon rain lashing her, soaking her to the bone. Yakima had taken her back to her house and, for good or bad, right or wrong, they'd made love that day, weathering the storm of each other's shared grief.

They'd made love many times after that,

and it was with a tug of lust in his loins now that he glanced toward her house as he rode on into what was now the heart of Apache Springs, at the broad, flat area atop the rocky pass. He couldn't see her house from this vantage, at the corner of Main Street and Third Avenue, because more houses had gone up recently, blocking his view. But the lovely Julia's neat frame house stood along the former unnamed trail that now bore the official moniker of Third Avenue.

Julia was likely home now, in the early afternoon, going about her chores. Yakima would pay her a visit soon, after he'd dealt with Goose McGowan and Curly Buck, and tended his and the dead men's horses. He'd stop by to tell her he was back in town, because she'd likely been worried about him.

Maybe he'd have a piece of pie and a cup of coffee, and they'd sit together out in the hanging wooden swing Lon had built for himself and Julia, beneath a brush *ramada* in their backyard. Just a short visit. Yakima had work to do. He would stop back later in the evening, and he and the pretty widow, and older sister of the wild Emma, would make tender love in her canopied bed.

Now he let Wolf pick his own way through the early afternoon traffic. There seemed to be more and more ranch wagons in town every week, for the land on the south side of the pass, with its springs and its wealth of grama grass and good hay pastures along the Rio Estrada, was coveted ranch country. Much of the traffic Yakima wove through now, however, was that of drays loaded with fresh, green-smelling lumber freighted up from the Southern Pacific rails and being off-loaded at the various building sites around Apache Springs.

There were also many prospectors' wagons and, in some cases, prospectors' handcarts being pushed by burly, bushy-bearded desert rats, some with a mongrel dogging the heels of their worn, high-topped leather boots.

There were all the sounds of a rollicking boomtown — men shouting boisterously; half-dressed painted ladies laughing on second- and third-floor balconies and on boardwalks fronting the town's numerous saloons, including the sprawling, rebuilt Busted Flush Saloon & Dance Hall. Piano music, some of it not bad, pushed through batwing doors. Dogs barked. Horses whinnied, and mules brayed. Hooves beat a steady rhythm all through the day and often into the night.

There was the hammering of nails from

all directions, and the cacophony of black-smiths' hammers, for all the wagons rolling through town often needed new axles or wheel rims, and the horses and mules needed shoeing. At last count, Yakima deemed there were at least three blacksmiths now serving Apache Springs, which had been little more than freshly charred ruins less than two years ago.

There was another sound. Others like it were growing more and more common despite Yakima's attempts at keeping the violence tamped down.

It was the sound of gunfire.

More specifically, it was the thunderous concussion of a shotgun.

Just then a man was blasted out the large louvered doors of the Busted Flush on Yakima's right, propelled across the saloon's broad wooden veranda without his feet even touching the floor, to hit the street not ten feet in front of Wolf, where the shotgun-blasted man rolled, screaming, in a cloud of dust.

CHAPTER 6

Yakima looked from the man in the street to the Busted Flush, a big, beautiful building in its new transformation, sitting across the side street from Señora Galvez's Place — a purple, mansard-roofed affair with red gingerbread trim, a broad front gallery painted glistening white, and a white balcony running around its second story. A red lamp shone in a window near the front door.

Boots thumped inside the Flush, the sounds growing louder.

Yakima began to reach for the Yellowboy, but then the Rio Grande Kid stopped just inside the louvered doors and stared out over the batwings, his big, beefy face, as craggy as a coffee tin used for target practice, flushed in anger. He looked at the man he'd apparently shot.

The man was no longer screaming. In fact, he was no longer doing much of anything except lying belly up in the street.

Yakima and a couple of wagons had stopped near him, while the rest of the traffic continued as usual.

Yakima looked at the Kid, who was pushing sixty or sixty-five. His age was a carefully kept secret, just as he shrouded his own identity in a myth of his own making. The half-breed lawman said, "I see you've been keeping busy. I was worried you might go fishing as soon as I left town."

The Kid shook his head as he stepped through the batwings and tugged his funnel-brimmed, badly weathered Stetson down low on his warty, liver-spotted forehead. "I was thinkin' about it, but then all hell broke loose up at the new Chinese brothel down by the wash. And then it was payday out to the Bridlebit, and all the boys rode to town to stomp with their tails up. As if that wasn't bad enough, that *hombre* there's been spoilin' for a fight in every saloon he's walked into. Snake-oil salesman, though I think he done drunk up all his inventory. Most places kicked him out, including Cleve Dundee over here at the Flush."

Dundee himself pushed out the batwings to stand on his broad front gallery beside the Kid. Like his saloon, Dundee had received a makeover. He stood a few inches taller than the Kid beside him, a big man, bald as an egg, now sporting a nattily tailored suit of clothes complete with pin-striped shirt with a poet's collar and arm bands, and creased broadcloth trousers. The black, gold-buckle shoes on his feet glistened in the desert sunshine from a recent polishing and buffing.

He once wore a tangled beard. The beard was gone — or at least transformed. Now, thick muttonchops dragged down the sides of his broad, pale, raw-boned face to angle over and connect in a thick, waxed, handlebar mustache mantling his mouth. Even the patch, worn over the socket of the eye he'd lost in Rebel Wilkes's sacking of the town, gave him a rough-and-tumble, big-city businessman's air of intrigue.

"But then he came back," the saloon owner said, adjusting the black patch over his left eye as he gazed into the street at the presumably dead man. "I guess he thought he'd start all over again. He pulled a gun on me, so I sent for the Kid."

"He pulled a gun on me," the Kid said, spattering a wad of chaw over the gallery's front rail, "so I aired him out a little." He held up his big, double-barreled Greener in both hands across his thick, lumpy chest and grinned.

The quick thuds of running boots

sounded, and Yakima began to automatically reach for the Yellowboy again, but stopped the motion when he saw Galveston Penny running toward the Busted Flush from the west, on the same side of the street the Flush was on. He was a slender, fresh-faced lad in dark-brown trousers, dress shirt, string tie, and bowler hat. The well-liked young Penny, or Master Galveston, as he was called by everyone in town, had had his fill of "wet-nursing beeves on the hoof," as he called cow-punching and which he'd been doing since not long after graduating from rubber pants on a west Texas tumble-weed farm.

That's why he'd applied for the job as second town marshal and burned his impossibly dusty, smelly, and faded range clothes an hour after he'd donned the badge. He'd burned everything but his worn brown boots, that is. He'd said the boots fit him like moccasins, and it was so rare to break in a pair of boots "so good your feet called 'em by their first names" that he couldn't part with the rundown, undershot Dan Posts, though they did stand in sharp contrast to the rest of his sharper, more city-bred attire.

Twenty-two years old, young Penny didn't look a day older than twenty. He was a slender, tow-headed, blue-eyed young man roughly six feet tall, two inches taller than the oldster, the Rio Grande Kid. The two pearl-gripped Colts he'd bought at a local gun store as soon as he'd landed the job, and for which Yakima was sure he was still in hock, sagged in thonged-down, hand-tooled leather holsters on both bowed thighs. In his hands just now was the brush-scarred Winchester carbine he'd carried on the range.

His blue eyes flashed anxiously as he stopped near the bottom of the Busted Flush's front steps, glanced from the Kid to Yakima and then to the dead man in the street.

"Heard the shootin'," he said, breathless from his run. "What happened?"

"That varmint tried to take me to the dance," the Kid told him.

"That snake-oil salesman?" young Penny said.

The Kid nodded as he broke open his shotgun and plucked out the spent shells. "He milked oil from his last snake."

Galveston laughed. He'd taken to the Kid like a toddler to rock candy. He thought everything the Kid said was at once humorous and wise, believed all the Kid's tales of his rowdy outlaw days, and the Kid basked in the younger man's admiration.

"Where you been?" Yakima asked Penny.

The youngest deputy jerked his chin to indicate the northwest side of town. "A coupla riders from the Bridlebit went hog wild this morning on their way out of town and busted up Mister Patten's picket fence. Mister Patten wanted me to check it out, and he wants the culprits run to justice. I was out askin' around if there were any witnesses, but it was awful dark last night. No one got a good look at the miscreants."

George Patten owned the First Bank of Apache Springs. He and his wife had moved here from the Midwest to open a new bank, replacing the one that had been looted and burned by Wilkes's bunch. Patten's wife suffered from consumption, and her doctor had prescribed the move to a dryer, warmer climate. They'd built a stately brick, Victorian-style house two blocks north and west of Main Street.

Yakima had pulled Wolf and the other two horses over to where the Kid stood in front of the Busted Flush and turned to Penny, standing on the broad main street's other side.

"Inquire with the bartenders around town," he told the young deputy as he swung down from the saddle, raising his voice to be heard above the clatter of traffic. "Find out which Bridlebit riders left town around the same time that fence was ruined. When you see those riders again, tell them they can either buy the materials and replace Patten's fence or spend a week in the hoosegow."

He jerked the Yellowboy from his saddle scabbard and rested the rifle on his shoulder.

Young Penny pinched his hat brim and started to turn away, but Yakima stopped him. "First, get that snake-oil salesman off the street. And take Curly Buck and Goose over to the undertaker's. Have 'em fitted for wooden overcoats. Tell Jenkins the town'll likely be paying for their planting, so his cheapest model will suffice. When you're done with that, you can stable Wolf and these other two horses."

He turned to the Kid, who'd come down the gallery steps to stand beside him on the boardwalk. "Me an' the Kid need to pow-wow back at the office."

When Galveston Penny had led the three horses off in the direction of the new undertaking parlor, Yakima and the Rio Grande Kid began slanting across the street to the east, heading for the barrack-like adobe-brick town marshal's office, identified by a sign stretching into the street on two cottonwood poles. The sign was the only thing new about the place. The fire had avoided the jailhouse, so it was the same rudimentary building that Lon Taggart had operated from.

There was a new city hall, but the parsimonious town boosters had seen no reason to make a jailhouse part of it when the standing one worked just fine for holding prisoners, never mind that it was often too small to hold all the criminals Yakima and his deputies found themselves arresting on a wild, drunken Saturday night.

"What're we powwowin' about, Marshal?" the Kid asked as he followed Yakima up the four steps to the adobe hovel's small, brush-roofed front gallery. "Don't tell me the town boosters caught wind of my criminal past and ordered you to fire me. Or, worse, arrest me!"

"No, no — nothin' like that." Yakima tripped the latch and opened the door.

"Whew!" The Kid shook his head as though with relief as he followed Yakima into the office flanked by four barred jail cages. "I thought I was gonna have to shoot my way out of another town. That gets old when you're gettin' on in years!" He turned to the window by the door and used his double-barreled Greener to slide the flour-sack curtain to one side as he stared out. "And, I don't know what it is, but I've grown to fancy this town."

Yakima hooked his hat on a wall peg by the door. "Maybe, at your age, you've just grown to fancy a steady, honest job and a roof over your head. Even if that roof does belong to a whore's crib most of the time."

The Kid wheezed a laugh, moving his heavy, rounded shoulders as he turned to face the half-breed lawman. "That might have somethin' to do with it — sure enough. And a steady paycheck is novel for this old border bandit." He chuckled again, then leaned his shotgun against the wall and hooked his thumbs behind his cartridge belt. "What're we powwowin' about, Yak?"

Neither man took much stock in formalities. They were partners first, town marshal and deputy second.

Yakima wasn't sure how to ask the question without arousing the Kid's suspicion. Maybe there was no way to do it, so he just came out with it. "Where's your map?"

The Kid's bushy, gray-stitched, red-brown brows slid down over his eyes. "Huh?"

"Your treasure map. You know — the one you keep in your Bible? The one your friend Eddie drew."

"The one I — ?" The Kid looked astounded. "How in tarnation did you know I kept it in my Bible?"

"You were a better bank robber than you are a secret keeper, Kid." Yakima moved to the roll-top desk that served both deputies and that sat against a wall by the line of jail cells, near a sandbox for chaw. The town marshal crouched, drew open a bottom drawer, and lifted out a one-foot-high stack of *Policeman's Gazette* illustrated magazines, the Kid's favorite reading material, though Yakima suspected he mainly looked at the pictures.

The Kid stared at the open drawer in shock. "How did you know — ?"

"That you 'hide' the map in your Bible, under these magazines?" Yakima snorted wryly. "Just check it."

"Huh?"

"Check the Bible."

The Kid crouched over the drawer, reached inside with his two ham-sized, dirt-colored, freckled and liver-spotted hands, and from within it drew an old, falling-apart Bible sprouting yellowed papers with spidery, inked writing, most in a woman's flowery hand. "This is the Bible my dear mother gave me on her deathbed, nigh on twenty years ago. One of the few times I wasn't doin' time in a state or territorial pen somewhere. It's the Day Family Bible."

"Check it."

"Huh?"

Yakima sighed in frustration. "Look in the back and see if your precious map is still there."

"How did you know — ?"

"Just check the damned thing!"

The Kid opened the book, looked inside the back cover, then flipped through the pages near the back, and his lower jaw sagged farther and farther toward his chest. He looked in wide-eyed shock at Yakima. "It ain't there!" He glanced around at the floor as though the old scrap of paper might have fallen out.

"Shit," Yakima said.

"How did you . . . how did you know it was gone?"

"Had me a feelin'." Yakima moved to the window and stared out in frustration.

"Come on, Yak," the Kid urged. "How did you know the map was there in the first place, and then how did you know it was *gone*?"

Yakima turned toward the beefy old deputy. "Hell, you sit there and ogle that map all the time. We can have a jail full of prisoners, and you still pull that old Bible out, bite off a chunk of wedding cake, and sit there and chew and spit and stare at that map like it's a picture of a half-clad fallen angel. When you're through, you always get that guilty look on your big, ugly mug, look around, then stick the map in the back of the Bible and stuff the Bible under your magazines. I've seen you pull that stunt a dozen times."

"Shit!"

"I hope you were a better bank robber, though all the time you did behind bars doesn't say much in your favor."

"I was a hellion at robbin' banks!" the Kid intoned, defensively. "I ain't been old an' stupid all my life! Now, tell me how you knew it was gone." He stepped up close to Yakima, like a bull ready to burst through a chute. He turned his head to one side and narrowed one suspicious eye. "Did you steal it? If so, all bets are off!" He brushed his right hand across the top of his old, hol-stered Remington, freeing the keeper thong from over the hammer.

"Yeah, I stole it," Yakima said with another wry chuckle. "That's why I just showed you it was gone. Because I'm no smarter than you are."

The Kid turned his head to the other side and narrowed his other eye, which flickered uncertainly. "You're startin' to confuse me now."

"That don't take much." Yakima walked behind Taggart's old desk facing out from the far adobe wall on which a framed map of Arizona Territory hung, flanked by flags of both Arizona Territory and a thirty-eight-starred red-white-and-blue.

He plopped down in the swivel chair behind the desk, peeled off his gloves, hiked his boots onto the edge of the desk, and crossed them at the ankles. The desk was littered with all kinds of paperwork, most of which he wouldn't have had any inclination of doing even if he'd known how to do it. To hell with it. His job was to keep the tough nuts from running wild and trampling the banker's picket fence.

And, since yesterday, to keep the Wildcat of the Sierra Estrada from getting herself or anyone else killed.

He glanced at the line of empty cells on his left, then turned to the Kid, who stood staring in open-mouthed exasperation at the old Bible in his hands.

"Who'd you have in here over the last two days?"

The Kid lifted his head slowly to stare back at Yakima.

"Huh?"

"Think about it. Who'd you have in here over the last couple of days? The day I left . . ." He let his voice trail off, then crossed his arms on his chest and shook his head. "Ah, hell. Whoever took your map took it a lot longer ago than that."

If the same person or persons who'd taken the map had also left the remains of the campfires Emma had spotted near the canyon, they'd have to have taken the map quite a while ago. At least a week ago. Probably even more than that.

"You think whoever took it was in one of our cells?" the Kid asked, his voice thin with bewilderment. He sounded like a little boy whose best friend had just left town for good.

"No doubt. Who else . . . besides myself, that is . . . would know you keep it in your Bible . . . and that you keep your Bible in the bottom drawer of that desk?"

"Ah, hell!" The Kid walked over to the window by the door, rested his elbows on the sill, and pressed his fists against his temples. "I'm such a damn fool!" He stared out for a time, then turned to Yakima again, his craggy face creased with suspicion and curiosity. "Say, now . . . how did you know it was gone?"

CHAPTER 7

Yeah, how did Yakima know the map wouldn't be in the Kid's Bible?

"Just had a feelin'," he muttered, running a fingernail along the edge of the desk and turning askance from the Kid's skeptical gaze.

"Just had a feelin', huh?" The Kid wasn't buying it. He walked slowly toward the desk, his face a mask of wariness and suspicion. "What was it that gave you the — ?"

Yakima couldn't have been more pleased when boots thudded on the front gallery and spurs rang, causing the Kid to break off his interrogation. Galveston Penny opened the front door and walked inside, poking his crisp new bowler hat, which appeared one size too small, back from his pale forehead. "Them two dead owl hoots and the horses done been taken care of, Marshal Henry. I ran into Señora Galvez on the way over here. She seen you was back in town, and she wondered if we told you about . . ." Young Galveston let the thought dwindle on his lips as he turned to the Kid. "You told him, didn't you, Kid?"

"Told him?" the Kid said, still preoccupied with his concern over the missing map. "Told him about what?"

"What Señora Galvez said. You know — about a possible holdup or somesuch. Somethin' big bein' planned for Apache Springs!"

Yakima dropped his feet to the floor and rested his elbows on the arms of the swivel chair. "What're you talkin' about, Galveston?"

"Oh, yeah!" The Kid snapped his fingers in the air, remembering. "I done forgot about Señora Galvez."

"What about her?" Yakima prodded the pair.

"She come in here yesterday all distraught," young Penny said. "She said one of her girls overheard a couple of fellas — a couple of customers — over to Señora Galvez's place talkin' about doin' a big job around here somewheres. Sounded like they was talkin' about a hold-up, and it sounded like it was gonna happen soon. She wanted to warn you."

"Yeah, yeah," the Kid said. "She said she'd like it if you'd go over and powwow with her personal."

"She seemed a mite concerned," Penny added.

"All right." Yakima rose from his chair, glad to have an excuse to clear out of the office for a while. At least until he could come up with a convincing lie to tell the Kid about how he'd known the map was missing from his Bible. He grabbed his gloves, stuffed them into a back pocket, then pulled his hat off the peg by the door and set it on his head. "You two mind the store."

"Uh . . ." said Galveston Penny, shambling toward Yakima. The young man smiled bashfully and said, "You . . . uh . . . wouldn't let me tag along with you, would you, Marshal Henry?"

"Tag along?"

"Yeah, you know . . ."

"Not exactly, no."

The Kid laughed.

Penny's smooth, open face flushed deep crimson.

Then Yakima understood. He'd seen young Galveston chinning with one of the girls in front of Señora Galvez's place — a pretty little Mexican girl named Clara, if Yakima remembered right. The younker had been lit up like a Christmas tree. He'd lit up even brighter when young Clara, clad in a black-and-red corset and bustier and long, fishnet stockings, had taken his bowler and set it on her own head and flounced around, modeling it for him.

"Galveston," Yakima said, genuinely puzzled, "why don't you just save up your pennies and buy yourself a poke?"

The young man frowned, flushed, shook his head, and waved his hands, palm out. "No, no . . . I couldn't do that."

"Why not?"

"I just couldn't, that's all."

"Well, hell, boy," the Kid said, "the rest of the town does." He laughed again.

"It ain't like that . . . between her an' me," Galveston said.

"Like what?"

"Like that," Yakima said, suddenly understanding, remembering how, long ago, he'd once tumbled for a pretty *dove du pave* himself. Only, his had been a tall, slender, buxom blonde with cornflower-blue eyes — eyes as blue as blue wildflowers in a sunlit spring meadow — named Faith. Despite her profession, he'd tumbled for her hard, every bit as hard, or harder, than young Galveston Penny had apparently tumbled for Clara.

He knew how love, the kind of love that bit you deep down at your core, penetrated way beyond thoughts of a mere mattress dance.

"I still don't understand," the Kid said, shaking his head and running a hand down his face in frustration. "The world's a-changin' a mite fast for this old Kid, I reckon. When a young, strappin' young man ain't savin' his pennies to bleed off his sap with a comely Mescin whore" — he shook his head again in defeat — "what in tarnation is the world comin' to?"

"Galveston," Yakima said. "You don't need to hound-dog me over there. You go over there yourself tomorrow morning, before you go on duty, and bring her a spray of flowers and ask her out for breakfast. The girl's likely sleeping right now, and she'll be busy later tonight. Go on over there in the morning, wake her gently, and take her out for breakfast. She'd appreciate that better than anything else you could do for her."

"You think so?" Galveston said, staring at Yakima now with interest, but also with skepticism.

The half-breed lawman curled a conspiratorial half grin and winked. "Take it from me. I know. Now, why don't you go on over to Patten's place and assure him we're workin' on his picket fence." He winked again, then stepped outside.

As he drew the door closed behind him, the Kid called from the other side of it, "I still wanna know how you knew my map was missin', *Marshal Henry*!"

Yakima winced as he drew his cartridge belt up higher on his hips and tramped down the gallery steps. He slanted across the street toward Señora Galvez's place sitting across the side street from the Busted Flush.

He went inside and found the place understandably quiet — as quiet as a crypt, in fact, with the drapes drawn over the parlor windows, no lamps lit, and not a soul except a long-haired, smoke-colored cat and the Chinese cook moving around on the first floor. The air was spiced with Spanish incense, also known as marijuana, as well as a cloying potpourri of cigar smoke, man sweat, and cheap bottled fragrances. Yakima gave the cat, lounging on the back of a red velvet sofa by a cold fireplace, a friendly pat, then went into the kitchen and learned from the cook that Señora Galvez was in her boudoir upstairs, enjoying *siesta* along with the rest of the girls.

Yakima should have remembered. The Spanish madam's *siestas,* which all her girls enjoyed, as well, were well known around Apache Springs. They lasted from between one and five in the afternoon.

Such nap times made sense, given a whore's hours. The cook, a stocky man named Gu Cheng, but whom everyone called "Chang," said he'd wake her if Yakima thought it necessary, but Yakima could tell from the man's expression that rousting the madam from *siesta* was not to be done without just cause and might very well be met with no little Old Country rancor.

Yakima shook his head.

"I'll be back in a few hours," he told Chang, who, clad in a long smock over threadbare balbriggans, a loosely rolled quirley dangling from his mouth, was chopping rabbit meat and tossing the chunks into a stew pot bubbling on his coal-black range.

Yakima took his leave and headed back outside. He studied the street for a time, wondering if what the madam had heard was true. He'd had to parry no hold-up attempts since his second time taking over the town marshal's job.

Then, again, the town was new. Newly reborn, anyway. Trouble was about to come from one quarter or another. The local lawdog would like to know which quarter he should be keeping an eye on.

Oh, well. He'd learn soon enough. He didn't want to wake Señora Galvez and risk rubbing her the wrong way. As owner of possibly the most lucrative business in Apache Springs so far, aside from the Busted Flush and the new mercantile, half-owned by Emma's and Julia's father, Hugh Kosgrove, the *señora* carried considerable weight. She tended to run hot and cold and could hold a grudge, fairly typical of South-of-the-Border ladies. At least, he'd heard she could cloud up and rain all over anyone who crossed her, or whom she perceived to have crossed her.

Yakima hadn't tangled with her so far, and he didn't care to. She was one of those women, not unlike the Wildcat of the Sierra Estrada, he'd rather wrestle a wounded grizzly bear than get crossways with.

He started retracing his steps to the marshal's office, then, thinking about the Kid possibly waiting there for him to continue grilling him about the map, Yakima switched course. He headed east, tramping across Second Avenue to the next cross street. Nearly to the edge of the business district, he headed north.

He swerved into a dry wash and followed its snaking course back west for fifty yards.

He felt foolish for taking this roundabout way to his lover's house — this furtive route — but he sensed it best if not too many of Apache Springs's citizens knew that the half-breed marshal was paying visits to Julia Taggart, the former marshal's widow and Hugh Kosgrove's older daughter.

Yakima might have been town marshal, but his skin hadn't grown any lighter since he'd pinned the badge to his shirt. In fact, he was probably crazy for continuing to see Julia. Where could it lead, anyway? Still, he felt compelled. Julia had been on his mind ever since he'd left town. He suspected he was on hers. He wanted to let her know he was back.

He didn't like it being that way, he and Julia hailing from opposite sides of the tracks, as it were, and knowing that their relationship would eventually have to end — probably sooner rather than later.

But there it was.

He stepped out from between two palo verdes and glanced around to make sure neither of Julia's two near neighbors were in their backyards. Then he strode past Julia's privy and the brush *ramada* Lon had built, with the two-person swing hanging beneath it, and mounted the small stoop at Julia's back door.

He glanced around once more, then knocked twice on the door lightly. He turned the knob. The door opened. He stepped inside, into the cheerfully sunlit kitchen at the rear of the house.

"Julia?"

There was a shrill gasp, and then he saw her. She'd just stepped into the kitchen from the parlor, wrapped in a heavy towel, her brown hair pinned in a rich, messy pile atop her head, stray strands curling down against her pale, beautifully sculpted cheeks. Now she leaped back against the wall, jostling several pots and pans hanging from pegs, and splayed a hand across the two mounds of her breasts pushing out against the towel wrapped tightly against her torso, leaving bare her legs from below her thighs.

"I'm sorry," Yakima said quickly, doffing his hat and holding it against his chest. He extended his other hand apologetically. "I didn't mean to frighten you."

"Well, frighten me you certainly did, Yakima Henry! You're lucky I don't have a gun in here. If I did, I'd likely have shot you!" Recovering, she pushed off the wall and walked lithely over to him on her bare feet. She shoved his hat back and leaned close, pressing her cheek against his chest. "I'm so glad to see you. I had a dream about you last night. I dreamed that you were in trouble . . . out there in the desert."

"No trouble. At least none this unlikely lawdog couldn't take care of."

She looked up at him. "You found those two men who cut the girl at Señora Galvez's place?"

"Sure did." Yakima tucked a stray lock of her hair behind her ear. "They won't be cutting any more whores."

"That's good to hear. Those poor girls have it tough enough as it is without getting cut by drunk border toughs." Julia stepped back and looked up at him curiously. "Why did you come to the back door, Yakima? You do know this house comes with a front door, don't you?"

Yakima shrugged. "Just figured . . . you know . . ."

"No, I don't know."

Changing the subject, Yakima ran his hands down her long, slender arms and looked at the towel barely covering half of her. "I like the new duds."

Julia lifted a mouth corner, wryly. "I was hoping you'd be back today. I wanted to be freshly bathed for the occasion. Also . . ." She glanced at a steaming round pan resting on a warming rack of the range. "I made sweet rolls spiced liberally with cinnamon."

She lifted her arms and placed her hands against the back of his neck, rising up on the tips of her small, pink toes, and kissed him. "Because I know you like cinnamon."

"Sweet rolls? What about pie?"

Julia stared at him for a moment, then shook her head slightly. "No more pie. At least, not for a while. You and I will be having sweet rolls with our afternoon coffee."

Yakima understood. The afternoon pie and coffee had been a holdover from her time with Lon. Making the buns instead of the pie was her way of saying she was letting go of the past and embracing the future.

Yakima dipped his head to kiss her wrist, which was fresh and clean from her bath and tasted vaguely of lemon. "Sweet rolls it is." He sniffed the air. "They sure do smell good."

"I took a little nap in the tub, and, when I woke up, I couldn't remember if I'd taken them out of the range or not. I came back down to check. I was just about to go back up and dress."

"I'll wait outside. I smell like sweat and horses, and I got enough trail dust on me to fill an Arizona canyon."

"You go on upstairs, and I'll heat water for a bath."

"You don't need to do that."

"I want to."

"Your water still up there?"

"Yes, but I'll throw it out."

"No need."

"What?"

"No need." Yakima snorted a laugh and drew her firmly against him, running his hands down her slender, curving back to her rump lightly encased by the towel. "I'd find it an honor to bathe in your used bathwater, Miss Taggart."

Julia laughed, her gray eyes flashing. "Don't be silly!"

Yakima kissed her forehead, stepped around her, and strode across the kitchen and into the parlor. "I'll see ya upstairs!"

"You idiot! I'll bring the buns and coffee!"

"Can't wait!"

CHAPTER 8

Upstairs in Julia's house, in her small but comfortably appointed bedroom — the bedroom she once shared with Lon, a fact Yakima did his best to try to forget, especially when they were making love in her and Lon's canopied bed — he unbuckled his cartridge belt and hung it over a chair back. He shucked out of his clothes and left them in a dirty pile on the floor by the bed. He'd take them over to a Chinese washhouse later, but, in the meantime, he needed to get his big, red, battle-scarred carcass scrubbed clean.

He was standing in the tub, lathering his legs with a chunk of scented soap and a soft cotton washcloth, when footsteps sounded in the hall outside the door, which he'd left open a foot. Julia nudged the door open with a bare toe and came in carrying a tray bearing two buns and two steaming coffee cups and saucers and a shallow bowl of creamy butter.

"Here we are," she said, setting the tray on a table near the bed.

She turned to him, sidestepped over to the bed, and sat down on the edge of it, tucking one long leg beneath the other one.

Yakima glanced at her twice, then his gaze held on hers. "What is it?"

"Nothing." She gave a coy little smile and nibbled her thumbnail. "I enjoy seeing you naked, that's all."

Yakima dropped the soap and the cloth in the water and straightened. "You have me at a disadvantage."

Her smile broadened. She cast her admiring gaze across his broad, wet shoulders, then down his hard, lumpy chest and across his flat belly to his soap-lathered, half-erect manhood and balls, hanging heavy now with raw male lust. She slid her bent leg out from beneath the other one and rose from the bed. She took one step away from the bed and, gazing deep into Yakima's eyes, reached up with one hand, pulled the towel free from her bosom, held it out to one side with aplomb, and let it drop.

She reached up and unpinned her hair. It tumbled in rich, auburn cascades about her shoulders and breasts, messily framing her face with its mysterious gray eyes, fine delicate nose, and warm sensuous lips. Again, a smile tugged at the corners of her mouth, and a playful light sparked in her eyes as, holding her arms half out to her sides, she turned a slow circle, so that he could feast his hungry eyes on every inch of her pale, beautiful body.

Finally, she stood facing him once more, her large, firm breasts up-tilted and swollen, nipples pebbling.

She slowly lowered her gaze from his eyes to just beyond his belly again, and then returned it to his eyes. "You like what you see, Marshal Henry," she said, huskily. It wasn't a question but a statement of fact.

Yakima swallowed down a tightness in his throat. His heart beat slowly but heavily against his breastbone. "Oh, yeah."

Remembering that he was covered in soap, he lowered himself into the water. Quickly, he rinsed off, squeezed water from his face with his hands, then rose once more to stand facing her in the tub. She'd moved up to him and stood not a foot away. She leaned forward and kissed him hungrily. Yakima placed his hand on her shoulders and drew her tighter against him.

"I missed you," he said, sliding her face away from his.

She smiled and averted her gaze shyly,

showing the tips of her white front teeth beneath her plump upper lip. Slowly, she lifted her gaze to his once more. As she did, she bent her knees and dropped just as slowly to the floor, running her tongue down between the twin slabs of his chest, down over his iron-hard belly . . . down . . . touching the tip of her tongue to the end of his almost painfully jutting cock.

She slid her tongue down the underside of the swollen mast until she was on her knees before him, gently cupping his balls in her hands, licking him, sucking . . .

When he could stand it no longer, he placed his hands on her shoulders, drew her to her feet, stepped out of the tub, took her hand, and led her over to the bed.

She rose onto her toes again and kissed him, smoothed his long, wet hair back behind his ears, then gave him a coquettish smile and crawled into bed, throwing the covers back. She spread herself out before him, extending her arms, reaching for him, a desperate cast of carnal desire making her eyes glisten.

Yakima crawled into the bed. He positioned himself between her legs. He pressed himself flat against her, feeling his staff pressing firmly against the triangle of hair between her thighs. It was warm and wet with desire. He lowered his head to hers, and they kissed tenderly, playfully, hungrily for a long time.

Groaning, she spread her legs and looked up at him, her eyes bright now with an even greater need than before.

"Oh, Yakima," she whispered in his ear as he slid his full length inside her. "Oh . . . oh . . . Yakima . . . you do know how to send me," she said in his ear.

She nibbled his lobe, then groaned as he pulled out of her, to the very edge of her portal, then slid back inside her — slowly, tenderly, enjoying every moment of their union.

When Yakima and Julia had finished making love, they snoozed for a time, entangled in each other's arms and legs. Yakima woke with a start, hearing gunfire beyond the bedroom's open window.

"Oh, no!" Julia said, lifting her head from her pillow.

Yakima sat up and turned to the window, listening intently. There were two more gunshots, neither one close. A man whooped victoriously, and a horse whinnied. Julia wrapped an arm around her lover's waist, drawing herself taut against him. Beyond the window, from the direction of the town's center, another man bellowed an angry roar.

Yakima let out the breath he'd been holding and smiled. He turned to Julia, pressed his lips to her forehead. "Just some drunk drover popping some caps. That last shout was the Kid. He'll take care of it."

Such commotion before sundown was growing more and more common in Apache Springs.

Still, Julia shuddered against Yakima. "I hate that sound. It reminds me of . . ."

"Wilkes?"

She nodded.

"Don't worry." Yakima ran his hand up and down her back, nuzzled her neck. "Wilkes is dead. Nothing like that will ever happen again. Not here. At least, not as long as I'm here. I promise you."

He continued to nuzzle her neck, rubbing her back with his right hand while massaging her breasts with his left. They were warm and supple, swollen with desire.

"You're wonderful — you know that?" Her hand had found his manhood, and she was playing with it, bringing him to life again.

"Because I killed Wilkes?"

"No." She was growing breathless with desire, moving her hand faster. "Because . . . of . . . what you do to me . . . here . . . in bed."

"Oh."

"But also because you killed Wilkes, that wretched bastard!" She threw her head back and squeezed her eyes closed, laughing throatily. Sometimes, in bed, when her guard was down, she reminded him of her more rustic, younger sister, though he shoved that bit of uncomfortable reflection to the back of his mind just now.

Yakima pushed her back down on the bed and made love to her once more.

When they were finished, they lay sweating together, hot from their toil as well as from the furnace-like desert air pushing in through the open window. The sun was angling into the room, laying a trapezoid of yellow-gold light across their sprawled bodies — his large and brown body, her delicate, white one, both glistening with sweat.

Yakima gave a long, luxurious yawn, his desire sated, a pleasing dolor settling over him. He wanted to lie here forever, but, judging by the angle of the light, it was probably nearly five o'clock. He wanted to talk to Señora Galvez.

"I'd best be goin'."

But he didn't move. He just lay there, staring up at the bed's canopy. He found himself feeling very much at home in this bed. Julia rested her head on his chest and was brushing her fingers over the hard slab of his left pectoral and slowly sliding her right leg up and down his thigh.

He dropped his chin to glance down at her. Her eyes were pensive.

"What're you thinking about?"

She rolled her eyes up toward his, and a Y formed in the skin above the bridge of her nose. "Why the back door, Yakima?"

He sighed. "I'm a back-door kinda fella."

She lifted her head to level a direct look at him, her gray eyes penetrating. "Next time, use the front door."

"I don't think that —"

"Yakima" — she sat up and slid her face up to within a foot of his, sandwiching his own face in her hands — "I don't care what anybody thinks. And you shouldn't, either."

"I just don't want them to be hard on you. It can happen if we're not careful. You'll see."

"I don't care."

He placed his hands on her shoulders and returned her gaze with a sincere one of his own. "You will care, Julia. People can be ring-tailed mean, even those you've known a long time and trust. So far, things have gone all right. The badge helps. But if the good citizens of Apache Springs know that

I'm, uh . . . *seein'* . . . a white woman, and not just any white woman but the previous marshal's widow *and* the daughter of Hugh Kos—"

Julia cut him off by placing two fingers over his lips. "Yakima, they already know."

He frowned. "What?"

"They know. At least, some do. I know they know. I can tell."

Yakima took her wrist in his hand, squeezed it gently. "How can you tell?"

"By the looks I get when I'm uptown shopping. Occasionally, I'll catch someone eyeing me as though they didn't think I'd notice." She lifted her head, defiantly shook her hair back from her face. "It doesn't bother me."

"Shit." Yakima turned away, thoughtful, a cold burning starting in the pit of his gut. He'd wanted to prevent such a thing. He hadn't wanted to expose Julia to the same sort of prejudice he himself had to deal with all too often. He was used to it. She wasn't, whatever brave face she wanted to put on it.

What had he been thinking? How long did he think he . . . they . . . would get away with it?

She placed a hand on his cheek, turned his face toward hers. "Yakima." She gazed deeply into his eyes and smiled reassuringly, her gray eyes fairly glowing in the bright western light from the window. "I don't care. It doesn't bother me. Don't you know why?"

His eyebrows furled. "Why?"

She paused, her gaze becoming even more penetrating. "Because I love you."

That set him back on his proverbial heels. He wasn't sure how to respond. *Love.*

Why had he become so afraid of the word? He hadn't realized it, but he had. What horrible torment that one simple word could cause. Torment of so many different kinds.

"Well?" Julia said, narrowing her eyes slightly, probingly. "What do you have to say to *that*, Marshal Henry?"

Yakima looked away again. "You shouldn't."

"Why?"

"Because you shouldn't, Julia. I didn't realize it until just now . . . until you said it." Yakima turned away from her, dropped one foot to the floor. She grabbed his arm, turned him back to face her. "You're not going anywhere. We're not going to leave it like this!"

He placed a hand gently along her jaw, caressed her delicate cheek with his thumb. "Julia, life could get tough. Very tough for

385

you if we —"

She placed her hand on his hand caressing her cheek. "My father is taking care of me. I mean, if it's money you're worried about. How I'm able to support myself. My father stayed out of my life when I was married to Lon. But, now, with Lon dead . . . and all that happened . . . he's paid me a few visits and offered help in keeping me here in Apache Springs. In this house. He paid it off, in fact. He's even offered to hire me to keep his books over at the mercantile. He's expanding his business here in Apache Springs, investing in several different ventures, and he needs all the help he can get. I used to do his books for him, before . . ."

Before Taggart, too lowly for her father's approval, married her and brought her to town and Hugh Kosgrove all but disowned her.

Julia glanced away, as though searching for the words to express what was on her mind. She turned back to Yakima, her eyes resolute. "You make me very happy, Yakima Henry." She smiled and wrapped her arms around his neck, brushed her nipples against his chest. "Very happy, indeed."

She kissed his nose. "I love you. There. I said it again. I love you. A third time!" She dipped her chin and shaped a teasing smile.

"Are you going to shame a girl for loving you?"

He gazed back at her.

Love.

What the hell?

There were worse words, he supposed. Worse ways to feel.

Ride it out, he told himself. *Ride it out, see where it leads. It might surprise you. You might surprise yourself. It happened once. It might happen again. No need to worry about tomorrow.*

Besides, can't you see how happy you — you damned badge-toting, half-breed, drifting fool — have made this woman after all she, like you, has lost?

Suddenly, he felt as though he were teetering atop the razor edge of a tall precipice. Afraid to move forward. Even more afraid to walk away. The room swirled around him. Life offered so few second chances, after all.

And here was one smiling at him now.

"I love you, Julia."

He wrapped his arms around her and kissed her, and they sagged back into the bed together once more.

CHAPTER 9

Later, as long shadows striped the town of Apache Springs, Yakima stepped through Julia's front door and out onto her gallery. He drew the door closed behind him, latching it quietly.

He turned to face the street beyond her yard, beyond the gate in her whitewashed picket fence, abutted on each side by palo verdes. He felt uneasy. The back door, the whole backside of the house, concealed from possible watchers, beckoned him.

He fought off the impulse to turn around and walk back through the house, to head for the concealment of the wash. He moved to the edge of the gallery's steps. A steely resolve tightened inside him. There was no damned reason he should use the back door. She loved him. He loved her. Anyone who didn't like it could go to hell.

He dragged his makings sack out of his shirt pocket and took his time rolling a smoke, standing there on Julia's front gallery, facing the street. He felt good, he realized. Better than he'd felt in a long time. It hadn't come from the mattress dance alone. True, there was nothing like a hot frolic in the proverbial hay with a beautiful woman, but he could get that at Señora Galvez's place, if he wanted to.

There was a lightness in him. A tenderness. The world didn't look as cold, harsh, and unfamiliar as it so often had in the past. His own life didn't feel so desperate.

Love.

Feeling sheepish, but then again not so sheepish . . . feeling good and light on his feet and at home here in Apache Springs . . . finally at home somewhere . . . he scratched a lucifer to life on the buckle of his shell belt and touched the flame to the quirley drooping from between his lips curved in a rare, sappy smile. He blew out the match with a puff of exhaled smoke, flipped it into the dust, and headed toward the gate.

Halfway through the small front yard, he turned to look up at a second-story window.

She stood there, waving, just as he knew she would be.

He chuckled and waved, then turned and opened the gate and stepped through it. When he'd drawn the gate closed behind him, he turned to the street. Two older women were just then walking along the avenue's far side, heading in the direction of Main Street. Both women, gray-haired and dressed in the wan colors and poke bonnets of their aproned lot, one bespectacled, gave him the wooly eyeball as they passed.

Yakima pinched his hat brim to the women and smiled. "Good afternoon, ladies!"

They turned abruptly away and continued walking, one leaning toward the other one, whispering. The disapproving biddies didn't bother Yakima. He had something they likely did not.

Whistling softly, feeling as light as an unabashed schoolboy in love, he followed the two biddies to Main Street, then hung a right and continued west toward Señora Galvez's place, identified by a single, understated sign under the gallery's front eave announcing simply, *SEÑORA GALVEZ.* The sign was enhanced by the red lamp burning in the white-curtained window to the right of the door. As Yakima started up the gallery's steps, he thought that above the horse and wagon traffic behind him he could hear a commotion inside — someone stomping around, girls gasping and yelling.

Inside, another, louder sound rose above

the others — a man's enraged bellow.

Yakima hurried across the gallery and was reaching for the door when it opened suddenly. Señora Galvez stood in the doorway, copper-brown eyes flashing alarm.

"*¡Mierda!*" she said in surprise, stepping back in shock at the big half-breed standing before her, placing one hand on her heavy breast clad in several layers of silk and lace.

Alfonsina Galvez had a long, black wooden cigarette holder in her beringed right hand, and the air around her was rife with the peppery aroma of Mexican tobacco. "I was just going to send someone to fetch you. It's dire. Such animals!" She turned to yell up the stairs rising just inside the foyer, against its left wall. "*¡Bastardos! Pigs!* What have I told you about fighting in my place?"

The commotion was coming from the second story — men's shouting, heavy foot thuds. A fight.

"I'll handle it." Yakima brushed past the madam and headed up the stairs, taking the carpeted steps two at a time. Several girls, most half-dressed in underwear and light, colored wraps, ribbons in their hair, had gathered at the near end of the second-floor hall, and they were spilling onto the landing, all looking anxious as they stared down the hall to their right.

"Excuse me, ladies," Yakima said, nudging one of the frightened doxies aside as he stepped into the hall.

Ahead were two men. One was dressed only in long handles. He was the bigger of the two, but they were both big men. Yakima recognized the long-handle-clad gent as a crew chief for the spur line laying rails south of Apache Springs, connecting the town with the Southern Pacific line.

This was Mordicai Gunnison — a big, red-haired, red-bearded Irishman with a swirl of garish tattoos on his thick neck. The second man was Jim Halsey, a big, black-haired, black-bearded Scot freighter working for Nordstrom's Freighting out of Tucson, which had just opened an office in Apache Springs. They'd been contracted to haul ties for the spur line. Halsey wore shabby, dusty fringed buckskins, a hickory shirt, and suspenders, his shirtsleeves rolled up his muscular, brown forearms. A black bowler lay on the floor near his feet.

Both men had knives in their hands, and they were skirmishing, slashing at each other in the middle of the narrow hall, circling one another and cursing loudly. The Irishman called the Scot a dog-fucking son of a bitch, and the big Scot jerked his head forward to spit in Gunnison's face.

That enraged Gunnison even more, who brushed a big hand down his cheek and lunged at his opponent once more, the savage-looking blade of the big Bowie slashing through the air before Halsey, causing the big Scot to leap back with a startled grunt.

The Irishman's blade had sliced across Halsey's shirt, showing a thin line of red. "Bloody bastard!" the Scot roared. "I'm gonna gut you dirty for that one, ya ugly mick — and choke ya with your own entrails!"

"That's enough now, fellas," Yakima said, moving forward. "Put the blades away and play nice, or I'm going to take you both over to the lockup!"

"Stay out of this, breed!" yelled Gunnison, keeping his eyes on his opponent, who'd recovered enough that he was parrying with his adversary once more, both men lunging forward to slash, then jerking back to avoid their opponent's slicing blade.

"What the hell's this about?" Yakima asked, continuing to walk slowly forward.

"None o' your business, breed!" Halsey made another swipe at Gunnison's belly, nipping a button from the front of the man's balbriggan top.

One of the girls behind Yakima said loudly enough to be heard above the men's stomping feet, grunts, and curses, "Halsey doesn't want the mick screwin' Kansas Kate!"

"I done warned him," Halsey bellowed, making another slash at Gunnison — this one aimed for the Irishman's throat. "I don't want him stickin' his slimy Irish dick in my gal!"

"I ain't your gal, Jim!" a girl who was obviously Kansas Kate screamed furiously behind Yakima. Her voice owned a definite Southern lilt. "I done told you that! I ain't givin' neither one of you two shit heels a poke ever again! I done had it with the both of you privy-skulkin' varmints!"

Halsey wheeled toward Yakima but cast his gaze toward the girls huddled on the landing behind him. "Why, you sassy little — *achhh-ohhhh, jayzuzzz!*"

Yakima had just stepped forward to kick the knife out of the man's clenched fist. The Bowie flew straight up to bounce off the ceiling before hitting the hall floor in front of Halsey, who grabbed his right wrist with his left hand and bellowed, crouching against the wall to Yakima's right.

"Ohhhh, sweet merciful Jesus — the fuckin' Injun done broke my wrist!"

Yakima had seen Gunnison, crouched low

394

and grinning devilishly, lunge forward, jabbing his own Bowie toward Yakima's belly. Ready for it, the lawman jerked back and sideways. The Irishman grunted, then stumbled forward, propelled past Yakima by his own momentum. When he was just beyond Yakima's right shoulder, Yakima chopped his own hand down hard against the back of the man's neck.

The Irishman bellowed, legs buckling, knees hitting the floor with a thunderous boom. He tried reaching for the knife. Yakima delivered two powerful left jabs to the man's right ear. Gunnison's head slammed against the wall.

He froze for a moment, on his knees, eyes rolling up in their sockets. Slowly, his arms sagged, and he leaned forward. He gave a shrill sigh, as though he'd suddenly become deeply tired, and crumpled like a pile of dirty laundry, out like a light.

"You red-skinned son of a bitch!" This from the Scottish freighter, Halsey, still holding his right wrist, which was cast at an odd angle and had a nasty-looking lump in it, with his left hand. He knelt on the other side of Gunnison. His big, bearded face was a mask of red fury, molasses-dark eyes sparking flames. "You broke my fuckin' wrist! I can't skin a team without my wrist!"

Yakima turned to him and pitched his voice with soft menace. "If you don't stop your caterwauling, Jim, I'm gonna break the other wrist and shove both hands so far up your ass you'll be able to scratch your tonsils!"

One of the girls behind Yakima muffled a laugh with her hand.

Another voice — this one a man's — said, "Well, I was just gonna ask you if you needed any assistance, but . . ."

Yakima turned to see the Rio Grande Kid standing behind him, holding his long-barreled, double-bore Greener up high across his broad chest and staring down at the two fighters — one out like a blown lamp, the other on his knees, glaring and gritting his teeth at the half-breed lawman. Yakima saw that Galveston Penny had come with the Kid, both deputies probably having heard reports of violence at Señora Galvez's place through word on the street.

Young Penny stood on the landing behind the Kid, his hat in his hands. He was grinning like a coyote with a mouth full of cockleburs as he chatted with a small, plump, Mexican girl with a heart-shaped face and wearing a little pink corset under a powder-blue wrap as thin as a butterfly's wing, and not a whole lot else.

Señorita Clara — barefoot, her hair in braids — smiled coquettishly up at young Penny, who was a good head taller than the comely young *puta*. The pair could have been on a separate planet, for all the awareness either seemed to have of the dustup that had just occurred a mere ten feet beyond the landing.

Yakima loudly cleared his throat and said, "Excuse me, Casanova."

He had to say it two more times, each time a little louder, before Penny finally looked at him, his face and ears suddenly turning crimson. He bounded forward and said, "You callin' me, Marshal?"

"If you're not too busy, I was wondering if you could help the Kid cart this brainless sack of Irish shit out to the street. Dump some water on him. When he wakes up, make sure he understands that he's been banned from town for two months."

Yakima glanced at Halsey. "That goes for you, too, Jim. If I see either of you two chuckleheads in town within two months, you're gonna be spending that long in the lockup — when I don't have you volunteering your time mucking out stalls in one of the livery barns, I mean."

Halsey hauled himself to his feet and, grimacing over the broken wrist he held against his chest like an injured sparrow, stumbled up to Yakima. Keeping his voice low, but hard with menace, he said, "I'm gonna kill you for this." He winked. "You can put money on that . . . *breed*!"

He'd shoved his face up close to Yakima's before spewing that last.

Yakima smiled. Then he drew his right arm back and shot it forward, plunging his clenched fist deep into the Scot's midsection. Halsey jackknifed, his wind gushing out of him with the ferocity of a cyclone, and hit the floor again on his knees.

"You can't say I didn't warn you not to try, Jim."

"Ohhh!" Halsey cried, bowing his head as though genuflecting in church. *"Ohhhh!"*

The Kid, working a wad of chaw around in his mouth, stepped up beside Yakima. "Want I should lock this one up, boss?" He stared down at the miserably groaning Scot. "Might be a good idea. Keep an eye on him, you know." He looked at Yakima, then leaned toward him and said quietly, "Or take him south of town an' blow his head off? Give him a *proper* burial?"

He smiled deviously, sucking the chaw against his gums.

"No need," Yakima said. "I think Jim got the message."

Señora Galvez had been watching the hall's festivities from the landing with her girls. Now, wielding her cigarette holder like a weapon, she walked up beside Yakima, and, holding a lacy cape about her otherwise bare, freckled shoulders, glared down at the burly Scot. "The marshal might have only barred you from town for two months, Señor Halsey. But you are banned for life from these premises. *¿Comprende, amigo?*"

Halsey looked up at her, black eyes bright with rage. He opened his mouth to spout an ungentlemanly retort, but then he saw Yakima staring down with a menacing half smile, and he merely gritted his teeth and averted his gaze.

"Out!" the Kid yelled at the Scot, stepping back and clicking his Greener's hammers back. "Before I revert to my old outlaw ways!"

When the Kid had shepherded Halsey down the stairs and he and Galveston Penny had carried the still-unconscious Gunnison down the stairs and onto the gallery, Señora Galvez turned to Yakima, removing the cigarette holder from her painted mouth and blowing smoke toward the ceiling.

She looked the half-breed lawman up and down speculatively, taking his measure, and said, "I would warn another man to watch his back. Halsey is a killer. He might skin mules for a living, but on the side he's a killer. I should have banned him long ago."

"What do you mean you'd warn another man?"

"You can take care of yourself just fine." She drew on the cigarette holder again and crooked the other half of her mouth with approval. Her gaze fell to Yakima's hand hanging at his side. "Do you need something for that?"

Yakima lifted the hand and inspected the knuckles, some of the skin of which he must have left on Halsey's ear. Before he could respond, a young blonde with henna-rinsed hair stepped forward, extending a length of white flannel. She wore only a thin chemise — so thin that it made her small, pert breasts appear all but bare.

"Here," she said. "And . . . thanks, Marshal."

Yakima accepted the cloth. "Kansas Kate?"

The girl nodded, smiled. She was tall and slender and rather plain-faced, but there was an attractive earthiness in her pale-blue eyes. A pale, white scar curved down over her jaw on the right side of her face, two inches in front of her ear.

"He won't be back," Yakima said, wrapping the cloth around his hand. "I'll see to it."

"Like I said," Kansas Kate said, shaking her hair back from her cheeks, which had colored a little, "thanks."

"You can go, now, Kate," Señora Galvez said crisply and blew another plume of smoke toward the ceiling. "The marshal and I have something to discuss."

Kansas Kate smiled at Yakima once more, then turned, let the strap of her chemise tumble off her shoulder, and flounced away down the hall and into a near room, casting one more coy look back at the big lawman before closing and latching her door.

When Yakima and the Mexican madam were standing alone in the hall, Señora Galvez said, "You can have her for free if you like. For what you did here today and for the two you hauled in dead. I'll give you two hours. You can do what you like, just don't leave any bruises. I have trouble getting girls way out here, even more trouble keeping them."

Yakima shrugged, shook his head. "Not necessary."

Señra Galvez frowned as she studied him probingly. "Is it the scar?"

"Hell, no. I got plenty of those myself."

"What, then?"

Yakima put some authoritative steel in his voice as he said, "Let's just say it's not necessary, Señora Galvez, and leave it at that."

"All right." The madam smiled a little woodenly, looking him up and down once more, obviously puzzled.

Señora Galvez was a woman who liked to get a firm handle on those around her, to know who or what they were exactly, probably so that she could manipulate them when needed. She wasn't pleased when Yakima's handle didn't come as easily as she would have liked.

"Have it your way, big man," she said with more than a little frustration. "Can I buy you a drink?"

"I'd take a beer."

She arched a brow, again taken aback by the man before her. "Just beer?"

"The firewater turns me into Halsey," Yakima said with a wry smile.

"¡Cristos!" Señora Galvez laughed, then turned and beckoned with her smoldering cigarette holder. "Come!"

CHAPTER 10

Yakima followed the madam along the whorehouse's third-floor hall, her tail wind rife with the smell of peppery Mexican tobacco and a not overly cloying perfume.

The half-breed wasn't an authority on fragrances, but he had a feeling what he was smelling now wasn't the cheap sort sold for a dollar or two a bottle at the mercantile. This, like the freight wagons that had pulled up to the whorehouse not long after the last shake shingle was nailed to its roof, its paint still drying on its clapboard siding, had probably come from Mexico City, which was from where the madam was rumored to hail.

Señora Galvez was also rumored to be a refugee of a scandal of some sort, likely involving powerful men in the Mexican government. Very little bonded fact was known about Señora Galvez beyond that her opulent furnishings had been shipped from Mexico City, and that the madam herself had followed them a week later in a fine carriage guarded by dusky-skinned, mustachioed Mexican men dressed in wagon wheel *sombreros*, brightly colored and ruffle-fronted *camisas*, bell-bottomed and elaborately embroidered *charro* slacks, and short leather jackets. Her *caballero* entourage had also been heavily armed.

Her men had lingered in town for a few days, presumably helping the madam settle in to her new abode. They left early one morning before anyone else in Apache Springs had been out and about. Aside from its newly reappointed town marshal, that is . . .

A door opened ahead of the madam, and a girl came out of a room, stretching sleepily. She was a young, tall, impossibly slender Mexican with vaguely Indio features and long, coarse black hair, some of which was braided with strips of dyed rawhide. Señora Galvez grabbed the girl's arm and said in rapid Spanish, "Eva, summon Clara, *por favor*. Tell her to fetch a bottle of cool ale from the springhouse and come to my office *pronto*."

"*Si, si, Señora,*" said Eva, all painted up and decked out in a pink corset and black and silver bustier for the night ahead. Sleep lines from a pillow remained in her otherwise smooth, dark-brown cheeks.

In passing, she gave Yakima a long, slow blink with her muddy eyes and brushed the very tips of her fingers across his arm, smiling devilishly and flouncing off down the hall.

"Eva, don't act like a child!" the madam admonished the girl, who was already on the stairs, chuckling throatily.

The madam sighed and threw open the door at the end of the hall, on the hall's left side.

"They are like herding cats, these girls. *Por favor,*" she said, extending an arm to indicate the small but nicely appointed office before her. "There is some dust, but I can't find a girl who cleans to my preferences. They are barbarians, mostly. Nothing like the girls in the city. Have a seat."

Yakima approached a leather armchair angled in front of a leather-topped desk adorned with a pink lamp that resembled an exotic, long-legged water bird. Likely shipped all the way to the Sierra Estrada from Mexico City.

"No," the madam said, brusquely. "Not there. There." She indicated a short, red velvet sofa fronting a cold, brick fireplace and a small table topped with a cut-glass decanter and two brandy snifters atop a polished silver tray.

Yakima considered the sofa, shrugged, and doffed his hat. He walked over and sagged into the sofa, angling toward Señora Galvez as she took a seat beside him, on the sofa's other end. She gazed at him with a vague curiosity as she drew on her cigarette holder, making the tip of the cigarette glow.

She was an amazingly beautiful woman, Yakima saw now, in the light of two large windows facing them. She was probably in her late thirties or early forties, judging by the crows' feet around her almond-shaped, light-brown eyes, and around her plump-lipped mouth.

Her cheeks were still firm and smooth, the color of varnished walnut. Her lashes were long and dark. Yakima had never been this close to the madam — in fact, he'd only seen her from a distance a handful of times in all the months she'd been in town — but he saw now that she had at one time been ravishing and was still beautiful. Handsome, he supposed is what most would call her now. He himself would still call her right fetching.

No wonder she'd gotten in trouble with the rich and powerful in Mexico. A woman as beautiful as the one before him could cause quite a war down south of the border.

"What's funny?"

Yakima hadn't realized he'd been smiling.

"Oh, uh . . . nothing."

She smiled with faint, good-humored sarcasm and poked the cigarette holder between her rich, bee-stung lips once more, drawing deeply, then holding her breath. "Share your thoughts with me, Marshal," she urged, letting smoke trickle out her nostrils.

"I was considering the rumors about you. Stacking them up beside the woman I see now."

"Rumors, eh?"

"Sure."

"And who is the woman you see . . . just out of friendly curiosity?"

"A most beautiful one, Señora Galvez."

She turned her head slightly to one side, smiling with one half of her mouth, skeptically. "Are you flirting with me, Marshal Henry?"

"Not at all, Señora. You asked me what I was thinking, and I told you. You're a beautiful woman. A mysterious one."

"I see. Well, do you know that you are shrouded in your own cloud of rumors, uh . . . what was your first name again?"

"Yakima."

"Yakima. Interesting. Indio, I take it."

"Half."

"I see." She frowned again as she nibbled the end of her cigarette holder. "Don't you want to know what the girls say about you?"

"The girls?"

"The girls in my employ. Oh, they are quite interested in the handsome, Indio town marshal. They watch from the balconies, muttering among themselves like lovelorn schoolgirls. Few have seen a red man wearing a badge. They are partly fearful, remembering the Apache depredations of recent history — some of my girls were orphaned by the *Coyoteros* — and partly attracted. *Intrigado,* I guess would be the right word. Intrigued."

Yakima chuffed with self-deprecation. "I won't spoil the mystery for them."

"They'd love to have it spoiled. In their beds, of course. They get tired of the more common fare around here." She flipped a hand, lit with several sparkling rings, toward a window, indicating the town beyond.

She smiled more broadly, showing her fine, white teeth, brown eyes flashing more than a little coquettishly. Still, Yakima didn't think she was flirting with him. Maybe building an alliance? Against what or whom, he didn't know. He had a feeling the mysterious, beautiful Mexican madam was in the habit, shaped by necessity, of building allegiances.

"How come I never see you over here, Marshal? You might wear a badge, but you're still a man . . . with a man's needs. I certainly don't take you for a Nancy-boy."

Yakima chuckled. "No. Nothin' like that. Frankly, Señora, I'm just too damn busy to think about it all that much."

"How terrible for you!" She feigned a pout, pooching out her erotic lips. "Anytime you want, I'll stake you to a couple of free hours with the girl of your choice. Any time at all, Marshal Henry." She held his gaze, continuing to probe him, her curiosity about him fairly boiling over inside her.

He had to admit feeling more than a little curious about the madam, but she owned the air of a woman who held her own cloak of secrecy very closely about her shoulders. He was only mildly curious, anyway. He had enough to worry about in the here and now in Apache Springs.

"I'll keep that in mind, Señora," Yakima said. "But I'll probably be passin' on it, just the same." Julia was enough for him.

A knock came at the door.

Señora Galvez winced slightly, as though she wasn't ready for their conversation to be over just yet. As though there was more she wanted to know about Apache Springs's half-breed marshal. Or maybe there was more that she wanted to discuss.

Fatefully, she sighed. "That will be Clara." She turned to yell behind her, "Come, Clara!"

The door latch clicked, and the door opened. The pretty little Mexican girl — the apple of Galveston Penny's eye — came in holding a tray a little uncertainly before her, a beer bottle wobbling atop the tray. Clara chewed her lower lip with concentration. The young *puta* was dressed for the night ahead in an intoxicating black velvet negligee that dipped so low in front that it covered only the tips of her small, tan breasts. The girl wore a small, black, velvet box cap pinned at an angle atop her head. The cap was adorned with a black velvet bow. Dark-brown braids trailed down over her shoulders.

Several strands of *faux* pearl necklaces hung down her chest. Her brown legs were bare between long, black, sheer stockings that rose to just above her knees, held in place with a red velvet and black garter belt, and a pair of very short, red lace bloomers edged in silver.

On her feet were black satin shoes with

pointed toes and three-inch square heels, black buttons running down the insides.

Yakima felt a pang of chagrin at the male heat rising in him as the girl walked past him, nearly stumbling over her own shoes, and leaned down to set the tray on the table. The negligee dipped away from her chest, giving him a complete picture of her tender, brown-nippled breasts. Her necklaces swung down and would have tipped the beer bottle she was trying to balance on the tray if Yakima hadn't reached forward to catch it.

The *senorita,* dolled up to entice the gentlemen of Apache Springs, had the air of a small girl playing dress up. A small girl filling out nicely, however. There it was again — the twinge of lust in the half-breed's denims. His ear tips warmed in shame. Now he saw up close what had so attracted Galveston Penny to the pretty little *senorita* whose sensitive eyes betrayed a tender heart.

Penny likely had the urge to take her away from all this.

"Oh, Clara, *please,*" admonished the madam. "I have shown you girls so many times how to set down a tray." She glanced at Yakima. "See what I mean? Barbarians!"

"*¡Lo siento, Señora!*" the girl cried, straightening and covering her breasts with the tray.

411

"You wanted to see me?" she continued in Spanish, glancing a little shyly at Yakima as she stepped back toward the cold fireplace climbing the wall behind her.

"*Si, si* — I did not summon you to show off your serving skills." Señora Galvez had plucked a ready-made cigarette from a wooden box on the table before her and was sticking it into her holder. "Go ahead — tell Marshal Henry what you overheard the two *gringos* discussing last night."

Clara shifted her eyes again to Yakima. "They thought I was asleep," she whispered. "When the one had finished with me, the other one came in and sat in a chair."

"Clara, speak up," the madam urged. "We can't hear you."

Yakima leaned forward, resting his elbows on his knees, and smiled reassuringly at the obviously anxious doxie. "It's all right. You're safe in here, *senorita.* What were these two *gringos* discussing?"

"A job of some kind," she said, clearing her throat and squeezing the tray in her hands. "A hold-up job, I think. They didn't say that, but I could tell it was something like that. Something against the law."

Clara took an anxious step forward, staring down at Yakima. "*Senor,* er . . . Marshal Henry . . ." She swallowed, hesitating, squeezing the tray even harder in her small hands.

"Yes, *senorita,*" Yakima prodded gently, dipping his chin. "Continue."

"They were men from the fire. From the men who set the fire. Two years ago. Remember? These two were part of that bunch, and, from what I heard, I think there are more men from that gang in Apache Springs."

Yakima's heart quickened. Six from Wilkes's original gang of twelve hadn't been brought to justice. The bunch had split up out in the desert, and Yakima, the Rio Grande Kid, and Emma Kosgrove had gone after the bunch led by Wilkes, because Wilkes had kidnapped Julia. Yakima had assumed the six survivors had continued on to Mexico, where he'd figured they were still cooling their hills after burning the town.

"How do you know?" he asked the girl.

"From what they said about the fire. And . . . because I remembered one of them." Clara's voice lowered again, and she looked downward, eyes bright with remembered horror. "The one who lay with me last night."

A wetness glazed the girl's eyes. A tear rolled down her cheek. It tumbled off her chin and onto the toe of her left shoe. "I was working the line then, too. Here in Apache Springs . . . when they came to town that day. Two of them broke into Mrs. Fitzsimmons's house and shot some of the girls." Mrs. Fitzsimmons owned a brothel the gang had burned, killing the madam herself. "They savaged the girls. Raped them brutally, making them cry, making them scream! I hid under a bed upstairs and watched in horror. I will never forget that night. I remember the man who came to me last night from that night two years ago. He savaged a girl in front of me, in the room we shared, and cut her throat before my eyes."

Clara hardened her jaws and gritted her teeth, more tears rolling down her cheeks. "I was terrified when I saw him. I recognized him right away. He has very black hair. It waves down across his forehead." She brushed one of her own hands across her own forehead. "A black mustache, too. A thick one. But it is his eyes that stand out. They are the deepest, darkest blue I have ever seen. There is no good in them. No good at all. Do you know what I mean?"

"I know what you mean."

"When he finished with me last night, I pretended to fall asleep. In reality, I was terrified that he would cut my throat. He took a long time, and he was very angry by the end. He was dressing when the other one came in, a blond man with black *chaparreras.* He sat in a chair, and the blue-eyed man sat down on the bed, and while I feigned sleep they shared a jug of whiskey and smoked and talked about the big job they had planned."

"But they weren't specific? They didn't say exactly what this big job was?"

"No." Again, Clara lowered her eyes to the floor and hesitated before adding, "But they said they had one important task before they did that job they were talking about."

"Did they say what that task was?"

Clara lifted her chin and looked at Yakima directly. "To kill you . . . the Indio lawman. They said they were looking forward to 'settling up for two years ago.' "

"Ah," Yakima said. They must have learned that the current town marshal, the badge-toting half-breed, had been one of the men who'd chased them into the desert two years ago and killed half their bunch, including Wilkes.

They were probably still chafed by that. And wanted revenge, as well as to get him out of their way.

What else did they want? What big job did they have planned?

"Is there anything else, Clara?" Señora Galvez asked the girl sharply. "Come, come — out with the rest. Don't let the cat get your tongue!"

The girl jerked, startled by the madam's own sharp tongue. She shook her head. "That is all."

"You didn't get their names?" Yakima asked. "The two men in your room?"

Clara furled her brows, thinking. "The blue-eyed man didn't tell me his name. But I heard him call the blond-haired man Les."

"Les?"

"*Si.*"

"All right, then," Yakima said. "I'm much obliged, Clara. If you happen to see either of them in town again, let me know, will you?"

"*Si,* I will." She glanced at the madam. "May I go, Señora?"

"*Si,* you're excused." Señora Galvez waved the smoldering cigarette holder at the door. "Go down and play the piano. That will calm your nerves."

"*Si.*" The girl walked to the door and went out.

Señora Galvez glanced at Yakima. "You'd better watch your back."

"I reckon," Yakima said with a sigh, rising. "I appreciate you letting me know about this, Señora." He started toward the door.

"You haven't even opened your beer. Why don't you stay a while, drink with me? A woman gets lonely in this big house with all these young women running about half-dressed, reminding her how old and ugly she's getting."

Yakima stopped at the door and turned back to the madam still sitting on the sofa, half-turned toward him. "Is that why you're so . . . so . . . ." Yakima looked around as though searching for the right word. "So short with these girls? You resent their youth?"

She studied him from the sofa. Yakima saw a fiery light blaze in her light-brown eyes, but then it dwindled, and she said, "Being a man, you wouldn't understand what it's like being a woman. Being an aging woman."

"You're a beautiful woman, Señora."

"*Gracias*," she said automatically, as though the compliment were no real comfort.

Yakima studied her, turning his hat slowly in his hands. He considered what he'd heard about her relationship with Cleve Dundee, and then decided to go ahead and ask the impertinent question: "No man in your life?"

She shook her head, and suddenly her eyes, once ready to catch fire, betrayed a deep inner sorrow. "No man. At least, not in the way you mean." She turned her head forward and drew on the cigarette holder.

He thought that was a shame. He didn't know Señora Galvez very well, but he thought he could like her. And he knew how important it was to have someone in one's life. He couldn't help feeling at long last fortunate in that regard.

"Good night, Señora," Yakima said, setting his hat on his head.

"Oh, call me Alfonsina, won't you?" Glancing at him over her shoulder, she shaped a slow smile, adding, "Yakima . . ."

"Alfonsina it is. Good night and thanks."

"Good night, Yakima. Be careful out there. Wolves are on the prowl, and this town is getting wilder by the day."

Yakima opened the door and left the somber madam on her sofa, smoking, hearing the wolves yipping and snarling inside her own head.

Chapter 11

Yakima went downstairs and stepped outside onto the small gallery fronting the whorehouse. He'd heard a deep rumbling while he was inside the house, and now he saw what was causing it.

One of Hugh Kosgrove's ore trains was pulling through town, heading from east to west along Main Street. The pass upon which Apache Springs sat was the only negotiable route from the Conquistador to the Southern Pacific line to the southwest. From there the ore would be transported via train to the smelter at Tucson. From the smelter, the ingots would be sent to the US Mint in San Francisco.

Soon, the spur line would transport the gold, but until the rails had been laid, Kosgrove had to move his ore via the large, mule-drawn ore drays now moving past Señora Galvez's place. The heavy-wheeled, stout-axled, high-sided Bascom wagons kicked up as much dust as a Texas twister. In fact, standing on the gallery, Yakima couldn't see much *except* the dust. He couldn't smell much of anything except the mules.

He could hear the mule skinners yelling at their six-hitch teams, hear the blacksnakes popping above the teams' backs and the thunderous clomping of the mules' shod hooves, as well as the noisy, squeaky clatter of the wagon wheels that were nearly as tall as Yakima himself. Vaguely and occasionally, he could see one of Kosgrove's heavily armed outriders trotting past in the roiling dust, a vague figure holding a rifle or shotgun on his shoulder or high across his chest, neckerchief drawn up over his mouth and nose.

Yakima knew that many of the town's inhabitants would welcome the day that Kosgrove's wagons no longer bisected Apache Springs. The townsfolk complained about the earthquake-like shaking and the din of the monstrous teams and wagons, and about the dust that sifted for nearly an hour after the last team and wagon had passed on out of town, after pausing for water at the springs at the town's edge. Two years ago, the town had preferred the ore trains passing through once every two or three weeks to the spur-line train that would likely come and go through the very heart of town at least twice weekly.

Now, with a mostly new population in the wake of the marauders' burning of the original town, the sentiment had changed. The new folks, mostly lured here by gold in the surrounding mountains, wanted the growth and prosperity a railroad would bring.

Yakima himself was wary. He'd seen what "prosperity" had done to other towns across the west. Then again, he'd found himself unexpectedly liking it here, though Julia Taggart had played no small part in that, and prosperity meant his job was reasonably secure. It was also nice to see folks living relatively happily and comfortably, and he liked being a part of such a community.

"You Henry?"

Yakima hadn't realized someone had ridden up to the gallery he was standing on. Now he saw the gent materializing from the swirling dust, holding a Colt revolving rifle across the bows of his saddle and tugging a red bandanna down beneath his chin. He was a tall, mustached man riding a high-stepping Arabian steeldust.

"I'm Henry."

"Jake Salko, foreman on Kosgrove's ore

train." His horse was prancing around, excited by the commotion of the wagons and mules and other outriders moving behind him. "Mister Kosgrove wanted me to invite you out to the Conquistador tomorrow for noon dinner. Twelve sharp." He put some slack in his horse's reins, and the Arab bolted on down the street like grapeshot fired from a cannon, Salko calling over his shoulder, "Don't be late!"

"Invitation, huh?" Yakima said, mostly to himself, running a hand across his cheek and staring after Salko and the last of the five ore wagons rocking and thundering on out of town.

"Sounds more like an order to me."

Yakima turned to see the Kid walk around from the end of the gallery on Yakima's left and stop at the gallery's left corner, gazing after the ore train. Thick dust blocked the view in that direction.

"Yeah," Yakima said, thoughtful. "Me, too."

"You suppose he's got trouble out there?"

"I reckon I'll find out tomorrow."

As town marshal, Yakima's official jurisdiction ended at the edge of Apache Springs. But since the county sheriff was quartered in Tucson, sixty miles away, Yakima assumed the role of deputy sheriff when trouble beckoned from the far reaches of the county. The sheriff, Henry Stafford, had swung through Apache Springs to swear him in. The growing city of Tucson and its surrounding environs kept the portly, middle-aged sheriff and his deputies hopping; they had no time to investigate every rustled cow or jumped mine around Apache Springs. Such problems were up to Yakima and his own two deputy town marshals.

"Want me to ride out there with you?" the Kid asked, setting his Greener on his shoulder and squinting one eye at his boss. "That's trouble country. Outlaws hole up in them canyons between town and the Conquistador. Some renegade 'Paches, too. I know all too well. When I was lookin' for Eddie's treasure, a coupla them bronco 'Pache braves got the wrong idea that this old man would be an easy mark for his hoss and the change in his pockets."

The Kid spat to one side. "Let's just say they was wrong. They're snugglin' with the diamondbacks now for their foolishness." He ran a stout, freckled forearm across his mouth and grinned.

"Don't doubt it a bit," Yakima said. "But I need you here in town."

He told the Kid about what he'd learned from young Clara in Señora Galvez's office, about the two men who were likely survivors from Wilkes's gang of town-burning marauders.

"You don't say?" the Kid said in astonishment. "You know, I was wonderin' what became of the second half of that bunch."

"I figured they were in Mexico."

"I reckon I figured as much. What job you think they might be plannin'?"

"I got no idea. Maybe the bank. Maybe the Busted Flush. Lord knows Dundee's got enough money movin' through his swing doors every day an' night. He'd be a tasty target."

"I'll tell him to keep his cash box locked."

"You do that. Inform Galveston. You both be on the lookout for that black-haired gent with the dead blue eyes and his sidekick, some blond-headed fella named Les." Yakima stepped down off the gallery's front steps and into the street, where the dust from the ore train was still sifting. "I'm gonna take a stroll around town, see what I can see. Then I'll head back to the office and make like I'm catching up on some of that consarned paperwork."

"Sounds good, boss," the Kid said. "But, say, about Eddie's treasure map . . ."

Yakima glanced over his shoulder at the older man. "Kid, didn't you hear what I just told you? We got more important things to worry about than Eddie's treasure map!"

Yakima quickened his step as he headed east along the main drag.

"All right," the Kid yelled behind him. "But we'll be powwowin' on that very topic soon enough, by Jim! This old outlaw don't cotton to claim jumpers!"

Yakima knew he could prolong the Kid's inquiry only so long. The old outlaw had a right to know about the treasure map. Yakima's predicament lay in how to tell the Kid about the missing map — or about how Yakima figured it was missing — without telling him about the canyon full of cursed Apache gold.

The next morning, at nearly midday, the sun straight up and nary a shadow anywhere around, the sun beating down to the rhythm of several hidden cicadas, Yakima reined Wolf to a halt on a low pass littered with boulders and saguaros as well as several other varieties of cactus and wiry desert shrub.

A few minutes ago, he'd started hearing a loud but distant din from dead ahead, issuing from a broad canyon between whose natural stone gates he was now. The din consisted of drumming and squawking sounds. The industrious cacophony told Yakima that he was nearing Hugh Kosgrove's Conquistador mine. As he'd continued to ride toward the canyon gaping before him, the sounds had quickly grown louder.

Now, sitting atop the low pass at the canyon's mouth, he stared off over a devil's playground of up-thrust rock and knife-slash arroyos to a distant sandstone and limestone ridge with a large black hole in it — the Conquistador itself.

Yakima had not been out here to these far reaches of the Sierra Estrada, a good two-hour ride on a good horse from Apache Springs. He'd never had reason to ride this far into the high and rocky — no previous invitation to join Kosgrove for his midday meal or any other meal. In fact, while the half-breed lawman had seen Hugh Kosgrove in town more than a few times over the past months, now that the man was investing largely in several Apache Springs businesses, Yakima had never been formally introduced to the former eastern speculator and general mucky-muck turned Arizona mine owner.

And father of two lovely daughters, Yakima couldn't help reminding himself, though it wasn't something he was liable to forget, both young women having played fairly large roles in Yakima's life in that he'd slept with both of them. And had fallen in love with one.

He eased his mind away from that bit of unnecessary distraction and concentrated on the canyon before him.

He saw what was making the thundering, squawking sounds. Ore cars were being rolled out of the mine's black mouth onto what appeared to be a short trestle bridge sprouting from the side of the rocky cliff. The ore cars were rolled by hand by two or three men, little larger than ants from this distance, out to the end of the bridge and then upended.

The upending was what caused the squawking. The thundering sounds, owning several variations in pitch, were caused by the ore from the rail cars striking the giant wooden bin jutting from the shoulder of the mountain below the bridge. The thundering was also caused by the louvered steel doors of the ore cars slamming shut before being latched by one of the attending miners.

Then the cars were wheeled back into the mine on a separate return track for another load of gold-rich ore.

"Damned hot, dirty, bone-grinding job," Yakima muttered to himself now.

He knew that for a fact, for he'd worked for such a mine a time or two, for as long as he could take it, which hadn't been long.

He'd just touched Wolf with his spurs to start down the far side of the pass, following a trail cut deep by the shod rims of many ore wagons, when he pulled back on the reins again sharply. Hooves thudded, growing quickly louder. Two horseback riders were approaching at a fast clip.

He could see them converging on the main trail from about fifty yards ahead and to either side of the trail. Mostly, he could see dust and brief glimpses of the riders' hats as they raced over the harsh, broken terrain.

Both riders converged on the main trail and continued toward Yakima before galloping around a sharp bend in the trail, dashing out from behind a bulging belly of white rock, and reining their own mounts to skidding halts.

Both men carried rifles.

The man on the left took his Winchester in both hands, loudly cocked it, glared toward Yakima sitting atop the pass, and yelled, "Who in the hell are you, and what in the hell do you want?" He lowered the rifle, aiming the black maw at the newcomer. "Make it fast or swallow lead!"

Yakima gave a wry snort. The poetic gent had been reading too many dime novels for his own good.

"Get the hump out of your necks. I'm Yakima Henry. *Marshal* Yakima Henry from Apache Springs. I was given a dance card."

The rider not aiming the rifle at Yakima leaned toward the one who was and whispered something. They were obviously mine guards, probably two of many keeping a close eye on this canyon. When the second man stopped whispering, the first one raised his rifle and depressed the hammer.

"Well, why in the hell didn't you say so? Come on!"

Both guards reined their horses around and headed straight off down the trail.

"Some folks were just born with burs under their blankets," Yakima muttered as he put Wolf into a trot behind Kosgrove's men.

CHAPTER 12

Yakima galloped Wolf into the dust of his two-man, rifle-wielding welcoming committee.

They passed a broad, deeply rutted trail that obviously led off toward the rocky ridge wall and the mine and continued along the main trail that followed a broad wash, before swerving sharply left and climbing up and out of the wash and into another, secondary canyon fingering off from the main one. The riders climbed a broad, low bench and then another, even higher, bench. Spreading out across the bench before him, Yakima saw what appeared to be a Mexican *hacienda* complete with brightly white-washed adobe barns, stables, and pole corrals, including a round stone breaking corral with a snubbing post at its center.

Last, but certainly not least, a sprawling, low, Spanish-style *casa* hunched behind a six-foot-high whitewashed adobe wall boasting a broad, wrought-iron gate with the name *KOSGROVE* fashioned of wrought iron in the gate's center.

The house fronted the barns and other outbuildings, quartering off to the right and flanked by a steeply slanted mesa wall shimmering in the midday heat haze. There was a veritable orchard of what appeared to be lemon and orange trees and maybe a few nut trees behind the wall. The trees spread welcoming shade over a courtyard patio.

Yakima and his chaperones reined up before the gate.

The man who'd done all the talking a few minutes ago now turned his frisky grullo gelding back toward Yakima and said in a habitually sneering voice, "We'll corral your horse. Just hang your pistol belt from the horn."

Yakima looked at him.

The man smiled without an ounce of humor. "Kosgrove house rules. No visitors with weapons get through that gate."

Yakima gave a caustic snort. It wasn't like he'd invited himself out here. And he certainly wasn't here to assassinate Hugh Kosgrove. But he was here now, and he had a feeling arguing his point wouldn't do him much good. Besides, Wolf needed water and rest before making the long, hot ride back to Apache Springs.

Yakima swung down from the saddle, tossed his reins to the ill-tempered gent, removed his holstered Colt and cartridge belt, buckled the rig, and hooked it over his saddlehorn.

"Enjoy your meal, Marshal Henry," the ill-tempered gent said in his ill-tempered tone, accentuating "marshal." He obviously didn't think a man with Yakima's skin tone should be wearing a badge.

"If I enjoy it even half as much as your company, I'll have a leg up on the rest of the day."

The ill-tempered gent's partner laughed at that. He looked at the ill-tempered gent, who wasn't smiling, so his partner tugged his hat brim low, obliterating his own smile.

Leading Wolf by his bridle reins, the ill-tempered gent galloped off toward one of the corrals, his partner galloping after him and casting a skeptical glance back over his shoulder at Yakima.

"Don't mind them," came a girl's seemingly disembodied but familiar voice. "If you had to ride around all day in the hot sun trying to hold the wolves at bay, getting paid pennies and piss water, allowed to visit town only once a month to bleed off your sap, you'd have a knot in your tail, too."

Yakima swung around to see her standing on the other side of the wrought-iron gate, staring through the slender, black bars at him.

Emma smiled.

"Shit."

"Hi, Yakima." She smiled more broadly, showing her perfect white teeth, and gave a slow, flirtatious blink.

"I thought you'd be out keeping the raptors away from that gold-laden church."

"I'll probably ride out later and check on it." Emma slipped the gate's latching bolt, closed her hands around the angling bars, and pushed the gate open. It groaned on its hinges. The girl stepped out with the gate and wrapped her arms around Yakima's neck, rising up on her toes to kiss him.

He drew his head back, pushed her away.

"Knock it off."

"Spoilsport."

He stared down at her. It was almost as though he were looking at someone else — a completely different girl from the Emma Kosgrove he'd come to know. Gone were her dusty riding clothes and brown Stetson. Today she wore a conservatively styled, cream, gingham housedress printed with tiny yellow sunflowers. The frock was buttoned clear up to her throat and was trimmed with a narrow, lace-edged collar. The collar was closed with a gold cameo pin.

The dress was not meant to be sexy, but on this girl, how could it not be? The gingham was pulled taut across her high, firm breasts, and the cream color accented the tan, earthy beauty of her face. Her hair, bleached the color of flax straw by her hours riding through these mountains in the harsh desert sun, was freshly washed and brushed. Sausage curls hung down against her cheeks. Several strands from each temple had been drawn back around behind her head and secured with a gold clip to tumble down her slender back.

His admiration must have been plain in his expression.

She broke the pout off, smiling, eyes flashing. "I clean up right well, wouldn't you say?" She shook the sausage curls back from her cheeks, threw her shoulders back, and thrust out her breasts. He tried not to remember cupping the bare, sweet orbs in his hands and sticking his nose between them, inhaling her natural aroma, like an intoxicating elixir.

"Is your father here?" he asked, changing the subject.

Emma snagged his left arm in both of her

arms and led him through the gate and along a flagstone walk through the shady orchard in which desert songbirds piped. "Of course. He invited you out here, didn't he?"

Yakima pulled his arm free and said, "What's it about?"

"Who knows? Poppa doesn't tell me anything about his business. Maybe he just wants to meet the marshal of Apache Springs."

"I doubt that."

"Well, I reckon you'll know soon, then. Right this way, Marshal Henry," Emma said, raising her voice as she led him onto a broad, deep patio flanked by two heavy oak, ornately scrolled doors propped open to the midday air.

The deeply shaded, low-slung house had an old, Spanish air about it — one of Old World refinement — though judging by the good shape it was in, it had been built recently. The walls, probably comprised of native adobe bricks, had been finished in stucco and coated with whitewash that reflected the desert sun. Clay *botillas* hung from strips of dyed hemp from the patio's cottonwood rafters, the evaporating water cooling the air scented with the sharp tang of lemons.

As Emma led Yakima through the open doors, the citrus aroma was replaced by that of *piñon* smoke, likely from previous fires that had held the desert evening chill at bay. There was also the fragrance of a good cigar. Voices emanated from the house's dusky recesses, and then one voice — deep and masculine — fairly roared with anger:

"Tell them if they want to strike, I'll do everything in my power to break it! I'll drive those ungrateful bastards to their knees! Every last one! They'll never work in this country again. They can go back to fucking the diseased *putas* in Mexico, where most of them hail from! They can try to find a *patron* down there who treats them half as good I always have!"

Another man spoke briefly in a dramatically lower voice before the shouting man shouted once more, after slapping his hand hard on something solid — a desktop, perhaps: "They'll get paid in a couple of days — when Salko returns from the Southern Pacific tracks! Salko is transporting the payroll! Tell them if they strike now, they won't get paid a fucking dime!"

The man with the softer, less passionate voice spoke again, and then footsteps sounded. A door opened on the far side of the salon, or parlor, that Emma had led

Yakima into. A slender man in a three-piece suit and handlebar mustache stepped through the door, walking quickly, setting a black bowler hat on his bald head.

He appeared to be in his early forties or so — a dapper gent with a skinny neck and prominent Adam's apple and, at the moment, a very flushed face with glassily anxious eyes. As he moved into the salon he slowed to a near stop, his gaze taking the measure of the big, badge-wearing half-breed standing beside Emma.

"Oh," the man said, continuing to walk past Yakima, as though he were reluctant to come to a full stop and risk more of the previous tirade. "Oh . . . you're . . . you're *him,* aren't you?"

The dapper gent raised his curious gaze to Yakima's face, no doubt studying the piercing jade eyes set deep in red sockets.

"The rock-worshippin' town marshal from Apache Springs?" Yakima asked, dryly. "Yep."

"Ah, well . . . I see." The dapper gent dipped his chin to Emma and pinched the narrow brim of his crisp bowler in parting. "Miss Kosgrove."

"Luther," Emma said.

Luther retreated back through the house, using the same route Emma had led her guest along.

"Luther Hammersmith is the superintendent of the Conquistador," Emma told
Yakima, keeping her voice low as though in
deference to the obvious fiery emotion still
emanating from the door Luther had left
open behind him. "Poor bastard has his
work cut out for him. He's the fourth one
since Poppa brought me and Julia out from
the east — nearly seven years ago now. They
don't last long."

"Who's that?" came the same voice as that
of the shouter, though he was no longer
shouting but yelling. "Emma? Emma, is that
you?" A silhouette appeared in the hall
outside the open door through which Luther
had fled. A short, stocky silhouette wreathed
in gray cigar smoke.

"It's me, Poppa."

"What're you saying?"

"Nothing, Poppa." Emma canted a rebel-
lious smirk up at Yakima.

"I heard you!"

"Oh, for chrissakes!" Emma retorted, her
own eyes flashing furiously. "It's nothing
that isn't true. I was just telling Yakima . . .
er, Marshal Henry, who has arrived, by the
way . . . how things fly out here at the
Conquistador!"

"You know I don't like talking out of

school, young lady!"

"Then you should keep your voice down, you long-winded old tyrant!" Again, Emma smirked up at Yakima, who was more than a little taken aback by the daughter-father exchange, as heated as it seemed.

Hugh Kosgrove walked out of the shadows of the short hall branching off from the salon and into the light angling in from the tall, deeply recessed windows lining both sides of the large, high-ceilinged room appointed in heavy Spanish furniture upholstered mostly in dark cowhide. Yakima was surprised by the man's appearance. He'd seen Kosgrove only in passing from afar, but somehow he'd envisioned a much different sort than the man moving toward him now — a portly gent shaped like a rain barrel and standing well under six feet tall.

Despite his girth, Hugh Kosgrove moved quickly, taking short, mincing steps, swinging his hips and shoulders far to each side, throwing his arms back as though he were moving through water. He had short, curly, gray hair, bright-blue eyes teeming with ironic good humor, a small, plump nose that was a patchwork of broken and frayed blood vessels, and a ruddy face mottled red from the sun. Untrimmed muttonchops the same color as his hair trailed to his lower jaw.

He was smiling brightly, more than a little ironically, an expression his face seemed entirely comfortable with and accustomed to.

The mine owner appeared of English or Irish extraction and spoke in a thick eastern brogue, but he wore a Spanish-style white, silk shirt open halfway down his mottled, red chest, and Spanish-cut corduroy slacks tucked into the tops of polished, black, Spanish-style boots adorned with lavish red and white stitching. Yakima's immediate impression was of a boisterous easterner, possibly a former street fighter from an east-coast city, who'd made a fortune probably working both sides of the law and come west to amuse himself by trying on a new culture like a fresh suit of clothes — and digging for gold.

"How do you like how this high-blooded little filly talks to her old man, Marshal Henry? I guess it's fairly obvious I spared the rod on this one, eh?"

Yakima could see now that the heated verbiage Kosgrove and his comely daughter had exchanged had all been bluster, and that such forms of communication were the custom of the country out here. Probably had been since his two girls had moved out here to live with their old man after their mother, from whom Kosgrove had been divorced, had died back east.

"It's never too late," Yakima said, cutting his wry gaze between father and daughter.

"Oh, it's far too late," Emma said, sidling up to Hugh Kosgrove and brushing her open hand over the tops of their heads, indicating that she was taller than her father by a good two or three inches.

"A big girl," Kosgrove said. "Just like her mother."

The sudden switch in tone to a biting sharpness was likely customary with old Kosgrove, as well. Yakima could tell the barb — probably an oft-used weapon — hit its mark. Emma flushed but, a veteran of such skirmishes, recovered quickly.

With aplomb, gesturing at her father with her open hand, she said, "Yakima Henry, Hugh Kosgrove, blustering son of a bitch and my father, as well as owner of the Conquistador. Hugh Kosgrove, also known as Poppa Bear" — she leaned down to plant a warm kiss on the old man's right cheek while glancing ironically up at Yakima — "this is Yakima Henry, marshal of Apache Springs in the Arizona Territory."

"Yeah, yeah," Kosgrove said, apparently growing irate at his daughter's overly patronizing tone. "I know what territory I'm in. And I know where Apache Springs is, as well. Lord knows I've put enough money into that town of late. Those bastards are strapping me for cash, say there's gonna be a big payoff after the railroad chugs into town. Well, we'll see, we'll see. Anyway . . ."

Kosgrove held out his thick, little hand, and Yakima shook it. "Pleased to meet you finally, Marshal Henry. I've always meant to thank you for what you did to get Julia back safely from that devil Rebel Wilkes." He frowned from Yakima to his daughter still standing beside him, Emma's arm draped across the old man's thick shoulders. "And managing to keep this one alive while doing it."

"Couldn't have done it without her . . . and my deputy."

"Pshaw!" Emma said with ironic self-deprecation, then changed the subject. "Three wolves told me several minutes ago that dinner is ready and waiting, gentlemen. It's probably cold by now. Shall we?"

The young woman swung around, skirts swirling, and strode through a broad arched doorway in the salon's far wall. Kosgrove gestured with his hand, and Yakima followed the girl from the salon into a dining room boasting a long, solid wooden table surrounded by high-backed wooden chairs.

A slender man with the features of a full-blood Indian and dressed in a white silk jacket and string tie was just then setting a silver coffee pot in the middle of the table. Already on the table were the victuals of the noon dinner — a large turkey roasted to a golden brown and stuffed with oyster dressing, a bowl heaping with snowy mashed potatoes, a steaming china boat chockfull of rich brown milk gravy, a bowl of creamed corn, and another of the greenest green beans Yakima had ever laid eyes on — obviously picked and cooked fresh from a nearby, irrigated garden.

There were two straw-basketed demijohns of dark-red wine. Crystal wine glasses glistened before three large platters set upon the table's far left end — one at the very end and two at the corners, one across from the other. The silverware shone with almost painful brightness in a shaft of golden sunlight angling through a long window to the right.

"Marshal Henry," Emma said, indicating the plate on the table's near side. "Father will take his throne at his customary place at the end there."

She swung around and placed her hands atop the shoulders of the Indian just then filling her wine glass across the table from where Yakima was now standing. "This is Three Moons, our, uh, butler, for lack of a better word."

She glanced at the slender Indian, roughly her own height, who had long, almond shaped eyes and a broad, round face with a beak-like Apache nose hooking down over his thick, slightly upturned upper lip. The abundant silver streaks in his hair said that he was maybe Kosgrove's age, which Yakima assumed to be late fifties to early sixties. Still, the Indian was board straight, and there were few lines in his handsome, aboriginal face with its coal-black eyes set beneath thin, gray-black brows and a high forehead back from which his raven-black hair had been pulled. It trailed down his back in twin braids.

"Three Moons, this is Yakima Henry, town marshal of Apache Springs," Emma said, glancing with a little more charm and faintly jeering humor than Yakima would have liked.

"Pleased to meet you, Three Moons."

"The pleasure is all mine, Mister Henry," the Indian said, shoving a cork into the mouth of the wine bottle. He owned not a trace of the customary clipped-vowel and rolled-consonant accent of the usual Native American. He spoke like a white man — a well-bred and -educated one, at that. "Con-gratulations on the position. I expect it keeps you hopping?"

"It does at that," Yakima returned.

"Yakima was the lawman in Apache Springs when that bunch burned and looted the town a couple of years back," Hugh Kos-grove told his servant, who stood as though at attention, hands folded before him, chin up, near the far corner of the table. "He ran them down, killed every one, brought the loot and my oldest daughter back safely."

"So I heard," Three Moons said, dipping his chin respectfully.

"I had a little help from the Rio Grande Kid and someone else." Yakima crooked a smile across the table at Emma, who'd taken her seat.

Emma smiled with a little too much double meaning at him and shook out her napkin. Yakima glanced at Kosgrove. The old mine owner didn't seem to suspect just what exactly his dinner guest and his comely daughter had meant to each other out in the high-and-rocky of the Sierra Estrada.

But then Yakima turned his glance to the Indian servant, Three Moons, who quirked a crooked smile. Kosgrove might not have known, but his Indian servant sure as hell did.

Yakima's ears warmed.

"Three Moons and I," Kosgrove said, standing behind his chair, resting his hands on its back, his cigar smoldering between the first and second fingers of his right one, "we been through a lot together over the years. I met him back east, though he grew up here in Arizona. He was educated in Boston after bein' taken in by missionaries with money. We came west together nigh on twenty years ago now. He knew the Apaches — or, at least he knew the Chiricahuas — well enough to keep us both from getting slow cooked over a low fire. And, by hook and by crook, I learned about rocks from books — after I taught myself to read, that is — while fighting the Germans and Italians in the old neighborhood. And so" — Kosgrove smiled admiringly at his Indian companion — "here we are now. Two old men sipping bourbon at night by the fire, remembering the wild old days."

Emma turned to Three Moons and rattled off several sentences in what Yakima recognized as the language spoken by the Chiricahua Apache.

Three Moons looked down and snorted a laugh.

"What?" Kosgrove said, scowling at his daughter. "What'd she say? Consarn it,

Emma — haven't I told you it ain't polite for you two to speak that in front of me when you know I don't know a lick of it!"

"She said the old coyote is getting sentimental in his old age," Yakima said.

All eyes turned to him, arched in surprise.

The half-breed shrugged. "I was a scout at Fort Hildebrandt not all that long ago," he explained. "Heart of Chiricahua country."

"Fort Hell." Three Moons nodded in acknowledgement. "Appropriately named. Or so I hear. God didn't dwell there."

"He means it true — about God," Kosgrove told Yakima. "Three Moons is an ordained Lutheran minister, though you wouldn't know it by lookin' at him."

"And you wouldn't know that by looking at you, you old whore monger," Three Moons said in Chiricahua, grinning between Emma and Yakima, "that his mother was a horny old coyote and his father was a three-legged armadillo!"

Emma and Three Moons threw their heads back, laughing.

Yakima chuckled.

"You cussed Injun!" Kosgrove railed in mock fury. "I think I smell your dog stew burning out in the kitchen!"

CHAPTER 13

Yakima couldn't remember when he'd last enjoyed a midday meal as much as he enjoyed dinner at the Kosgrove house. Three Moons was one hell of a cook. Yakima had no complaints. At least, not about the food.

While Hugh Kosgrove rambled on about rocks and geology and Mexican liquor — his favorite being *bacanora* — as well as about his frequent trips deeper into the mountains looking for another gold-rich vein, Emma kept casting lusty looks across the table at her and her father's guest. She obviously took great pleasure in making Yakima remember their nights together under the desert stars, making him squirm now in his chair in her father's elegant, Spanish-style *casa.*

At the same time, remembering those nights against his will, he couldn't help feeling a hot pull of lust deep in his nether regions, which made him keep his eyes on his plate as he forked the succulent food into his mouth, nodding automatically, chuckling occasionally at the long-winded Kosgrove's tales of his gold-hunting exploits.

Despite these distractions, a vague curiosity catfooted around inside his brain.

Why was he here?

He knew he hadn't been summoned merely to enjoy Three Moons's cooking or to become acquainted with Hugh Kosgrove. Those were merely the gold braid on the envelope of his invitation. The old gold miner had called Yakima out here for a different reason, and, as Three Moons cleared the dishes of the main meal and then served peach cobbler and coffee, it became clear Kosgrove was waiting till later to broach the purpose of Yakima's visit — likely when he and his guest were alone.

Sure enough, as soon as dessert was over, Kosgrove licked his fork clean, like a dog polishing off a particularly sweet bone, tossed it onto his empty plate, belched, farted, leaned back in his chair, and turned to Yakima. "Marshal Henry, why don't we repair to my office? I have a particular matter I'd like to discuss with you."

He glanced at Emma with a patronizing

smile and patted her hand atop the table. "Boring business talk, child. Why don't you help Three Moons with the dishes?"

Emma rolled her eyes.

When Yakima had taken a seat in a leather-upholstered guest chair fronting Kosgrove's large desk in an office easily the size of a suite in a fancy big-city hotel, Kosgrove offered him a cigar from a cedar humidor.

Yakima declined. His curiosity was piqued. He wanted the man to get on with business. Or whatever the hell it was he'd lured Yakima out here to discuss.

Taking a cigar for himself, Kosgrove removed the tip with a silver clip, then strolled over to a long, open glass door looking out onto the *casa*'s shaded patio, where a large, tiger-striped cat lay sunning itself near a birdbath. Between the cat's paws lay the remains of a dead yellow-headed blackbird — a few tufts of down and yellow feathers, part of a black wing.

A cabinet clock ticked woodenly against the wall behind Yakima, metronomic beats that, in his languor following the heavy meal, threatened to make him sleepy.

When Kosgrove had got his stogie going, he blew a long plume out onto the patio and said, "I want you to stop seeing her."

The order, given so casually, was puzzling

at first. Then, when he'd understood the words, Yakima thought: Oh, shit — he knows about Emma and me. His heart thudded, remembering those intoxicating, erotic nights at his old stone cabin in the Javelina Bluffs, in which he'd holed up after first coming to the Sierra Estrada. Damn her. Her brash glances across the table had given them away.

Kosgrove turned to Yakima, one brow arched, a bitter smile on his thin-lipped mouth. "You think I didn't know?"

Yakima winced with embarrassment. "Look, Mister Kosgrove, I —"

"Of course it got back to me. Everyone in town knows."

"In town?" Yakima rarely, if ever, saw Emma in town.

"You're making me a laughing stock."

"I . . . I don't understand."

"I can't ride into the Springs for a business meeting without hearing the whispering behind my back, see the townsfolk snickering." Kosgrove's ruddy face grew gradually red with anger as he took a few puffs from his cigar and said, "My oldest daughter nearly marries Rebel Wilkes — the man who double-crosses me by staking out his own mining claim on *my time,* when he *should have been working for me*! — and then burns and murders half the town. That wasn't enough for her, though, was it? *Then* she marries an even lesser sort — Lon Taggart — the marshal of Apache Springs. A workaday man from a bad family who was going no farther than that badge!"

He pointed at the five-starred chunk of silver-chased tin pinned to Yakima's buckskin tunic.

Kosgrove took another few puffs off the stogie, his face red and swollen now, blue eyes bright with rage. "Then, when Taggart swallows a pill he can't digest, she takes into her bed the next marshal of Apache Springs — *a half-breed Indian!*"

It was all clear to Yakima now. Kosgrove didn't mean Emma.

He meant Julia.

Yakima rose slowly, choking back the fury rising inside him. He glared at the older man facing him from the open doorway, wreathed in a thick, gray cloud of aromatic cigar smoke.

Calm, he told himself. *Calm. This isn't a saloon, and you're not drunk on firewater. No tearing the place apart!*

He had to repeat the silent admonition several times.

"She told me she loves me. I love her."

Kosgrove laughed without mirth and narrowed his blue eyes caustically. "Come on! What could come of it? *Marriage?*"

Yakima didn't respond. He just stood glowering at the man sneering at him.

"*Children?*" Kosgrove added with the same derision.

Still, Yakima glowered at him, fighting the rage building and building inside him, his ears ringing like a boiling teapot.

"What would such children look like? How would they be treated in Apache Springs? If you love her, imagine how she would be treated in Apache Springs, or anywhere else, for that matter!"

"That's a decision for her to make."

"My daughter, Marshal Henry . . . well, you probably know by now. Julia is not always the most sensible in these matters. For God sakes, she almost married the man who double-crossed me, then burned the town when the town boosters wouldn't let him run a train through town to his proposed mine!" Kosgrove laughed as though it had all been an insane joke. "And then she marries Taggart against my wishes, against my threats to cut her out of my life as well as my will!"

Yakima didn't point out that Kosgrove himself had arranged for Julia to marry Rebel Wilkes, Kosgrove's mining engineer, as part of an informal business deal. It would have been a waste of time. Kosgrove had revised his point of view on the topic, and, having dealt with such arrogant, self-centered men before — many of them, in fact —Yakima knew there was no changing it. The man had made up his mind that his oldest daughter had been born to defy him out of spite, and he'd go to his grave with that opinion, however wrong.

Yakima knew — at least *sensed* — that Julia actually loved her father and, deep down, wanted nothing more than to please him. That's why she'd agreed to marry Wilkes. After that had soured, with no little relief to Julia, who'd never loved Wilkes in the first place, she'd realized that pleasing her father was an impossible feat. Having nearly driven herself mad with trying, and knowing the lengths Kosgrove would go to to make her toe his line, she'd gone to the other extreme.

Not that she hadn't loved Taggart. She had. Not that she didn't love Yakima. He knew she did. But a part of what had first attracted her to both Taggart and Yakima was knowing that her father wouldn't approve. Yakima didn't hold it against her in the least. It was the result of her strained relationship with her father and an ironic fact of her life.

Yakima walked slowly across the office to stand before Kosgrove. He consciously relaxed his muscles. He didn't want to seem any more threatening than his size already made him appear. This was not an occasion for violence. Sober, he was above all that. Especially now that he wore the badge.

"Mister Kosgrove, I know you're —"

"Even Three Moons agrees!" Kosgrove continued, staring up at Yakima through his smoke cloud. "Ask him yourself if you think this is only about you. It's not. Three Moons married a white woman back east. You know what happened? The girl's father took a gun into his attic and shot himself out of shame! Shame despite that Three Moons had gone to none other than Harvard University and earned a degree in divinity! Now, I'm not saying I'd shoot myself," Kosgrove added, laughing loudly, caustically. "No, no. Not me. I relay the story merely to illustrate the scandal such a union can cause. Especially in these parts, with so many folks so recently terrorized by the Apaches. Not that you're Apache, but —"

"Kosgrove, shut up and listen to me."

The old man glowered up at him, his blue eyes flashing as though from a fire burning inside his head.

"I know you love your daughter and you think you know what's best for her. But you don't." Yakima set his hat on his head and started walking toward the door.

"One thousand dollars."

Yakima stopped at the door and turned back to the old man now taking another couple of draws off his cigar and grinning shrewdly. Yakima laughed. He grabbed the doorknob and started to turn it but stopped when Kosgrove said, "I do apologize, but you're forcing my hand here, Marshal Henry."

Yakima drew the door open but glanced over his shoulder at Kosgrove again, vaguely curious. The man had pitched his voice with an ominous edge.

"I really didn't think it would come to this." Kosgrove walked toward his desk. "Close the door."

Yakima sighed and closed the door only because he was curious about what the man was going to pluck out of his basket next. However, a cool breath of apprehension blew against his ears.

Kosgrove walked around behind the desk and pulled open the middle drawer. He withdrew a swollen manila envelope and tossed it to the opposite side of his desk.

"A thousand dollars, and this conversation goes no further. A thousand dollars to stay away from my daughter. I'm not ordering you to leave town. By all accounts, you're a good lawman. We need a good lawman in Apache Springs."

"I gave you my answer." Yakima turned to the door again.

"I'm sorry to have to do this."

Once again, Yakima turned back to Kosgrove. He half expected the man to pull a gun out of the same drawer. It wasn't a gun he produced, however. It was a quarter-folded sheet of paper. He tossed it over by the money.

Yakima walked to the desk and stared down at the folded, slightly yellowed cream leaf.

Again, that cool breath of apprehension blew against his ears. It was as though he were staring down at a dagger with his own blood on it.

Slowly, haltingly, he picked up the paper and unfolded it.

A cold stone dropped in his belly when he saw the word *WANTED* splashed across the top of the paper in large, heavy black letters. Below, in a box taking up roughly a third of the sheet, was a penciled likeness, or a rough likeness, of himself, complete with long hair and low-crowned, flat-brimmed hat. Between *WANTED* and the penciled picture was a block of regular-sized type in capital letters:

$2500 REWARD FOR INFORMATION LEADING TO CAPTURE OF UNKNOWN KILLER OF DEPUTY US MARSHAL LEON MYERS IN BURLINSON HOTEL, ESTELLE, KANSAS, ON NIGHT OF JUNE 6. GREEN-EYED HALF-BREED. NAME UNKNOWN. LEFT TOWN NEXT MORNING ON A BLAZE-FACED BLACK STALLION.

Yakima hadn't realized he'd been holding his breath. Now, slowly, he released it as he just as slowly set the Wanted circular back down on the edge of Kosgrove's desk.

"Mighty bad business — killing a deputy United States marshal," the gold miner said. He was leaning forward, fists on his desk.

He stared with menace across the desk at Yakima. "They didn't have a name, and it's not a very good likeness. That's probably why no one has run you down. Yet. My good friend, Lloyd Barstow, who runs the Western Union and Wells Fargo office in Apache Springs, was cleaning out a drawer in his office when he found this near the bottom. He decided to turn it over to me. Asked me what I thought should be done about it."

"And you said . . ."

"Nothing. As long as there's no need."

Kosgrove shrugged his heavy shoulders. "Kansas is a long ways away. This happened three years ago. And . . . I'm thinking maybe this Myers fella, federal lawman or not, needed killing."

"He did."

"I'll take your word for that . . ."

"As long as I stop seeing Julia." Yakima heard the emotional quaver in his voice.

Kosgrove's only response to that was a slow blink as he lifted his cigar to his mouth once more and let several more puffs blossom around his face set with a subtly victorious smile. Yakima stared at him, that ringing in his ears now rising to the din of cracked bells echoing from a near tower. His urge was to swing his arm across the desk, to smash his fist into Kosgrove's smugly smiling face.

If he'd had a few belts in him, he'd have done just that. But he was as sober as a judge, so he didn't have the firewater for an excuse. Still, he felt as though he were about to explode. Instead of waiting around to find out what he'd do, given enough time and rage, he willed himself away from the desk, stumbling a little on his spurs, the rowels raking the flagstone tiles.

The room was a little blurry, and the floor was rising and falling around him. He didn't feel drunk so much as drugged, or as though he'd been thrown on his head.

He turned toward the door. He had to reach for the knob twice before he finally grabbed it, opened the door, and stumbled out into the hall. He steadied himself against a wall, then strode back through the house, hearing Emma call his name distantly from somewhere behind him.

Then he was outside, crossing the front patio, pushing through the wrought-iron gate with the *KOSGROVE* name scrolled in its center, striding quickly across the yard toward where his horse waited in the corral, staring over the gate at him, as though Wolf had sensed the trouble inside the house and was expecting his rider to come for him.

Julia.

Yakima slung his saddle onto the black's back, slipped the bridle over its ears. He kicked open the gate and galloped out of the corral, out of the yard.

A mile, maybe two — hell, maybe three — slid by in a blur of blind emotion.

What snapped him out of it, albeit briefly, was a searing pain in his left arm and the following crack of a rifle from somewhere in the bluffs above the trail he was following.

Wolf whinnied and lurched up off his front

hooves, scissoring his front legs furiously at the sky.

Another bullet plumed dust near the stallion's prancing hooves. Yakima had let the reins slip out of his hands when the first bullet had punched into his arm. He reached for them now, but then the reins and Wolf were gone. There was nothing around him but air. The gray-brown slant of a steep slope rose up quickly to smack him hard about the head and shoulders.

He cried out in shock and agony.

And then he was rolling . . . rolling . . . rolling down an endless and endlessly brutal, rocky slope.

CHAPTER 14

Yakima lifted his head, groaned.

He opened his eyes. The world was a tan blur around him, the sun slashing at his corneas.

He closed his eyes, rested his head back against the gravelly ground. He felt as though he'd been run over by a runaway ore dray. His back and neck felt broken. His shoulders and arms, too. Legs and hips — same thing. Multiple bruises probably made by the rocks and gravel and sandstone lumps he'd rolled over when falling from the steep slope converged to make his entire body feel like one massive, generalized, purple, fast-swelling slab of misery.

Gradually, he became aware of a slightly different ache in his left arm. It was a sharp, searing pain. He turned and dipped his chin, saw the blood stain around the tear in his tunic sleeve, about seven inches down from his shoulder. He also saw the blood dribbling onto the rocks and red sand and gravel beneath that arm.

He remembered the bullet. Alarm rose past the physical agony hammering his bones and muscles. Quickly, he took stock of his condition, tensing and then slackening various parts of his body, moving his arms and legs, turning his head. Despite the pain he was in, he didn't think anything was broken. Now that he had that decided as best as he could at the moment, before he'd done any real moving around, he considered his situation.

He'd been shot out of his saddle. From the left side of the trail. He wasn't sure how long ago that had been. In his addled state, he wasn't sure how long he'd been lying here, unconscious. Or maybe he'd *just* landed here.

As his body was a mass of agony, his mind was fuzzy with confusion. Judging by the sun's angle, he hadn't been here all that long. Whoever had shot him was likely somewhere atop the ridge he'd fallen from, possibly still looking to finish the job they'd started.

Still lying flat, chest expanding and contracting quickly as he breathed, tension rising in him, Yakima looked down toward his right thigh. He knew a moment's relief to see that his stag-butted .44 was still in its holster. He dropped his hand over the revolver, used his index finger to free the keeper thong from over the hammer.

He tensed with a start when a voice, ominously clear in the dry desert air, said with menacing matter-of-factness, "Go ahead and put another bullet in him, Les."

The man who must have been Les said, "Why don't you do it?"

"You got the better angle."

"Yeah, but the footing here is for shit."

"Just take the goddamn shot! Finish off the bastard!"

Yakima lifted his head and squinted up the long, steep slope before him and down which he'd tumbled. It took a while for his vision to clear.

Then he saw them — two men on the slope about fifty yards above him, spread out about thirty feet apart. There was a thumb of ground just above Yakima, giving him partial cover from one of the two rifle-wielding bushwhackers. The other man was moving daintily along a talus slide, crouched low and carefully setting his boots, heading toward a boulder humping out of the slope just below him.

Yakima grunted as he slid the .44 from its holster. He wished like hell he had his Yellowboy, but the rifle was still in its scabbard on Wolf's back, wherever Wolf was . . .

Yakima grunted again as he clicked the hammer back, narrowed one eye, and aimed down the barrel of the pistol. He drew a bead on the bushwhacker just then dropping to a knee atop the boulder, raising his rifle. Yakima nudged the barrel of the .44 a little higher, adjusting for the distance as well as the steepness of the slope. It was a long shot for a handgun.

Yakima held his breath, squeezed the trigger.

The .44 bucked and roared.

The bullet plumed rock dust off the edge of the boulder near the bushwhacker's boots. The man jerked back with a start, yelling, "Shit!" He dropped to his butt.

The other man laughed jeeringly.

As the shooter rose again, getting his boots beneath him, Yakima's Colt barked again, smoke and flames jetting up the slope. The man on the boulder jerked once more, even more violently this time.

For a second, he crouched there on one knee, staring down the slope toward Yakima. Slowly, his Winchester wilted in his right hand.

"Les?" the other man said.

Les lowered his head and fell slowly

forward. Dropping the rifle, he tumbled over the edge of the boulder. He hit the slope on his back, his black hat tumbling away, his black chaps flapping like wings as he rolled. Twenty feet from where Yakima had dropped him, the man bounced off a boulder with a dull smack and veered down the slope nearly straight above where the half-breed lay, crowding the base of the slope to stay out of view of the second bushwhacker.

Les rolled and rolled, arms and legs flying, dust billowing around him. Longish, red-blond hair danced around his head. He grew larger and larger before Yakima until the half-breed pulled his head back, and Les flew straight over him to land on the canyon floor just beyond him.

Yakima turned to his left, staring out across his own wounded left arm.

Les lay ten feet away on his back. His head was turned toward Yakima. He had coarse, straight, blond hair and a blond mustache. His chaps were black. *Chaperreras* was what the Mexican whore, Clara, had called them in her native tongue. This was the man who'd visited her room to talk about an upcoming job with the blue-eyed man. "Eyes with no good in them," Clara had called them.

Yakima looked at Les's face. The man's eyes were open and staring at Yakima. Blood trickled out both sides of the man's mouth to dribble down over his chin. The hole in his upper right chest oozed blood down the front of his blue and red checked shirt. His chest rose and fell slowly.

He stared at Yakima, but it was impossible to tell if he was seeing anything. His chest was still moving, so there was still some life in him.

Keeping his head below the hump of sand and gravel, Yakima said, "Les, what job you boys got planned?"

Les moved his lips a little. He moved them again until finally a choked whisper escaped them. "Fuck you, you dog-eatin' Injun. You . . . you killed me . . . you *fucker*!"

Les Reese made a strangling sound, and his eyes brightened in horror until they grew opaque, and his chest fell still.

Yakima turned and edged a cautious glance up over the hump of ground covering him from the other man — the man with the dead blue eyes? Apprehension swirled in his belly when he saw the man was no longer standing where he'd been standing before, about halfway up the slope and between two talus slides.

Yakima looked around, his heart thudding.

No sign of the man. After carefully perusing the slope above and to both sides and seeing nothing moving, not even a cloud shadow, he tossed a look along the canyon in which he'd fallen. A jumble of large boulders lay to the south. They littered the slope to that side of the chasm. That must be where the second bushwhacker had gone, maybe trying to work his way into a better position to send a killing shot into his prey.

Straight back behind Yakima stood a narrow corridor between two jagged walls of broken rock. The corridor apparently led deeper into the canyon. It was Yakima's only way out. Or at least his only way from where he lay now, certain prey to the second son of a bitch with a rifle.

A light breeze rose, lifting sand and other debris and swirling it around the canyon. Somewhere in the brassy sky above, a *zopilate* gave its chilling carrion cry.

Yakima pressed a hand against the ground, heaved himself to a squatting position, looking around quickly, feeling the crawling sensation of having rifle sights being planted between his shoulder blades. He still wasn't sure he could move as well as he needed to

— his body cried out in misery as he continued to straighten — but he had no choice but to lurch forward and move as quickly as possible toward the gap in the wall of fallen boulders.

Something shredded the air just behind him.

The bullet hammered the ridge to his left, three feet back.

Yakima cursed, grinding his molars against the pain burning through him, and quickened his pace, lunging into a shambling run. Two more shots screeched behind him, spanging shrilly off rocks. Then Yakima was in the corridor, jogging along a high-sided arroyo, following its twists and curves.

When the wall on his right lowered, something moved beyond it.

Yakima jerked his head in that direction, saw a man standing on the steep slope on that side of the narrow canyon — a potbellied, dark-haired, dark-mustached man wearing a dirty, sweaty, pinstriped shirt and suspenders. Fringed, brown leather chaps buffeted about his denim-clad legs.

He snapped a Henry rifle to his shoulder. Yakima threw himself forward, dropping to his knees behind a four-foot-high snag of brush and rock.

A bullet sliced through the air where his

head had been and slammed into the slope to his left.

The bushwhacker's rifle cracked, echoing.

Yakima winced as he again lurched to his feet, swung his right arm up, hastily aimed his .44, and sent two quick shots toward that side of the canyon. Both bullets tore up gouts of rock and sand where his stalker had been standing before he'd thrown himself with a curse behind the cover of a small boulder.

Yakima continued running, boulders and rock snags now shielding him from the canyon's far side.

He followed the canyon's course around to the left.

His pursuer shouted, "You're a dead man, breed!"

Two quick rifle shots, the bullets sailing high over Yakima's head.

He kept jogging, glancing up and to his right, occasionally swinging around to look behind him. Silence fell over the canyon, interrupted occasionally by the breeze snagging on the high cliff walls to each side, rustling the brush of the old flood snags choking the canyon floor, creating natural bottlenecks.

He was following a meandering game path now, breathless, his arm feeling as though a razor-edged, hot blade were sawing into the wound. He was losing too much blood. He needed water. He needed to clean the wound and bind it.

But at the moment, all he could do was run. He had only his .44, and his stalker had a Henry repeater. The bastard also had the advantage of not having a bullet in him.

Yakima ran under a natural stone arch. Beyond the arch, the arroyo dropped severely to the right. Yakima followed it down to where the air was cool but also fouled by the smell of something dead and rotting in the sun. The gravel was damp beneath his boots. Water dribbled from a crenellated wall of rock crusted with minerals and dark-green moss.

Yakima crouched to slurp water from two thin streams, licking the cold substance into his mouth and swallowing. The water braced him. He needed more, his thirst awakening now at the taste of it. He heard the faint, quick jingle of spurs behind him.

The second son of a bitch was dogging him. Maybe fifty, sixty yards back, but closing fast.

Yakima brushed cool water across his face, then continued running, following the old streambed's twisting course between canyon walls of various heights. When the canyon floor dropped again, abruptly and steeply, the air smelling of damp rock and mushrooms, he had the uneasy sensation that the earth was swallowing him.

Still, he ran. Jogged, rather.

He chewed his cheek against the ache in every bone and muscle, against the raw, hammering pain in his left arm, that sleeve now soaked with dark-red blood.

He wasn't sure how much farther he'd run before his legs gave out under him. It was as though he'd been tripped. He dropped to his knees and rolled. He rolled onto his back and, still clenching the Colt in his right hand, lay breathing as desperately as a landed fish, staring at the sky. His vision had darkened, and he didn't think it was only because clouds had now slid over the canyon.

He was on the verge of passing out.

By force of will, he sat up and looked around. Ahead, choking off the floor of the canyon was a broad pile of boulders that had likely tumbled down the rocky ridges. He cursed as he heaved himself to his feet, lumbered forward, and threw himself over the first, slanted boulder. He crawled over it and onto the next one, glancing into the dark gaps around him, dreading the appearance of a rattlesnake or a scorpion, possibly a gila monster calling such a cavern home.

Something peeped in one of the gaps but it sounded like a packrat. A gecko slithered up and over a rock nearby, expanding its tiny green cheeks.

Grunting and sighing and muttering oaths under his breath, Yakima continued climbing until he'd crested the jumbled pile. He slipped over the crest and dropped five feet nearly straight down to the next boulder below, landing on his hip and shoulder with a loud, anguished groan.

Damn, that was a hard landing . . .

He choked off another groan and pricked his ears, listening, wondering if the groan had been picked up by his stalker.

He held very still, staring up at the crest of the boulder snag five feet above him, holding the Colt barrel up in his right hand, thumb on the hammer. He breathed through his mouth, chest rising and falling sharply. Sweat bathed him, streaming down his cheeks and into his shirt. The tunic was pasted against his chest and back, but the air was so dry, he could feel it evaporating even as it oozed from his pores.

Faintly, he heard movement above him.

The sounds continued to grow — the soft scrapes and dull thuds of boot leather on rock. The man was moving up on him.

Yakima drew a deep breath, then consciously slowed his breathing. He could run no farther. He'd make his stand here.

Tensely, he stared up the crest of boulders above him.

A minute passed. Then another.

Then the rake of a boot on rock touched his ears. Pebbles and red dirt dribbled down from a flat-topped boulder above and to his right. A shadow angled out across the boulders beside Yakima — stretching long in the dull, gray light. The shadow was capped by a broad-brimmed, high-crowned hat.

Yakima's heart quickened. His trigger finger tingled.

He ran his tongue across dry lips.

The man above him stepped into view. The man looked around, then dropped his chin, and Yakima saw the black mustache and cobalt-blue eyes set beneath the brim of a tan Stetson. Quickly, Yakima aimed the Colt. His arm and hand were weak, his aim uncertain. The man's eyes snapped wide in sudden fear, and he jerked his head back a half a wink before the Colt roared, stabbing flames and smoke straight up toward the crest of the boulder pile.

A miss — shit!

Yakima triggered the Colt again.

Ping!

In all the commotion, he hadn't remembered to fill the chamber he usually kept empty beneath the revolver's hammer. The wheel was empty.

CHAPTER 15

Somewhere above Yakima, the man laughed.

The blue-eyed son of a bitch stepped back into view, raising his iron-framed Henry rifle to his shoulder and squinting one cobalt eye as he aimed down the octagonal barrel at Yakima's head. The man's body trembled, dropped a couple of inches. At the same time, the Henry thundered.

The bullet ricocheted off the rock Yakima knelt on, a foot to his left, causing the half-breed to flinch and jerk backward. When he looked up again, he saw that a rock that his assailant was standing on was tearing loose from a small chunk of sandy ground it had been embedded in.

"Oh, shit!" the man cried, crouching and throwing both arms out as though to balance himself.

The rock tore free, and the bushwhacker fell straight down at Yakima, who jerked back once more and twisted around, putting his back to the wall of boulders. The man and several rocks and a good bit of dirt and gravel dropped onto the boulder where Yakima had been a second before, and the blue-eyed bastard went flying several feet forward before rolling up against another, larger boulder.

Dust sifted through the air, obscuring Yakima's view.

The man sat up, hatless, grunting and groaning, shaking his head. His thick, black hair hung in his eyes. He shook it away, looked at Yakima, jerked with a start, and clawed at the six-shooter residing in a holster positioned for a cross-draw on his left hip.

Automatically, the half-breed's hand flung up behind his neck, sliding his Arkansas toothpick free of the hard leather sheath he wore under his shirt, behind his neck, strapped to a short, stiff leather lanyard.

He was so practiced in throwing the toothpick that he not so much aimed as merely watched the stiletto-like knife — five inches of Damascus steel tapering to a needle-like point — leave his hand to smoothly cleave the air, quickly closing the gap between him and the bushwhacker now aiming a long-barreled Smith & Wesson.

The knife plunged into the man's chest,

just right of center.

He made a hiccupping sound as the Smithy bucked and roared, the bullet sailing skyward as the bushwhacker fell back against the boulder behind him. He dropped the pistol and looked down at the round, smooth, wooden handle of the toothpick bristling from his chest. Blood oozed up around the blade embedded nearly to its brass hilt.

As the dust cleared, the son of a bitch looked up at Yakima. His cobalt eyes appeared bleary, the light quickly fading in them. He leaned against the rock behind him, turned his head to one side, dropped his chin to his shoulder, gave a shudder, as though deeply chilled, and just sat there, his legs straight out before him.

He was as dead as his eyes had always been.

The thudding of horse hooves sounded, quickly growing louder.

Yakima jerked his knife from the dead man's chest, cleaned it on the man's shirt, and returned it to its scabbard. He picked up his Colt and quickly began reloading, his hands feeling as though he were wearing several pairs of bulky gloves. The light in him was diminishing fast. But he didn't have time to pass out. At least one more rider was heading toward him.

He'd just fumbled a third cartridge into the Colt's wheel when he saw a horse gallop out of the mouth of an off-shooting canyon. A blaze-faced black. Yakima squinted, studying the beast that stopped at the base of the boulder pile, near the mouth of the off-shooting canyon. As its dust caught up to it, the stallion shook its head and whinnied.

"Well, I'll . . . I'll be goddamned," Yakima raked out, chuckling despite his weariness. "Wolf, you son of a bitch, I . . . I thought you'd headed back to . . . to t-town." He smiled, pleased indeed. He finished reloading the Colt, filling every chamber, then flicking the loading gate closed and spinning the wheel.

"Hang on," he told the horse. "Be down in . . . three jangles of a . . . of a whore's bell . . ."

He heaved himself heavily to his feet. It took him a minute to get his balance. He was as weary and sore as he'd ever been, and he still leaked blood. Maybe not as much as before — the wound appeared to be clotting — but it was still running down his arm.

Thunder growled like a giant, angry dog in the sky.

Yakima looked up. The clouds were settling lower. He thought he felt a few small raindrops blowing against him on a fresh wind. The wind felt good. It blew his sweaty hair behind his head, dried the buckskin tunic pasted to his chest and shoulders.

He made his slow, cautious way over the rocks, choosing his steps carefully, avoiding possible snakes and cactus clumps. When he reached the canyon floor, Wolf trotted over to him and blew a greeting.

"How'd you find me?" Yakima slurred his words as though drunk.

The horse whickered, sniffed his rider's bloody shoulder, and shook his head again.

"Just a nip," Yakima said, walking around to the horse's side to reset and tighten the saddle — not an easy task in his light-headed, badly fatigued condition.

When he'd managed to reset the saddle and tighten the latigo, the rain began to fall harder, splattering on the rocks around him and on the red *caliche* paving the canyon floor. Yakima had just turned out a stirrup and was about to poke his left boot through it, when lightning flashed on the canyon's far ridge — a piercing blue-red light.

Yakima lowered his foot and peered up at the rim.

A sprawling cedar was limned in a bright,

electric blue, smoldering. Red flames and sparks burst from where the lightning had struck the tree, which now jackknifed forward over the canyon edge, cut in half. An earth-shuddering thunderclap followed the strike that left the tree a dancing ball of red flames.

The top half of the tree, cut away from the rest, plunged down onto the slope about fifty feet below the rim. It struck with a great crunching sound, exploding, and then its several burning and smoking pieces continued to roll down over the rocks strewn across the slope's shoulder.

Sidling close against Wolf, Yakima clung to his saddlehorn like a drunk to an awning support post as he peered up the ridge in amazement. "Shittt! You see that?"

Another rumbling sounded. At first, Yakima thought it was more thunder.

But then he could feel the ground quavering beneath his boots. He felt it shuddering through the stallion's body pressed up hard against his own. He looked up at the ridge again. It seemed to be moving — shaking.

His gut flip-flopped when two rocks dropped off the lip of the ridge. They were followed by another one, and then two more and then even more, and they were rolling down the ridge, crashing into others and causing those to break loose from their own moorings and roll, too.

They were maybe two hundred yards from where Yakima stood but heading toward him fast!

"This day isn't turning out so well," he said, trying to stick his left boot through his stirrup.

Wolf was skitter-hopping, nervous about the growing thunder of the boulders heading down the canyon wall. Yakima hopped on his right foot, cursing.

"Hold still, damn it, you broomtail cayuse!"

His right foot struck a stone sideways, and Yakima went down with a loud curse.

Hooves thundered. At first, he thought Wolf was galloping away from him again, but then he saw another horse and another rider gallop toward him from the off-shooting canyon, long hair the color of flax stems blowing back in the wind, beneath a brown Stetson.

"Yakima!" Emma cried.

The girl leaped from the saddle of her rangy buckskin. She glanced at the boulders rolling toward the canyon floor and crouched beside the half-breed, who was huffing and puffing like an old man as he tried hoisting himself back to his uncertain feet. His knees felt like putty, and he wasn't making it.

"You've been shot!" Emma cried as she grabbed his wounded arm and draped it around her neck, heaving them both to their feet.

"Ah, Christ, woman!" he yowled as the agony of her manhandling of his arm ripped through him.

"Don't be such a crybaby, and get into your saddle, you idiot!" She'd grabbed the prancing Wolf's reins and quickly led the horse over to where Yakima crouched, squeezing his wounded arm in his right hand. "Hurry!"

Emma held Wolf as steady as possible while Yakima toed the stirrup and swung up onto the stallion's back. Emma ran over to where her buckskin was sidling away from the boulders he watched tumble toward him, sounding like a runaway freight train on a steep downhill grade.

The ground was leaping and bounding, pitching like the deck of a storm-tossed ship.

"Come on!" Emma swung the buckskin around, touched spurs to its flanks, and crouched low over its buffeting mane as the horse lunged off its rear hooves and into an instant gallop.

Wolf needed no prodding from Yakima.

Giving a shrill whinny, knowing that the boulders were nearly to the bottom of the canyon wall, the black bolted off its own rear hooves and took off after Emma and the buckskin as though tin cans were tied to its tail. Emma and the buckskin flew into the side canyon, and then Yakima and Wolf were in the side canyon, as well, the half-breed gritting his teeth against the agony every lunging stride evoked in his arm, sending poison-tipped Apache spears of misery shooting all through his battered and bruised body.

By force of will, he turned his heavy head to peer behind him, feeling a cold chill drape itself around him as he saw a large, tan boulder bouncing toward him across the floor of the main canyon. It bounced twice, quickly doubling in size, before slamming into the canyon mouth not fifty feet behind Wolf's lunging hooves. The rock, too large to fit into the mouth — thank God! — had been stopped dead and was now obscured by a thick curtain of dust billowing up around it and even before it, reaching into the smaller canyon toward Yakima.

The dust cloaked him, heavy as a blanket.

The drumming of the boulders tumbling into the canyon continued, sounding like a massive war played out in heaven. Or maybe hell . . .

Yakima turned forward with a sigh, shaking his head, blinking against the dust that thinned the farther he rode away from it. "Damn — that was close!"

He sagged forward against Wolf's buffeting mane and slipped into a merciful semi-consciousness. He wasn't sure how much time had passed before the black stopped.

Yakima lifted his head, wincing as the pain in his arm again bit him deep. They were in the open desert. At least it was open to his left. To his right was a tall, wave-shaped escarpment with a concave belly and several boulders at its base. Ahead, near an arroyo cutting around from the far end of the formation, mesquites mixed with tamarisk, greasewood, and ocotillo.

It was still raining, although not as hard as before. The sky was a deep, stormy blue, but the pale-yellow, low-hanging sun brushed it with a clean, lens-like clarity from beneath the western clouds. Thunder rumbled in the distance, but Yakima didn't see lightning. The air was cool and fresh and perfumed with the smell of rain-washed desert, though it didn't appear that much rain had fallen here, wherever they were.

Ahead of Yakima, Emma swung her right

boot over her saddle horn and dropped to the ground. She wore a white-and-red checked shirt, a tan Stetson, and blue denims that caressed her curves as lovingly as an appreciative man's hand. The cuffs were stuffed into the tops of her men's brown boots. Her pearl-gripped, 41-caliber New Line Colt bristled on her right hip.

"Where are we?" Yakima asked her as she strode toward him.

"A mile or so from being buried under a few tons of solid rock."

Yakima gave a snarl against the pain in his arm as he swung down from his saddle and turned to her, frowning. "How did you know . . . ?"

"I followed you out from the ranch. Heard the shot. I saw Wolf from a distance dropping into that canyon and followed him." She gave a wan smile. "I figured he was headed for you."

Emma poked her hat brim back off her forehead and inspected his bloody arm. "I can't see a thing through all that blood," she said finally. "How does it feel?"

"As bad as it looks. But I think the bullet missed the bone, or I'd be out by now."

"I have to get it cleaned." Emma looked around, then turned to Yakima once more. "Go sit against that scarp over there. I'll

486

gather wood and build a fire to heat some water."

Yakima grabbed his canteen from over his saddlehorn, popped the cork, and took a long drink and then one more. That made him feel a little better. It fueled him for the short walk to the scarp, anyway.

He shoved the cork back into the flask, hooked the lanyard over his arm, and dragged his boot toes through the brush and boulders to the base of the tall escarpment. He leaned back against the sandstone wall and slid slowly to the ground.

He raised his knees, draped his arms over them, and hung his head. He dozed until he heard her spurs chinking. He lifted his head to see her walking toward him, studying him, frowning with concern, several branches of sun-bleached mesquite in her arms. As she dropped the wood ten feet from where he sat and went to work arranging it for a fire, she glanced up at him.

"Who were they?"

Yakima shook his head. "Bad *hombres.*" He didn't have the energy to go into it. He wished he had a flask of whiskey in his saddlebags to dull the pain, but he didn't.

"Why did you follow me?" he asked her later, after he'd dozed again and wakened to find her kneeling beside him, gently cutting the bloody sleeve away from his arm with a folding Barlow knife.

A small fire crackled before them, in a ring of rocks. Emma had heated water, and it steamed now in the small pie pan she'd found in his saddlebags and which he usually used for a plate. Several strips of flannel lay on the ground by the plate. She'd set his coffee pot on the flames, as well. It chugged and hissed softly as the water heated. Nearby lay his sack of Arbuckles.

It was late afternoon or early evening. Yakima had lost track of time. Shadows had grown long. The storm seemed to have passed. Somewhere, a coyote yammered.

"I know what Poppa threatened you with."

He arched a brow at the girl. "Eavesdropping?"

Emma hiked a shoulder as she soaked the cloth and began gently cleaning the blood from around the wound. She glanced at him and smiled. "I'm a curious girl."

"Did you know about that ace he was holding?"

"The Wanted circular?" Emma nodded. "I saw it several weeks ago. He forgot it on a table in the salon. I had a pretty good idea what he was going to use it for." She looked up at Yakima, and her eyes glittered with devious delight. "And, boy, he sure did, all right!"

CHAPTER 16

Yakima spat to one side, then sat brooding while Emma cleaned the wound. He almost enjoyed the pain. It was a nice distraction.

"I think you're right," Emma said, when she had the blood washed from his arm. "I think the bullet missed the bone. Might have grazed it. There's an exit hole. The holes'll need to be cauterized."

Yakima's innards recoiled at the term. It sent a chill down his spine. The wound already felt as though it were being cauterized constantly. A big, red heart was throbbing just below his right shoulder.

He pulled the Arkansas toothpick from the sheath behind his neck, held it to her handle first. Emma took it and set the long, tapering blade in the flames.

She gave a sigh and glanced at Yakima again. "Tell me about it. The circular. The lawman you killed."

"Forget it."

"Tell me."

Yakima drew a deep breath and looked off beyond the flames, but he was seeing the main drag of Estelle, Kansas, lit by burning oil pots roughly three years ago. "I didn't even know he was a deputy US marshal." Yakima chuffed ironically at that. "Of all the rotten luck."

"Myers?"

Yakima nodded. "I was on my way down here from up north, stopped for the night in Estelle, little town in western Kansas. Middle of nowhere. After supper I went to a little saloon for a beer and a smoke, and I heard a commotion outside. Stepped out to see a big man tying a smaller man — smaller and younger, nineteen if the kid was that — to a big wagon wheel leaning against a livery barn.

"They were surrounded by several drunk tough nuts egging the big man on. The big man, Myers, grabbed a bullwhip, and he laid into that kid with a vengeance. Through the shouting, and hearing what Myers was sayin' to the kid he was whippin', the kid had whooped him at poker several nights ago. Won a gold watch off him. The kid had been wearing the watch around town. Myers thought he was showin' off, needlin' him. From what I could tell, the kid was a tad on

491

the simple side. I don't think he meant to chafe Myers the way he did. Anyway, this night Myers was drunk. Dangerous drunk, face all puffed up red, fire in his eyes. He laid into that kid over and over again with the goddamned bullwhip until I couldn't take it anymore. I intervened. Myers drew on me, and I beat him to the punch."

Yakima shook his head. "No one told me his name, let alone his profession. I thought he was just some big, mean no-account. No one seemed all that sad to see him lyin' dead in the street. So I went back into the saloon, finished my beer, bedded down with Wolf in the livery barn, and rode out of town early the next morning. Hadn't spared a single thought on Myers till your pa showed me that circular in his office."

While he'd told the story, Emma had dumped a handful of ground Arbuckles into the boiling pot and let it come to a boil again. Now she filled two cups, glancing at Yakima through the fragrant coffee steam. "I'm sorry."

Yakima gave an ironic snort.

"I don't want you to be unhappy," Emma said, sharply. Then her voice lowered, and she frowned. "I guess I'd just rather it was me you were happy with." She blew on her coffee and sipped. "Ironic, isn't it, that he probably wouldn't mind if I was the daughter you were seeing?"

"How's that?"

"I'm a hopeless cause in Poppa's eyes. I'm more boy than girl. He's always said that — the way I ride all over these mountains, critters my only friends, stay outside most of the day. He says I'm out in the sun too much, says no man is going to want a 'boy-wife with an Injun tan and horse muscles.' " She took another sip of her coffee and shook her flaxen hair back from her face. "Besides, Julia's the pretty one. I'm big-boned and ugly. All my life, every man has looked past me to Julia."

"That's just goddamn ridiculous, Emma, and you know it." Yakima's patience was growing thin. He'd assured Emma before that, while Julia was more traditionally beautiful, more the kind of young woman you'd see at a debutante's ball or behind a parlor piano, Emma had a rawer, almost purer beauty all her own. An outdoor beauty. A rugged beauty, but a feminine beauty just the same.

He remembered watching her dance naked in the rain, remembered them making love together with Emma propped on the edge of the well at his old cabin in the Javelina Bluffs, and winced at the old male pull in his loins. It was as though his own body were conspiring with Hugh Kosgrove himself to derail Yakima and Julia's relationship.

"I don't think it's all that ridiculous. After all, you looked past me to Julia . . . didn't you?"

Guilt flickered in him. He supposed he had, in a way. But his relationship with Emma had been a frivolous affair. An occasional night spent together in the Javelina Bluffs. At least, that's how he'd seen it. He couldn't help it if Emma had seen it as more than that. Besides, when he'd tumbled for Julia, after Lon had been shot in front of them both, he hadn't even known that she was Emma's sister.

"Ah, Jesus," he said, climbing clumsily to his feet. "I can't think about this now. I got bigger fish to fry. I gotta get back to town."

"Hold on, hold on!" Emma stuck her hand in his back pocket and gave it a tug, trying to pull him back down. "I gotta cauterize those wounds, or you'll open up again an' bleed out!"

Yakima resisted her pull. He took a step to one side but grew dizzy and bent forward, resting his hands on his knees.

"See?" Emma said. "You're too weak to ride. You're a good hour from town, Yakima.

You'll never make it."

"Ah, Christ." He dropped back down to his butt. He had to get to town, but he was trapped out here by his own weak condition. The men he'd shot in the canyon had been planning a job. He had to assume they were part of a larger group, and that the rest of the group was still planning that job.

His killing the two in the canyon might have delayed the holdup, or whatever it was they were up to. But he couldn't bank on that. He needed to get back to Apache Springs and help the Kid and Galveston Penny keep a close eye on the town. All three would no doubt be working around the clock for a while.

"Just sit there." Emma climbed to her feet and walked out into the growing darkness beyond the fire, toward their two horses. She returned with a roll of burlap, a smile growing, the low flames reflected in her hazel eyes.

"What's that?"

Emma unwrapped the burlap and, letting the wrap fall to the ground, held up a bottle. "I swiped a bottle of Spanish brandy from Poppa's liquor cabinet."

"What'd you do that for?"

"I hoped to catch up to you. I thought we'd have a drink together . . . and talk."

"Oh, shit." Yakima had a bad feeling about this. About her. About her and him together. Still, he yearned for a few slugs of that brandy. Nothing like hard liquor for killing the fire in his arm and the aches and pains in assorted other regions of his battered body.

She knelt and handed him the bottle. "Have a couple slugs, and I'll cauterize those wounds."

Yakima looked at her dubiously. She smiled, one eye turning inward, deviously. He took the bottle from her and looked at the Arkansan's toothpick resting in the fire. The tapering blade glowed red. He gave a shudder of revulsion, anticipating the raw burn of the blade laid against his already aching arm.

Yakima sighed, popped the cork on the bottle, and took a deep pull.

"Good stuff," he said, though he preferred bourbon. "Won't your father miss it?"

Emma sat back on her butt, knees raised to her chin, watching him. "Nah. He has the stuff hauled in by the case. Never mind he's so cash poor, he can't even afford to pay his own men. He was raised so poor — barefoot poor in the streets of Boston — that he doesn't know a thing about money.

About saving it, that is. And spending it wisely."

Yakima took another pull from the bottle. What Emma had just told him about her father being out of cash reminded him of something he'd considered earlier, before he'd been distracted by Hugh Kosgrove's ultimatum.

The Conquistador's payroll was being delivered tomorrow, hauled from the Southern Pacific line by Salko and Kosgrove's other cold-steel men, on their return from delivering the ore. Could the payroll contingent be the "job" Clara had overheard the now-dead bushwhackers discussing in her room?

"Better have one more pull," Emma said, nudging Yakima from his reverie and plucking the hot knife from the fire by its round wooden handle. She held it up before him, grinning malignantly.

"You're enjoying this." Yakima took another deep drink of the brandy, and then one more. He wasn't nearly as worried about the cauterization as he'd been only a few minutes before. The wonder of alcohol. He ran his sleeve across his mouth, then set the bottle between his boots.

"A lover spurned," Emma said, not so vaguely threatening, grinning, staring brashly into Yakima's eyes. She waved the knife in front of his face, then slipped it into her left hand, picked up the bottle with the right one, winked at him with impish deviltry, then took a drink of the brandy.

"You're supposed to be the sober one," Yakima pointed out.

Emma lowered the bottle quickly, choking back a laugh. She pressed her hand against her mouth. Her rich lips were wet, brandy oozing between them, dribbling down her chin. Her eyes were alive, and a beautiful flush shone in her cheeks.

Yakima looked away from her. A byproduct of the alcohol's soothing affect was the tempering of his inhibitions. He was losing his ability to control the feelings — the lust — rising inside him. He'd have to make more of a conscious effort to suppress it.

"Just get on with it."

"Okay, okay, Mister Bossy." Emma set the bottle down between his boots, took the knife in her right hand, scooted around on her knees to his left side. Either inadvertently or not, she brushed her breasts against his forearm. A tingling sensation rippled his lower belly.

He could feel the warmth of her body, smell her sweet sage odor mixing with the fresh smell of the desert after the rain . . .

"What's takin' so damn long?" he growled, turning to her angrily. "Just do it, will you?"

"It's getting dark out here, I have to get a good look at what I'm doing," Emma said in exasperation. "Jesus!" She took his left hand and laid his arm across her knees. Again, she pressed her breasts against his forearm and held them there as she slid the knife up close to the wound. He looked away, trying to ignore the soft pressure of the tips of her nubile orbs against his bare flesh.

"Here we go," she said. "Ready?"

"Jesus Christ — will you just — ah, *shittttt*!"

As the burn bit him deep, he could smell the nasty odor of his own burning flesh.

"One more!" Emma slid the blade around his arm to the back, then pressed the hot blade over the exit wound.

"Fuck!" Yakima cried through gritted teeth, tensing his jaws and throwing his head straight back to stare up at the kindling stars. As he did, Emma dropped the knife and wrapped fresh flannel strips around the wound. She tied the bandage taut, then lifted the bottle. Yakima took it and threw back several more swallows, noting that the level in the previously fresh bottle had dropped dramatically.

He could feel the brandy working its spell.

Emma took the bottle back, had a couple of sips, then ran the back of her hand across her mouth.

Yakima lay back and stared at the sky, hearing the flames crackling before him. Emma lay down close beside him, brushing her thumb playfully across his mouth, drawing his lower lip down. The feel of her flesh on his bit him hard. Almost as hard as the bullet.

"How do you feel?"

"Drunk."

"Did your owie go away?" she asked in a little girl's voice — a sexy one, at that.

"Stop talking like that."

She scowled at him, pooching out her lips. "Why are you mad at me? I doctored that wound as well as any sawbones could have done."

The stars swirled above him, making him a little dizzy. "I know what you're doing."

She leaned even closer, staring into his eyes. "What am I doing?"

"You're trying to get my blood up."

Emma laid her hand over the semi-hardness bulging the crotch of his tight denims. Her hand was a soft, hot pressure. He jerked with a start. "Goddamnit, Emma!"

"I'm not sure, kind sir," she said in a mocking sing-song, "but I think your blood is already up. Something else, too, I might add. I think it likes me."

Yakima flicked his right hand, waving her away. "You run along home now. Your old man's gonna get worried."

"He's got a night meeting at the mine. He won't be expecting to see me again till breakfast, if then. We go about our own schedules, Poppa and me. I got all night, Yakima. Just like you do."

He didn't say anything. He just lay staring at the stars, feeling the raw, aching burn diminish by degrees as the alcohol coursed through his veins. He felt better. If it hadn't been for the nettling rake of lust, he'd have felt just fine, albeit drunk.

Emma smoothed his hair back from his forehead, ran her fingers through the long, thick, sweat-damp strands curling behind his ears. Her hands were oddly soothing. In a quiet, intimate voice, she said, "Poppa doesn't make idle threats. It's over between you and Julia. You have to let her go. If he calls the law on you, you'll have to leave or go to jail for a long time. You don't want to leave. This is your home now. Even if there wasn't any consarned bounty on your head, it couldn't work — between you and Julia, I mean. You know it's true. It's just like Poppa said it was. The folks around here would never accept you marryin' up with Hugh Kosgrove's daughter. At least, not his *older* daughter."

Emma smiled. He heard the faint crackle of her saliva as she stretched her lips back from her teeth. "Now, it might just be possible to marry up with his wilder, younger daughter." She reached up and pinched his nose between her thumb and index finger. "No one cares what the Wildcat of the Sierra Estrada does as long as she stays away from the men in town!" She smiled again, impishly. "At least, that's what the women-folk think."

"Go away, Emma. I don't want to talk anymore. I don't want to think anymore. Leave me here. I'll ride back to town when I sober up."

"I don't want to talk anymore, either. But I don't think you want me to go away, Yakima."

Again, her hand pressed warmly down on his bulging crotch. Again, he gave a start.

He lifted his head and glared at her. "Goddamnit, Emma!" His breath caught in his throat. He stared at her. She'd opened her shirt and lifted her chemise off her head. It lay in a frilly white pile beside her. The firelight played across the sides of her full, pale breasts that sloped toward his chest.

Keeping her hand on his crotch, she smiled.

CHAPTER 17

"Yakima!"

The half-breed lifted his head from his saddle with a start.

He blinked, looked around. Had someone called his name, or had he been dreaming?

For a moment, he couldn't remember where he was or what he was doing out here in the desert, flanked by the sandstone outcropping. The fog of pain and alcohol was slow in yielding to consciousness. Then he remembered the bushwhacking, the bullet in his arm, and his tumble into the canyon.

Guilt raked him when he remembered last night, Emma writhing naked beneath him, her long, willowy, buxom body colored Indian-copper in the flames of the dancing fire. Her lips twisted, eyes bright with passion as he bucked against her, between her flapping, wide-spread knees, hardening her jaws and digging her fingers and heels into his back with delight at their rugged coupling.

Oh, shit . . . Julia . . .

Now the fire was a small mound of gray ash and bits of charred log in the gray dawn light. The air held a late-summer morning bite. Emma was not around. Her buckskin was not standing near where Wolf stood between two boulders thirty feet away, hobbled and staring off toward Yakima's right, twitching his ears and making a low rumbling deep in his lungs.

Emma must have woken early, gathered her gear while Yakima had slept the sleep of the dead, and ridden quietly off.

"Yakima!"

The half-breed's heart quickened. That was Emma's voice.

It was followed by the distance-muffled belch of a rifle.

Yakima's heart lurched. "Shit . . ."

He flung his bedroll aside and rose.

"Oh!" His blood plunged to his feet, and a nasty little man with a big hammer banged away inside his head. He stumbled backward on his bare feet, pressing the heels of his hands to his temples. His left arm hurt like a son of a bitch.

Another rifle shot was preceded by the sharp squeal of a bullet off a rock.

Suppressing the countless miseries barking like angry dogs inside him, Yakima stumbled around, gathering his clothes. The blade-like chill portending the desert autumn added to his raging discomfort. Fumbling and stumbling, hearing more rifles crackling somewhere off toward where the sun was lifting its pale head above the eastern ridges, he dressed.

Again, Emma shouted his name. There was no little fear in her voice. Her echoing cry was followed by the hiccup of another rifle.

Quickly deciding that riding would be a faster way of getting to Emma in his still half-drunk and badly battered condition, he hauled his gear out to where Wolf stood, whickering his worry at the shooting and the girl's shouting, and threw the blanket and saddle over the black's back. His scabbard and Yellowboy repeater were strapped securely to the saddle, the rifle's rear stock angling up over the right stirrup. Yakima would leave his saddlebags and blanket roll for now.

He stepped tenderly into the saddle, wincing against the barrage of miseries coursing through him and, holding his tender left arm against his side, touched Wolf's flanks with his spurs.

"Oh, Jesus!" he cried as the horse lunged into a gallop, riling up that demonic little man with the big hammer in his head.

The shooting continued sporadically in the distance, somewhere to the east and south. As Yakima rode, gritting his teeth and crouching low in the saddle, he began to hear the cracks of what sounded like a pistol returning the rifle fire. A small-caliber pistol. Emma's pearl-gripped, .41-caliber New Line Colt.

Yakima and Wolf stormed across the desert, which slowly gained definition as the sun continued to rise, spreading buttery rays across the desert far ahead and beyond some steep, sawtooth ridges. Yakima reined Wolf up and, as the stallion's rear hooves skidded across the sand and gravel, turned to his right.

A steep trail dropped into a canyon to the south. Yakima had seen the trail before. Suddenly, he recognized the rocks and brush around it, as well.

It was the trail into the canyon in which the gold-laden church sat. He hadn't realized he and Emma had been so close to the chasm. This vast mountain desert of the Sierra Estrada looked vastly different from every different angle, and he was far from familiar with it yet. The shooting was coming from the canyon.

"Let's go, boy!"

Yakima reined the stallion down the steep trail that turned sharply to the left at the canyon bottom. Wolf picked his way around rocks and other debris, hugging the canyon's north wall. The wall climbed higher the deeper Wolf and Yakima rode into the canyon, heading southeast toward the church. The sporadic shooting continued, growing louder, until Yakima could see occasional smoke puffs rising from behind rocks ahead of him.

He checked Wolf down in a fringe of mesquites. The horse blew warily, shook its head.

"Easy, easy," Yakima said, running a gloved hand along the mount's left wither.

He stared straight ahead of him, across a field of white rocks and chaparral. Getting the general lay of the land as well as the situation, he urged Wolf ahead once more. The stallion galloped full out, though its rider could feel in the tense muscles beneath the saddle the beast's fear of the flying lead.

Yakima didn't blame him a bit.

Yakima jerked the reins to the right, and, as Wolf swerved in that direction, his rider shucked his Yellowboy from its scabbard and leaped out of the saddle. He yowled as he hit the ground, got his boots tangled, fell, and rolled.

The nasty old man in his head was really going to town now with that hammer. His twin, even nastier brother, was following suit in Yakima's bullet-torn left arm.

The half-breed gave another yelp as he gained his feet. As two bullets plumed dust to his right, he ran ahead and dropped behind a boulder a little higher than a wheelbarrow.

He looked to his right. Emma crouched behind a rock about thirty feet away, looking at him with a haughty expression that said, "It's about time!" Her hat was off, and her hair was tangled. One sleeve of her checked shirt was torn, leaving her shoulder bare. Her buckskin must have thrown her.

Yakima rose with another yelp, and, as two or maybe three rifles cut loose ahead of him, he sprinted across the rough terrain toward Emma. Ten feet away from her covering boulder, a bullet nipped his left pants cuff. Again, he dropped and then rolled up against Emma's boulder, breathing hard and sweating. He'd lost his hat in the roll, and now he slid his own tangled hair back from his face and turned to the girl.

"What the hell's goin' on?"

"What's it look like?" Emma said in fiery

exasperation, holding her pearl-gripped Colt barrel up in her right, gloved hand. "Some nasty sons of bitches have found the church!" Her eyes blazed wickedly, as though somehow this was his fault. "I told you this would happen!"

"Well, I didn't do it!"

"I don't think you have any idea what this means!" She was talking about the Apache curse.

"Like I said, I didn't leave no trail of bread crumbs for anyone to follow into your precious canyon." Yakima drew his head down lower behind the boulder as a bullet smashed into the other side of it. He looked at Emma again, concern in his gaze. "Are you all right?"

"They fired on me. The buckskin pitched an' threw me. The bushwhacking sonso'bitches!"

Emma jerked her head up above the boulder and triggered two quick rounds at the bushwhackers.

"Keep your head down," Yakima scolded her. "That pea-shooter of yours isn't going to do a damn thing from this distance except get you killed!"

Emma flicked open the Colt's loading gate and shook spent cartridges onto the ground beside her. "What are we gonna do? Those shooters obviously don't like us being down here in this canyon any better than I want them carrying off that treasure."

Yakima didn't know what to believe about the curse. What he belicved or didn't believe about the witch's hex didn't matter. Obviously, the three men shooting at him and Emma didn't intend to let them leave the canyon alive. They'd likely discovered the treasure and didn't much care for the idea of sharing.

Yakima turned onto his right shoulder and edged a look around the rock. One of the shooters, outlined against the sun rising up from behind the canyon's eastern wall, was just then running up toward Yakima and Emma, tracing a zigzag pattern through the chaparral and holding an old Winchester rifle up high across his chest. He appeared dark-skinned, and he wore a cream shirt and suspenders, a palm-leaf *sombrero* topping his head.

Yakima aimed quickly and fired, but his bullet merely blew up dirt and gravel as the man dropped behind another boulder a dozen or so yards to Yakima's left, maybe half that many yards ahead of his and Emma's position.

Too damned close for comfort. Out of the corner of his right eye, the half-breed spied more movement and turned to see another man running toward the arroyo on his and Emma's right.

"Goddamnit," Yakima bit out. "They're tryin' to get us in a whipsaw!"

Yakima swung his Yellowboy around and fired over Emma's head at the man to the south. The half-breed couldn't see the bastard, but only the brush and rocks he'd gone to ground in. He just wanted to discourage any more crowding, hold them off for as long as possible.

Yakima had just ejected the spent, smoking cartridge and pumped another one into the Yellowboy's action when another lurch of sudden movement drew his gaze straight out before him. The third man was running straight up toward Yakima's position, weaving between mesquites and boulders. Quickly, Yakima aimed and fired. The slug blew rock dust from a boulder far beyond where the man had just swerved behind a stout barrel cactus.

A rifle cracked in the distance downcanyon, in the direction of the treasure-laden church. Yakima stared toward it, a butterfly of dread flapping its wings against the back of his neck.

As if the three bushwhackers working their way around him and Emma weren't enough,

512

there was a fourth shooter!

The thought had just passed through Yakima's brain when deep lines of incredulity cut across his forehead as he watched the third man stumble out from behind the barrel cactus. The shooter staggered to one side as though drunk. His bowler hat tumbled off his shoulder. His rifle slipped from his gloved hands to clatter on the rocks around his high-topped, mule-eared boots. He fell to his knees and then to his face and lay still. Blood glistened up high on his back.

Yakima and Emma shared a look.

What the hell?

Yakima whipped around toward the man standing behind the boulder on his left. The man was aiming his rifle at him, from over the top of his covering rock. The man's head jerked violently to one side as smoke and flames lapped from his Winchester's barrel. The bullet sizzled through the air over Yakima's head to spang off a distant rock.

The shooter fell forward, head lolling on his shoulders as though his neck were little more than a thread. He fell forward, on top of his rifle, and lay still.

He, too, had been shot from behind.

Yakima glanced over his and Emma's boulder, staring off down the canyon. Smoke puffed from a low pinnacle of eroded rock about fifty yards away. At almost the same time, the man in the arroyo, hidden by wiry shrubs on an island in the arroyo's center, screamed shrilly. From that same island, a rifle thundered, flames lancing out of the brush to the east, in the direction of the fourth shooter.

The distant shooter fired again, smoke puffing from the same spot as before on the finger of rock.

Again, the man in the arroyo screamed.

Another hit.

There was a wild crunching of brush, and then the man appeared, staggering out of the thicket, grunting and wheezing. He dropped his rifle, ran a few more steps before getting his boots entangled. Then he dropped and crawled a few more feet on all fours before collapsing. Blood spotted his light-blue work shirt between his shoulder blades.

Emma stared at the man in the arroyo. Slowly, she turned her head toward Yakima, eyes cast with wonder.

The half-breed shrugged. Slowly, he rose as he stared off toward the finger of rock. No movement over there now. Yakima shouldered his rifle and stepped out around the boulder, walking slowly down-canyon, head canted to one side, eyes narrowed in wary curiosity.

He stopped when a horse trotted out from behind the finger of rock. A wide-shouldered, heavy-set gent rode toward Yakima and Emma, who'd just stepped up to the half-breed's right, staring after the big man riding toward them on a beefy sorrel with a spray of white spots across its withers and chest.

Something shiny was pinned to the new-comer's vest.

"Well, I'll be hanged," Yakima said.

The Rio Grande Kid continued riding toward them, head canted to one side.

CHAPTER 18

The Rio Grande Kid brought the sorrel up to within ten feet of Yakima and Emma and checked it down. The Kid didn't look happy. In fact, he looked vexed as hell as he said with uncustomary formality, "You okay, Marshal Henry? Miss Emma?"

Emma's cheeks colored, and her jaws hardened angrily. "Don't 'Marshal Henry' him and don't 'Miss Emma' me, you old outlaw. How did you know about this canyon?" She'd spat the words out like four-letter epithets, leaning slightly forward at her waist, gloved hands bunched at her sides.

"How'd *you* know about it?" the Kid returned in an indignant tone.

"I've known about it for years!"

"It's her canyon," Yakima said, canting his head toward Emma. "Leastways, that's how she sees it."

Emma opened her mouth to offer a bitter

retort, but Yakima held up his hand, cutting her off. He kept his curious gaze on the Kid. "What're you doing out here?" He glanced at the dead man lying in the gravel by the barrel cactus, adding, "Not that I mind, mind you, but . . ."

"When you didn't come back to town last night, I decided to ride out and have a look. Galveston can keep the lid on the town on a weeknight. I rode out to the Conquistador, talked to a coupla ornery characters ridin' roughshod along the place's perimeter. They told me you left hours ago, so I headed back this way. It was too dark to track you, so I decided to hole up at the old church back yonder" — he gave Emma a sour, suspicious glance before returning his gaze to Yakima — "and wait till daylight to continue lookin'. Heard the shootin' come first light, and Miss Emma yellin' your name."

"You spent the night at the church?" Emma said.

"That's what I said, Miss Kosgrove."

"Don't 'Miss Kosgrove' me, you old outlaw. How did you know about the church?"

Before the Kid could respond to the girl's question, Yakima smiled knowingly and said, "You didn't lose that map out of your Bible, did you? You just put it away for safe keeping."

The Kid puffed up his lumpy chest as he sighed. "I realized how valuable it was" — again he cut his defensive gaze at Emma — "after it finally brought me to this canyon about three months ago." Keeping his eyes on Emma, he said, "How did you say you knew about it?"

"Never mind," Yakima said. "Who're these fellas?"

"Hell if I know," the Kid said. "I just seen 'em slingin' lead at you and Miss Kosgrove. I recognized you when you galloped in on Wolf. So I climbed up that rock there — damn near fell an' broke my neck, don't ya know! — and lined up the sights on 'em." He ran an appreciative hand down his Spencer repeater. "Not bad shootin' for an old catamount — would you say, Yak?"

"Not bad for an old catamount," Yakima agreed.

The Kid winced and shook his head as he studied the dead man by the barrel cactus. "Last night I saw that someone had been here and found the church. There's the remains of a recent campfire out front of it. These three dry gulchers must've found the canyon on a previous trip an' were comin' back this mornin' to start packin' out the treasure, gallblast their hides anyways!"

He hooked a thick thumb over his shoulder. "I seen their horses back yonder — an' three mules outfitted with pack frames and *aparejos.*"

"Shit!" Emma said. "This is terrible!"

"I'll say it's terrible!" the Kid complained, slapping his battered, weather-stained hat against his canvas-clad thigh, causing dust to waft. "Here I thought I found the mother lode of riches all by my lonesome. Wasn't gonna have to share it with nobody. I thought I was gonna be richer than a half-dozen Jay Goulds for the first and last time in my life. Hell, I was gonna go down to Mexico and find me a whorehouse an' . . ." His gaze fell on Emma, and his ears turned pink. "Oh . . . never mind . . ."

Emma stomped up close to the potbellied Kid and looked up at him pointedly, narrowing one eye suspiciously. "Did you take anything out of that church? Any ingots or anything in the box atop the altar?"

"Not yet," the Kid said, curling his upper lip and flaring one nostril defiantly. "I thought it might be safer right where it was . . . till I could think of a way to haul it out of there without raising suspicion." He canted his head to one side and returned Emma's suspicion-slitted stare. "How 'bout you? Did you take anything out o' that church?"

"I certainly did not, and you can't, either. Not ever! And you can't tell a single soul about what's down here in this canyon." Emma trotted around Yakima and the Rio Grande Kid and strode over to where the dead man lay by the barrel cactus. She kicked him over on his back, slid a lock of hair back from her cheek, and stared down at the dead man. "Oh, no."

Yakima had just whistled for Wolf. He'd spent enough time in the canyon. His focus now was on getting to Kosgrove's riders before they were hit for the payroll they were carrying back to the Conquistador from the Southern Pacific tracks. But now, waiting for the stallion, he turned to Emma. "What is it?"

Emma turned to him and pointed at the dead man at her feet. "This is one of my father's men."

"Sure enough?" said the Kid.

Emma ran over to the second man the Kid had shot. "This one, too."

She ran into the arroyo and kicked the third man over on his back. She looked up again at Yakima. "This one's name is Hale. I don't know the others, but I recognize them. They're professional packers. They ride with Poppa when he goes off deeper into the mountains looking for gold-rich quartz veins."

"You think your father knows about this canyon?" Yakima asked, hearing Wolf's hooves drumming behind him.

"Ah, hell," the Kid lamented, again slapping his hat across his thigh, causing even more dust to billow. "Who *doesn't* know about it?"

Ignoring the stout deputy, Emma kept her eyes on Yakima. "I don't know. Maybe they found it on their own." She turned slowly to stare curiously, darkly down at the man lying dead at her boots. "Maybe not . . ."

Yakima grabbed his reins and swung up onto Wolf's back, wincing again at the pain the maneuver sent through him in waves. This excursion into the canyon hadn't done his condition any good at all, but he didn't think his arm had opened up again.

"Where are you going?" Emma asked.

"Yeah, where you goin', Yak?" the Kid echoed.

"I think I know what job those two bastards from Señora Galvez's place were talking about. Those two are buzzard bait, but I'm thinking they were part of a larger group. And I'm thinking that larger group is fixing to hit the Kosgrove payroll on its way back from the Southern Pacific tracks. Fetch your horse, Kid. We got work to do!"

"Work?" The Kid stared at him, hang-jawed, astounded. "How can you think of *work* when there's all that gold back there! We gotta get it out! We gotta get it out right now before others get onto it!"

"Oh, no you don't!" Emma drew her Colt. She climbed up out of the arroyo, looking as mad as a peeled rattlesnake, and stood glaring and aiming the pistol at the Kid. "You try to take one trinket out of that church, and I'll fill you so full of lead you'll rattle when you walk, old man!"

"Ah, Christ!" Yakima reined Wolf around and spurred him back down the canyon.

He was halfway back to Apache Springs when, after slowing Wolf from a lope to rest him, he heard hoof thuds growing louder behind him. He reached for the Colt holstered on his right thigh but stayed the motion when he saw that the two approaching riders were none other than the Kid and Emma. They looked as owly as two school kids after a nasty dustup behind a buggy shed.

The Kid checked his mount at Yakima's left stirrup, matching Yakima's pace. Emma checked her buckskin at his right stirrup, also matching the half-breed's pace.

"I was listening for gunfire," Yakima said, "thinking you two might shoot each other back yonder. It's a wonder what gold will do to a person."

"We came to an agreement," the Kid said tightly, staring straight over his horse's twitching ears.

"Well?" Yakima said when neither one elaborated.

"We agreed that I wouldn't shoot him if he left that gold alone," Emma said, looking past Yakima at her newly minted nemesis, the Kid.

The Kid turned to Yakima, his eyes indignant beneath the brim of his battered Stetson. "I think she woulda done it, just like she said. She woulda gut-shot me an' left me there to bloat up an' rot with her old man's gun wolves!"

Emma winked at him. "My trigger finger is still itchin'."

The Kid said to Yakima, "She's purtier'n a speckled pup, Miss Emma is. But I've come to believe she's meaner'n a back-alley cur with fourteen sucking pups!"

"When it comes to that gold, you better believe it," Emma agreed.

"What's the plan?" Yakima asked her. "You going to hound-dog him for the rest of his days to make sure he doesn't ride back out to that canyon?"

"If that's what it takes."

"What about you, Yak?" The Kid studied the half-breed lawman, puzzled. "Don't you want none o' that gold?"

"Nope."

"How come?"

Yakima hiked a shoulder. "Believe me, when I first saw that church, I felt the fever. But how would you ever get that treasure out of that canyon without every seedy-eyed border snake in Arizona getting word and running out here to 'help'? No one could ever be satisfied with only an ingot or two. You'd want the works, or you'd never sleep at night."

He spat over the side of his saddle and chuckled. "Anyone tries hauling that gold out of that canyon is going to go up against an army of desperadoes intent on relieving them of it. Shit, there'll likely be a war that'll make the Misunderstanding Between the States look like a game of schoolyard kickball. Besides, look what that gold has done to you two."

Yakima looked from the Kid on his left to Emma on his right. "An upstanding deputy town marshal and Hugh Kosgrove's purty, polite daughter goin' at each other like a wolf and a mountain lion trapped in the same privy. You two oughta be ashamed of yourselves."

"It's not the gold I'm after," Emma said, defensively. "What I'm after is keeping it where it belongs!"

"What do you think, Yak?" the Kid said after they'd ridden in silence for a while, the sun really burning down on them now at nearly midday, not a shadow in sight. "Do you believe that gold is really cursed like this purty wildcat says it is?"

"From the trouble I've seen it cause so far?" Yakima said, raking his gaze again between his two trail partners. "Hell, yes, I do!"

The Kid glowered, sheepish. Emma did the same.

"Say," the Kid said after another brief silence, "were you two together out here last night?"

Now it was Yakima's ears that turned red. He cut his eyes at Emma, who smiled at him lustily. "Oh, yes," she said. "We certainly were."

Guilt battered Yakima nearly as badly as his tumble down the canyon wall.

"Could we stop all this consarned chinnin'?" He raked spurs against Wolf's flanks, urging the black into a gallop. "I got a job to do!"

CHAPTER 19

Yakima rode into Apache Springs around one o'clock in the afternoon.

He weaved Wolf through the early afternoon traffic, of which there was getting to be more and more. As he drew up to the town marshal's office, he saw Galveston Penny another block to the west, helping an old, gray-bearded prospector — of whom there were also getting to be more and more around here lately — wrestle a shod wheel onto the oldster's rickety-looking farm wagon while the mule in the traces craned its head around to watch and offer comment in the form of an occasional bray.

Around them, shoppers and shopkeepers and other businessmen milled. Hooves thudded, and the wheels of wagons and buggies creaked and clattered. A low din rose, comprised of those sounds, as well as the conversations of men and women on the street and on the boardwalks, and of the painted young ladies lounging or flouncing on several second-floor balconies or leaning over the balcony rails, trying to drum up business on the street below.

Yakima waved his hat at the young deputy, letting him know he and the Kid were back in town. Penny returned the gesture, then continued helping the prospector. The Kid drew up to the jailhouse behind Yakima. Emma rode up beside the half-breed lawman, sidled the buckskin up close to Wolf, turned to Yakima with a sultry smile, then reached out to flick some dust from his cheek, letting her gloved hand linger on his shoulder.

"Buy a thirsty girl a drink?"

Yakima grabbed her hand and squeezed it, not with affection but annoyance. "Like I said, I have a job to do, and you need to get one thing . . ."

He let the words trail to a stop when his office door latch clicked. He turned to see Julia step out of the office clad in a ruffle-fronted, light-yellow day dress with small feathered hat pinned to her piled, glistening brown hair. A matching reticule hung from her right wrist. As she drew the door closed behind her, she looked forward to see Yakima sitting Wolf by the hitch rack, and a smile of unabashed delight began to lighten her gray eyes and draw her lips away from her teeth.

But then she saw Yakima holding the hand of none other than her younger sister, who sat her horse uncommonly close to his own — so close that their thighs were pressed taut against each other — and Julia's smile faded as quickly as it had arisen.

Emma's voice was toneless as she said, "Oh . . . oh."

Yakima froze. He looked down to see Emma's hand in his, their legs touching.

He looked up again at Julia, who stood on the gallery, her face now ashen with shock as she slid her gaze between Yakima and Emma, then back again.

Yakima drew a breath and let it out slowly, saying, "Julia . . ."

He couldn't continue. He wasn't sure how.

Behind Yakima, he vaguely heard the Kid breathe out a hushed, "Oh . . . shit . . ."

Yakima tried again. "Julia —"

She cut him off by shaking her head. "Don't say anything." She looked at him and then at Emma once more, her eyes becoming two cold, gray stones at the bottom of a shallow stream, and shook her head again. "There's no need."

She placed her hand on the gallery rail and carefully trod down the three steps to the street. She did not look at Yakima or Emma again but kept her eyes lowered as she hurried off down the street to the east. She glanced over her left shoulder, waiting for a break in the traffic. When one came, she crossed Main Street and disappeared down Third Avenue toward her house.

Yakima turned to Emma. She stared down at her saddle horn.

"Happy, now?" he asked her.

She turned to him. He was surprised that she didn't look happy or even satisfied. She looked sad.

Quietly, she said, "You underestimate me, Yakima."

She backed the buckskin away from the hitch rack, then turned the mount and gigged it westward along Main Street, threading her way through traffic. She was probably heading for a livery barn to put up her horse. Her father owned a hotel on the west side of town, The Conquistador Inn, and she'd probably spend the night there before heading back to the Conquistador in the morning. A livery stable for hotel patrons flanked the large, three-story building outfitted with a tony saloon.

Yakima watched her ride away. As he did, the Kid put his sorrel up beside him.

"Uh . . . sorry about that . . . Yakima."

The older man brushed a sheepish fist across his mouth and sighed, looking away.

Yakima swung down from the saddle and handed his reins to the Kid. "Take our horses to the Federated, will you? Pick out a couple of good fresh ones. We'd best get started south and see about Kosgrove's payroll."

"You got it."

When the Kid was gone, Yakima climbed the gallery steps, then turned to look off toward where Julia had disappeared. A rusty knife of loss stabbed his belly, twisting.

He'd loved another one, and he'd lost another one. It was probably best for Julia that it had happened this way. He'd decided to break it off with her despite how desperately he didn't want to. The Wanted dodger really had very little to do with it. What Kosgrove had said before he'd pulled that ace out of his sleeve had convinced the lawman that the man was right, although he hadn't realized it until just a while ago, when he'd been riding back to town.

What kind of future would they have had — him and Julia? Marriage? Kids — *Kosgrove's half-breed grandchildren?* The town would shut down around Julia and those kids, and Yakima couldn't put her through it. He could have taken her away from here, he supposed. But her family was here. Her roots were here.

Besides, Yakima was a drifter. Julia was not. She was not like Faith. Faith had hit bottom before she'd met Yakima, and he'd picked her up on his own rebound from his own bottom. Faith could have been happy anywhere, as long as she and Yakima were together. That wouldn't hold true for Julia. She was more delicate than Faith was. She needed stability. She was bound here in Apache Springs, where her father could take care of her until she found another man.

The right man.

The knife twisted a little more.

Feeling wobbly on his feet, Yakima went into the office and pegged his hat by the door. He found a bottle amongst the Kid's gear, took it over to his desk, and slacked into his chair. As he plucked the cork from the bottle with his teeth, he looked down at his desk. His heart thudded, and the knife in his belly twisted again.

She'd left a note for him on a lined tablet. She'd left the tablet in the middle of the desk, facing him, so that he'd be sure to see it. In her pretty, feminine writing, it read:

Dearest Yakima,
    I hope you've made it back safely. If

you can spare an hour or two . . . or three . . . please stop by the house for a meal. I'm sure you're famished, and you need to eat. Besides, I yearn to feast my eyes again on your handsome face.

All my love,
Your Julia.

"Goddamnit to hell!"

He raked the note from the tablet, wadded it up in both hands, and tossed it into a wastebasket. He pushed his chair out and leaned forward, elbows on his knees, and raked his hands back through his long, sweaty, trail-dusty hair.

"Goddamnit to Christ!"

For several seconds he felt as though he would vomit.

Finally, he sat back in the chair. He looked at the whiskey bottle. He'd been going to use the whiskey to clean his bullet-torn arm. Now he didn't care about that. He needed the whiskey more on the inside, to quell the ache in his heart, the dull rusty knife in his belly. He plucked the bottle off the desk and took several deep swallows.

He set the bottle back down on the desk, brushed his sleeve across his mouth. He didn't feel any better than before the drink. He looked out a front window. The Kid was riding up to the jailhouse on a broad-barreled bay. He was trailing a light-footed blue roan. Yakima lifted the bottle again, took another couple of deep swallows.

Those eased the aches and pains in his battered bones and muscles, but they did nothing to remove the knife from his belly. In fact, he thought the blade had become even duller and rustier.

He rose with a curse, stomped wearily over to the door, grabbed his hat, and went out.

"You look like death warmed over," the Kid said from atop his rented bay. "Maybe you better let me an' Galveston ride out to meet the payroll train."

"You'd like that, wouldn't you, you old bandit?" Yakima swung up onto the roan's back and grinned at his beefy deputy. "Then you could rob those riders yourself and be in Mexico by morning."

"Damn," the Kid said, scowling. "You must be able to see right through me!"

Yakima turned the roan out into the street. He rode over to where Galveston Penny was just then tightening the hub on the prospector's wagon while the prospector leaned against a *ramada* post, drinking from a clay jug.

"The Kid and I are heading out again,"

Yakima told Penny. "We're going to meet Kosgrove's payroll train."

Penny brushed wheel dope from his hands on the side of the prospector's wagon, which was loaded with mining implements and feed for the oldster's mule. "You think it's gonna get hit?"

"I think there's a good chance. In the meantime, keep a sharp eye out around here. The bank *might* be the target, but I'm thinkin' it's the payroll."

"Don't worry, Marshal Henry," young Penny said, picking up his Winchester carbine from where it leaned against the wagon. "I'll keep these peepers peeled!"

"You stay away from Señora Galvez's place," the Kid warned him, leaning forward against his saddle horn.

Galveston Penny flushed. The old prospector spat out a mouthful of who-hit-John, laughing.

Yakima swung the roan back into the street and gigged it west. The Kid riding off his right stirrup, he galloped on out of town and up the rise to the pass through the red rocks of a dyke that curved down over the shoulder of the mountain, like the spine of a half-buried stone dinosaur.

He beat it down the other side of the pass, then leveled out on the desert below, following the old stage and mail road west. Then he turned south through chaparral-bristling desert, the dark humps of purple mountains surrounding him in every direction, the Sierra Estrada and the Chiricahuas now flanking him.

He and the Kid dipped down through a broad, flat-bottomed arroyo paved with black volcanic rock still damp from a recent gully washer and then climbed a knoll on the other side. Atop the knoll, they checked their mounts. Yakima stared along the trail before him.

A black mass of wagons and outriders lay roughly a mile ahead.

"That must be them," Yakima said. Just before touching spurs to the roan's flanks, he cast a habitual glance over his right shoulder. Someone was riding up behind them — a rider coming fast, tan dust rising from the galloping hooves of Emma's horse. It was her, all right. Yakima could pick that succulent figure and dancing flaxen hair out of a crowd of any size.

Goddamn her!

"What the hell are you doing?" he asked her as she drew rein before him and the Kid, her dust billowing over all three of them.

Emma tossed her hair back defiantly. "It's

my father's payroll that might be hit. That makes it *my* payroll, too."

Yakima shook his head. "Nope. Get back to town. First thing in the morning, you ride back to the Conquistador."

Emma scowled, puzzled. "Why do you care about the Conquistador payroll? After that stunt my father pulled."

"It's my job," Yakima said, leaning forward in the saddle, his dark eyes grave. "Go on home!"

Emma said softly but pragmatically, "It had to end one way or another, Yakima. This way it's a clean break."

Frustration as well as embarrassment burned in his cheeks. He glanced at the Kid, who was tactfully looking away while fidgeting around as though ants had invaded his saddle.

"Christ!" was all Yakima could think of to say.

He reined the roan around and galloped on down the hill toward the shadowy column lumbering toward him beneath a tan dust cloud. He felt eyes on him and turned to see the Kid, galloping off his right stirrup, staring at him incredulously. The Kid looked away.

"What?" the half-breed said, peeved.

"Nothin'," the Kid said, the wind bending

his hat brim back against the crown. "I was just thinkin' to myself that there goes a fella with a complicated life!"

"Yeah, well, it's about to get a lot less complicated," Yakima grumbled, sliding his eyes to one side. Emma followed close behind him, lips pursed with customary defiance. He didn't look at her closely, but he thought he glimpsed a faint smile in her feral blue eyes.

CHAPTER 20

Yakima and the Rio Grande Kid rounded a bend in the trail and continued straight toward the wagon train.

Two men rode out front of the train, maybe a hundred yards from the train's first wagon. Two more men rode about fifty yards behind the first two outriders. Yakima spied more outriders to each side of the train, weaving their way through the chaparral, on guard for a possible attack.

When Yakima was roughly fifty yards from the first two outriders, he saw both men tense and raise their rifles.

"Let's hold up here," Yakima yelled to the Kid and Emma and checked the roan.

The first two outriders glanced at each other. One turned his head as though to issue orders to the other men behind him, and then he and his partner kicked their horses into rocking gallops, intent on checking out the newcomers for possible threat.

When they were halfway between Yakima's group and the other two riders behind them, they slowed and walked their horses up to Yakima's threesome. Both men held their rifles up high across their chests. The half-breed lawman could see that the hammers of both rifles were rocked back to full cock.

"Easy, easy," he said when he saw that the rider on the left was Jake Salko, the contingent's ramrod.

Salko jerked the red bandanna from over his nose and mouth and, glancing at the five-pointed stars winking on both Yakima's and the Kid's chests, and seeing Emma Kosgrove flanking the lawmen, stitched his dusty eyebrows curiously beneath the broad brim of his hat.

Yakima said, "Any trouble, Salko?"

"No," the man said, glancing skeptically at his partner scowling beside him. "Why do you ask, Henry?"

"We got word in town that someone's fixing to pull a job of some kind. I thought it might be Kosgrove's payroll."

Salko canted his head warily to one side. "How did you know I was haulin' payroll?"

"Kosgrove." Yakima raked a thumb down his cheek. "Thought I'd check it out."

"Well, we ain't hit trouble so far . . ."

Yakima glanced at the Kid, who arched a puzzled brow.

Yakima turned to Salko. "Who all knows when Kosgrove's going to haul his payroll up from the Southern Pacific?"

"Just me and the other men in my crew. Hell, I don't even know when I'll be haulin' payroll till the night before we leave the Conquistador with a load of ore."

Yakima pondered the information.

Salko pursed his lips and shook his head. "I think you're barkin' up the wrong tree, Henry. There's no way anyone outside of my men with me now could know that we're hauling payroll. I'm surprised Mister Kosgrove even mentioned it to you. He runs a pretty tight ship, Kosgrove does."

Yakima saw no need to inform the ramrod he'd only overheard Kosgrove speaking about the payroll to his mine superintendent. He looked behind Salko and Salko's partner. The other two forward outriders had stopped their horses about fifty yards away. The wagon train was also stopped on the two-track trail, weaving its way through the desert rocks and scrub.

Yakima looked around warily. He'd kept a close eye on both sides of the trail out of Apache Springs and hadn't spied anything suspicious.

Salko said, "Like I said, I think you got it wrong, Henry. Now, if you wouldn't mind stepping aside, we're late gettin' back as it is. We lost a wheel rim only a few miles north of the tracks, and two mules threw their shoes at almost the same time. We won't be getting back to the Conquistador till late."

"Yeah, I probably have it wrong." Yakima studied the man riding beside Salko and then glanced back at the others. Two of the other outriders just now rode out of the chaparral to rein their mounts to a stop on the trail behind Salko and his partner and stared curiously at Yakima's group and their foreman.

"Everything all right, Jake?" one of them asked after pulling his bandanna down from over his nose and mouth. He was holding a double-barreled shotgun, and his left cheek bulged with chaw.

Salko glanced behind him. "Tell the drivers to come on — we're rollin'!" He turned back to Yakima, brows ridged impatiently. "Well, Henry?"

Both men behind Salko beckoned to the wagons.

Yakima could hear the mule skinners popping their blacksnakes over their teams as the big ore wagons rocked into forward motion. One of the mules brayed. The mule skinners yelled, whistled, and cursed. The wagons clattered loudly over chuckholes.

"Any new men on the crew?" Yakima asked Salko.

Salko studied him, his brows stitching more tightly, forming an upside down V between his eyes. He glanced at the man riding to his left — a fair-skinned gent with a badly sunburned and peeling nose. Rust-red hair dropped from the man's Stetson, which wore a bullet hole in a corner of its crown, right up along the crease.

"Yeah, we got a few greenhorns," Salko said. "It's the kinda job a fella stays with till somethin' better comes along. That usually don't take long." He turned back to Yakima. "You think . . . ?"

"How many new men on your roll here, Salko?"

"Five. Er, six, I mean." Again, Salko glanced at the man to his left. "All in one new bunch," he added, studying the rusty-headed man with sudden gravity. "Including you — ain't that right, Clavin?"

"That's right," Clavin said, staring hard at Yakima. "What's your beef with new men, breed? Me an' my pards got cut loose from a ranch that went under up north, on the rim. We needed work, so our boss wrote us a recommendation to Mister Kosgrove, and he was good enough to hire six capable outriders."

"Who was your boss?" Yakima said. "This rim rancher."

"Benson." Clavin spoke the name tightly, adding just as tightly, "Why?"

To Salko, Yakima said, "Do you know a rancher named Benson up on the rim? I used to have a ranch near Bailey Peak, and I never heard of any Benson up that way."

"So what are you sayin' breed? Chew it up a little finer."

"A young whore in town recognized two men from the bunch that attacked and burned Apache Springs nearly two years ago. There were six men of the bunch who got away. I figure they went down to Mexico. They might have returned by now, gained a couple more men, and headed this way to kill me and make another play. They would have known about the Conquistador from their now-dead leader, Rebel Wilkes, who was once a mining engineer for Kosgrove.

"The two men the whore recognized are lying dead in a canyon back in the Sierra Estrada. I figure they were trying to trim my wick to keep me from spoiling the new game they and the rest of their bunch found to play around here." Yakima paused and stared hard at Clavin. "Ain't that right, Clav—?"

He didn't have time to finish the sentence. Clavin's hands became a blur as he suddenly raised his Winchester, swinging it toward Salko. The carbine thundered and stabbed flames toward the foreman, who jerked back in his saddle as his pinto squealed and pitched.

"Take 'em, boys! Take 'em!" the wild-eyed Clavin bellowed as he swung the Winchester toward Yakima, whose horn-gripped Colt came up quickly and roared.

His bullet took Clavin in the shoulder, causing the man's own shot to sail past Yakima's right ear. Clavin bellowed and sawed back on the reins of his own pitching mount. He tried to level his rifle again, but he didn't get another bullet off before the lawman's Colt bucked twice more, blowing Clavin back over the arched tail of his pitching horse, which kicked his left shoulder as he hit the ground.

Yakima held his rented horse's reins taught as he punched a killing shot through the howling man's left ear.

The thunder of a wagon grew louder behind Yakima. Pistols popped, and rifles belched loudly, men shouting and screaming as the robbers who'd infiltrated Kosgrove's guards began shooting the others. Yakima swung the roan around and was about to kick it back toward the wagons but stopped when Emma shouted, "Yakima!"

He jerked his head toward where she and the Kid sat their horses behind him, staring toward four riders galloping toward them from the direction of town. The four had rifles raised to their shoulders, their reins in their teeth. Smoke puffed from the maws of their rifles, bullets kicking up dust around Yakima's, the Kid's, and Emma's prancing mounts.

The Kid turned his anxious gaze to Yakima. "They're tryin' to get us in a whipsaw!"

Yakima punched his Colt into its holster, shucked his Yellowboy from its scabbard, and swung down from his saddle. The Kid did likewise as Emma dropped smoothly off her buckskin's back.

As the roan and the other horses ran off, buck kicking, Yakima dropped to a knee and levered a cartridge into his Winchester's chamber. He stared at the four riders hammering toward him. He'd have bet gold ingots to goose eggs that those four had been waiting for the payroll contingent in the broad arroyo he'd crossed half a mile back. That's where they'd intended to cut down the legitimate guards and take the payroll, probably turn the wagons south along the arroyo paved with black rock before transferring the money to mules and heading south to Mexico.

Bullets chopped the chaparral on both sides of the trail. They plunked into the dirt around Yakima, the Kid, and Emma and spanged off rocks.

Quickly, Yakima dropped belly down. The Kid followed suit to his left, Emma to his right, extending her New Line Colt and thumbing the hammer back.

Yakima centered a bead on one of the fast-approaching riders, squeezed the Yellow-boy's trigger, and watched with satisfaction as the rider jerked backward and sideways in his saddle, drawing his reins back so quickly that both he and his horse went down in a thick, churning cloud of bright-red dust. Yakima quickly fired again and again, until all five horses were galloping off into the chaparral on both sides of the trail, their riders rolling in the dirt behind them.

He hadn't realized the Kid and Emma had moved away from him until they shouted his name at the same time, their voices nearly drowned by a hammering, near-deafening thunder.

"Get off the trail!" the Kid wailed.

Yakima jerked a look behind him. A four-hitch team of sweat-lathered mules was bearing down on him fast, foam from their open mouths whipping from their leathery snouts. The ground vibrated. There were two men in the driver's box. One was whipping a blacksnake over the team's backs. The other stood with a Winchester raised to his shoulder. He was aiming over the front of the team at Yakima sprawled in the trail's dead center.

"Yakima, get out of the way!" Emma screamed.

Yakima hurled himself off the trail just as the lead mules' scissoring hooves were about to rip him to shreds. A rifle thundered, though it sounded little louder than a derringer above the team and wagon's roar.

The bullet tore across the outside of Yakima's right ear as he rolled into the brush. When he looked up, squinting against his own swirling dust and that of the wagon's large, churning wheels, the man with the rifle turned quickly, tracking him.

Yakima snapped up the Yellowboy and fired three times quickly, punching the shooter over the driver and out of sight down the wagon's far side. As the wagon flew past, Yakima dropped his rifle, leaped to his feet, and, reacting more than thinking, took off at a dead run.

He leaped up and grabbed the top of the wagon's rear wooden gate. Grunting and groaning and running along behind the wagon, he hoisted himself up and over the gate. He dropped into the wagon, hitting the floor of the box with an indignant groan.

A steel-banded strongbox containing Kosgrove's mine payroll was fixed to the box's middle by stout log chains hooked to rings in each of the wagon's four corners. Yakima looked up from the box to see the driver hip around in the high seat and extend a cocked Remington revolver at him, baring his large, yellow teeth like a snarling, rabid cur.

The Remington roared.

The wagon was bouncing around too much for accurate shooting. The bullet screeched over Yakima's head to bury itself in the tailgate. The man glanced forward, keeping one eye on the trail, then fired again . . . and again.

Both bullets thumped loudly into the bed of the wagon within inches of where Yakima crouched. He raked his own Colt from its holster and, bracing himself with his free hand against the side of the wagon box, lined up the Colt's sights on the driver's head.

The man turned again toward Yakima, intending to fire another round. He hesitated when he saw the half-breed's six-shooter aimed at his head. He opened his mouth to scream but didn't get a sound out before a quarter-sized hole was blown into his forehead, just above the bridge of his nose. He jerked back and disappeared.

The wagon lurched violently right, then left.

Then right again.

Ah, shit.

The only problem with Yakima's tactic was that now the wagon was a runaway on one hell of a curving trail between thick chaparral and unforgiving boulders.

The cold thought had just buffeted across his brain when the wagon lurched again to the right, then the left.

Back to the right again, ricocheting off something hard.

It caromed wildly back across the trail before again smashing into something unyielding — probably a boulder — on the trail's left side. That front corner leaped up as Yakima heard the wagon breaking free of the team, and the mules brayed raucously.

For what seemed a long time but was likely only a second or two, he was aware of nothing but a sense of flying through air, then rolling in dust and over rocks and cactus patches. The world was a gray-brown blur swirling around him. He saw his Colt fly out of his hand. His right knee came up to smash his left cheek.

He yowled and grunted and cursed through gritted teeth.

Vaguely, he heard the thunder of the wagon rolling wildly on down the trail, bouncing off rocks and being turned to little more than kindling.

Beneath a shrill ringing in his ears, there was only silence.

He lay still. Mercifully still. He felt his cheek pressed against the ground.

Hooves thumped. He could feel the reverberations in the ground beneath him. When the hooves stopped, he rolled onto his back with a ragged groan to see Jake Salko staring down at him, eyes wide beneath his hat brim, from which clay-colored dust dripped.

Salko shook his head and grinned, eyes flashing. "Well, you're a crazy sonofabitch, I'll give you that!"

Yakima spat dirt from his mouth, cleared his throat. "I thought . . . you were dead."

Salko reached into the breast pocket of his pinstriped shirt, near a rawhide suspender, and withdrew a smashed, gold-washed pocket watch. "The bullet glanced off my old turnip. Can you beat that?"

Yakima shook his head. "Nope . . . don't reckon . . . I can."

Salko laughed.

Yakima spat dirt to one side. Blood was mixed with his spit. "The . . . robbers . . . ?"

"All dead. They killed two of my men, wounded four more. They likely would have taken us all if you hadn't warned us. I'm much obliged, Henry. I know Kosgrove will be, too." Salko frowned down at him with obligatory concern. "How you doin'?"

"I, uh . . . I don't, uh . . . reckon I know . . . for sure."

"Ah, hell, you're fit as a fiddle!" Salko laughed again, then galloped on up the trail to where the wagon likely lay like a boxful of strewn matchsticks, the strongbox nestled inside the rubble.

More hoof thuds sounded. "Yakima!"

Emma galloped out of the chaparral. She'd lost her hat, and she was coated in dust. She reined the buckskin to a skidding halt and leaped out of the saddle.

"Yakima!"

"Ah, shit."

She ran over and dropped to a knee beside him. She stared down at him, pressing her hands to his face. "Are you all right? Please tell me you're not dead."

"Do I look dead?"

"How do you feel, you idiot?"

With a grunt, Yakima sat up, trying to blink away the fog in his brain. A hundred aches and pains were awakening in him, adding to the multitude that had plagued him since his bushwhacking and tumble into the canyon. "I don't know. Not so good, but . . . I'm still kickin', I reckon . . ."

"I thought you were dead for sure!"

Emma kissed him, wrapped her arms around his neck, and hugged him. He'd be damned if, in spite of everything, she didn't feel good in his arms. Warm and supple and . . . good.

Damn her!

More hoof thuds.

When the thuds grew louder and then died, Yakima looked up to see the Rio Grande Kid scowling down at him. The Kid shook his head, brushed a sheepish fist across his mouth, and looked away. "No, sir. Never did see a fella with a more complicated life."

The Kid shook his head again, touched spurs to his bay's flanks, and galloped away.

ABOUT THE AUTHOR

Western novelist **Peter Brandvold** was born and raised in North Dakota. He has penned over a hundred fast-action westerns under his own name and his penname, **Frank Leslie.** He is the author of the ever-popular .45-Caliber books featuring Cuno Massey as well as the Lou Prophet and Yakima Henry novels. The Ben Stillman books are a long-running series with previous volumes available as ebooks. Recently, Brandvold published two horror westerns — *Canyon of a Thousand Eyes* and *Dust of the Damned.* Head honcho at "Mean Pete Publishing," publisher of lightning-fast western e-books, he has lived all over the American west but currently lives in western Minnesota. Visit his website at www.peterbrandvold.com. Follow his blog at: www.peterbrandvold.blogspot.com.